Praise for Caroline Roberts

'Pure comfort – warmth and cosiness exude from every page'
Woman

'Cosy and uplifting – a real treat!'
Debbie Johnson

'Family, friendships, farming and fabulous food'
Heidi Swain

'Warm, romantic, emotional . . . gave me ALL of the feels. A truly lovely read'
Carmel Harrington

'A delightful, life-affirming story. I wanted to retreat to a cottage by the sea after the first chapter!'
Ali McNamara

'Such a wonderful book, heart-wrenching and uplifting and joyful!'
Cressida McLaughlin

'Cakes, castles and oodles of charm: this book is huge fun and pure escapism'
Cathy Bramley

Family, friends, food, a glass of bubbly and, of course, a good book make me smile. I believe in following your dreams, and my love of writing led me here to HarperCollins Publishers. Stunning Northumberland is my home – golden sandy beaches, castles and gorgeous countryside that have inspired my novels.

Also by Caroline Roberts

The Second Chance Supper Club series:
The Second Chance Supper Club
Christmas at The Second Chance Supper Club

The Desperate Wife
The Cosy Teashop in the Castle
The Cosy Christmas Teashop
My Summer of Magic Moments
The Cosy Christmas Chocolate Shop
The Cosy Seaside Chocolate Shop
Rachel's Pudding Pantry
Christmas at Rachel's Pudding Pantry
Summer at Rachel's Pudding Pantry
The Seaside Cocktail Campervan
Mistletoe and Mulled Wine at the Christmas Campervan

The Seaside Supper Club

CAROLINE ROBERTS

HQ

ONE PLACE. MANY STORIES

HQ

An imprint of HarperCollins*Publishers* Ltd
1 London Bridge Street
London SE1 9GF

www.harpercollins.co.uk

HarperCollins*Publishers*
Macken House, 39/40 Mayor Street Upper,
Dublin 1 D01 C9W8
This edition 2026

1

First published in Great Britain by HQ,
an imprint of HarperCollins*Publishers* Ltd 2026

A catalogue record for this book is available from the British Library.

ISBN: 9780008807399

Printed and bound in the UK using 100% Renewable Electricity by CPI Group (UK) Ltd

FSC www.fsc.org MIX Paper | Supporting responsible forestry FSC® C013604

Remembering Lorna and Prue,
and with thanks to all my writing friends

Chapter 1

'Wow, it seems an age since we last had a supper night!' Andreas was stood on the cottage's steps, grinning.

'Hello! And doesn't it,' Cath agreed, holding open the dove-grey wooden door in welcome. 'A get-together is well overdue.'

'Well, thank you for organising, petal. And for getting us all out of our far too cosy living rooms,' Andreas added. Despite it being a rather cool Northumberland April, there was already a hint of tan about his olive skin.

'Hi, gorgeous.' His long-term partner, Dan, stood behind him, smiling broadly. 'Oh and here's a little something by way of thanks.'

Cath spotted the label, a fancy champagne, no less. 'Ooh, lovely. What a treat. Well, good evening, lads.'

'We've gone all out to celebrate the spring!' explained Dan. He was shorter than Andreas, dressed smartly casual in dark denim jeans and a striped shirt beneath a navy jumper, his ice-blue eyes striking below the cropped silver-fox hair.

They were the first friends Cath had made when she'd moved into the village a year ago. Both in their late forties, they were fabulous and fun, and ran the village stores – the shop at the hub of their community. The dashing duo followed her through to the galley kitchen, a sunshine-inspired blast of yellow walls and oak-wood units, at the back of the cottage.

'Any excuse for bubbles,' Andreas elaborated. 'It was a New Year's gift. Been sat in our flat for months. We needed someone to share it with, and this seems the perfect occasion.'

'No need to look for an excuse on my account,' added Nikki, who was a bubbly blonde-haired whirlwind in her late thirties and, having been the first to arrive, was already settled at the kitchen table with a glass of chilled pinot grigio. 'Anytime is fizz time.'

Cath started getting flute glasses down from a cupboard, when there was a rat-a-tat on the door, so she left Andreas to finish that task. Next to arrive, hot on the heels of Andreas and Dan, was Lily, the latest recruit to their unofficial supper group. Lily – Nikki's recently turned eighteen-year-old niece – was busy studying for her A levels and Food Science Diploma, and was hoping to turn her love of baking and cooking into a career, with dreams of becoming a patisserie chef, or running her own artisan bakery one day.

The young woman arrived in a dash, her green eyes heavily kohled, pixie-cropped hair, sporting a red tartan mini-skirt, which she'd teamed with thick black tights and Dr. Martens boots. 'Hi, guys. Hey, Auntie Niks. Hope I'm not late. Everyone okay?'

'Good, thanks, Lily,' replied Cath. 'And no, I'd say you were right on cue.'

'Phew, it's been a mad rush. I thought I had loads of time, and then I got caught up with posting a reel about the restaurant on Insta; I'm helping them with their socials, and suddenly it was time to get changed and get here.' Lily did some part-time work at an up-and-coming bistro in nearby Alnwick.

'No worries. And we're doing great, petal,' said Andreas.

'Well, your cousins are doing my head in, but I'm fine,' Nikki groaned dramatically, as she tossed her blonde ponytail. 'Better now that I've escaped for a few hours. Left Kev to deal with them. They were arguing about the game controllers as I made my exit.' Nikki had three boys aged between nine and fourteen. She juggled a busy life running her own cleaning business with looking after a houseful of lads, including husband Kev, who whilst handy with an electrical task, was not overly keen on chipping in with the household chores. It was a work-in-progress. A long one – they'd been married for almost sixteen years.

'This is so lovely, asking us over. Thanks, Cath,' said Lily. 'Oh, and I've brought some chocolate truffles with me. Made them myself.' She took a small sparkly-silver square box out from her rucksack, handing it to Cath.

Cath peeked in to see, and smell, the most scrumptious coco-dipped dark and white chocolate truffles, all in individual petit four cases. 'Delightful. Thank you. They'll be ideal with coffee after supper, I reckon.'

'Spoilsport,' said Nikki. 'They look amazing. I'm ready to dive in now.'

With that, the cork popped dramatically in an arc across the kitchen, leaving a small dent in the ceiling, that only served to make Cath laugh.

'Ooh, that's a lively one,' exclaimed Andreas, as a 'Whoop!' followed from Nikki.

'Fizz, anyone?' Andreas was soon offering out the filled flutes.

Cath reached for a glass, with a 'Cheers!'

'Cheers, lovelies,' added Dan.

'Gosh, the last time we were doing this was at Christmas,' said Andreas, clinking glasses with Cath.

'Really? Crikey,' responded Cath. 'It *has* been a while. We're into April already. Supper club has slipped a bit. I think the mammoth Christmas event must have wiped us out. Or have we all just been hibernating for the winter, or something?'

'Feels like it,' said Lily.

'Think so,' agreed Nikki.

There was only one more person in their recently formed supper group to come, and that was Will. Hmm, Cath mused, perhaps she had been doing more than her fair share of hibernating with the handsome and rather lovely Will, of late. Her new partner – oh, it still felt a bit strange saying that.

Just thinking of him made the corners of Cath's lips crease upwards into a gentle smile. It was still early days, but things had been going so well between them lately. Though the supper club hadn't met as a group for months now, the two of them had been quietly nurturing their romance; walks in the woods with a carpet of crisp bronze, frost-crusted leaves underfoot, chatting by the log fire in The Star Inn village pub, catching up on their lives over a glass of wine or two. Being a small, rural village here in Tilldale, there wasn't a lot of choice socially, but that was fine. It more than made up for it with its stunning countryside; the valley with its meandering river and rolling patchwork of farmed fields, small woodland copses and hawthorn hedges abundant with birdsong, and the moorland twin peaks of the Cheviot Hills as its grand backdrop.

Actually, Will was slightly late, Cath mused. She hoped all was well. Perhaps he'd just been held up at the cycle repair shop he owned in nearby Kirkton.

As she sipped her champagne, her thoughts lingered on Will. That delicious getting to know each other, over winter's cosy nights in, taking time to discover each other's bodies beneath the duvet. Well, you had to keep warm somehow.

After her divorce, Cath had thought her middle-aged body would be wrapped up for good, and left to perish in its comfy old M&S undies. But with Will, she'd felt the fear and done it anyway, discarding those greying panties with a flourish across the bedroom, and then setting off to buy some new and far prettier sets. Still M&S, mind. These past few months of getting to know each other had honestly been beautiful – as well as scary, naturally, after all that hurt – with evenings of pleasure and moments of pure joy, as Cath had gradually begun to open her heart once more.

But had she tempted fate? After all the pain – her ex, Trevor, letting her down in the most clichéd and cruel way with an affair, leading to the failure of her long-term marriage – she was struggling with the angst that she may have jumped in too soon. You couldn't help it after that kind of emotional battering. One part of her kept cheerleading her on with a fresh start, telling her to go grab the rest of her life by the balls, while the other part, the one that lurked deep in her soul, warning her not to get hurt again, that romance wasn't all it was made out to be. Those rose-coloured glasses had been cracked years ago, and they could easily be stomped on and crushed again.

Her big concern was what would happen to her fabulous supper club friendship group then? When in time, she and Will didn't work out, had to go their separate ways, would the whole group feel the ricochets of their failing love story? Would it make it too difficult to carry on with the supper club? This group had been her saving grace, her sanctuary, filled with warmth and laughter, when first arriving in the village.

She switched the naysayer in her soul off, as she took a large sip from her flute of fizz. Enough! What she needed was to enjoy the here and now with her gorgeous friends.

'Cheers again, everyone. Thanks so much for the bubbles, lads. We do indeed need to celebrate the supper club being back together, *and* up in the summerhouse.' She raised her glass.

'Oh, fantastic. So, we're going to be in the sassy shed,' said Nikki with a smile.

'We are, indeed,' Cath confirmed.

'Ooh, I loved it up there,' added Lily.

Cath had converted the old potting shed of Reggie's – the cottage's previous owner – last spring. Now painted a soft sage green, with mix-and-match dining furniture within, and Cath's pretty and thoughtful touches, it had become their special place last summer and autumn. A place for chat, laughter, a cheeky glass or two of vino, and the most delicious suppers.

'Glad I've brought my fleece, then,' quipped Nikki.

'And I've donned my warm socks and a vest for the occasion,' said a sensible-sounding Dan, with a hint of his warm humour.

Evenings in Northumberland could cool substantially, especially in April. The al fresco life took a little more effort here.

'Cath had already given us the nod,' Andreas explained. 'Earlier on in the shop.'

Eleven years ago, the couple had moved up from London, where many of Andreas's Greek-Cypriot family still resided. The characterful pair had become an integral part of the community here in the Northumbrian village of Tilldale, and had helped form the supper club along with Cath, when she'd arrived freshly divorced and in need of a new start. Their friendship, and a shared love of good home-cooked food, had been the start of something very special at its core.

'Never fear, the cosy blankets are up there, just in case.' And this time around, she had Will to snuggle up to, Cath realised. Hmm, it wasn't like him to be late. She hoped everything was okay.

Shifting her thoughts on to the evening meal and her cooking, she swapped her glass for her oven gloves. As she opened the oven door, the kitchen filled with mouthwatering savoury aromas. She lifted a large casserole dish out and onto the hob, ready to give it a stir.

'Oh, and what's on the menu this evening, my lovely?' asked Dan.

'Mmm, it smells divine,' added Andreas.

'It's my one pot wonder. Kind of an all-in-one roast chicken dinner,' Cath explained. It was one of her son Adam's favourites, especially in the chilly winter and spring months. How she still missed cooking those family meals. The times spent chatting and catching up around the dinner table back in Leeds. With her and Trev now divorced, and Adam having been off to uni, done some travelling, and now starting his new wildlife park job in Yorkshire, family life wasn't the same at all. Would never be the same again, after the bomb of divorce, she'd realised. But they were finding a new normal between them. And she was still close to her son, which was lovely.

'Spring chicken, then,' commented Dan. 'Sounds wonderful.'

'Well, that's none of us anymore, except Lily,' added Nikki wryly.

'You're certainly a bit of an old rooster by now, Daniel,' chipped in Andreas, mischievously, Dan being older than him by a couple of years.

'Cut the cheek. You're no spring chicken yourself.'

Cath smiled at the banter as she stirred the dish; aromas of chicken-herby gravy filling the cosy cottage kitchen.

'Well, whatever kind of chicken it is, it smells absolutely delicious,' said Lily.

At that point, the doorbell rang. With her hands full at the hob, Cath shouted out, 'Come on in.'

A few seconds later in waltzed Will. Dark conker-coloured hair with just a hint of salt and pepper to the sides, and his expressive hazel-brown eyes – sometimes they looked like rich toffee to Cath, and at others a myriad of verdant shades like the greens and browns of the woods. This evening, he was dressed in dark indigo jeans, teamed with a pale-blue T-shirt, under a navy-and-black-checked lumber-style jacket.

She couldn't help it; her heart still gave a leap every time she saw him. Flipped like a bloody pancake in a pan, in fact. It felt like being a teenager again, just like when they'd first ever met, way back when . . . A long story, and for another time.

'Hi, sorry I'm a little late, Cath. Hey, guys, hope you're all fine.'

'Hi.' 'Hey, Will.' 'Good to see you, mate.' Greetings rang out around the kitchen.

Will paused to catch his breath, as though he'd been rushing, then moved towards Cath at the hob, leaning in to give her a kiss on the cheek.

'Woohoo!' Nikki called out, still delighted with the outcome of the group's matchmaking.

'Ah, you're so cute, you two,' added Lily, grinning away.

Cath half turned, wooden spoon in hand, finding herself blushing, though more than happy to be wrapped in his brief hug. His aftershave smelt gorgeously woody and citrus fresh. She loved the smell, the feel of him near to her, even in a kitchen filled with friends, she relished those few simple moments of togetherness. 'Hi.'

She still couldn't believe her luck. Finding Will again after all these years, and then, rather unbelievably, moving on to form a relationship together.

'Sorry,' he began to explain, 'Sophie was on the phone. A bit upset about something that's happened at uni. Nothing major, she just needed a sympathetic ear. I didn't want to cut her off too soon, though.'

'Ah, it's no problem.' Cath knew how important his girls were to him. Sophie, aged twenty-one, was studying law at York University. His elder daughter, Maddie, was an oncology nurse, working and living down in Newcastle. He was a good dad. Cath knew how hard he'd been trying with his two daughters, the three of them navigating their way through a minefield of grief, since losing their mother to pancreatic cancer almost three years ago. 'I hope she's okay?' Cath asked caringly.

'She will be, I'm sure. And oh, something's looking good.' He moved the conversation on.

Cath had to smile, as he was no longer looking at her but gazing down at the huge dish filled with crispy chicken, potatoes, carrots and herby-gravy sauce, now out on the stove top.

'Chicken à la Cath.' Years back, she'd kind of made this recipe up, from a mix of roast chicken dinner ingredients, and a splash of wine, all in one dish. As a busy working mum and teacher, it had seemed easier than the faff of cooking all the roast dinner components separately.

'Looks delicious . . . I can't wait.' He looked rather sexy, excited by her cooking and giving her a cheeky grin.

'Sounds delightful,' said Andreas.

'My tummy's rumbling already at the scrummy aromas,' added Nikki.

'Glass of fizz, mate?' offered Dan.

'Yes, please. And can I help with anything?' Will asked, looking to Cath.

'Ahm, yes, can you uncork the bottle of white wine that's chilling in the fridge, please,' she responded. 'Then we can take it up with us, as we'll soon be heading up to the summerhouse.'

'Perfect.'

And she hoped it all would be. She loved cooking and hosting, but there was always an edge of anxiety just before serving, that the meal would work out well, and the guests would enjoy it.

Cath had spent a happy hour this afternoon getting the garden shed back in order, after having shut it down for the winter months. She'd swept it out, dusted high and low – how did those tiny leaves, grains of soil and bits of garden debris find their way in? – and cleaned the glass of the windows and doors. It was all ready for her garden supper with crockery, cutlery, wine glasses and more.

With bowls of nibbles to hand, and each guest now carrying a fresh glass of wine, the fizz savoured and gone, she led them up the garden path (literally!) and the half-dozen stone steps to the pretty sage-colour culinary retreat. The wood-framed glass-panelled doors were left welcomingly open, the sanded-down table all set and mix-and-match chairs – some painted in a dove grey, others a natural faded pine – at the ready. It all looked very much the part for this evening's supper.

'Welcome back!' Cath stood proudly at the entrance. This little garden shed meant so much to them all.

Nikki was first through the open doors. 'Wow, this looks gorgeous, Cath. Oh, I've missed it.' She beamed.

'This is *soo* lush.' Lily stepped in behind her. 'One of my fave places.'

Cath had placed sprigs of delicately scented freesias and primroses from her garden into two posy vases, which sat alongside some green-glass tea-light holders on the table, which she now lit, watching them glow and flicker. The wooden shelves had their vintage terracotta pots (basically Reggie's old ones) filled with fragrant herbs back in place; they'd been nestled on Cath's kitchen windowsill through the chilly winter months.

And the views from the shed, at this top level of the garden, out and across the rolling green countryside and to the moorland hills beyond, were gorgeous. Dusk would soon be settling, and it was wonderful from up here to watch the colours of the day fade through to cooler blues, then into peach and mauve hues, finally changing to the dark indigo of night-time.

'Right, well, no need to stand on ceremony, folks. Take a seat. Nibbles, anyone?' Cath passed around some crispy cheese snacks, purchased earlier from the lads' shop: delicious bite-sized biscuits made with strong cheese from the dairy at the nearby market town of Kirkton.

'Cheers, lovely.' Dan raised his glass.

'This is fab-u-lous, thank you so much for having us,' added Andreas, sounding very like the judge Craig Revel Horwood from *Strictly Come Dancing*. It was, of course, one of the lads' favourite TV programmes.

'The supper club is back! Yippee!' Nikki grinned. 'I've missed you guys.'

'Yes, after the Christmas festivities, we've all been holed up through the chilly winter,' Dan took up.

Will gave Cath a knowing glance across the table, quirking an eyebrow. The cheeky spark was back in his eye once more, which was lovely for Cath to see. They shared a secret smile. Oh yes, they'd certainly been doing their fair share of staying in . . . together.

'Yeah, well, after that mammoth village event, think we all felt a bit knackered,' admitted Nikki.

'Aw, it was hard work, but it was fab though. The residents at the care home are still talking about it,' Cath added with a smile.

'Oh, I loved doing that. The oldies were so sweet,' said Lily.

They'd put on a huge Christmas lunch with turkey and all the trimmings for the local community and elderly – also doing up the old village hall in the process. And though bloody hard work, what a fantastic, heartwarming celebration it had been. It wasn't surprising they'd all needed some downtime after that.

Having taken up their seats at the supper table, with Cath nestled beside Will at the end beside the door, the conversation rolled on.

'So, how's life at the village stores, guys?' asked Will.

'Well, the baking never stops. Just today, I was on the go first thing with a big batch of walnut and honey baklava, and some feta and Mediterranean veg quiches. And then, there's the never-ending whirl of provisions deliveries, customers, the post office counter to sort out . . .'

'You love it really,' said Dan.

'I do, of course. The stores are our lives. That's why we moved up here, after all.'

'And I bet he was in that apron again!' Nikki laughed. Andreas's naked Greek statue apron was the talk of the village, and had brightened many a shop visitor's day. You went in for a newspaper and a takeaway coffee, and got an eyeful of far more than you bargained for, some chirpy conversation, and came out chuckling.

'Your little shop is the heart of the community,' confirmed Cath.

'Aw, thank you,' said Dan.

'Well, I wish I had time left for some baking.' Lily puffed out a sigh and rolled her eyes. 'I'm full-on with revision. The exams are looming ever closer. It all kicks off mid-May, and I'm feeling the pressure now.' Lily was in her final year taking A levels, and her all-important Food Science and Nutrition Level Three qualification, at the local high school in Alnwick.

Cath responded caringly, 'Hey, take a breath, lovely. You'll be fine. I'm sure you'll have made a revision plan by now. Stick to it, little and often, and be sure to get some exercise to clear your head each day.' Her advice, as a teacher, for getting through the exam period was sound. 'Oh, and plan some treats into your revision. That'll keep you motivated.'

'Thanks, Cath. I'll try and remember that.'

'Well, the very best of luck, petal,' said Andreas.

'Go smash it, Lils,' Nikki added.

'Good luck, Lily. Keep going, and Cath's right, don't forget to look after yourself, too. I remember my two girls at that stage . . . not so long ago.' Will paused, seeming a little floored by his thoughts for a second or two.

Cath felt for him, catching his eye, whilst giving the gentlest of supportive smiles. He'd previously told her how Sophie had struggled badly at that A-level period, with her mum's devastating illness hitting hard at the same time. Sophie had made it through with hard work and sheer determination, whilst Jane, her mum, had not. It must have been a horrendous time for the whole family.

Will gave a small cough before adding, 'Well then, very best of luck, Lily,' his voice sounding a little hoarse.

With everyone settled, and having caught up on the latest group news, Cath rose to her feet, saying she was heading back down to fetch the main course. This was the tricky part of hosting supper in your garden shed – bringing the hot food up the garden path and all the way from the kitchen. Will and Dan stood up too, ready to go and give her a hand. Teamwork was key, plus a good strong pair of oven gloves.

Back at the hut a few minutes later – after some sprightly step-negotiation from pan-carrying Will, and Dan bearing the buttered greens in their covered dish – Cath lifted the lid on a huge red casserole pot that was now set on a board in the middle of the table.

'Ta-dah.'

Aromas of chicken and herbs and a white-wine gravy tantalisingly filled the space.

'That looks amazing,' said Dan, with eyes wide. 'You, and the meal.'

'Hah, well, thank you.' Cath chuckled.

'It smells absolutely wonderful,' added Will. 'Can't wait to try it.'

Cath served out hearty portions of the main dish, and they helped themselves to the greens.

Tucking in, Andreas announced, 'Oh my, you are the goddess of comfort food, Cath Taylor. Honestly, this is divine!'

Will was nodding in agreement with a big smile on his face.

'Bloody scrumptious,' added Nikki.

'De-lish,' said Lily. 'This is unreal.'

To add to the comfort levels, they finished with warm chocolate brownies topped with a confectionery mini egg – a chocolatey nod to Easter approaching – served with fresh raspberries and a blob of thick melting cream. Delish!

Relaxing back into their chairs with happy tummies, they all needed a rest after that. Some of the gang were wrapped in fleeces, some with blankets on their knees, as the inevitable evening garden chill drifted in. With top-ups of wine, a lovely buttery chardonnay that Cath had chosen to go with the main course, the conversation rolled on until late in the evening.

Cath caught up with Will as the two of them cleared the dessert plates from the hut to the kitchen, finally catching a few minutes on their own. She used the opportunity to ask about Sophie. He'd obviously not wanted to go into any detail with the others, especially at the start of a social evening.

'She's feeling the pressure right now,' he began to explain. 'A bit like Lily. That revision and exam strain can hit hard. It's a big year for her law degree. And I think it all just came to a head with one of her flatmates.'

'Oh, dear.'

'One of the girls, Jess, really doesn't pull her weight in the flat,' he added. 'Sophie's mentioned that before. Well, she told me how she'd come back from a heavy studying stint in the library to find heaps of unwashed dishes and dirty mugs left all over the kitchen surfaces. Some of it was even mouldy, so it must have been shifted out from the girl's bedroom. Bless Sophie, all she'd wanted to do was go back, make a simple healthy supper for herself, and then chill out. She hadn't counted on having to clean the whole kitchen first.'

Whilst the issue was concerning, it was a relief that Will was opening up on this with Cath; sharing details not only about his own life but his daughters' too. He'd seemed rather guarded in their early months. This felt like a breakthrough.

'And, to make matters worse,' he continued, 'a lad was staying there, too. Jess had put her music on thumping loud, probably to drown out other noises from the bedroom. I think Sophie flipped at that point. There were words, a falling-out. Sophie sounds exhausted to be honest, and just needed to let off some steam with me. It'll blow over, for sure. But it's tough, all those different personalities in one flat. Like a melting pot, especially when she needs to study.'

'Yeah, that's hard on her, though. On the build up to exams, too. Some people are so damned inconsiderate.'

'I had to laugh, mind, she told me how she'd stacked the whole lot of dirty dishes back outside the lass's bedroom door, so she and lover boy would find them on their way out. She must have been fuming.'

'Good on her. Student life, hey.' Crikey, she'd been going out with Trevor back in her student days, starting their adventures together, filled with hopes and dreams. She could never have imagined where life would end up taking her as she'd hit her fifties. Making a whole new chapter for herself.

But hey it wasn't so bad, she looked over at Will who was loading the dishwasher as they chatted, those cannon-style curveballs had led her into the arms of this gorgeous chap. As he straightened up, she moved to give him a quick peck on the cheek, just as Andreas and Dan came in carrying the empty casserole pan and several glasses.

'Hey, I thought you two were clearing up not canoodling.' Andreas was grinning as he spoke.

'We were doing both.' Cath laughed. 'I can multitask.'

'Well, that meal was a-maz-ing. Another incredible supper night, thank you. But we really ought to be making tracks,' said Dan.

'Yep, time for our beauty sleep,' announced Andreas, stifling a yawn.

'Some need it more than others.' Dan gave a wink, as Andreas poked him in the ribs.

The girls arrived in the kitchen too, bringing yet more glasses and a couple of empty vino bottles with them. 'Eeh, those steps are lethal in the dark,' said Nikki.

'Nothing to do with the amount of wine you've quaffed, lovely,' said Dan drily.

'Nothing at all,' she responded, trying and failing to keep a straight face.

It was soon time for jackets on, hugs in the hall and fond farewells.

'We mustn't leave it so long for a supper night next time,' said Andreas.

'Agreed,' said Nikki.

'Oh yes, we'll get our thinking caps on,' added Dan. 'I quite like a themed evening.'

The lads were great at coming up with ideas for hosting.

'Ooh, I'd love that. But why don't you all come over to mine first, maybe in the next couple of weeks, before my exams are full-on. I'll see what Mum and Dad reckon.' Lily, naturally, still lived at home. 'I'm doomed to become a recluse for a while after that.'

'Sounds lovely, but don't pressure yourself, Lily. Whatever works best,' Cath responded.

‘Yeah, just let us know, Lils. See you then, folks,’ said Andreas, addressing Cath and Will, giving a wave.

‘Bye all,’ replied Will, who was now stood with his arm gently around Cath.

‘It’s been wonderful, thanks again,’ added Dan. ‘Come on then, girls, we’ll chaperone you up the street.’

And the four of them set off, arm in arm.

‘They’re great, aren’t they?’ Cath was always left with a warm glow after their get-togethers. Will was standing beside her at the threshold, seeming reluctant to head off himself. And that was lovely, too. Hopefully he’d want to stay. Another night of getting to know each other, both body and mind.

The mental monkey on her shoulder cranked things up again. Though everything seemed great, and she was in such a happy place right now, was it almost *too* good? Past experience had taught her that love could fail, even when you’d thought it was there for the long term. Despite the strength of feeling she had for Will, and that he appeared to have for her, those nagging fears of whether this could last were hard to shake off. Where the hell would it leave the supper club, and her new life in the village, if the two of them broke up? Had she been a bloody fool to rip the plaster off her torn-up heart so soon?

Chapter 2

'The washing up can wait . . .'

They'd reached the kitchen, after having closed the cottage door on their friends. There was a look of longing in Will's eyes that now appeared the shade of molten toffee. 'I'll do it in the morning, I promise.' His smile was soft and sexy, as he moved to face her. The house now still, just the two of them. 'There's something I've been wanting to do all night.'

He reached out, and after pushing away a strand of her dark wavy hair that had fallen across her face, gently brushed his thumb over her lips, and then moved in for a deliciously slow kiss. Cath's whole body went on tingly high alert. Oh yes, the washing up could *absolutely* wait.

A deeper more passionate kiss followed, as he pressed against her, the pair of them shifting back towards the kitchen unit for support. She could feel the heat of him, warm and firm against her. And ooh, that felt so good. A soft moan escaped her mouth, as they shifted their bodies even closer.

Cath had never imagined sex could be like this in your fifties. She'd thought slow and sedate, if anything. Her love life had dwindled and then died – a sorry, petered-out death – within her failing marriage. She had learned how damned lonely and soul-destroying a double bed could get, even with your lifelong partner there next to you. But of course, she later learned that he wasn't there at all, not really; no doubt thinking of his new fling, impatient to go, to be with her.

Will's kiss brought Cath back to the now. His tongue teasing her lips, tasting of brownies and coffee and wine. This was no place for bad-old-day thoughts, she told herself. *Live for now, Cath.* Enjoy this gorgeous man, who's right here, the one who wants you so – oh my, that's so damn good – very much. Every nerve end in her body was tuning in and tingling.

Might he take her right here? Lift her up onto the work surface? Good heavens, would her middle-aged joints even manage that? But hey, she was willing to find out. Beneath her red paisley dress and leather long boots, she had her best new maroon lacy knickers on. Fully prepared; just last week she'd had that very satisfying trip to the lingerie department. Had her bra size checked and everything; discovering that she'd gone up a size since the last (years ago) day of cup-size reckoning. And, praise the Lord, her pilates classes were finally helping to tone her tummy area. Yes, she was still a 'comfy' size fourteen, but she did have ins and outs in vaguely the right places. Hourglass, at a push. And Will seemed, rather miraculously, to love her body just as it was. She couldn't wait for him to discover these new lacy undies and bra. No more shying away under the duvet.

She undid a couple of buttons on his shirt, and slid her hand in to touch his warm, lightly muscled chest. Will's cycling hobby kept him trim and lean. She knew beneath those clothes there was an extremely fit body for a man in his middle age.

He gave a sensual sigh, as she brushed her fingertips over his skin.

'Now then, Goddess of Comfort Food . . .' A smile played on his lips, which had momentarily left hers. His tone was laced with love and humour, and *want*.

She braced herself against the kitchen surface – the bottles and glasses still there, a sign of their sociable night – and watched, holding her breath, as he lifted the skirt of her dress.

'Now, what have we here . . .?' She could hear the delight in his tone. Hah, he'd discovered the ruby-red panties. Ooh, he was touching the lace, gentle fingers gliding to trace sensual lines inside the fancy fabric. She felt the delicious tension ramp up.

Now, they were being slowly peeled down over her thighs. And before she could dwell – okay, panic – on how her upper legs might look in the full beam of the kitchen spotlights, he had moved in once more to press against her. In a whirl of excitement and tension, with a heap of insecurities still to batten down, her brain on high alert, her body was saying 'Hell, yes'. There was no way she was stopping him now. Relax. Go with the flow, Cath. Her inner cheerleader had struck up. So, she did . . .

And wow, she really did feel like a kitchen goddess, in more ways than one.

Sunday morning, and Cath woke before Will. She'd slept well, waking only once, when she'd heard Will get up in the middle of the night to use the bathroom. These past couple of years spent alone, she'd missed the warmth, the comfort of having someone beside her. It had happened unexpectedly, finding a new partner, but being with Will had turned everything around.

Lying here in her cottage bedroom, a world away from the hurt and betrayal of the past few years, Will's dark hair all mussed up on the pillow next to hers, she still had to pinch herself that this was really happening. When she'd moved up here, just a year ago, it hadn't entered her mind that she'd be in another relationship so soon. She'd pictured herself content but rather holed up, keeping herself safe and secure in her new single life.

It was admittedly scary putting herself back out there, emotionally and physically, again. It felt unsettling. Yet with Will it had happened so naturally, the feelings coming with such force, that she couldn't help but risk it all on the chance of happiness. It seemed like the kind of relationship she might only have dreamed of, that she didn't really believe might *ever* exist for her at this later stage in her life. Whilst him being handsome meant little in the big scheme of things it was rather wonderful to fancy someone again, to take pleasure in each other's bodies. Life was short, so why the hell not?

But the feelings of vulnerability still lurked. After all, she'd broken her promise to herself, at the beginning of her fresh start, not to get involved romantically with anyone. She'd been torn apart by love not so long ago, and those feelings of hurt remained, a stark warning. By opening herself up to love, was she also opening herself up to pain?

Not wanting to disturb Will, she crept out of bed to nip to the bathroom across the landing, but by the time she'd slipped off her dressing gown and was ready to get back in under the covers, he was stretched out with his arms above his head, looking at her.

'Morning.' He gave a warm smile from his nest of pillows.

'Hello.' She snuggled in next to him.

'Well, that was a very nice night, indeed.' He looked happy, relaxed.

'It was,' she agreed, tracing a fingertip over his chest. Was she ready for a morning re-run? She wasn't quite sure; she was just relishing this closeness. Despite her fears about embarking on this new relationship journey, she was determined to enjoy the now. Not quite ready to leave the haven of their bed and start the day, Will gently kissed her forehead, as if acknowledging that, and nestled in close.

Not everything needed to be rushed in life. They had time. And a life of experiences behind them; some good, some bad. A cuddle and a kiss could mean so much, too. Togetherness. They held each other close, and dozed off for a few more mellow minutes.

Around forty-five minutes later, the bell jangled as Cath entered the village stores. She'd left Will making coffee, but after that busy night, and perhaps a touch too much alcohol, the yearning for something baked and sweet had drawn her to the shop.

There, behind the counter, was Andreas with a jolly smile but slightly weary-looking, giveaway eyes. He must be feeling the same way, too. 'Good morning, petal. And how are you at this early hour?'

'Mmn, good, I think. I need sugar.'

The aroma of warm, fresh-from-the-oven croissants filled the stores. There were definitely buttery baked goodies on the go, thank heavens. The lads must have been up early despite their night of entertainment.

'Oh, don't we all, lovey. That was such a wonderful evening, but we may have overindulged a tad. So, what are you craving?'

'Croissants? What flavours have you got?'

'Plain, almond or chocolate. All freshly baked.'

'Fantastic. You're a star.'

'And will you be needing one, or perhaps two, for this morning?' he said pointedly, as he cheekily quirked an eyebrow.

Cath blushed, knowing exactly what he meant by that. Blimey, there were no secrets around here. Honestly, she loved her new small village community, but crikey, everybody liked to know everyone else's business. She knew there was no point hiding the truth, they were grown adults, and she had a feeling Andreas had their best interests at heart. 'Two,' she answered with a smile. 'Or perhaps make that four. I'll take a selection.'

'Wonderful. And your secret's safe with me, petal. Mum's the word. Honestly, it's just lovely to see the two of you so happy. Our matchmaking was meant to be.'

The supper club had been instrumental in getting the pair together, after a few false starts. Andreas took pride in his matchmaking achievements.

'Thanks, Andreas.'

It was a good job Will hadn't left his car outside last evening, she mused, or they really would be 'the talk of the town' otherwise.

They might well have ended up as part of the agenda for the next village hall meeting. Point of interest 6(a): There has been news of a romantic dalliance between resident A, William Matthewson of 18 Main Street and resident B, Cath Taylor of Cheviot Cottage. Evidence of Blue Audi hatchback spotted outside of Cath's residence overnight.

'And hey, thank you so much for last night.' Andreas pulled her back from her humorous musings. 'We had a ball. And the food, that roast-chicken-in-a-dish was divine. You must share the recipe.' As he chatted, he placed one of each flavoured croissant into a large brown paper bag with tongs.

'You're welcome, it was wonderful having you all around again.'

'Ah, we loved it.' He looked up, gesturing at the croissant stack with his tongs. 'So, what's the fourth going to be? You'll need to double up on one.'

'Let's go with the chocolate,' Cath replied.

'I should have guessed that. There you go, petal. Is there anything else I can do for you today?'

'Ah yes, some more milk, please, that's getting low.' She'd made a round of frothy-milk coffees to go with the brownies and Lily's chocolate truffles last night. Cath moved to take a large carton from the stand-up fridge. 'Oh, and I'll pick up a Sunday newspaper.' She hadn't done that for ages; curl up on the sofa and flick over the news, travel pages and the book section. A slow leisurely breakfast with lots of strong coffee was absolutely in order.

'Any plans for the rest of the day?' Andreas asked, as he rang the prices into the old-fashioned till.

'A chilled breakfast, a slow morning, and then I've got four online tuitions booked back to back for this afternoon. It's all ramping up with exam season looming. So, I'll need a clear head by then.'

Cath had been a maths teacher for the past thirty years, reaching deputy headship in the last few years at her secondary school in Leeds. It was a demanding and very satisfying role.

When her early retirement plans for travel and a new chapter with hubby, Trevor, went belly up after his fling – which surprisingly and hurtfully had lasted – she found herself in a dark and unexpected place. Her brave move to the tiny Northumbrian village of Tilldale for a solo fresh start was lifting her back up, slowly but surely, with a whole new set of friends and adventures that she could never have imagined just a few years before.

How life can change. The wrecking balls came, smashed into you, then you started off in a whole new direction. She was learning, gradually, how to embrace these new opportunities. And here she was, standing in a traditional rural village shop, chatting away with her gorgeous new friend who was part of her supper club group, a lover (whoop!) – a rather hunky one, too – in her bed, and warm flaky crisp croissants in a bag. Life was very much looking up. She handed over her payment with an 'I-can't-quite-believe-it' smile lacing her lips.

'Well, don't waste time. Get yourself back to lover boy. Your croissants will get cold.' Andreas gave a wink.

Cath chuckled, as she turned on her heels; this morning her steps were light and hopeful. The jingle of the bell sounded chirpy, as she walked back through.

'Thanks, Andreas. Catch you again soon.'

And she was thanking him for far more than his freshly baked goods. When her world had tilted on its axis, it was Andreas, Dan and the supper club gang who had helped her stand upright again.

Will was freshly showered, his hair damp and ruffled, and the coffee was smelling good, as she walked back into the cottage and through to her kitchen.

'Hot milk or cold?' he asked as he stood at the counter. Oh, *that* counter . . .

'Hot, please.' Her lips creased into a smile.

They shared a knowing, sensual look.

'Yum, something smells great. What treats have you got?'

'Freshly baked croissants. Chocolate, almond or plain?'

'Ooh, almond for me.'

Cath fetched two tea plates, and popped the baked goods onto them.

'The lads all good?'

'Yep, I saw Andreas. They enjoyed their night.'

'Of course, they did. Goes without saying, hosted by our domestic goddess here.' He smiled proudly, which slipped into a cheeky grin, as if he too was remembering their kitchen antics. He handed her a frothy-milk coffee.

It was just what she needed. Caffeine and a gorgeous sweet treat. The chocolate chunks were still slightly melty, as she bit into the flaky butter croissant. Delish. 'Ahh.' She couldn't help her satisfied sigh. Small pleasures.

'I bought a Sunday paper, too. I'll look at the magazine first if you fancy the main paper to flick through.'

'Yeah, sounds good.'

And they settled at the table in the galley kitchen, sipping coffee, savouring their croissants. Anyone looking in through the glass of the back door, might think they were a well-established married couple. Not all new and shiny, and still a little nervous of where this relationship might lead them.

Mid-morning, though he seemed rather reluctant to leave, Will said he'd better be making a move. Even though it was a Sunday, he intended on catching up on some urgent admin for the cycling shop – explaining that it was often too busy to start on that kind of work whilst dealing with walk-in customers. He was a one-man business, after all, and lots of his time and skills at the shop were taken up with servicing and repairs.

He'd also organised to go out on a thirty-mile bike ride this afternoon with one of his pals, a strenuous one by the sounds of it, up and away in the hills. His favourite hobby; he loved getting out in the fresh air, with the scenic countryside whizzing by, and the sheer physicality of pushing his body.

'Time to head off . . . I'll give you a call.'

'Yeah, of course. Enjoy the bike ride.' It wasn't her thing at all, cycling, but hey it kept him fit, and she was gaining the benefits in other ways. A smile formed at that thought, as she moved in for a goodbye kiss, which was warm and lingering, with a hint of almond croissant.

With Will away, it was a good time to do some prep for her tuition classes, all back to back this afternoon. Sundays were popular with the sixth form and GCSE pupils she coached, no doubt being a quieter day for them socially. She enjoyed her work supporting them with extra tuition, helping these youngsters to achieve their goals by passing their exams, and much more. Maths was key to so many careers, and a great life skill. It was wonderful, and felt very much a privilege, that she now got to focus on helping students directly, without all the worry of the internal and external politics that being a deputy head at a busy school involved. Teaching had always been a huge part of Cath's life, and it still felt like her vocation.

It was just after 8 p.m., and with her last online lesson of the day completed, Cath headed down from her little office in the spare bedroom to make herself a cup of tea, ready to curl up with on the sofa with her latest read. As she reached the bottom of the stairs, her mobile phone buzzed in her pocket.

She took it out to see the caller ID: Susie. Ah, lovely, it was her sister, and ideal timing. She had the chance to put the kettle on, and have a good old catch-up and a goss. Susie was two years older than Cath, and throughout their lives, despite or perhaps because of the occasional minor sibling fallout, they'd always been there for each other.

Susie's first marriage had broken down only a few years in, leaving her as a single parent with two very young girls. Cath's determined and inspiring sister found her feet, a job as a PA, and her self-belief, and was already doing a sterling job of bringing them up, when her now-husband Mark came along. The man she probably should have married in the first place, but life wasn't like that, was it. Lessons were learned, and this steady, supportive grown-up kind of love was appreciated all the more. Beth and Hannah adored him too, with their biological father only sporadically showing up in their lives. Mark was more of a father to them than their blood relation.

Susie had been there for Cath, time and again too, especially these past few years when the shit hit the fan with Trevor, and her marriage had folded.

'Hi, Suz,' Cath answered, as she reached the kitchen, moving to click the kettle on and grab a cup.

'Hey, Sis, how are you? And, how's it going with Mr Pellow?' Susie quipped. Her sister had met Will in the village when she'd come to visit a few months earlier, and commented on the likeness to Marti Pellow, lead singer of the band Wet Wet Wet back in the 80s, immediately. There was something there, Cath had to agree. A handsome, rather cheeky sparkle across his green-and-brown-flecked eyes. The look that had made her stomach flutter on many occasions since.

'Hah, yes, and Will's fine, thank you,' she responded with a smile. 'We had a really nice get-together here last night with the supper gang actually. I cooked; my roast dinner in a pot. We were out in the garden shed again – it's back in action after the winter.'

'Sounds a bit like you,' her sister jibed.

'Hah, well, I can't really argue with that.' Cath chuckled. It was exactly how she felt, to be honest . . . back in action after a very cold and dismal spell in her life.

'Well, the lucky things. Your roast chicken dish is amazing. I still remember when you made it for us, a while back. And hey, it's really great that you're finding your feet in the village. You sound so much happier, Cath.'

'Thanks, and yes, I am.' At last life was turning itself around.

'How're your tribe? The girls doing okay?' Cath asked. They were both grown up now; Beth worked in corporate legal and lived in Sheffield, and Hannah was at Bristol Uni doing maths.

The sisters chatted away, as Cath brewed her tea, moved to the lounge and sank down on the sofa. After catching up on Beth, Hannah, plus Adam's latest antics, they reminisced about their trips to Northumberland with their parents (who'd sadly now both passed away) in the 'good old days' and then generally put the world to rights between them, an hour quickly disappearing.

'You'll have to come down and visit us again, soon. Come for a long weekend or something,' suggested Susie.

'Yeah, that sounds a lovely idea.' It had been too long, she knew that. She'd been feeling fragile and somewhat reclusive, initially holing up in her cottage whilst she found her feet again. Susie had come to visit her, but maybe it was time for Cath to test her wings and do a bit more travelling again. They'd been clipped for far too long.

'Well, I'd better get going. Believe it or not, I'm in the bath. Mark'll think I've gone down the plughole. I'm also getting that shrivelled-prune look. And don't you say that's my norm.'

'I wouldn't dare.'

The pair of them laughed.

'Well, you take care, Sis.'

'You too.'

'Say hi to Mr Pellow . . . ah, Will from me.'

And that shifted Cath's thoughts back to a certain Marti look-alike. After last night, she was absolutely still feeling it in her fingers, toes and much more.

Chapter 3

Will was at the door. Cath's heart gave an involuntary lift. It was early evening, a couple of days later, and his visit was a surprise. He hadn't mentioned he was calling by.

'Hi.' Cath smiled.

Even though they'd only been together on Sunday morning, she couldn't help but feel a fuzzy glow, the one she got whenever he came around. Especially a bonus visit, out of the blue, like this one.

'Hey.'

'Well, this is a nice surprise. Coffee? Something stronger?' She offered.

'Ah, yeah. A coffee would be good, thanks.' He sounded upbeat, as he followed her into the kitchen, but there was something else to his tone that she couldn't quite work out. As if he might be about to tell her something. She hoped his girls were okay.

She popped the kettle on, choosing a decaf for herself; hopefully warding off the 3 a.m. caffeine-induced whirl.

'So, I've had some news,' Will started, a bemused look crossing his face.

Cath looked up from her coffee-making, now curious. 'Oh?'

'Yeah, it's a bit of an unusual one. Certainly unexpected . . . uhm, it looks like I'm about to inherit a beach hut.'

'Oh, wow, that sounds exciting. Where?'

'Not far away, actually. Just at Low Newton. One of those bungalows in the dunes there.'

'Well, that's a gorgeous spot. Lucky you.' She knew that part of the coast well. The two of them had shared a picnic there just last summer. They'd also walked the beach from Low Newton to Embleton with Will's girls over Christmastime. 'How's that come about?' Cath had always been fascinated by the old wooden chalets and huts of varying shapes, sizes and styles, dotted about the dunes near the Dunstanburgh Castle Golf Course and beach. They seemed to be a rare commodity; you hardly ever heard of them changing hands.

'Well, it should really be going to my dad.' Will began to relay the story, as Cath handed him a cup of strong white coffee. They headed for the little bistro table at the galley kitchen end. 'He had a distant cousin who had the lease on one. I do remember going to visit it years ago, when I was just a kid . . . and playing in the dunes. Now then, don't get too excited, even from my childhood memory, it was very basic. A wooden shell, really. And I don't think it can have been used much since those days, as we never went back. In fact, I'd almost forgotten all about it. It wasn't a side of the family we saw much of.'

Cath was fascinated. What a wonderful surprise; the chance to have a beach hut of your very own. 'It sounds an amazing opportunity, though. That part of the coast is just fabulous, too.'

'Well, it is pretty cool. The National Trust own the land,' he elaborated, 'and there's several years left outstanding on the lease. Mum and Dad didn't think they'd get the use out of it at their ages, and to be honest, I think there'll be a fair bit of work to do, to even make it usable. Not the kind of project they want to take on in their eighties. The solicitor advised them of a way of passing it on, directly. So, hey, being an only child, I'll be the one who inherits. You're looking at the soon-to-be owner of a slightly ramshackle beach bungalow.' He gave a quirky grin.

'Ooh, we'll have to take a drive over and have a look. When do you think you'll get the keys?' Cath couldn't wait to go and see it.

'I'm not quite sure. It's all yet to finalise legally. But fairly soon, I imagine. Perhaps in a couple of weeks.'

'Exciting.'

'Yeah, it is, isn't it?' He took a sip of his coffee. It seemed like the news was only starting to sink in for him, too, telling someone making it all the more real. 'I haven't mentioned it to the girls as yet. Wanted to make sure it was all going to go ahead okay. Mind you, I think when they do find out, they'll be picturing a luxury seaside retreat – all New England grey-painted clapboard. There are one or two a little like that, but I fear this one will be as far from that as you can get. More garden shed.'

'Hey, there's nothing wrong with a garden shed.' Cath gave a wink, alluding to her own recent supper club venue renovations.

'True. Well then, cheers.' He raised his mug with a hopeful grin.

'Cheers! To new seaside adventures,' Cath replied, lifting her coffee mug.

'Good times . . . and lots of DIY.' Will gave a knowing yet happy smile. He didn't seem the sort to be put off by a bit of hard work.

'And of course, I'll be happy to give you a hand,' added Cath with a grin.

They clinked their mugs, both of them feeling a frisson of excited anticipation mixed with a let's-not-get-carried-away-with-it dose of reality.

Will stayed a while, and they chatted about how lovely it had been catching up with their supper gang the other evening. Cath then asked how things had been going for Sophie since the episode at her uni flat, last weekend.

'Yeah, things seem to have calmed, somewhat,' Will responded, looking relieved. 'Jess's been a bit more thoughtful, trying not to leave so much mess in the kitchen. And I think Sophie realised it had all just got to her, built up over time. There's a lot of pressure on them with exams coming soon, looking at career paths, hoping she's made the right choices with her options. And you know, I bet at the bottom of it all, she's still missing her mum.'

'Of course, she has to be. That's who you'd naturally go to when life gets tough.' Cath remembered chatting with her own mum back in her uni days. Warwick to her home town of Sheffield had seemed so very far. And they'd had to queue for a pay phone back in the day, too.

Will managed a soft smile. 'Anyway, it was touching that she chose to let off steam with me. My advice may not be quite as sound as Jane's would have been . . .' His voice trailed.

'Hey, sometimes it's just about having someone you trust to vent at,' Cath reassured. 'We're all just doing our best in this parenting game. Doesn't get any easier as they get older, does it?'

'No, not really.'

'From what I've seen of the girls so far, they're growing up to be great young adults. My Adam, too. So, we must be doing something right.' As Cath spoke, she felt proud that this was true. With all the recent ups and downs with her son, he was coming through it well. His new job at the wildlife park was the spur that he needed to get out there, revel in some fresh experiences and enjoy life once more.

Cath had already eaten, but suddenly wondered if Will had managed to have anything as yet. 'Do you fancy any supper? Can I fix you a toasty or something? I had mine earlier, a salad. There's plenty of ham and cheese left.'

'No, I'm okay, but thanks. I'll head back in a while. Feel a bit knackered. Think that long bike ride's taken it out of me, to be honest.'

That was two days ago.

'Oh, are you sure you're okay? Not coming down with something?' Cath wondered.

'Hmm, now you mention it . . . I can usually cope with those hill cycles easily, but I just felt kind of flat on Sunday. I managed it, thirty miles, but nowhere near my usual time. Mind you, I had had a bit to drink at supper club and a late night. That might help explain it, but yeah, still feel like my batteries are a bit low.'

Will usually made light of his cycling challenges, being as fit as a fiddle, so Cath felt a touch concerned. He did look a little pale in the face. There were plenty of bugs about, maybe he'd picked something up when they'd all gathered on Saturday. He might just need a few quieter days. Best not to push himself, however. 'Well, make sure you take care of yourself.' She gave a gentle warning.

'Right, well, I'll get away, back up the street.'

He nipped to the loo, and whilst he was in there, Cath made up a mini packed lunch for him, turning the last of the cooked chicken into a sandwich with some salad, and popping some fruit and a leftover brownie into a greaseproof bag, too. If he was feeling slightly off, at least he'd have some easy pickings for supper.

He was very grateful for them. 'Thanks, you really do spoil me, don't you?'

She wrapped him up in a hug before he left. 'Let me know if you need anything. And get some rest.' She kissed the top of his nose, before moving her lips down to meet his.

Their kiss was warm and tender, and edging towards sexy after a few sensual moments. The all-over tingles were off again. Well, if he did have a virus, she'd probably be sharing it by now, she mused. But it was worth every delicious second.

'Catch you soon. And thanks for my goodie bag.'

'You're welcome. And take care. Sounds like you'll be needing to be fit and well again soon, for your new beach hut DIY project.'

He gave a smile. 'I will indeed.'

Chapter 4

The next day, it was a sunshine and showers kind of morning. Cath had already done a spot of weeding around the bluebells and primulas that had burst into life in the small garden area to the front of the cottage, and with no tuition booked until late afternoon, she decided to take a drive out to make her weekly visit to the care home in the nearby town of Kirkton.

Working in the garden always made her think of elderly Reggie, the cottage's previous owner, who'd evidently toiled away, nurturing the plants and shrubs here. There was a pot of bold-pink tulips stood in welcome at the side of her front steps; the ones he'd planted just before he'd had to leave. One fall too many meant that he was no longer able to care for himself or the house and garden, which he'd loved so much.

Cath got into her racing-green Mini Countryman and set off, driving past the village stores and on through the short main street of Tilldale with its pretty stone cottages, heading out and on through winding countryside roads towards the hills. Mid-April sunshine was peeking out from behind bulbous clouds. The hawthorn hedgerows were now bursting into life, with a sprinkling of delicate white blossom. Sparrows and finches, busy darting in and out of their hedgerow nests, were adept at skilfully negotiating the sharp thorns. A huge blue tractor was trundling, ploughing the rich brown earth in a field beside the road, a flock of seagulls swirling eagerly behind it, ready to settle in its ridged-mud wake and peck up the worms.

Kirkton was a small, traditional market town, nestled in the valley at the base of the rolling, predominately moorland Cheviot Hills. It was a town very much at the heart of its rural farming community with its sheep and cattle mart, a couple of small supermarkets, butcher's shop, cafés, hardware store, three pubs, and one remaining bank left on the high street. The care home for the elderly was set on the outskirts of the town, bordering green country fields.

Cath had first visited the home last summer, when she'd helped out Andreas by visiting his frail-in-body but sharp-minded mother, Maria, when he and Dan had needed to spend a few days away. Though going into a home could be a tricky time for the aged and their families, Cath felt this was a truly lovely place to while away your latter years. It had once been a vicarage, and had been extended. The rooms were large and airy with high ceilings. The staff were evidently kind, and there was an interesting array of characters in residence, whom she was getting to know, one by one. The day room seemed to hold a world of varying life experiences between its walls.

She'd recently volunteered as a 'friend of the home', and enjoyed her regular visits, aiming to get there most weeks, and taking turns to chat with the various residents. She tried her best to share her time fairly, but had to admit she always loved her chats with Reggie. Since meeting Reggie, Cath had felt like she'd become the cottage's custodian, taking on the legacy of the little house and its pretty garden with its flower and shrub borders and small vegetable patch, all planted by Reggie many years ago. The cosy kitchen had been his late wife Elsie's domain, she'd learned, and Cath still sensed her and Reggie's light and warmth through the house. As soon as she'd walked in for the viewing, the cosy cottage had had a wonderful feel about the place.

After Elsie's passing, living there on his own those later years, Reggie had done his best to keep it all going.

Now, Cath was buzzed in through the front doors of the home. A vase of cheerful yellow, pink and white chrysanthemums, set on an elegant dark-wood table, made the reception area feel welcoming. The staff knew Cath well by now, and carer Linda nodded for her to go on through to the day room.

'Hello, everyone!' Cath gave a warm smile and waved to the twelve or so residents who were sitting in the room. She spotted Joan, who'd lifted her bowed head to smile and wave across at her. She'd been a Land Army girl, drafted up from Newcastle-upon-Tyne to the Northumberland countryside, and her stories from her Second World War days were always fascinating, though she often struggled to remember what she'd had for breakfast. It was obvious the elderly lady was looking for a bit of company.

Cath headed over. 'Hi, Joan, and how are you today?'

'Oh, doing fair, pet. Nothing to grumble about. And it's lovely to see you.'

Cath was soon settled in the empty wingback chair beside her, and hearing all about her past, shawing turnips, backbreaking work by the sound of it, and then found herself smiling along with Joan who was remembering the fun they'd had dancing at the nearby RAF base in Milfield.

After half an hour of chat, with Joan becoming tired, Cath moved on to sit next to Reggie. He was dressed smartly in grey flannel trousers and a checked shirt. He'd given a broad smile and a nod as Cath had come in, and had then continued reading the local newspaper, *The Northumberland Gazette*, whilst Cath was busy chatting.

'Ah, dear Cath, wonderful to see you.' His blue eyes twinkled as she approached.

'You, too. And how are you today, Reggie?'

'I'm grand. All the better for seeing you. And how's the old girl? Not causing you any bother?' Reggie asked.

The 'old girl' was in fact his cottage, as Cath had come to learn rather cryptically on one of her earlier visits.

'Yes, all's well at the house. She's looking after me. And your garden is bursting into life. The pink tulips by the door are blooming, and the daffodils and bluebells have been gorgeous this spring.'

'Well, it's good to hear all that hard work hasn't gone to waste.' He gave a grin. 'Now then, be sure not to cut the grass too soon over the daffodils. Let them die back naturally. Knot the leaves into a twist, if you like, that'll keep them tidy.'

'Will do.' She gave an 'aye aye, Captain' style salute.

'And how's that young man of yours?' Reggie asked kindly.

'Ahm, Will's good, thanks.' She had to smile, only an eighty-eight-year-old would call Will 'a young man'. Like her, Will was in his early fifties.

'Will, that's it. Nice chap, I remember him well from the village. Fireman, he was. So very sad about his wife, and the girls . . . they were all so young when it happened. Such a terrible illness, cancer. Doesn't matter if you're young or old . . .' He gave a sigh.

'I know. It's awfully sad.' Life, and death, could be so precarious, thought Cath.

'And here *we* all are.' Reggie glanced around the room, his eye snagging on the wall clock. 'Biding away our time. Watching the clock tick by.' The irony, the randomness of it all, apparent.

'But that's why we shouldn't waste it. Any of it,' Cath responded, as Reggie nodded in agreement.

Jane, Will's late wife, was several years younger than Cath was now, when she'd passed away. Will had shared some of the struggles they'd gone through facing her devastating illness, and eventually her death. He was, of course, still left reeling from it all. The world could seem so cruel, at times.

'Well, then, pet. I'm glad he's found some love again.' Reggie lifted the conversation. 'You're a good girl, too. You'll be just the tonic he needs. We all need a little joy in our lives, after all.'

'We do indeed. Thanks, Reggie.'

'Right, well no use us sitting here getting all morose,' he added, his eyes giving their usual twinkle. 'Let's get the teas in. Where's that lovely Linda when you need her?'

Cath was sure that Linda, the care assistant, would have plenty enough to do. 'I'll go and fetch us one.' She knew the care home set-up quite well by now, and was familiar with the little kitchen area that the more able residents and their guests were welcome to use. As she stood up, ready for her tea-making mission, she called out, 'Anyone else for a cup of tea?' Several frail hands went up, along with a few cries of 'Yes, please.'

'Oh, and don't forget the custard creams, lass.' Reggie gave a cheeky wink. Despite the rather sad start to the conversation today, it was great to see that his spark was in no way diminished.

With tea and biscuits duly served, Cath settled down to chat with Reggie once more.

'Oh, this is nice.' He gave a gentle smile as he tucked into a biscuit. 'Nothing like those gorgeous buttery mince pies at the Christmas do, though. Ah, what a day that was. We're still all talking about it here, the food . . . the dancing. Magical, it was, lass.' His smile had broadened and his eyes held a nostalgic sparkle. 'Be wonderful to have something like that again. A proper get-together, and a trip out for us lot. We need a bit of waking up and shaking up, at times.'

'It was a really special day,' Cath reminisced. She, the supper club gang and a host of village helpers had put on a big Christmas lunch bash, with turkey, trimmings and all the works. The village hall had been renovated for the cause, and they'd managed to turn it into a real winter wonderland. But it had also been a huge, snowballing project, and had been a ton of work. 'Well, let me have a think on it, Reggie. No promises, but I'll see what me and the village gang might come up with.'

She didn't particularly want to commit to another huge project. At the time, she'd very much needed something else to focus on and distract her, but now that she had Will in her life, and she'd managed to build her tuition business, plus helping out occasionally in the village stores, she was plenty busy enough. She very much needed the funds from this extra work too, to support her new cottage and the ongoing costs of solo living. Her post-divorce savings had started to dwindle. Whilst she'd loved putting on the festive event, it had taken a hell of a lot of organising and energy, which had in turn taken a lot out of her.

But it did sound lovely . . . another event. As long as she didn't jump in feet first, biting off more than she could chew. She'd have a chat about it with her supper group team. Without their input and support, a further social function would be a non-starter, anyhow. But her mind was already beginning to mull with the seeds of something. With only twenty minutes left of her visit, and Cath aware that the home's lunch preparations would soon be started, she made her farewells to Reggie, and moved on once more. It was a bit like playing musical chairs to cheer up the guests.

'Morning, Betty.' The elderly lady was positioned just a few seats along, and Cath took up the chair next to her. She had thick white hair and vivid blue eyes. She was always well groomed, with her hair neatly styled, her floral lilac dress teamed with a jacket-style cream cardigan. She had a touch of glamour even in her late eighties.

'Good morning, Cath.'

She loved to talk about her family, and the latest antics and achievements of her many grandchildren, proceeding to tell Cath about her grandson who had secured a new job over in Zurich with his accounting office. Whilst being naturally disappointed that she might not get to see him quite so often, Cath could hear the tone of pride in her voice. 'It's lovely to hear of the young ones doing well.'

'Oh, yes, and he's done brilliantly,' agreed Cath. 'What an

experience for him. A whole new culture and lifestyle.'

'Yes, pet. There are so many stories of doom and gloom these days. You almost don't want to see the news. But there are so many other any stories they don't tell, the happy ones, the successful ones. The younger generation are not the lost cause that they often make out. It does make me cross.'

'Very true.' Over her years of teaching Cath had seen the good, and of course, sometimes the bad. She'd felt she'd played a crucial part in those young people's development, in encouraging many and varied talents, hopes and dreams. It was a constant source of pride for her, too. 'We need to inspire the younger generation, not slam them down.'

'And I so loved meeting young Lily – well, all of you – at your wonderful Christmas lunch. Oh, and the kind gifts the Brownies had made; I still look at my sweet little wooden robin. He's perched on the dressing table in my room. Oh, when will you be having one of those lovely dos again in the village?' asked Betty, smiling hopefully, from her wingback chair.

'Ah yes, that was a grand day, that was,' agreed Reggie loudly, with a big cheesy smile on his face – he'd clearly been earwigging.

With that, a sudden chorus broke out from around the day room, like a flock of birds twittering to life. Dozing heads lifted, and eyes shone, as though everyone had suddenly perked up at the memory.

'Eeh, I loved the dancing,' said Edna. 'Took me right back.'

'And singing along with the carols . . .' added Peter.

'And all that bloomin' marvellous food . . .' said Reggie with glee.

'Such a delightful day,' added Betty warmly.

The Christmas lunch event had been fabulous. Cath thought back, still amazed at how they'd managed to convert the run-down Tilldale Village Hall into a magical festive venue in a mere matter of weeks. But it had taken a huge amount of organising and hard work to pull it off, though it had been so worthwhile seeing all the happy faces there.

She'd definitely have a chat with the gang and see what they might come up with. Perhaps something lower key organisation-wise, but it would be nice to use the newly renovated village hall once more. She smiled, any excuse for another get-together with her lovely supper group.

'Okay, well, leave it with me, folks. No promises, but I will have a think on it.' She mustn't get carried away, she warned herself.

But there was a sea of frail, and very hopeful, faces sat before her. Oh dammit, her heart was melting just looking at them, and she was already excited at the prospect of another community event.

Chapter 5

Cath was in her back garden, secateurs to hand, tidying and deadheading a pink-blossomed rhododendron that had rather taken over one of the borders. Bursts of its delicate sweet scent surrounded her, as a message popped up on the WhatsApp supper group thread. She straightened up, with a slightly creaky back, and pulled out her mobile phone from her jeans pocket. It was Lily.

> *Anyone up for a Final Fling before my exams? Please help save my head from exploding!*
>
> *Tea and treats in the garden at The Barn next Sunday 27th. Mum's helping me host. 2pm start! Xx*

Ooh, that sounded delightful. And luckily next weekend, with one of her regular pupils away, after a morning tuition line-up, Cath's Sunday afternoon was free until 5 p.m., when she had a couple of evening sessions.

She swiftly messaged back, a big smile on her face, with a: *Yes, please. I'd love that. C x*

Back to the task in hand once more, she continued filling her trug basket with spent blooms. Hah, a year ago she'd have felt like that was her, abandoned in her fifties like 'a spent bloom'. But here, in this rural village, in her flourishing garden, with new friendships formed, she was having her own second flowering. She wasn't done yet, by any means. The gut-wrenching changes which had felt very much like an ending to all the good things she'd known, had merely meant the start of a brand-new chapter. Life was filled with hope and happiness again.

And one by one, the messages rolled in from those very friends, until they were a full supper club house of 'Yeses'. Brilliant! And an afternoon tea to look forward to, how wonderful.

It wasn't long before her phone began buzzing once more. Oh, lovely, it was Adam. After her gardening stint, it was the ideal time to head in for a reviving cuppa, and a chat.

'Hey, Mum.' His tone was cheery.

'Hi, Adam. How're things going with the new job?' He'd recently landed a new role in 'Research and Education' at the Yorkshire Wildlife Park near to Doncaster. His dream of working with animals, and particularly in conservation, finally coming true.

'Great, actually. Three weeks in, and already I'm working on building links with local schools and colleges. I've even been looking to establish more meaningful connections with conservation researchers at a few universities. It's cool.'

'Sounds great.' She was so pleased for him, hearing the joy in his voice lifted her so much.

'Yeah, I also have to monitor current educational visits – hah, some of those are pretty full-on, I don't know how you managed in school for all those years, and I've been tasked to come up with ideas for improvements, to move the "visitor experience" forward.'

'Wow, you sound busy, and happy.' His clear enthusiasm was brilliant.

'Yeah, there's a lot to think about, but I'm loving the challenge. And the team are really good. Helping me find my feet.'

'That's great, Adam. I'm so pleased for you. It's all come

together, at last. All those applications and interviews were well worth it in the end.' His perseverance and resilience in the face of many rejections and interviews, some that seemed hopeful but then led to a dead end, had finally paid off.

'Yeah, I still can't believe my luck.'

'Hey, not just luck, your love of animals and your wildlife work and volunteering put you in the frame. And your zoology degree, of course.'

'And my sparkling personality . . .' he took up, half-jesting but sounding delighted.

'Of course, Son.' And she thought with much relief that he was sparkling again, with his tone upbeat, and his cheeky sense of humour back on track.

He asked about village life, and Cath chatted about their recent very sociable supper evening. She also mentioned that things were going well with 'the cycling guy' Will – whom Adam had met briefly in the village – hoping to make her son aware that her new relationship might be one to last the distance. Adam was well aware of the tough time his mum had been through. He had been there through the worst of it, witnessing the pain and destruction within the family unit. Though gutting at the time, he had gradually learned to accept the situation. And he'd always been supportive of his mum moving on.

With her tea brewing in a mug, she squished out the tea bag as she continued to talk, then added a splash of milk, before heading back outside to take up a garden chair on her crazy-paved patio. She could hear the sparrows chattering in the hedgerow too, as she listened to her son chat away.

'Right, Mum, I'd better get going. I've got a primary school landing in precisely ten minutes.'

'Ah, well, good luck with that.'

'Thanks.'

'It's been lovely to catch up. You take care.'

'Will do. And you. And once I get settled in more and find my feet here, I'll have to make another trip up to good old Tilldale.'

'You know you're always welcome here, any time.'

'Cheers, Ma. Love you.'

'Love you, too.'

And knowing that Adam was happy and doing well career-wise, her heart felt like it had been topped up. Even when your children became adults it didn't stop you worrying about them, or wondering how their lives were panning out in their new roles and residences far away. Parenthood was a permanent and precious thing.

'I can get the keys . . . *tomorrow*. Do you fancy coming along to view the beach hut with me?' Will's voice came animatedly down the line. Crikey, her phone was a hotline this morning.

'Oh, yeah, absolutely. What time are you thinking?' She wouldn't want to miss this opportunity.

'Well, my mate Josh has offered to help out in the cycle shop in the morning, and we can fetch the keys from the solicitors any time from 9 a.m. So shall we leave around a quarter to?' He sounded excited about the imminent viewing of his seaside inheritance. 'I'll come and pick you up.'

Cath's response echoed his buoyant mood. 'Yep, of course. Great. I can't wait to see it.'

She loved that part of the coast; it held some cherished memories. Walking at Low Newton and Embleton Bay on family holidays, then this summer's picnic with Will sat in the dunes, followed by that almighty downpour and the mad dash back to the car, holding hands in the rain. It was already a special place, and now it was lovely to think that lots of new memories might soon be made there, too. Hopefully, together.

It was Will's beach house, of course, but a part of her couldn't help but hope they might be sharing a future of some kind. That they'd be having more time as a couple, and what an amazing place to spend time getting to know each other.

Chapter 6

The keys were in Will's hands. Two of them hung on an old-fashioned leather fob, both for the front door, apparently. They'd just left the solicitor's office in the main square in Alnwick town, and were heading back to Will's car.

'That's it.' He grinned. 'I'm the proud owner of a beach hut.'

'Or a "beach bungalow" as Mr Wright advised is the appropriate name,' added Cath.

'Beach bungalow 12A. I'll have to take some photos for Mum and Dad to show them what it's like now.'

'Oh yes, and for the girls. I bet they can't wait to see it, too.'

'Ahm, I haven't actually mentioned it to them, yet. Wanted to see what kind of condition it's in, before I go getting them all excited about it.' He seemed cautious in sharing this news with them, but perhaps he just wanted it to look the part before surprising them, and fair enough.

'Yeah, perhaps that's wise.' The excitement about the location had perhaps meant she'd got her rose-tinted glasses on.

The drive from Alnwick to Low Newton-by-the-Sea was a journey of winding lanes, the occasional sharp bend, hawthorn hedges and stone walls, with the odd tight squeeze past a touring caravan or tractor. As they neared the sea, with glimpses of it shimmering a metallic blue-grey on the horizon, there was a sense of anticipation building.

'Nearly there.' Will glanced across at her momentarily, his hands tightening on the steering wheel.

'We are.' Cath gave a hopeful smile.

'I wonder what's it like?'

'We'll soon find out.'

They travelled through the upper village, passing The Joiners Arms pub, on past the little corrugated steel church of St Mary's, and were now coming up to the brow of the hill where Cath well knew the view that always took your breath away for a second. Looking out as the road dipped down the hill, ending at the original white-painted fishermen's cottages, the view then stretched along the golden-sand bay which curved in and on in an arc to the far headland where the ruins of Dunstanburgh Castle stood in rugged fingerlike peaks of majestic decay.

This trip really did feel momentous. Very different from coming here for a stroll, or a pint at the historical and quaint Ship Inn which nestled in the corner of the three-sided square of coastal cottages. Ooh, their new 'local' to be.

With the huts literally being built in the middle of the marram grass dunes, there were no parking spaces next to them, nor even a road or track to take you directly to them in a vehicle. Will had been advised by the solicitor to use a small private parking area down a narrow lane, that was behind the pub and before the dunes.

'Okay, so this is it.'

They pulled up, and got out of the vehicle to a waft of cool sea breeze and a mostly cloudy sky. April showers were looming once again on the horizon, but nothing could quell the sense of anticipation.

Cath took out her bag. Being ever practical, she'd packed a small rucksack with a flask of coffee and a couple of shortbread biscuits, plus a loo roll for good measure. The hut wouldn't have been used for years, and who knew what condition it might be in, after all.

They'd learned today that the only utility available at the bungalow was water, and even that was only supplied for six months of the year through the spring and summer seasons – they were lucky it was mid-April, then. No electric, no oil tanks, only gas bottles where they'd been fitted, and their bungalow didn't at present have that facility. There was, apparently, a small log burner for heating purposes within the property, and that was it. It'd be candlelight if they ever decided to stay, Cath had mused in the solicitor's office, or perhaps less romantically, their phone torches.

'Let's go, then,' Cath responded, feeling a bit like a child on a treasure hunt as Will took out and unfolded a sketchily drawn map of the various buildings, by which to locate his plot. There was a rough path heading in to the dunes, which trailed beside a large marshy pond area.

Cath's hopes for this coastal haven filled her thoughts, as they made their way along the track and then weaved through the spiky marram grass of the dunes. Will's beach bungalow; she couldn't help but feel that this was going to be a part of their new adventure as a couple. It'd make a fantastic little hideaway for day trips. And if they managed to get it shipshape, perhaps even the odd overnighter. A place where they could listen to the surf rolling in, lying in each other's arms . . . the dusky-peach glow of the morning sun rising over the ruins of the castle on the distant shores of the bay. She finally had the chance to dream again.

Ahead was a large greenish-grey clapboard-style renovated hut. Oh, and they'd even installed solar panels on the roof. 'Look at that Will, solar panels an' all. Looks fancy this one.'

'Doesn't it just. And yeah, that's a good idea for an electric source. Might have to find out more about that.'

They passed another two dark-brown wooden bungalows that appeared well maintained. And a more traditional-looking one, which on closer inspection appeared to be covered in dark-greenish flaps over all the walls, that oddly reminded her of an armadillo's skin.

Will paused for a second, screwing his face up as he read the map, trying to work out the bungalow numbers. 'Well, these are twenty-four and twenty-five so we've a little way to go. Right then, this way.' He marched on.

The trail they apparently needed, snaked its way into a bracken and bramble patch. He stamped down and held back what he could to clear the pathway for Cath, but the spiky branches still managed to snag at their coats. Cath made a mental note to bring her secateurs next time, and trim back a decent path for them.

They came out into a clearing of dune area to find a single wooden hut positioned on a rise with a lovely porch and covered front deck, and a gorgeous view of the bay. She could picture the owners sat on the two wicker chairs there, perhaps with a contented dog at their feet, after a long stroll on the beach, hmm, yes, with a glass of wine to hand. But this wasn't Will's. Two further huts were nestled in the patch behind them, as they could make out the black of their corrugated metal roofs. Will shook his head, and gestured for them to move on. Onwards again, crikey, Will's place must be a right trek.

'Can't be far now.' His voice carried back to her on the salty breeze. He scanned the map once more.

Then just ahead and set slightly back from the rise where the dunes led down to the beach, was a fairly large . . . and oh, very dilapidated-looking . . . well, all you could describe it as was a shed. And, nothing at all like the smartened-up garden shed she had at home.

Cath caught up with Will. The two of them stood together and stared. Oh my, how her fanciful dreams had just been dashed. *OMG*, compared to all the other buildings they'd just walked by . . . this, well . . . words failed her. It was built of brown-weathered wood, that had possibly lost its stain, and oh, some of its slats, many years ago.

'Ah,' Will managed.

'Hmmm,' Cath added mutely.

They remained frozen for a couple more seconds, trying to smother their disappointment. Perhaps they'd been rather over-optimistic in their expectations.

'It's not great, is it?' admitted Will.

'Well, that's the understatement of the year,' responded Cath wryly.

'It has potential . . .' Will arched an eyebrow.

Cath merely raised both of her eyebrows in response.

They had to chuckle.

'Well, we have keys, we may as well go in.' Will gingerly crossed the front deck area that faced the sea, noticing that several of the wooden boards were rotten and had sunk. Reaching the pale-blue peeling-painted door, which was central to the bungalow, and had seen better days, Will took a breath, steeling himself.

Ironically, a key seemed hardly necessary, with the amount of rotten timber on the frame, one strong push and you'd most likely be in. The lock was rusty, and Will struggled for a while to free the bolt. Then, with a shoulder barge, it gave way. With a poof of stale-scented and mildewed air, and a cloud of sandy dust, they were in.

With a sense of trepidation, they entered. What were they about to discover?!

They walked into a large living space, the walls still the original brown wood, the same as the outside. Concerningly, the odd crack of light came through the rotten slats. Some artwork made of shells which had been stuck on driftwood – Cath guessed from the beach here – still hung there. Cath wondered who had made them. There was a faded-red sofa with two sunken floral-patterned cushions, set before the log burner which had grey ash and a half-burnt log inside. An ancient sideboard had a couple of old photos – Will picked one up, pointing out his father's cousin – along with a boxed game of Scrabble, a soggy pack of cards and several paperbacks with mildewed edges. Cath pulled out a Georgette Heyer classic and a book on bird spotting. It was like the world had stopped here decades ago. Fragments left from another life, another time.

Against the far back wall an old 'fitted' unit acted as the kitchen area, with a bucket to one side, rather worryingly positioned, it seemed, to catch drips from the ceiling. In the unit, there was one drawer with a cupboard below, painted in the same pale blue as the door, with a frilly-edged curtain on a wire drawn across below the stainless-steel sink. Above the sink, was a white-tiled area. And on the wall above that was an old-fashioned wooden plate rack, still holding a few aged items of crockery and a traditional brown teapot. Cath's nan used to have one just like it.

Cath moved cautiously to take a look under the sink, shifting the stained curtain to find a grubby white plastic bowl, and oh yuck, several mouse droppings.

They'd hardly said a word since walking in. Merely looking at each other with eyebrows raised, and faces strained. It was fascinating, but nothing like as idyllic – even being aware there'd be plenty of work to do – as they'd hoped.

Next, they took a quick look through a door that led off from the living space to find a bedroom area with an old pine double bedstead and a manky mattress that you really wouldn't want to go bouncing on. A further door, again heading from the living area, revealed a once-white porcelain toilet with a dried up green-and-brown-stained bowl – hopefully, just years of stagnant water and nothing more sinister.

'Bloody hell,' muttered Cath.

'Jeez,' puffed out Will. 'I really need to pee, but there's no way I'm chancing it in here.'

They fled back to the 'airier' space of the living room, where that sofa, as Cath peered closer, had several ruffed-up holes in, and fluffy bits of stuffing coming out. Evidence of gnawing . . .

'Ekk, don't even think about sitting down . . .' Cath warned, as Will moved nearer to it. 'I think that's a hotel.'

He quirked an eyebrow, quizzically.

'A mouse hotel,' she continued.

And with that, there was a scurrying from beneath the sofa, and right on cue, one of the smooth brown-grey furry critters scampered off, its tail a thin flash behind it.

'There's a *moose* in the *hoose*.' Will put on a strong Scottish accent.

'You'll need to call in pest control before you even start thinking of doing any work here,' said Cath.

'Yeah, and then a joiner. There's so much rotten wood, it's dangerous. And I'll need to check the roof for leaks.'

'The bucket in the kitchen's a bit of a clue, and I bet there's more than that one. And that sofa will need to go, and the mattress . . . the bedstead and sideboard, too. Could be full of woodworm or anything.'

'That'll be some job ferrying it all out across the track.' Will's brow furrowed further.

'Bloody hell, yeah. They'd certainly not allow a bonfire in the dunes. Looks like our work's going to be cut out.'

'It is indeed. I'm beginning to understand why my parents wanted to pass it on to me so swiftly.'

'Yep, there'll be lots of work,' agreed Cath. 'But hey, I bet that's never held you back. And of course, I'm more than happy to lend a hand. I got stuck in with my little garden hut project, and think of the massive difference we made at the village hall.' Along with the supper club gang, they'd tackled the community hall renovations with aplomb.

'True.' A glimmer of a smile flickered on his lips.

Will took a few interior photos for his parents, without zooming in too closely on anything. Cath took a couple of images too, hoping one day to be comparing a very different 'after' image against these 'before' ones.

'Time for a pint, and a glass of wine?'

'Absolutely.'

They re-scanned the shabby, partly rotted interior. Will took a slow breath, the air so very musty. They certainly weren't going to be hanging around here for long. It wasn't a space for relaxing, well, not for a good while yet, and there wasn't a lot they could tackle today, anyhow. It needed clearing out and thoroughly cleaning the next visit, mused Cath.

They turned at the same time and oh, spotted the view out of the open front door.

'Wow,' said Will.

'Oh my,' Cath gasped.

When they'd arrived, they'd been so focused on finding the hut and getting inside, neither of them had looked out to the sea. The short grass of the dunes before them formed a small garden patch, from which a track led down to the wheat-coloured sands and the sea, now all milky-green and pewter-grey tones with gently rolling crests of white surf. The sky was awash with bulbous cloudy greys, aquamarine and shades of gold. And there, right opposite their front deck, on the far side of the sweeping bay, stood the dramatic stony ruins of Dunstanburgh Castle. The view from here was incredible. Cath took a couple of snaps on her phone, wanting to capture this moment.

'Wow,' Will repeated. 'There's hope for the old place yet.' He stood simply gazing, a spark of optimism filling his eyes.

'Hah, no need to worry about the manky inside,' added Cath. 'We just need to put a blanket down here on the front deck.'

'Absolutely. That'll be next time.' The corners of Will's lips shifted into a cheeky grin. What was he imagining might happen here?

'A blanket and a picnic,' Cath clarified, smiling, feeling a frisson of fresh excitement at the prospect of the project, and the hope of some magical times to come. 'I brought some coffee. We could sit for a few minutes.' The rain had held off for now, and they were sheltered and mostly out of the breeze here.

'Go on then. We'll go and have that pint after.'

Cath took off her rucksack, found the cups and flask, and poured. They sat for a few precious minutes, sipping coffee as they gazed across that amazing vista, watching oystercatchers dipping their beaks and sanderlings scurrying at the shoreline, with the shushing sounds of the sea rolling onto the sands, the smell of salt and a gentle breeze teasing Cath's hair.

Embleton Bay was already casting its calming magic.

Cath packed away the empty cups and flask, and they walked from the bungalow out and down the dune to the front and via some rather rickety wooden steps, onto the sands, where Will took her hand. Whilst realising the huge practical, and no doubt costly, project the beach hut would be, they still gave each other smiles filled with hope. For both of them, this felt like a new adventure in life, timing perfectly with their blooming relationship.

They strolled back to the village along the beach, passing a couple walking their Labrador, a few hikers with sturdy boots and rucksacks, and a sand-encrusted toddler building sandcastles with his mum. Cath and Will made their way around the headland, where a far smarter bungalow than theirs graced the dune point. Along they went, hand in hand, and up the concrete causeway where small fishing and pleasure boats could be pulled in. Then, they passed the white-painted former fisherman's cottages; one with vivid-purple petunia flowers in pots on the sill, another with an old conifer-green glass float and a lobster pot positioned outside the porch.

They found a corner table in The Ship Inn, nestled between an old sash window and a stone hearth with a cast-iron log burner. Dried hops and twigs trailed high above them from the ceiling. Paintings of moody seascapes and sepia pictures of boats were displayed on the uneven grey-and-honey stone walls.

This characterful cosy pub had been a social hub and refuge for its fishing community for hundreds of years, and more recently for local residents and tourists. It must have a few stories of its own to tell, plus secrets to guard in its time, having been part of this coastal village life for over two hundred and fifty years.

Cath sat down on a wooden settle, whilst Will headed off to the bar in the hunt for a much-needed pint, still trying to absorb the reality of the task ahead with his new inheritance. He soon came back, bringing a real ale from the pub's microbrewery for himself and a cider for Cath, along with a couple of packs of sea-salted crisps.

'Thanks.'

'Cheers.' He took up the seat opposite Cath. 'Well then, that was an interesting escapade into my inheritance. And jeez, there's a whole load of work to do to make it shipshape. Excuse the pun.' That was an understatement, but Will was clinging on to positivity.

'There is indeed,' agreed Cath, thinking drily, *a mountain of work*.

'Yeah, we'll need to get the professionals in to check the roof and sort out any major external joinery issues. We have to make it structurally sound first, and then . . .'

'And then . . . there's the inside to tackle,' Cath added, her eyes wide.

They looked at each other. The task was actually monumental. There was a pause, as the reality of the renovation project began to sink in. If she'd been hoping to find some time to put on a social event for the elderly, then she'd likely just lost it to this project.

'Hmm, I think we might need a few helpers with this one,' said Will, before taking a large sip of his pint.

'And hey, we know just where to find them,' Cath mooted, remembering the village hall renovations. 'Our trusty supper clubbers, and perhaps a handy DIY tradesperson friend or two.'

'Yes, they were brilliant at helping with Tilldale's hall. But this is more of a personal project,' Will noted. 'Perhaps, I'd be better just ticking away at things myself.'

'True. Or, maybe we could hold a Seaside DIY SOS,' Cath added with a grin. 'Do you think we might be able to lure them in with an offer of a seaside supper or a beach picnic?'

'Hah, sounds a good idea. Definitely worth a try, anyhow.' He gave a smile, which lifted her hopes. With so much to do, they needed to keep positive, after all.

Cath then glanced out of the pub's sash window, which lifted her spirits even more. 'And hey, it's certainly got one thing going for it, big time.'

'What's that?'

'Location, location, location.'

The two of them gazed out, past the grassy green of the village square, the fishermen's cottages, to the golden beach and the rocky outcrop near the headland, and on to the North Sea which was rolling in in hues of greys, blues and greens.

'Well, it's got that in spades,' Will agreed.

'Buckets and spades.' Cath grinned.

'And, it also has a very good local, which serves an exceedingly good pint.'

'Absolutely.'

'Well, I'll drink to that.'

'Cheers.'

They clinked glasses.

The Beach Hut Challenge was on. And it certainly *was* going to be a challenge.

Chapter 7

The end of April was here in all its spring glory. The weather fair, being a breezy sunshiny Sunday afternoon, as Cath strolled up the village, wicker basket to hand, ready for Lily's al fresco 'Final Fling' tea. Cath had chosen a cream-and-red ditsy-floral-patterned dress, thinking it would suit the garden party theme. Her legs were bare and admittedly rather pale beneath the skirt. Well, it was the first time they'd been on show in months. But it was nice to feel that summer was just around the corner.

With Lily's exams due to start in two weeks' time, she and her mum, Anna, had decided a few hours' break with some friends around would be the perfect tonic to help her relax. The young woman had been working like a trojan for months now, after all. Studying hard for her exams, whilst still managing to hold down her Saturday-night waitressing job at Saveur, the restaurant in Alnwick, where she was eagerly picking up the tools and tricks of the hospitality and fine dining trade. As well as serving, and learning to deal with the public, she'd even helped in the kitchen at times, delighting in the desserts, gaining tips and new skills to help her create wonderful patisserie and puddings. Her dreams of one day running her own bakery or patisserie-inspired café were still holding firm. If she could pull off her A levels and her crucial Food Science Diploma, she had ambitions to fulfil.

With a skip in her step at the thought of a lovely social afternoon with friends, Cath spotted Andreas and Dan coming up on the other side of the street. 'Hello,' she called out cheerily.

'Hi, lovely,' Dan responded, with a grin.

'Gorgeous afternoon for it,' added Andreas, as the pair began to cross the road towards her.

'It is indeed. Can't wait.'

The lads looked suave and summery, dressed in beige chinos teamed with brightly patterned shirts; Dan's with small daisy flowers and Andreas's with blue and white stripes. Andreas had the addition of a neckerchief in navy-floral-patterned silk. Little Shirley who was trotting alongside them, was also sporting a floral neckerchief. Her invite a must, as Lily adored their white West Highland terrier. The little dog was an unofficial member of the supper club, of course. Their canine companion was always happy to step up to the role, at the ready to scoop up any stray crumbs that might come her way.

They turned into the lane that led off from the main street, which was sun-kissed with dappled light through leafy trees, and were soon approaching Lily's home; a beautiful cream-stone and wooden-beamed converted barn. Crossing the gravel driveway with crunching steps, a pair of bay trees, groomed into leafy globes in large terracotta pots, greeted them each side of the oak front door.

Before they had a chance to ring the bell, Lily was already there at the door, looking quirkily gorgeous with her trademark angular cropped dark hair, heavily kohled green eyes, and bold-red lipstick.

'Hi, come on in, guys.' She welcomed her guests with a warm smile. 'I'm so ready for this.'

'Hello, and how are you, petal?' Andreas asked. 'And dare I ask, how are the studies going?'

Lily gave a small groan. 'Okay, I think. I've put in a shedload of work, and my brain is fried. But hey, let's not mention it today. I'm having an afternoon off, and I want to chillax.'

'Okay, we'll say no more, other than best of luck.' Dan gave a wink.

'Yeah, well done, Lily. It sounds like you've been working really hard. And the very best of luck from me too,' Cath added, understanding well the stresses of sixth form studies from her many years in teaching, and of course being a mum.

'Oh, and we've brought some feta and spinach pastries to help out. I made them fresh this morning,' said Andreas.

'Tantalising triangles of tastiness,' Dan added.

'Mm, they sound delicious. Cool, thanks.'

'And I've made some millionaire's shortbread.' Cath had also been busy baking. It was lovely to bring something along to add to the occasion; the supper clubbers happy to help each other out where they could. And Cath's little chocolate-caramel biscuit squares were always a winner.

'Come on through. We've set up outside in the garden. Mum's been great, and helped me get everything organised. And, I've made a cake for the occasion. It's been a welcome diversion.' She rolled her eyes, as if the studying had got to her.

Anna was there in the kitchen as they followed Lily through, arranging dainty finger sandwiches on a platter. She looked up with a smile. 'Hello, folks.'

'Hi, Anna,' said Cath.

'Hello,' added Dan.

'Hi,' chipped in Andreas.

'Thanks so much for this. Looks like you've been busy,' commented Cath, seeing all the goodies on the countertop.

'Ah, not too much. Keeping it simple really. Sandwiches and scones on my part,' she elaborated. 'Wanted to give Lily a little break, that's all. She's been working hard. Though I couldn't stop her from getting up early to bake a sponge for today.'

And there, on the side, was the highest, creamiest, most

scrumptious-looking Victoria-style sponge loaded with fresh strawberries and cream.

'That looks incredible, Lily.' The baking queen was evidently back on it, and Cath couldn't wait to sample a slice of that golden-sponge deliciousness.

'It's my Victoria sponge with a twist,' announced Lily. 'It's made with a custard cream and strawberries.'

'Oh, how fabulous. It's looking very much like we're being treated to a full afternoon tea,' Dan said with delight. He adored a high tea, considering it quintessential English summer dining at its best.

'Come on out to the garden, guys.' Lily led the way through open double glass doors to the patio, where a teak-wood circular table was set out with vintage tea plates, cups and saucers, crisp whitelinen napkins, cutlery and Prosecco flutes.

'Mum got a bit carried away with herself,' Lily commented, raising her eyebrows whilst giving a big grin. After the stresses of the past year, trying and struggling at first, to get her parents on board with her dream of becoming a chef or artisan baker – and her wish to go to a specialist catering college rather than traditional uni – they'd finally become more open-minded and supportive of the idea. With a promise that she kept her options open, and had taken a look at some university courses and campuses, as well as the cooking schools she'd researched – Prue Leith's School of Food and Wine being the dream, she had her name down there already. And there was the cutest college in Devon that did a diploma in patisserie, but it was a short course, so perhaps something she could add to her repertoire later. And as well as her sixth form Level Three in Food Science and Nutrition, she had also remained committed to her A-level studies.

Out on the patio, Nikki was already there, with her shades on and dressed in a bright yellow-and-white-polka-dot dress with black kitten heels. Very different from her day-to-day cleaning company attire. She could, in fact, have been dressed for a day at the races.

She spotted the look of surprise on their faces. 'I know, but when the hell else will I get a chance to dress up? Can hardly put the heels on to go off cleaning, can I? I've only worn this outfit once to my cousin's wedding, so it's getting an airing.'

'It looks gorgeous, very summery. Good for you,' said Cath. Glad she'd made the effort to dress up a bit herself, and put her own floral dress on for the occasion.

'Stunning, darling,' added Dan. 'And I totally agree. Why keep things for best, when you can go out there and *be* your best.'

'Exactly. Well then, the Prosecco's chilled and ready in the cooler. I've been holding back, waiting for company,' said Nikki.

'Hah, that's so not like you, my love.' Andreas gave a wink.

'The cheek of it,' came her retort, and she snorted with laughter.

'Right, let's celebrate my afternoon off and pop that cork!' Lily announced.

Dan did the honours, whilst Lily gathered the flutes ready to fill.

'Sounds like I'm right on cue.' Will appeared at the patio, having been ushered through by Anna.

'Perfect timing, mate,' said Dan.

'Hi, Will,' said Lily.

Cath felt her happiness level notch up even more.

Greetings were made, with high fives from the lads, hugs from the girls, and a close-up kiss on the cheek from Cath, who couldn't help but notice how dashing he looked in a short-sleeved white linen shirt and his trademark dark jeans. He'd obviously got the smart clothes memo too, Cath thought with amusement. Al fresco afternoon teas were evidently for wearing your Sunday best.

'Cheers, Lily.' Will raised the glass he'd just been offered. 'Thanks for having us all over. And hey, good luck with those exams.'

'Thanks.' She gave a slow steadying sigh, then took a gulp of her bubbles.

Aware Lily didn't want to dwell on her impending exams, Andreas and Dan moved the conversation on to the incredible cake waiting for them all in the kitchen, and they were soon chatting easily as they sipped the refreshing fizz.

'Oh, this is the life,' said Nikki. 'The boys are out at football training in Alnwick, and luckily for me, it's their friend's parents' turn to do the taxiing and hanging around today. And Kev'll be lazing on the sofa by now, after his "extra-busy" week. Recharging his batteries, so he insists.'

The group gave a chortle at the pun; they all knew he was an electrician.

'Oh, look, and it's about to get even better,' Cath added, spotting Anna heading out with a platter of dainty sandwiches – having prepared thinly sliced cucumber, cream cheese and smoked salmon, and mustardy ham – along with a three-tiered cake stand piled high with freshly made scones, small pots of strawberry jam and clotted cream, graced on the top tier by some delicious-looking mini chocolate cakes, and individual pots of lemon posset. 'That looks amazing. Can I give you a hand?' Cath took the stand from her, setting it carefully down on the table.

'Oh, let me help you too, Mum.' Lily stood up and nipped into the house, coming back soon afterwards with two big pots of tea on a tray, a jug of fresh milk and a bowl of white sugar cubes with dainty tongs, and a tea plate of Cath's shortbread. 'Here you go, guys.'

'Sit yourself down again, love. This is your day. I'll pour,' offered Anna, lifting one of the teapots, evidently keen to wait on them. It seemed like she wanted to make it a special afternoon for all of them.

'This is so lovely, thank you. Are you joining us?' asked Andreas, concerned that Anna was doing all the work and missing out herself.

'Um, I might grab a sandwich and one of your delicious-looking feta pastries before I head out. But I've got to dash over to the Kirkton Co-op shortly. On a mission for my mother. She hasn't been feeling quite herself this week, so I'm fetching her a few groceries, and then I'll stay with her for a bit of a natter. So, I'll have to love you and leave you.'

'Oh, I hope she's okay,' said Cath, with a note of concern.

'I'm sure she'll be fine, thanks. I think Grandma Liz just needs a bit of company and a helping hand.'

Cath had the feeling that setting them up with their afternoon tea and then nipping away, might have been part of Anna's plan all along. The supper club had always been Lily's thing, rather than her parents'.

'Tell Grandma I'll be over on Tuesday, after school,' called out Lily.

'Will do, love.'

'Well, thank you so much for this,' added Will warmly. 'And pass on our best wishes.'

'I will. And you're all very welcome.' Anna gave a cheerful smile. 'I've seen how much your friendship has meant to Lily these past months. And everything you've done for the village, with doing up the hall and the wonderful Christmas event. Well, today's a bit of a thank you from me, really.'

'No need at all. But thanks, we appreciate it,' said Cath. 'And I have a feeling we're going to have a deliciously sociable afternoon.'

After delivering a top-up of freshly made sandwiches and the feta pastries, Anna made her exit. 'Enjoy, folks!'

'I'm sure we will!' Nikki raised her Prosecco glass. 'Thank you.'

'You're a star, Mum. Thanks.' Lily gave her mum a peck on the cheek.

Talking of Lily's grandmother and the Christmas event reminded Cath of her visit to the home earlier in the week. 'Oh, by the way, I went to see Reggie and the residents at the care home on Monday. Think I'd better warn you, they keep asking for another "do". They loved that Christmas party so much.'

'Ah, it was such a brilliant day, wasn't it? The Big Christmas Bash,' Nikki remembered fondly.

'Crikey, I'm still reeling from it now.' Andreas wiped his brow, dramatically. 'I've never cooked so many roast potatoes in my life, and don't even get me started on the oversized turkeys . . .'

'Aw, but it was lovely, though. You and Cath did such a great job, heading up the kitchen,' said Nikki. 'Even my lads liked helping out.'

'It was a great day, and everyone who went said how much they'd enjoyed it,' added Will.

'It *was* like feeding the five thousand,' Andreas declared with a grin.

'Well, if we do have a round two, perhaps we need to think of something a little lower key this time,' added Dan sensibly. 'We have a busy summer ahead as it is.'

There were nods of agreement from around the table. Lily had her exams, Nikki her cleaning company work and hectic family life, Will his shop . . . and now the beach hut to renovate. *Should she really push forward with this?* wondered Cath. But then she remembered all those eager wizened faces in the day room, filled with the hope of something sociable to look forward to . . .

'Well, it would be lovely to use the village hall again,' mooted Cath, feeling the weight and the joy of their expectation, as she passed the pot of jam around, ready to top those fluffy soft scones.

'We've done all the hard work with the renovations, so we may as well get the use out of it,' said Andreas.

'I've heard it's doing well now, the hall,' explained Will. 'We'll need to book a slot in early, if we intend doing something. The Brownies are using it regularly, and I believe there's pilates and carpet bowls.'

'Not to mention the "Pop in and Play" session for the mums and toddlers,' added Dan, who'd chatted with several of the young mums in the shop.

'Ah, that's so cool. To think what we've started,' said Lily with a smile, her hand hovering over a feta pastry.

With top-ups of tea served by Cath, fizz flutes refilled by Nikki, plates piled high with sandwiches, and scones dolloped with thick fresh cream and gloriously glossy sweet jam, the gang sat back in their chairs in the balmy sunshine, contemplating the idea of a new community task.

'Hmm, I am pretty busy over the summer months,' confessed Nikki, with an edge of reserve. 'Just taken on an extra job with a holiday cottage too.'

'And I've got my exams for weeks to come. Just saying . . .' Lily added.

'The shop's full-on with tourists and locals at this time of the year.'

And Cath's own online maths tutoring was finally getting established and building nicely, which, though very positive, meant she had less free time, especially during the coming exam weeks. Her brow creased as she considered the matter. Everyone seemed to have something on. Did their group really have the time or inclination to take on another community task? She really didn't want to let the old folk down by disappointing them. But without her trusty team . . .

'Sorry, guys, let's put it on hold as an idea. I realise it's a lot to ask . . . especially so soon after the last big effort from you all.' Cath felt that was sensible in the circumstances.

'Oh, for goodness' sake, what are we all fannying about for?' exclaimed Andreas. 'We're busy, yes, but who the hell isn't these days? Dear Mama loved coming out for a treat, and so did all the others from her home. The oldies need us.' His beloved mother, Maria, who'd spent many happy years at the Kirkton Care Home had sadly passed away just last year.

'The care home residents were *so* happy that day at the Christmas party,' added Lily.

'And it brought everyone together, young and old,' commented Will. 'I'd be up to help,' he offered, taking the lead.

Cath could have kissed him . . . hmm, perhaps she would later.

'And of course, I'm in,' said Andreas.

'If he's in, I'm in.' Dan laughed. 'I'd be in such trouble otherwise.'

Shirley gave a woof in support from under the table, too.

'Okay, okay . . . go on then, twist my arm. Pour me another Prosecco, if you must.' Nikki sounded unsure. Her life was already manic, yet she couldn't help but feel a sense of duty and kinship with her friends.

'Hah, that's FOMO for you, Auntie Niks.'

'Yeah, whatever. But I can't let you lot down, can I?' She raised a smile.

'Honestly, Nikki, we can take on the lion's share,' added Cath understandingly, sensing her friend's trepidation.

'And I could help too, if we set the event date post exams,' Lily said, through pastry-flake-dusted lips.

'That would be good. So, July or August, then? Into the school summer holidays. That'd give us time to get organised and think of a fresh new event idea. Nothing quite as complicated this time, I promise,' said Cath, feeling relieved that these timings would work better for her tuition schedule, too.

Her thinking cap was on. She took a sip of tea, and nibbled on a cucumber sandwich. It had to be a sociable event, with great food, yet easy to organise. She had to concede that the Christmas lunch had rather taken over all their lives.

A bee buzzed by, and the leaves on the nearby silver birch tree rippled in the breeze. It was lovely here in the garden, munching away on these scrumptious homemade treats, chatting with friends, whilst sitting in the sun. A wonderful way to relax for the afternoon. *Perfect*, in fact.

'That's it . . . *this* is it!' Cath scanned the table of delicious goodies before her with an inspired beam of a smile. 'Afternoon tea to be served in our newly renovated Tilldale Village Hall.'

'Well, it won't be anywhere near as complicated as cooking a full Christmas roast with all the trimmings. I must admit I was feeling a shudder of trepidation, and a sweat coming on when you first mentioned another event,' Andreas confessed. 'I loved doing that gig, don't get me wrong, but boy, did it take some planning and cooking.'

'An afternoon tea sounds a brilliant idea,' added Will.

'Finger sandwiches, scones and cakes . . .' Dan joined in.

'Tea galore, served in the original Women's Institute teapots and all those china cups we found in storage in the hall.' Lily grinned. 'And yes, I can bake!'

'And we can make the hall look so summery and pretty. With flowers in bud vases, and crisp white tablecloths . . .' Nikki added, picking up on the buzz.

'Oh, and why don't we dress up 1950s style? That was the tea dance era,' Andreas took up. 'All grace and glamour.'

'Now you're getting carried away,' Dan chided, yet smiling. 'And who said anything about dancing?'

'But why not? You always say you love a theme, Dan. This is perfect. A tea dance.'

Lily's face lit up. 'I love that vintage 50s look, too. And the oldies can waltz.'

'Or jive,' added Nikki, getting into the swing of it. 'Though that might prove hazardous considering most of them will be octogenarians.' She gave a grin.

'We can swish around in tea dresses, serving sandwiches,' Cath added. 'Aw, I remember Reggie talking about tea dances with his Elsie. He'd adore this.'

'Yes, 50s music and dancing. Why not, indeed, it sounds a splendid idea,' agreed Will.

'It'll bring back so many memories for the older people, too. They'll love it,' said Andreas. 'And Dan, just think, you can bring out your gorgeous old black leather jacket and go all Danny Zuko!'

'I adore the sound of this!' Nikki was grinning.

'Okay, so shall I check out some possible dates? I take it a Sunday afternoon's generally good for us all, with the village stores and your cycle shop closed, lads. And of course, I'll make it *after* your exams are all done, Lily,' said Cath, taking a sip of fizz. 'So, yes, later on in the summer. I'll check some dates with the hall committee, and also coordinate with the care home,' offered Cath, feeling excited at the prospect. 'Any dates you know you can't make, gang?'

'We have a family holiday late July, I'll check the timings on that,' said Lily.

'Nothing major for us at that time of year,' said Dan. 'Other than good old work.'

'Okay. Great, let's get a date fixed in the diary, then,' said Cath.

'A Tilldale Afternoon Tea . . . has a lovely ring to it, don't you think?' Andreas smiled. 'Simple, but it works,' he added.

'Sounds a bit like you, Andreas,' chuckled Dan.

Andreas then swatted his partner as if he were a wasp. 'Cheeky git.'

'It sounds perfect,' confirmed Cath.

Andreas continued animatedly, 'And we can let the village folk know about it, too. Get a poster up in the shop window, get the community involved.'

'The supper club strikes again!'

'It's going to be tea-licious,' said Andreas.

'Tea-lightful,' added Dan.

The group's groans turned into big grins.

'This calls for cake!' And with that, Lily went off to fetch her showstopper of a sponge.

They celebrated their great idea over slices of moist buttery Victoria sponge, with fresh juicy strawberries and a hint of custard in the cream.

'Oh my,' Andreas said dreamily, after taking his first bite.

'You've excelled yourself with this one, Lily,' said Dan.

Cath was left speechless momentarily, as she savoured the perfect combination of bouncy soft sponge, creamy custard and sweet strawberry. 'That is heavenly,' she finally managed. Honestly, it was like having the best-ever trifle in a cake.

Lily gave the brightest of smiles.

It was, in fact, the perfect cake for an afternoon tea event.

* * *

Cath felt sun-kissed, content and very full. A relaxing while later, sat beside Will, he reached for her hand where it rested on the table top, giving it an affectionate squeeze. Life felt good, with everything on the up, at last. They certainly had some great things to look forward to, and life as a couple was beginning to take shape – with a community afternoon tea event now to plan, and the beach bungalow project to forge forward with.

Oh, they hadn't mentioned the hut as yet to the others, so perhaps this was the ideal time. 'We've got a bit of exciting news, too,' Cath started, as she looked to Will. It was his inheritance and project, after all. Will gave an affirming nod, seemingly guessing where she was going with this.

Before she could begin to explain, Andreas blurted out gleefully, 'Oh, we've not got wedding bells ringing out, already?'

Crikey. 'Of course not, we've only just got together.' Cath firmly batted down that idea, feeling herself blush. Though she was surprised to find herself secretly lifted by the thought, but then equally terrified that Will would get spooked.

Will too went rather pink in the cheeks, and it wasn't just the effect of the sun.

'Shame, I was looking forward to buying a new hat for the occasion,' Andreas continued.

'Pipe down, Cilla,' Dan warned. 'After that set-up of a supper club for two, he thinks he's some kind of matchmaking hero.'

With that, Andreas was off singing, 'I need a hero . . .' As the group collapsed into a fit of the giggles.

'Aw, it would be lovely, though,' chipped in Nikki. 'A wedding in the village . . . Now that would be some event to organise.'

'Behave, you lot.' Cath suppressed a smile as she tried to steer the conversation back on track, and steady her matchmaking pals.

Will took over, swiftly changing the subject. 'Well then, the news is . . . that I've just inherited a beach hut.'

'Ooh, how fantastic,' said Dan.

'Sounds great . . . and more than a little intriguing,' added Nikki.

'Tell us more. Where is it?' Lily was curious.

'Now don't go getting yourselves too excited. It is in a beautiful spot on the coast. In the dunes over at Low Newton, but the building has been left empty for a while, so it's rather shabby and neglected,' explained Will. 'It's not really habitable just yet.'

'Think ramshackle,' added Cath. 'We went over to have a look. And, put it this way, the only guests of late have been mice and spiders. So, we won't be staying there any time soon.'

'Sounds lush,' Lily noted sarcastically, raising a neatly drawn eyebrow.

'Yep, there'll be lots of work to do to get it shipshape,' confirmed Will. 'But it certainly has potential.'

'Oh, it does sound exciting, though,' said Dan. 'And that's such a beautiful spot.'

'Yeah, it is. Once we've had a chance to get the main structure sound and rainproofed, you'll have to all come over and see it sometime,' offered Will, the sense of excitement apparent in his tone, despite all the work to come. And that was lovely, thought Cath.

'Oh, a supper club trip to the coast. I can feel a picnic coming on . . .' Andreas grinned.

'A picnic sounds like the way forward. The kitchen facility is limited, let's put it that way,' added Cath.

'Cool,' said Lily. 'But oh, please, don't clash with my exams . . .'

'It'll take a while to get the initial work done, I'm sure,' responded Will. 'But of course we'll bear that in mind, Lily.'

'Yeah, that sounds great, we'll give it a few weeks – a supper club gathering by the sea to look forward to. But back to the mission in hand, we've an afternoon tea to organise, don't forget. I'll contact Julie at the home in the morning, and try and get a date for early August fixed in the diary.' Cath felt a tingle of anticipation.

Reggie and his fellow residents would love this idea for sure. Oh, and she might even look to organise a live band, though she realised that might prove expensive. Finances had yet to be considered. But how wonderful would a proper 50s-style tea dance be?

'A Tilldale Afternoon Tea' was in the making!

Chapter 8

Though they'd had the most wonderful afternoon with Lily, since the two of them had been back at Cath's, Will hadn't quite seemed himself.

'Will, are you okay?' Cath couldn't help but feel a little concerned about him. Surely, he hadn't been scared off by Andreas's wedding bells jibe?

After saying their farewells and thank yous at The Barn, Cath had wondered if he'd like to come back to hers for a glass of wine and to chill out for the evening. It seemed a shame to go their separate ways after having had such a gorgeous time. She'd explained that she had a couple of online tutorials to take from 5 p.m., and had left him in the living room. After an hour and a half, when she'd come back down from her upstairs study, she'd found him fast asleep on the sofa. That in itself wasn't so bad, an early afternoon glass of fizz could easily do that to her, too. But he'd looked a bit pale in the face when he'd woken, and had gone straight off to the bathroom. He'd been tired last week, too. It was all minor stuff, so she wasn't sure why she felt uneasy.

'Yeah, I think so.' He gave a small yawn, then admitted, 'I still haven't quite got my usual energy levels back.'

‘Hmm.’ So, maybe her instinct was right. ‘Perhaps it’s something viral hanging around in your system? That can take it out of you.’ Cath hazarded a guess. She took a sip of the white wine that she’d just poured out for them.

‘Maybe.’

‘Just take it steady, hey. Give yourself a bit of a break,’ Cath spoke softly, caringly. ‘You do seem to push yourself on these long bike rides, and there’s your work to keep up with, as well as everything else you’ve had to deal with . . .’

He’d been through so much. Grief could do strange things to you. Will’s body and mind had been put through the mill these past couple of years. Constantly worrying about his girls, no doubt burying his own sorrow deep down in the process. He’d been trying to hold everything together for so long. Bless him, was it affecting his health? It wouldn’t be surprising.

She felt a tug of emotion within. Her love for Will was growing daily. However much she’d tried to keep those feelings down and listen to the voice of ‘been there, done that, got the T-shirt and ripped it off again’ experience, and however weary her heart had become over Trevor’s devastating betrayal, believe it or not, it was all revved up again and ready to go. There seemed to be no stopping it.

‘Yeah, I’ll try,’ he responded.

She lay her hand over Will’s in a silent gesture of support. Leaning in close beside him on the sofa, his arm wrapped around her, she felt his wonderfully solid warmth. They hadn’t made any rash promises, nor said too much, too soon. There was an element of caution at this midlife stage, leaving you wary of making those bold statements that you might not finally be able to keep. No one was yet talking about moving in together, or anything as close to plunging into a commitment as that. They were taking their relationship day by day. It seemed to be the best way. But oh, did she feel it, that love. It seemed to have a tender language all of its own, a language that she treasured deep within.

She took a slow breath, taking in the scent of his woody-citrus aftershave. Sitting so close, she could feel the beat of his heart below her other palm where it now lay on his chest. She wanted so much for him to stay over tonight, to be able to sleep in his arms. That felt like the very best place to be, just now. She'd never imagined she might feel like this again. But love wasn't exclusive to youth. And how wonderful was that revelation.

Might this second chance at love really last? Dare she hope as much?

Will had stayed the night, the pair of them settled together in the cosy double divan under the ancient eaves of her cottage bedroom. It was more than she could ever have imagined when she'd first moved in over a year ago. After the hurt and pain of divorce, she'd pictured a solo life, quietly getting on with her middle age. But that was absolutely not the way it was playing out at all. Her fresh new start had been full of surprises. And this relationship with Will was one of the loveliest. Who knew where life might take her, *them*, next?

Will had gone off to sleep like a log after a cosy cuddle, he had evidently felt too tired to make love. And that was no problem for Cath, they were beginning to settle into their relationship; it didn't have to be fireworks every time. They'd had many gorgeous passionate nights in these early months of discovering each other, and she was happy to snuggle up for a change.

Over a breakfast of coffee, toast and honey, Cath asked, 'Did you sleep well? Feeling a bit fresher?'

'Yeah, thanks . . . I think I just needed to crash, sorry . . .'

'Hey, it's fine, honestly.' Whilst the naughty nookie in the kitchen had been a gorgeously spicy surprise the other day, they didn't need to be competing in the sexual Olympics.

As Cath took a sip of her coffee, she considered that this shift might signify a deeper commitment forming between them, one that nurtured real life, with all its ups and downs. It was a good feeling. She really couldn't cope with a fly-by-night lover at this point in her life.

Will headed back to his own place mid-morning, after a hug and a kiss, and a promise to see each other very soon. If they didn't have a meet-up scheduled, then they'd taken to calling each other every day, catching up on the little details of their lives. It was nice just to hear the warm tones of his voice, to be honest. She'd definitely be calling later to check on how he was feeling.

Finding herself with a little free time on her hands, Cath took the plunge with finding a date for the 'Tilldale Afternoon Tea'.

She looked up Veronica's number – queen of the village hall committee – and called. Sat at the kitchen table Cath had her pocket diary to hand, opened to start browsing from the beginning of August, and preferably a Sunday.

'Veronica, hi.'

'Hello, Cath. How are you?'

'Good, thanks. How are you, and how's the hall doing?'

'I'm well. And the hall's doing fantastic, thanks to you and the troops. We have some regular groups using it now. The Brownies, Lyn's yoga, pilates, carpet bowls, and there's even been some interest from the Autistic Society. It's becoming a bit of a hot spot, actually. Oh, and that reminds me, the heating's been working marvellously since all the repairs, too.'

'Ah, that's wonderful to hear. Our hard work has paid off.'

'It has indeed. Now then, how can I help?' Veronica got to the point, sounding a busy lady.

'Well, I'd like to make a booking, please. For another event.'

'Oh, do tell me more. That was such a super day for the community at Christmastime. I so enjoyed seeing everyone, the elderly and the young ones, chatting and dancing. I still don't know how you managed to pull it all off.'

'Thanks, well, it was teamwork. And our supper club group have mooted 'A Tilldale Afternoon Tea', focusing on the elderly once more, but also open to everyone. We'd like to fix a date for the summer, perhaps early August time, and start the ball rolling.'

'Sounds delightful, and if it's anything like the last one, it'll be a joy. Give me a mo, I'll just fetch the diary for the hall.' There was a scuffling, and then a rustling sound. 'Right you are, fire away. Was there a particular date you were interested in?'

'A Sunday in August would be good.' Cath literally crossed her fingers. To have all the team available to help, a Sunday was the only day, and August would give them plenty of time to get organised.

A further rustle, as pages were turned. 'Right-io. Oh, there's only one Sunday left – goodness, we are busy – Sunday the third. Shall I pencil you in?'

'Absolutely. That's perfect. Yes, book us in, please.'

'How exciting. I can't wait to see what you come up with this time.'

'Me too.' They had a lot of planning to do. 'Oh, well that's fantastic. We have a date.'

'I look forward to it. And do let me know if there's anything I, or the committee, can do to help out.'

'Oh, that's good to hear. I will. Thank you.'

They then bade their farewells.

Cath hoped the care home didn't have anything on that day, or they might be stumped at first base. She felt a buzz of excitement about the new event, laced with a touch of nervousness. There'd be a hell of a lot of work to get this set up. And with it being her idea, and as team leader, the bulk of the responsibility was on her shoulders. Could they pull off another big social bash? Was she bloody crazy to even try? Nothing like giving herself a task, when her life was busy enough. But then she thought of all those elderly faces looking at her so hopefully in the day room, and she remembered the smiles and chatter at their village hall festive lunch, the impromptu dancing, the joyfulness of bringing people together.

Dancing . . . and music. Ooh, and wouldn't it be lovely to find a band, or some kind of live music; the thought kept flickering in her mind. Give the event an old-style music hall feel, while they ate the most gorgeous cakes, bakes and sandwiches. Well, she wasn't known to do anything by halves, she may as well throw herself in hook, line and sinker.

With no time like the present, she dialled the number for the Kirkton Care Home, ready to check the date with them. Fingers crossed once again.

Cath felt a little nervous as she waited for the call to be answered.

'Hi, it's Cath Taylor, can I speak with Julie, please?' Julie was the care home manager, a lovely lady who kept a tight ship, as well as having a heart of gold.

'Hi Cath, it's Linda. I'll just pop you through.'

A click and a pause, and then Julie's voice came through. 'Morning, Cath. And how are you?'

'I'm good, thanks.'

'Are you calling in to see us this week?'

'Of course. Can't let Reggie and the others down. That's exactly why I'm phoning, actually. We've had an idea, myself and the supper group that is, with more than a little prompting from your residents, too.' She couldn't help but grin, as she pictured all those eager faces.

'Oh, tell me more . . .'

'Well, as the Christmas lunch went off so well, lots of your residents keep talking about it. In fact, several have been asking for another event . . .'

'Hah, they're not backwards in coming forward, are they.' Julie chuckled. 'And yes, I've heard them talking about it too. They so enjoyed it.'

'Well, I suppose when time's at a premium, you have to pack it all in while you can,' Cath agreed with a smile. 'Anyway, after chatting with our group, we'd love to host another social event.

And this time we've come up with a summertime afternoon tea.'

'Now that sounds a delightful idea. How wonderful.'

Cath was cheered by her positive reaction. 'And if, like last time, you could organise transport over to the Tilldale Village Hall, then we'd be happy to host the tea and cover all the other expenses.' She realised that she hadn't actually discussed this directly with the group, but they had done it as a charity event last time. It felt right to continue in the same vein. Fundraising was going to be the next task on her growing list. 'We need to set a date. I've pencilled something in with the village hall and was wondering if Sunday, third of August might work?' She held her breath, knowing that was the only Sunday left in the village hall calendar for the whole of August.

'Uhm, give me a mo. We've got a diary system on the computer here. Oh . . .' The line went quiet for a second or two.

'Ahm, it's just that a Sunday's better for our helpers,' Cath explained. 'Several have businesses that open during the rest of the week.'

'Yes, I can quite understand that, and we're so grateful to you all putting yourselves out to host another function, but . . . oh dear, yes, we seem to have a clash of dates. There's already a residents' outing booked for that day. We're going on trip to Seahouses for fish and chips. It's been set in the diary for a while, and a deposit has already been paid for it. Now let's see . . .' There was a short pause before Julie added, 'We can certainly do the Sunday after?'

'Ah, that's booked up already. The village hall's become very popular, which is great, but it means we're limited to dates. It would be so lovely to host the event there again, and support our village community, though.' After all the hard work they'd put in last year with its renovation, it seemed a shame to have to use somewhere else. The newly revived hall felt so personal to them all. It was a part of their community.

'Yes, of course. What a shame about the timings,' said Julie.

'Don't worry, I'll just have to go back to the drawing board. Are there any alternative Sundays that might work, perhaps early July,' she mooted. 'Or possibly a Saturday.' A Saturday would cause all kinds of issues for the shop lads and Will, Cath mused, but she really wasn't sure where to go with this now. Lily had mentioned her family holiday planned at the end of July, and if she made the date any earlier in the summer, then that would leave exam-laden Lily out of the equation. With Lily being the baking queen, and so excited about the whole thing, it didn't seem fair to miss her out.

Julie mooted a couple of alternative dates, which Cath noted, but knew she'd have to discuss them with her supper team. With so much happening between them all, it was going to be a bit of a juggle, and inevitably someone might not be able to help on the day, putting further pressure on the others. But she was not going to let herself feel deflated.

The pair of them then had a brief chat about the latest escapades at the home, with Cath closing the conversation with, 'Okay then, leave it with me.' Trying to sound bright and cheery, despite her hopes having been somewhat dashed. 'I'll go back to the drawing board, speak to the team, and try and get a date that suits us all.'

She'd have to put out a message to the supper clubbers, and have a further chat with Veronica. With timings and logistics to consider for the home, the hall and all six of them, the challenge was on.

The next day, after speaking with Veronica and pencilling in an alternative Saturday in August and a possible Sunday in early July, Cath held a video call with the supper group early evening, to discuss the date dilemma they were faced with.

Cath explained the care home's diary clash for the Tilldale Afternoon Tea, and then mooted the Saturday date, with Andreas responding apologetically, 'Oh, I'm so sorry, petal, I really wanted to make this event work, but Saturdays in summer are so difficult to cover for the shop. And you're our usual port of call, so that won't help at all.'

'Yes, we'd have to bow out on the Saturday date,' Dan confirmed.

'Okay, yes, I knew a Saturday was a long shot. It wouldn't have been good for you, nor Will either, so that leaves the first Sunday in July then,' Cath proposed.

Will then piped up, 'Sorry, I've got a big cycling event on that day, The Cheviot Challenge. I'm booked to be on hand as a marshal, and I'm the main man on the mobile cycle repair squad – well, that's basically me and Josh. We've done it for the past ten years.'

Cath held down a sigh of frustration.

She then spotted Nikki shaking her head. 'And we've got Kev's mum and dad's ruby wedding do that day. They're having a big celebration lunch. There's no way we could miss that.'

'No, of course not.' Dammit, so as well as Will being AWOL, the whole of Nikki's family wouldn't be able to help either.

This was going from bad to worse, and really wasn't looking good for a summer event at all. Should she start looking at dates in the autumn? But then Lily would be off and away on her studies, Cath realised. She began to feel a bit headachy. But she wasn't one to give in. There was always a way. There had to be . . .

She'd go back to Veronica and Julie and start the whole process again. Perhaps try late June? When was Lily's last exam? Or early September, at a squeeze?

'Sorry, Cath,' said Dan kindly.

'We seem to be going around in circles, don't we,' added Nikki, rather dejectedly.

'Where there's a will there's a way,' Cath added, without realising her pun, in no way ready to give up on this. And then she had to laugh as she spotted Will giving a goofy smile from his thumbnail image.

'There is indeed.' He grinned at the group, and gave a wink.

'Right, so we'll chat again soon. I'll go back to Veronica on dates, and check with the home too, then I'll come back to you all.'

'We'll make it work somehow,' Andreas said positively.

And that gave her the extra lift she needed to get on with the task. The first of many tasks, of course. And well, if it was this hard finding a date . . . her work was well and truly going to be cut out.

A day later, and Cath was back at the care home for her weekly visit, trying her best to add some cheer to the residents' day room. But beneath her jolly chat, she was hiding her concerns that their much-longed-for event might not yet happen.

She'd had a conversation with Veronica last night, after the video call with her tribe, and free Sunday dates were few and far between; the June ones clashed with Lily's essential exam schedule, and the autumn availability began in November! Bloody November, it'd end up being another Christmas do at this rate.

Back in the day room, after spending some time chatting with Christopher about his working days, and Vera telling her the exciting news of a new great-grandchild in her family, Reggie caught her eye and beckoned her over to come and sit beside him.

'Hello, lass. Now then, a little bird told me you're planning another shindig for us old 'uns.' He gave a big, sparkly-eyed smile.

Oh dear, had he heard something on the grapevine about the tea event plans, perhaps through Julie or Linda, she wondered? Or was he second guessing? Either way, she really didn't want to have to disappoint him.

'Umm, well.' She lowered her voice, not wanting to raise the other residents' hopes merely for them to be dashed. 'Yes, me and the team were mooting something, but . . . well, it seems timing's a bit of an ongoing issue.' Cath's shoulders wilted.

'You seem troubled, lass. And that's a real shame when you're trying to do a good deed. So why don't you go ahead and tell me what the problem is. My Elsie always used to say a problem shared . . .'

'Is a problem halved,' finished Cath, who then went on to quietly fill Reggie in on the diary clash they had with the home's special fish and chip lunch outing.

'Ah yes, well, that is always a good 'un, that trip. But . . .' And he paused, leaving it there, as though pondering.

A new face in the room was smiling over at them, at that point. She then gave a little wave.

'Oh, that's Janet. Just joined us. Bit batty, but seems pleasant enough,' explained Reggie, cheekily.

'Oh, well, perhaps I'll go and introduce myself. Make her feel welcome,' said Cath, rising to her feet. 'I'll catch you next time, Reggie. Take care.'

'You too, lass. And don't you go worrying yourself about this 'ere do. Things have a way of working themselves out, as you know . . .' And he gave a wink.

Janet was indeed new to the home, having arrived two days ago. She confessed to feeling a bit lost, bless her, and she was missing her cat, Tigger, a beautiful tabby, who'd been re-homed with her daughter. Whilst Cath and Janet were getting acquainted, and Cath was reassuring the old lady that her cat would have a nice new home with her family, she spotted Reggie getting up rather stiffly out of his seat, with Betty joining him. The pair of them then headed off out of the double doors to the entrance hallway, looking rather purposeful.

After a round of tea and biscuits served by the lovely Linda, with Cath diving in for a Jammie Dodger, Janet began chuckling as she told her how the last time she'd had one of those, it'd taken her dentures clean out.

Cath had to smile.

How she wished she could get this date ironed out, and give these wonderful people a 'Tea Dance' to remember. There'd be no Jammie Dodgers on the menu, however. The home wouldn't thank her if they had an influx of dentistry issues.

Cath was just heading out to the car park, when she heard a dash of footsteps crunching the gravel behind her. 'Hey, Cath, I'm so glad I spotted you. I wanted to catch you.' Julie sounded a tad out of breath. 'The date for the tea event, it's going to be okay, after all. I've managed to switch things around a bit. Some of the residents had got news of your afternoon tea plans, and well, now the word is out, it's become the talk of the day room. They are adamant they want to come, even to the point of foregoing their fish and chips.

'And well, if it makes it easier for you to stick with the original date in the first week of August, I've just managed to make a call to the chippy we were booked into. They can switch to the weekend before.'

'Really? Ah, that'd be amazing.' Cath grinned. 'Umm, this wouldn't have anything to do with Reggie and Betty scheming together, would it?' She remembered their joint exit just a half hour before.

'They were representing the views of the day room, they assured me.' Julie gave an affirming nod, accompanied by a wry smile.

Cath snorted with laughter. And she felt such relief. It seemed the tea event really was the talk of the town. 'That's fantastic. I'll let the others know right away. We've been struggling to find an alternative date. The last I'd heard, the shop lads were trying to sort out cover at work, and all sorts.'

'Yes, I wondered that. I really didn't want to make life difficult for you all, not when you're putting yourselves out. It's so very kind of you. And my residents had such fun at Christmastime. It seems this will be the highlight of their summer social calendar.'

'Ah, that's so lovely. Right, I'd better go. Thanks for sorting this out, Julie. That's brilliant.' And good old Reggie and Betty. Cath retraced her steps, to give the pair of them a big wave and a thumbs up through the day-room window. She couldn't wait to tell the supper gang the good news.

Naturally, expectations were high, and Cath was going to have to very much kick herself into gear. But first things first, she had to get back home ready for her next slot of pre-exam revision tutorials. She mustn't keep her students waiting.

Twenty minutes later, and still on a high about sorting the Tilldale Afternoon Tea date, sounding very like Buzz Lightyear as she mounted the stairs to the spare room where her laptop awaited, she roused herself by calling out, 'To trigonometry and beyond . . .'

Chapter 9

It was the first weekend in May, and Cath was feeling bright and positive after having spent a couple of days visiting Adam at his Wildlife Park.

Of course, they'd been chatting regularly on the phone, and Adam had popped up to see her for a couple of weekends earlier in the year, but this was the first chance she'd had to visit him in his new digs. She'd booked to stay over for a night in a nearby country pub.

Adam had had to work when she'd arrived at the park on the Saturday afternoon, so with a few spare hours to fill, he'd organised her a free pass to explore his wonderfully unusual place of work. Discovering the animal enclosures, she'd loved seeing the cheeky lemurs having fun among the trees and their rigging runways, and the big cats were entrancing – huge striped tigers with their massive padded feet, the spotty leopards very much in hiding and hard to see, and the spine-chilling wondrous roar of the powerful lions. Whilst it was a little sad to see them caged, the animals had lots of space and were evidently well cared for. She also understood from her chat with Adam, later that evening over a meal at the pub she was staying at, that many of the creatures would have been born into captivity and incapable of surviving in the wild, or were suffering extremely difficult circumstances in their native countries, perhaps having been found injured or having lost their territory. Many, such as the Northeast African cheetahs, were on the endangered list with less than six hundred individuals remaining in the wild.

Her son was proud of his new role and was evidently settling in well. He explained that his job as Research and Education Manager meant he was involved with organising and planning various school trips, higher education and special needs visits, as well as coordinating with several other organisations and research schemes, some worldwide. It was challenging for him for sure, especially coming fresh – and admittedly a little 'green' – from university, but his enthusiasm for spreading the word on wildlife conservation was infectious. Cath had loved sitting and chatting with him, enjoying all the details of his role, over a supper of steak pie and mash. It was wonderful to see him settled, happy and enthusiastic about the future again – one she knew would be bright.

And earlier, when they'd been heading out of the main admission area that afternoon, Cath had spotted a pretty brunette-haired girl smile over at Adam as she'd said hello. 'Ah, hi, Kirsty,' he'd responded briefly. Eagle-eyed, Cath was sure she'd seen Adam blush a little. Hmm, was there an early romance in the making, she'd wondered? He really did seem to be finding his feet here. New friendships, new challenges. In fact, she reflected, it felt like both mother and son were moving on big style.

Over dinner, Adam had mentioned seeing his dad recently, and talking about Trev didn't hurt half as much as Cath had thought it might. She was glad to hear that her ex was stepping up to his paternal role. Cath also found the confidence to open up to Adam about Will, telling him how well their relationship was going just now. Her son seemed genuinely happy for her, which was lovely, and with his open-minded attitude, it hadn't ended up feeling awkward at all filling him in about her new romance.

He'd met Will in the village previously, and they'd struck up a conversation about cycling and got along easily, but there was a sense that this budding relationship was entering the next stage for Cath, something more permanent. It was important to her that Adam was aware of this, and also that her son very much felt a part of her ongoing life, too.

His response was heartwarming, and Cath couldn't help but compare how very different that was from Cath's ongoing emotional trials with Sophie, Will's youngest daughter. Despite things improving slowly, when they'd last met, Cath could still sense the young woman's frostiness, that unwillingness to welcome Cath into her dad's life. Of course, with losing her mother to cancer and the tough times they'd been through as a family, it was never destined to be an easy journey.

From chatting with friends, Cath had learned that the 'stepmother' scenario was often a rollercoaster at the best of times. Though she was a long way off from becoming that officially, she'd wanted to try and understand how fitting into an established family might feel. And after a bereavement, the path was bound to be a particularly thorny one. Cath was empathetic and wise enough to realise that much, but sometimes she wished things might forge forward a little more smoothly. So that she could really enjoy her new relationship, and not feel like she had to be on her guard around Will's family. She very much hoped that the old adage about 'time being a good healer' would work in her favour in the long run. And in the meanwhile, she tried her best not to let it get to her. It was a complex situation, after all.

She enjoyed the rest of her evening catching up with Adam, talking and laughing, with memories of times gone by, of happier days with Trev, and Adam's animal antics as a boy. Including the night the tank for his worm farm cracked. He'd struck it by accident practising his golf chipping in his bedroom, and hadn't realised the damage until the wriggling army escaped. He woke to find them all over him, the bed and the carpet. It had been a long job collecting them all.

After Adam organised a taxi back to his shared digs just a few miles away, it was an easy walk up the stairs and to bed for Cath; the pub's bedroom being small but cosy and clean. Her heart had been warmed, and she began to doze off with a head full of happy memories of the day she and Adam had just spent together.

The visit had all gone too fast, but Cath buoyed herself up the next morning with the knowledge that Adam wasn't too far away – he'd been off travelling the world the year before, after all. Concentrating on the steady flow of traffic on the A1(M), she made her way back to her Northumberland village, settling into her journey that her satnav was advising might take around three hours. She tuned in to BBC Radio Two, and began to relax.

With the motorway section of the journey done, and the Angel of the North and Newcastle-upon-Tyne firmly in her rear-view mirror, the more intense part of the drive was completed. Her thoughts began to turn to home, to getting back to Tilldale, finding something easy in the freezer for supper. Might she invite Will around? Tell him all about Adam and her visit? That'd be nice.

At Morpeth, she made the decision to go the country route up the A697, a slightly slower and more winding road than continuing on the A1, but far more scenic as you skirted the moors and the villages beneath the Cheviot Hills. On an S bend, she felt a strange bump jar the vehicle from beneath one of her wheels. And then frighteningly, as much as she tried to steer normally, it all felt wrong. Her heart was thumping wildly as she tried to control the vehicle. She was out of the bend, but something was coming in the other direction. A huge bloody lorry. Steer, come on, Mini, do it! Shit!

She instinctively began to duck down, but she forced herself to look out over the dash at the road and lorry ahead, as she battled with the steering wheel. She knew she needed to get on to the left-hand verge and relative safety, in an effort to avoid the worst. The off-road area here, unfortunately, was the narrowest bit of rough moorland grass beside a stone wall.

Her vehicle was slowing as she braked cautiously, the weird wheel-thumping still going on beneath her. She spotted a slightly wider section of muddy verge, near a farm gate. She limped the Mini on towards that, and came to a bumpy halt half on the mud, but with the vehicle's tail-end still in the road, it wasn't a great place to stop, but woah, at least she hadn't been in an accident. Her heart was still thumping in alarm.

The oncoming lorry passed by slowly. He gave her a concerned look, but it wasn't a good place for its driver to stop and offer help. She fumbled fingers over her dash area trying to find the triangle warning sign, and managed to put on her emergency lights. With a massive sigh, she rested at the wheel trying to absorb all that had just happened in a mere matter of seconds. Then she steeled herself with the realisation that she needed to get out of the car. It wasn't safe to stay in the vehicle, like a sitting duck.

She was shaking as she reached for the door handle. Grabbed her bag. Checked no vehicle was coming from behind her on the road, and got out. Swiftly moving to reach the verge. The damage now apparent. Her front nearside tyre had blown out, with ripped black rubber, leaving a very wonky metal rim to her wheel. OMG, Cath felt so very lucky, and unlucky all at the same time. Relief and shock made her a little weak at the knees, as her eyes misted. Jeez, thinking about that lorry, the bends, things could have ended up so much worse.

She needed to find some help. Ring a garage. Oh, and thinking of how the car was stuck in a possibly dangerous place, tell the police. 101, that was it. This wasn't quite a 999 emergency. She rifled through her handbag for her mobile. The signal wasn't great here but a bar appeared on her screen. Standing still, ensuring she was well back from the road, she dialled. Cath began to explain her situation and location as best she could to the operator; considering she was in the middle of bloody nowhere between Longframlington and Kirkton. So much for the scenic route. The operator confirmed they were going to try and send a vehicle out to help alert other drivers, but advised it might take some time.

A car whizzed past her abandoned vehicle, and then her. Ah, great. It didn't even stop to help. Mind you, she didn't fancy getting into a vehicle with a complete stranger, either. She knew that the Mini only had a puncture repair kit and no spare wheel on board. Not that she'd have known how to change a wheel by herself, anyhow. It was a Sunday, and she didn't know any local garage or tyre companies' telephone numbers. Google was struggling with the lack of decent signal out here for any internet roaming, too. Will . . . ring Will, came to mind. And she did.

He answered within two dial tones. *Phew.* 'Hey, how's it going? Good trip to see Adam?' He sounded all cheery.

'It was . . . but ah, it's all gone wrong. I'm stuck, somewhere on the 697. Tyres blown, and the Mini's knackered.'

'*Shit*. Are you okay?'

'Yeah, yeah, I'm okay, just shaken up a bit.' She felt a bit teary all of a sudden, remembering how close a call that lorry had been. 'I just don't know who to call out. I'll need a new tyre, wheel probably, too. It looks pretty wrecked. Just missed a huge lorry by . . .' She puffed out a sigh, and then took a sniff, trying to hold back her tears.

'Hey, I'm coming out to get you. Where are you?'

'Umm, well, I passed Longfram' maybe five . . . ten minutes ago. I'm not exactly sure. There aren't really any landmarks . . . just moorland.'

'Ah, I've an idea where you are. Are you safe? Are you out of the car?'

'Yeah, yeah. I got out okay. I'm walking up the side of the road . . . on the verge. I've called 101. Perhaps I'd better stay near the car for when they send someone out.' A chill ran through her, even though it was now May, she found herself feeling cold in her light summer jacket. When she'd dressed for her journey home, she hadn't imagined she'd be stuck outside, nor on the edge of the moors. The shock may have had something to do with it, too.

'Okay, I'm on my way. And I'll call out the Kirkton garage from the car. I'm pretty sure they have a 24-hour recovery service. Stay safe, yeah.'

'Yeah. Thank you.' When someone then passed by in a car, she felt the whoosh and heat of it, it felt way too close. 'Damn, it's not the best bit of road here.'

She also feared another driver wouldn't spot the warning lights, and end up hurtling right into the back of her Mini. That would be so awful . . . and she daren't think of anyone getting hurt because of her having to stop there – even if it was through no fault of her own. Yes, she'd wait for the police, or whoever they might send. Scaling the stone wall, she looked for somewhere to sit this out in the rough moorland. Finding a rock to settle on, she had a feeling it was going to be a long, chilly wait.

Boy was she happy to see Will's blue hatchback appear along the road, twenty-five minutes later, and pull over with his hazards on beside the Mini. She waved from her bum-numbing rocky perch on the moorland grass rise, and headed down to the stone wall to meet him.

Wrapping her up first in a hug, and then a cosy sweatshirt he had to hand. 'You all right?' he asked, looking concerned. Aw, he'd even thought to bring her one of his fleeces.

'Yeah, it could have been far worse. The tyre's totally blown out. I lost control of the steering at that point.'

He looked down at the passenger side of the car, and puffed out his cheeks. 'Whoa! Looks like you had a lucky escape. Come on, get yourself into my car. I think I'll move it further down the road, somewhere safer. I spotted a layby just before.'

'What about the police? They're meant to be coming to put out some warning signs or something . . . I ought to be here, I suppose . . . oh, and the garage, did you manage to get hold of anyone yet?'

'Yep, all sorted. There's a tyre specialist coming out in the next hour, and if they can't sort it roadside, they say they can organise a recovery vehicle to follow.'

'Aw, thank you, Will.' She felt like a weight had been lifted. She was by no means inept. She dealt with most situations in life head-on, and managed to sort things out. But it was such a relief to have someone looking out for her, helping her through a difficult time. Someone who cared for her.

'Let's leave a note on the car window with your number and a message, and we'll sit it out together somewhere safer down the road. We'll no doubt spot the tyre van going past, anyhow. It'll be far better waiting in the layby than here.'

'Yes, of course. And are you sure you're okay waiting on with me? I'm not spoiling any plans?'

'It's fine. We'll get the car sorted, then I can take you home. In the meantime, you can tell me all about yesterday, and your trip to see Adam. How's he doing?'

The deft switch in conversation took her mind off the stress of the last forty minutes, which was no doubt Will's plan. A short while later, a police patrol car passed them and they watched it begin to slow. It went out of sight, disappeared for a couple of minutes, and then it must have done a U-turn to catch up with them. An officer approached, established that they were linked to the broken-down car, and advised that they'd put out some traffic cones and a warning sign.

The tyre van arrived soon afterwards. Will drove along to speak with them. It didn't take long for the two guys to ascertain that the Mini's whole wheel was knackered, confirming Cath's hunch. Changing a tyre was not going to be enough, so the next step was to call out the breakdown team. The lads offered to take the Mini's keys and said they'd coordinate the recovery, advising Cath that it was fine to go on home. They confirmed her mobile number with her and promised to provide an update later.

Arriving back at Tilldale village felt like coming home, and was such a relief after the trials of the day. As they passed the first cottage of the main street, Will asked Cath if she'd like to come in to his for a cup of coffee. He sounded caringly protective after all she'd just been through.

He always made good coffee, having a fancy machine that frothed the milk and everything. It seemed like just what she needed. 'Thank you, yes, that sounds great.'

'Oh, and Sophie's here. She's been up for the weekend,' he added casually.

'Oh, Will, you should have said. You've been away hours sorting all this out for me. I hadn't realised. I must have spoilt your day together.'

'Hey, of course you haven't, these things happen. I couldn't have just left you there at the side of a busy road. It's fine. Sophie will have been okay by herself for a while. Probably glad to get me out from under her feet.' Will pulled up kerbside, in front of his house. 'Come on in.'

Cath felt a little nervous walking up the path, hoping she hadn't spoilt the day for dad and daughter, especially knowing that Sophie could be bristly at times. She put on her best smile, however, as she stepped forward into the house. Will held the front door open for her, calling out, 'We're home, Soph.'

Cath wondered how the '*we're*' bit was going down, right now.

Sophie appeared in the hallway.

'Hi, Sophie, your dad's been brilliant today. Sorry if I've messed up any plans,' Cath brazened it out.

'S'okay.' Sophie didn't look that happy about it, to be frank. But her words weren't too harsh. They were going to have to learn how to get along. Both of them wanting Will's company, time and love. Better that they moved forward as a team. But that was easier said than done.

'Thanks for being so understanding, love,' added Will.

'Thank you,' Cath confirmed.

Sophie gave a small tight nod. If Sophie had been a hedgehog, her bristles would have been right on end, Cath mused.

'I'll go make that coffee,' said Will, leaving the girls alone.

Sophie was a bit sharper, however, once Will was out of earshot. 'Well, that's the afternoon almost over. Dad had mentioned about going to the pub for lunch, too,' she muttered sourly.

'I'm sorry, Sophie. I hadn't realised you were home, or that the two of you had plans. Your dad didn't say . . .'

'Well, that's typical,' came the young woman's retort.

Dammit, she'd evidently landed Will in it too, now. It must have seemed like Sophie's visit wasn't important to him.

But actually, after the afternoon she'd had, Cath was beginning to feel cheesed off with this. She loved Sophie's dad, and she wasn't going anywhere. This wasn't a twelve-year-old she was dealing with; Sophie was twenty-one. 'Look, Sophie, I've said I'm sorry. This wheel blow-out was bloody awful and dangerous for me. Your dad's been great, and I'm really appreciative of that. It's a shame it's spoilt your lunch plans or whatever, but please don't take it out on me . . . or him.'

Sophie looked up, somewhat startled.

'I know this isn't easy for you, me coming into your dad's life but we're a couple, and I'm in this for the long haul, Sophie. So, we may as well try to get along. It'll be very difficult for your dad otherwise, and I think after everything, he deserves more than that.'

Sophie didn't get time to respond, as Will came into the front room where they were, right on cue, with a couple of mugs of coffee. 'I made one for you too, Soph,' he said as he passed them over. 'You girls, okay?' He must have sensed an atmosphere in the room.

'Ah, yeah, fine, Dad,' came Sophie's response, as she managed to glance rather guardedly over towards Cath.

It might make the young woman think about their situation anyhow, mused Cath, who gave a small friendly smile, whilst hoping this might be the verbal kick-up-the-bum Will's daughter needed. She'd very much been the princess of the family, the youngest and 'daddy's girl'. It was time to grow up, step up and learn some respect. Enough said, thought Cath.

'Thanks, Will.' She took her coffee gratefully, at this point rather wishing it might morph into a gin and tonic.

Chapter 10

Plans were afoot in the village. The supper club gang were settled at Dan and Andreas's kitchen table in the flat above the stores, after closing time the following Tuesday. They had already spent a half hour discussing fundraising ideas for the tea event: a themed hamper raffle filled with gourmet afternoon tea goodies – this sounded a winner, and Nikki's boys had offered to go around the village washing cars for a fiver, and happy to put all the funds raised into the pot. Will was delighted with this idea, and he and Cath put their vehicles forward to be the first cleans. Thankfully, the Mini was all repaired and back at home.

Cath also advised that the Brownies group had volunteered to do a sponsored trampoline 'bounce-a-thon', and she told them about Julie's recent offer of a donation from the care home. When she'd visited last week, the manager had explained that the home had been left some money by Christopher, who'd sadly passed away a couple of weeks before. The elderly gent had loved coming to the Tilldale Christmas do, and had apparently been talking about it up until the end. It had seemed very fitting, that a part of his monies go to help another Tilldale event, one that was guaranteed to cheer the home's residents, Julie had said.

Lily – via a video call to the others, being mid-exams and

studying hard – was on the case with organising some live music for the dancing, telling them that she was in discussion with some members of the high school's band, and negotiating a small fee for their attendance. She laughed about bribing them with the promise of cake for a reduced rate.

'That'd be brilliant if you can get them involved,' Cath said, feeling the event was starting to come together. 'It would be wonderful to have live music for the guests to dance to. Oh, can you check if they can perform any 50s-style tunes?' she asked.

'I have already, and they've been practising "Swing", "Sinatra" and "Big Band" sounds for a school concert this year. They'll be the perfect fit.'

'Ideal. Thank you so much, lovely,' said Andreas, with a grin.

'And how are the exams going, dare I ask?' queried Dan cautiously.

'Ahm, okay, I suppose. I'm pretty much knackered. But I've just gotta keep going.' She seemed resigned to her revision-heavy fate.

'That's the attitude,' said Will.

'Go, girl!' encouraged Nikki.

'Thanks all, and on that note, I really had better go. Mum might come up at any minute, and realise I've not actually been studying for the past half-hour. Love you, guys.'

'Bye, petal! Love you, too,' said Andreas.

'Best of luck,' Will added.

'Bye, darling. Keep on going. It'll all be worth it in the end. And thank you for your help with sorting the band. Sounds brilliant.' Cath waved at the screen.

Dan had made a coffee and walnut sponge for this afternoon's meet-up, and there was also a plateful of Andreas's famous honey and walnut baklava before them. The conversation had gone off-piste from the tea event, with Andreas asking Will how the plans for the beach hut were going. He was angling for a coastal visit, and a nose around the inherited hut, for sure.

'Slowly,' answered Will frankly. 'I've yet to get someone

contracted to fix the roof and wooden wall slats. It's got to be weatherproofed before I can do anything else.'

'So, there'll be plenty of work on, then,' commented Dan, as they chatted over top-ups of tea and cake.

'There will, indeed,' confirmed Will.

'Yep, *lots* of work,' agreed Cath, visualising the dilapidated state of the place. 'It's rotting away,' she added openly.

'Sounds lush,' noted Nikki sarcastically.

'I've rung around a few companies already,' added Will. 'The structural repairs are needed before we can start thinking about any interior work. And before I can do any of that, I need to get permission from the National Trust regarding the exterior and roof work.'

'It has loads of potential,' added Cath more positively. 'And it does have the most beautiful location.'

'Oh, how exciting. Will you be open to interior design suggestions?' asked Dan, who loved a bit of creative input, and was already looking to the next stage.

'Now then, that's a long way off,' said Will.

'Ooh, well, I love a challenge me,' Nikki added. 'I'm more than happy to help, when the time comes.'

'I think we'd all be happy to help . . . and I'd love to take a trip to the coast to see it,' added Andreas, still angling.

'Well, once the initial repairs are made, of course, you'll all be welcome to come and take a look around. Don't get too excited, though,' warned Will. 'It's more of a wooden shell than a cosy beach retreat at the moment.'

'But in time . . . just think, it could be amazing,' said Nikki.

'It's going to be a great project,' said Dan warmly.

'Lots to plan and do,' added Will.

Cath chipped in with, 'The Tilldale Tea and a renovation by the sea. We've got our work cut out.'

Chapter 11

'Ahm, hey.'

It was now two days later, and Will was on the phone to Cath. She knew he'd been trying to get work started on the beach bungalow and wondered if he was calling with an update. Yet his voice sounded unusually hushed. A mere two words, and she felt an odd sense of unease.

'Hi, Will.'

'Ahm, I've been . . . to the doctors.'

'Oh, right. Well, is everything okay?' He hadn't mentioned making an appointment, but perhaps it had been on his mind about his ongoing tiredness.

'Umm, I've had a blood test,' he continued. 'A PSA.' The couple of seconds' silence that followed seemed disturbingly long.

'Oh.' She'd heard of that test. Cath felt a cold prickly feeling ripple through her like a shudder.

'Cath, they're referring me to the hospital, for an MRI scan . . . the result came back as "raised". There's a chance it might be cancer . . . prostate cancer.' His words came out in a rush now. He sounded like he could hardly believe it.

She could hardly believe it. *She'd been putting his fatigue down to some virus.* 'Bloody hell. Oh, Will, my love.' *Fuck.*

She wanted to hold him, to be with him. But he was on the other end of a phone. Okay, so this wasn't a diagnosis; she tried to reassure herself. This wasn't real, not yet. A PSA test, how accurate were they? It was an indicator. Her brain was scrambling, trying to make sense of this. She finally found more words. 'When do you go . . . to the hospital?'

'I'm not sure. I've been referred . . . Waiting for an appointment to come through. Actually, I think something was mentioned of around two weeks . . .'

'Oh, okay.' Crikey, she didn't want to sound negative, like this was already real. 'Shall I come round? Do you want some company? Where are you now?'

'I'm at the cycle shop. The test results have just come in. The surgery rang me . . . just before.' He sounded dazed.

'Are you all right?' *Stupid* question, she knew, but what the hell else did you say?

'I don't know. I really don't know. Depends what happens next, I suppose. I think I'm better keeping busy here for now. I've got a few services to be getting on with. That'll keep me occupied.'

'Well, it's just at the investigation stage, hopefully it'll all be fine.' She tried to be positive, but as she said the words, unease spread thickly in her stomach. 'Ahm, do you want to come round to mine after work? I'll get us some supper . . .'

Would either of them even feel like eating with this news on the table? But she didn't know what else to say, or do? This was a whole new experience. One she wished she wasn't bloody facing. Not Will . . . how could it be Will? After everything he and the girls had already been through . . . shit, that seemed too unfair.

'Yeah, I'll come round once I finish here . . . Thanks.' His tone sounded dull.

She didn't want to end the call and leave him on his own with this news – okay, so it wasn't news yet. It was about more tests. That's how they needed to think about it.

'Okay, see you later. Take care, my love,' said Cath.

And they closed the call like any other. But that was *so* not like any call she'd ever received. And her heart didn't know what to make of it.

Shock made her feel strangely numb, as she put down the phone. No point panicking . . . and yet, what if it was cancer? What if Will, her darling gorgeous Will, had cancer?

Oh, and, if she was scared – and yes, the initial numbness was swiftly shifting into fear – then what the hell must Will be feeling? He'd lost his wife to that terrible disease only two years ago . . . he'd seen first-hand what it could do, and he and his girls had had to go through that horrendous journey with Jane.

Cath went from feeling numb to sick.

She'd felt restless ever since Will's call. It was now after four-thirty, she'd already taken one tuition lesson, somewhat distractedly if she were honest, with another due shortly. She knew that Will closed the cycle shop around 5 p.m., so he'd be due soon, though he might decide to call at his own home first. After such difficult news, she really didn't want to be mid-lesson when he arrived, but equally, she couldn't let her student down who was about to take her GCSE maths, either.

Cath wrote a little note for him, and left it on the kitchen table next to an empty mug, a teaspoon and the cafetière which she'd already scooped some ground coffee into, along with a tea plate with a couple of choc-chip shortbread biscuits on. Simple things, small acts of love. Then she sent a brief text message to his phone, saying 'see you soon' and giving the time her lesson finished. She didn't want to put him off, but also didn't want him to arrive, perhaps ready to unload emotionally – though that might be unlikely knowing dark-horse Will, who'd kept his feelings close to his chest ever since she'd met him – to discover an empty room.

It was in the last ten minutes of her tuition session, from the upstairs study, when she heard the front door open and close. He was here. Her heart felt a strange pang. She managed to hold the end of the lesson together, whilst fighting the urge to run downstairs and scoop Will up in her arms. Oh, what must he be feeling?

'Okay, well, thanks very much, Caitlin. Keep practising those algebraic equations. And remember, on the exam day, keep calm, read the paper over first before you launch in, and breathe. It'll all be there in your mind if you give yourself a second or two to find it. And your GCSE will go off fine. Give it your best shot. Best of luck, lovely!'

'Thank you, and you've been great.' The auburn-haired girl on the screen broke into a smile. She'd been one of Cath's quieter students this year, far less chatty through the lessons than most. 'I'm still bricking myself about the exam,' she continued. 'But this extra time to go over things has been so helpful.'

'Ah, you're very welcome. It's been a pleasure.'

And didn't that 'thank you' feel good. Cath hoped the young woman would do well – she'd certainly had the right attitude with her studies – and that she'd now be able to move positively into her further studies, and her post-school aspirations, with a decent grade in her GCSE maths exam helping her along her way. A sound maths result was key to so much. This was what being a teacher was all about; giving these young people the tools to achieve their dreams, building their confidence and a good work ethic. Giving them building blocks for their future.

Cath finished their farewells, shut down her laptop and then rushed downstairs. She guessed Will would be in the kitchen; the scent of coffee already drifting through.

'Hi,' she called out from the hallway, trying to sound as normal as possible.

On hearing her voice, he'd stood up from his place at the kitchen table. A look of fear, that he was unable to disguise, shadowed his face. 'Hi . . .'

'Oh, my love.' At last, she was able to take him in her arms, and she felt his weight sink against her as she gathered him to her. They held each other for a silent second or two.

He pulled back to say, 'I can't believe that this is happening, Cath.'

'I know. I'm struggling to process this as well. But it's just the test stage, remember, Will.'

'I know, I know. I keep telling myself that, too. But my granda' had it, prostate cancer. I remembered in the GP surgery . . . there were a load of questions. I'd gone to ask about the fatigue, and mentioned needing to pee a bit more. They did a well-man check whilst I was in, I was due one soon anyway . . . the urine test was fine, and then there were all these questions. And Granda', yeah, he died from cancer . . . and I tried to remember what kind it was. Prostate . . . They suggested the test, and well, here we now are.' He released a long slow sigh.

'Oh, Will. At least, if there is anything, hopefully we've caught it early . . .' Cath knew Will would want to be realistic, and positive. Genetics did seem to play a part. Of course, she'd already been on to Google, between lessons, just to find out a few facts. See where they might start with all this. She'd found the Prostate Cancer UK website. There were many different stages of the cancer, several options for treatment, surgery being one . . . But for now, she needed to mentally put all that on hold. *Who* she needed to hold and support right now was Will.

'Christ, I hope this MRI appointment doesn't take long to come in,' he added. 'If it is cancer, I want them to find it and get it out, as soon as . . .'

'Of course. But hey, we'll cross that bridge when we come to it.' One day at a time. One stage at a time. It was all they could do.

He held her gaze, adding earnestly, 'Cath, we can't tell anyone, not yet. Not until after the scan, the tests and whatever comes next. It might yet be a false alarm. And the girls . . .' He was lost for words then. The pain, at the mere thought of having to tell them such devastating news, was etched across his face. He absolutely didn't want to be the one to drag them all back through hell.

'Of course, we can keep this to ourselves for now. No need to worry the girls. But hey, you can talk to me, at any time.' She had a strong feeling Will would keep this news, and the conflicting emotions he was bound to be having, so close that it would smoulder away inside.

He nodded. 'Okay.'

'Another coffee?' she offered. After fetching a second mug and the milk, she reached for the cafetière. Bloody hell, she felt like she needed a double gin, not another coffee. But that, of course, wasn't the answer.

They were both now sitting at the kitchen table trying to make sense of this. It was going to feel like a damn long two weeks until the scan – which he'd been advised it was likely to be – she knew that much. From looking up prostate cancer earlier, even if it was contained, there was a strong likelihood of surgery or radiotherapy, and there were a whole host of side- and after-effects to consider. If the PSA indicator was right, then the next chapter in Will's life, and naturally hers too, was going to be a difficult one.

After a light supper of mushroom and cheese omelettes with salad – something easy that she already had in – they moved to the lounge, settling onto the sofa together.

She leaned in against Will's chest, and he brought his arm around her. She could feel his beautiful heart beating below her, as he held her tenderly to him. This test, the scan . . . it was their secret to keep for now. He'd insisted there was no need to worry family or friends. She loved how he was doing his best to protect everyone else, whilst faced with this terrible dilemma. Beneath his sometimes cool exterior, lay a heart that cared so much.

'Whatever it is, we'll face this together,' Cath said in a calm, steady voice.

Chapter 12

Cath and Will could hear familiar voices chatting, giggling, and one – sounding very like Andreas – complaining about the weight of the cool box, and that his arms were feeling like they were ten feet long. Their supper club gang must be traipsing up the rather steep bank of the dune.

They couldn't help but smile at each other. It was the weekend after Will's troubling PSA test result. There was a hint of nervousness about Will's health secret between them, but they were both looking forward to an afternoon spent with close friends at the bungalow on the coast. The appointment for the scan had come through for the end of the following week, and there was no point sitting at home and dwelling on things.

The beach hut was still very much a work-in-progress, more or less an empty shell, but at least the National Trust had agreed to the initial external works, and the building contractor – a friend of Will's who'd fitted him in quickly after a last-minute cancellation, had managed to re-roof the bungalow and was coming back soon to replace several planks of rotten wood to its sides and floorboards. In fact, after he'd finished, there probably wouldn't be an awful lot of the original wood left, but that was no bad thing.

When the supper club group had last met up at the lads'

flat above the stores, moving forward the plans for the Tilldale Afternoon Tea, they'd ended up chatting about the coastal hideaway, with Dan desperate to take a look, and Andreas hinting again on the WhatsApp group that he'd love a trip to the coast to see the new inheritance, whatever its condition. With the invite made, they then leapt in, offering to cook and make it the next supper club meet-up; which was a relief to Will who was well aware of the hut's extremely limited kitchen facilities, or indeed, any other facilities at present. Nosiness and excitement were a driving factor for the lads, for certain.

As for today's 'supper' menu, well that was still under wraps. Something that 'reminded you of holidays and the sea' was all Dan had hinted at. Fish and chips, had come to mind for Cath, but unless it was a takeaway, that was more than a tricky task to create on a camping stove. With no electric, there was, of course, no fridge in the place, either. Cath and Will had warned the others, but they'd still insisted on coming over and cooking, rather than a picnic.

With it now being mid-May, they were having to use cool bags and ice packs for the fridge essentials. Will had just been out to buy some big bags of ice cubes from the local mini-market, to fill an ice bucket for the white wine he and Cath had brought over. And, not-standing on ceremony, a black plastic bucket in which to chill some bottles of beer and soft drinks.

'Over here!' called Cath, as the footsteps and voices approached. The dunes could be a bit of a maze, with the various huts dotted here and there.

The pair of them then spotted the top of Andreas's dark hair. 'At last.' A rather bedraggled Andreas, in striped-pink-and-navy short-sleeved shirt and beige chino shorts, was sweating his way along the dune ridge. It was a rather warm day. 'I feel like a bloody pack horse.'

'Oh, stop it. I'm sure you've managed fine. You keep telling me how you've got the biggest muscles,' Dan teased, appearing from behind him. 'Anyway, we're here now. Honestly, you'd think we've made him walk the Sahara Desert with that cool box. Hello, folks.'

'Hi, and welcome,' greeted Will. 'Can I help?' He got up from his chair – they'd brought over a few practical essentials – and reached to take one of the bags from Andreas.

'Thank you. And well, I am rather parched,' said Andreas, giving a hopeful wink. 'Hi, guys.'

'Hello, lads,' responded Cath, smiling at their banter. 'Brought the kitchen sink with you, I see.'

'Nearly. I don't think we'd figured quite how far the walk was,' admitted Dan, a few droplets of sweat beading his brow.

Will headed in to grab some cold beers, whilst Cath gave Andreas and Dan welcoming hugs.

'You'll be ready for one of these, then.' Will reappeared with a smile.

'Now there's a man who knows how to host.' Andreas beamed.

'As you all know, my pouring skills are better than my cooking skills,' said Will.

Nobody argued with that.

'Where are the girls?' asked Cath.

Nikki and Lily were in fact bringing up the rear, loaded with fold-up camping chairs, a picnic rug and yet more bulky cool bags.

'Welcome to the beach bungalow,' Cath greeted them warmly.

'Now then, don't get too excited before you look in. Remember, it's a work-in-progress,' Will warned.

'No worries,' said Nikki. 'And what a view.' She dropped down her bags and took a breath, gazing around her.

'Hey, Lily? You okay? How's it going exam-wise?' Cath asked.

'Ahm, all right, I think. At least, I've managed to escape . . . for just the day. I've got one food practical left and two more A-level written papers, and then that's it. I'm counting down. Nine more days, then I'm done. Exams will be over! I'm *soo* ready to stop and chill out. My brain feels fried.'

'Ah, well done, Lils,' said Nikki. 'You're nearly there, hun.'

'We'll be sure to help you with the R&R, today,' added Dan, with a smile.

'Yeah, well done, Lily,' said Will. 'Rest today, then you can refocus for one last big push.'

'My head is honestly done in.' Young Lily did look a touch peaky.

All that stress and study, thought Cath. 'Yeah, I bet you're tired. Exams can really take it out of you. Enjoy some time out today.'

'I will. I've done my best, and that's all I can do. I'm ready for a good yap and chill out with you lot. And for now, I'm going to park the worries about results.'

'Sounds a good idea,' Cath added warmly, thinking that's exactly what she and Will needed to do today, too.

'Ooh, and this place, it looks awesome,' Lily gazed about her at the wooden beach bungalow.

'Well, from the outside, perhaps . . .' Will smiled knowingly.

'But what an incredible spot. This has so much potential.' Nikki was hovering by the open door. She couldn't wait to get inside and check it out.

Not that there was a lot to see at this stage.

'I take it you want to look around,' said Cath.

'You bet.' Nikki was already on her way in.

'Here, give us one of your bags, Lily, and we can drop them down inside,' offered Cath.

'Thanks.'

Despite being noticeably fresher within, with Cath and Will having gone on a mission when they'd arrived today armed with brooms, cloths, disinfectant, mops and buckets, the interior was very much as it was. They hadn't had a lot of time, or funds, as yet to sort out the next stage of the refurbishments. Two director's chairs, which had been stored pretty much unused in Will's garage, were positioned each side of the log burner. And there was now a replacement, barely used, navy sofa bed that she and

Will had discovered on 'Kirkton Sales and Wants' and picked up for a bargain price of thirty pounds.

One of Will's cycling friends had come over with a van with him just over a week ago, before the doctor's appointment, and helped him dispose of the original sofa, aka mouse hotel, and a few other items, to the dump. 'Express Pest' controllers had been booked in to de-louse and de-mouse the coastal bungalow soon afterwards. And just yesterday, Will had deemed it safe to move the new item in with the help of the same mate. And boy, was that one hell of a carry from the car park and across the dunes! He'd been shattered when he'd arrived back at Cath's later. He hadn't told her what he'd been up to initially, and when the truth of his exertions came out, she'd been cross with him for overstretching himself.

'So, what are your plans for the place?' Dan asked, as they headed on in.

The newcomers dropped down their many cool bags, wine, food items, plus an extremely big pan along with a few cooking utensils; Will having warned them about the lack of facilities and cookware.

Gathered in the living space, and eager to take a look about, they soon began to realise that there wasn't actually a lot to see. The black-metal log burning stove, which was the nicest feature of the place, was positioned to the side wall of the living area, with the replacement second-hand sofa and Will's two chairs beside it. The compact 'vintage' kitchen zone took the space at the back of the hut with its basic cupboards within one unit, and old-fashioned stainless-steel sink.

There was the one bedroom which was sectioned off, just big enough for a double bed, but at present had nothing in it. Will having also dumped the original bed along with the sofa that day – nothing had been safe from those pesky mice! Plus, there was a small box-room of a WC with a wall sink and toilet, which Cath had now given a damned good scrub, armed with heavy-duty rubber gloves, a loo brush, bleach and disinfectant. Several of the wooden wall and floor slats were flaking with rot in there. At least, they were now in the summer months, so they currently had a water supply to flush the loo. After the end of October, they'd been reliably informed by the solicitor, that it all got turned off. So, other than a place to sit for a while with a flask after a chilly walk, the bungalow wasn't going to be a space to use over the winter months. And well, that was it.

The underwhelmed faces around the group said it all.

'It's cosy. Bet it'll be nice here with the fire on,' said Lily politely, trying her best to find some positives.

'Quaint, but yeah, it's basic.' Nikki was more realistic.

'Needs a bit of work, mate.' Dan was thinking practically.

Andreas merely came up with, 'Oh my.'

Not surprisingly the group seemed rather dispirited. They had been warned, thought Cath.

'On the plus side,' said Will summoning a hint of enthusiasm, 'we pretty much have a blank canvas to work with, as you can see.'

'Oh, and with a bit of imagination, I can feel the Hamptons coming on.' Nikki was suddenly perking up, gazing around her at the living space. 'White-painted wooden walls, maybe even the ceiling in white, too. It's the dull dark brown that's doing nothing for it. The sofa's navy so that'll work, yes, with some stripy cushions on. All blues and creams, and soft beige, the colour of old rope. And a driftwood-framed mirror, just over there.' She pointed to a bare brown wall space. 'Yeah, coastal chic, here we come.' She sounded quite pleased with her imaginings.

Cath could kind of picture it coming together with those seaside shades, too.

'Ooh no, it needs a splash of colour,' Andreas began. 'Bright floral paintings . . . Tiki style. Grass skirts and cocktails. Oh yes, Club Tropicana even. And a bar area, yes. Pina coladas . . . with those cute mini umbrellas. We're on the beach, baby.' Andreas was waving his arms as though casting a spell over the place, imagining a Tiki palace, whilst grinning.

'That's so cheesy, Andreas,' said Lily with a smile. 'But you know, it sounds kind of fun, too. Kitschy. If you do it stylishly, it might work.'

'Honey, I do everything stylishly,' he trilled.

Lily continued, 'So, like keep the white walls, but have tropical greens and touches of floral hot pink and orange in the cushions and soft furnishings. And yes, I'm totally in on the cocktails and bar, one hundred per cent.'

'Oh, and yes, a blow-up pink flamingo,' added Andreas, so warmed to his theme that he was smoking hot, whilst Dan spluttered into his bottle of beer.

'Good Lord, I'm not letting you lot get your hands on this place,' Will leapt in. 'Well, not until *I've* settled on a colour scheme, that is.' Yet he couldn't help but smile as he glanced across to Cath, who just held up her hands. He did actually think a little DIY help from his friends might in fact come in very handy, but he'd need to keep a bloody tight rein on them, and the colour scheme.

'Well, I'm more with Nikki on this one,' said Cath. 'Some cool coastal shades. It's a place to relax, after all, not a party shack.'

'Aw, shame. Spoilsports,' countered Andreas, pouting his lower lip.

'It could be both,' Lily mooted, raising her arched eyebrows hopefully. 'Somewhere to chill, of course, but also have something of a cocktail bar feel. There are some very on-trend places in town.' By that, she meant Newcastle-upon-Tyne. 'I could check out some colour schemes for you. When I finally have time on my hands again.'

'Ooh, yes, it could have a bar *corner*, at least.' Andreas was perking up again. 'With a hint of tropical, somewhere.'

'Mai Tais and a bowl of peanuts,' added Dan, with a smirk.

'Scampi Fries,' added Nikki, thinking of her favourite snacks.

'Okay. Well, we'll see.' Will cut them short, whilst Cath stood there grinning. She loved the daft banter of this lot. 'Enough about the decor. That can wait,' Will continued. 'Let's get back outside and enjoy a cold beer on the patio, and make the most of this wonderful May sunshine.'

'And after that,' Cath suggested, 'we could take a stroll down on the beach before getting supper underway, if that sounds all right with the chefs?'

'It sounds perfect,' said Dan. 'Supper's going to be exciting, too. And for a change, it's not Greek style, in case you're wondering.'

'He's such a man of mystery,' added Andreas, ironically.

It was time to hit the deck, literally, with bottles of bucket-chilled beer for all.

A relaxed, sunny Sunday afternoon stroll followed. Their group of six chatted as they wandered, taking in the salty sea air and feeling the soft golden sand beneath their feet. Lily had taken her flip-flops off, and Dan and Andreas had abandoned their trainers at the base of the dunes. Each of them pausing here and there to look across the beautiful bay towards the jagged-finger-shaped ruins of Dunstanburgh Castle on the horizon.

Children with buckets and spades were creating their own mini castles in the sands. Birds gathered along the shoreline; sanderlings scurrying, sandpipers skimming the waves before settling to wade, and black-and-white oystercatchers dipping their bold orange bills into the shallows. Cath pointed out a wise-looking heron to the group, who was standing still on one leg, intently perusing the rockpools. She'd spotted him in that very place before; it seemed to be his patch.

Back up at the bungalow, a half-hour later, they settled into their various picnic chairs on the front deck, with Lily perched on a driftwood log, that someone must have hauled up from the sands at some point in the past. Will found he was enjoying today. His health worries were, of course, still very much on his mind, but hosting for the first time at his beach bungalow, offering glasses of chilled white wine for those who fancied it, or a further bottle of beer, and having the company of the group, was serving as a nice distraction.

'So, what's the story, Will? How did you come by this cool place?' asked Lily. 'I know you inherited it, but tell us more.'

'Yeah, so this used to be owned by my dad's cousin. I've been wondering what the history of it is. All these seemingly random huts in the dunes. I've done some internet digging . . .' Will started. He'd been curious to find out more, once he'd learned about his rather unusual inheritance.

'Yes, these quirky huts in the dunes,' added Dan with interest, 'how on earth did they get built here in the first place? No vehicular access. No real planning, by the looks of it.'

There were indeed a hotchpotch of wooden bungalows nestled in the dunes behind the bay, perhaps thirty-five separate small buildings, stretching from the golf club at Embleton, in a scattered trail along to the headland point at Low Newton beach.

'Well, I've done a little research,' Will explained. 'And they were originally built by the Dunstanburgh Castle Golf Course that's positioned behind these dunes, back in the 1930s, as a place for the golfers to stay over.'

'Ah, okay, that makes sense.' Dan nodded.

'Then they were compulsory purchased in the war, as the country prepared for invasion. There were trenches and all sorts of coastal defences set up here. You can still find odd bits and bobs of metal about. After that, when the war was over, they were offered back to the original owners for repurchase, or otherwise sold on. Most likely at a cheap price back then, but now, they can go for big money, as they hardly ever come up.'

'That's so cool,' said Lily.

'I own the bungalow, but nowadays, the land is leasehold with the National Trust,' added Will.

'Ah, I see. So, you don't own the land just the building,' clarified Nikki.

'That's right. It was Dad's cousin, Bill, who owned it before. He and his wife. They didn't have any kids of their own. We came down here once or twice, I seem to remember, years back,' Will recollected. 'I can picture playing out on the front deck here, finding grasshoppers in the dunes and collecting shells down on the sands with Mum. There were a few other kids from the huts and I knocked about with them, too. But after that summer, way back, we never came back, not to the hut. I'm not really sure why. And I suppose, later on, it didn't get used much. It wasn't mentioned at home over the years, and in time I forgot about it. So did my uncle, by the looks of it, perhaps he and his wife couldn't keep it up. Didn't visit much themselves . . . Uncle Bill was never in good health,' Will explained further. 'After Auntie Brenda passed, he went into a care home. My dad would visit him every now and then. He was in there for years before he died recently.'

'I suppose it hasn't been used here for years,' observed Dan.

'Yeah, left to rack and ruin. Such a shame,' said Cath.

'Bet it was a cool place to hang out as kids,' said Andreas.

'It's a pretty cool place to hang out now. If you think of its potential, anyhow,' added Lily.

It was indeed in the most stunning spot. The gathering gazed out across the awe-inspiring gold and blue hues of the bay, as they chatted.

'Location, location, location,' called out Andreas suddenly, waking them all up from their history lesson, as though he was presenting *Escape to the Country*.

'This'd definitely be the "wildcard" house,' said Nikki.

'Hah, absolutely,' agreed Cath, knowing the TV programme they were referring to. The wildcard being the quirkiest and out-there kind of option.

Sat on the deck, looking out over the rhythmic swell of the pewter-blue North Sea, with a brief break in the conversation, they could hear its hushing and rushing as it rolled in, breaking in a froth on the shore.

Families were playing on the sands beneath them; laughter, chatter, sandcastles, ball games, dipping toes and splashing in the chilly sea. Dog walkers strolling. Terns and gulls circling above giving their iconic coastal cry; looking up, you could see the white of their underbellies as they turned and dipped. All set against the backdrop of a Northumberland almost-summer sky of azure blue, with plump cumulus clouds in the exact same white and grey shades as those birds.

Aromas of fried garlic and onions began wafting from the hut. Dan had started cooking the supper. Andreas was busy in the cramped kitchen area too, setting out a platter of olives and breadsticks, Manchego cheese and mini chunks of chorizo. Outside on the deck, a small plastic table, that Will had brought from his garden shed at home, was set out; ideal for propping their glasses and the snacks to come. Sunshine was streaming in on them.

'Ah, this is the life.' Nikki stretched out her lightly tanned legs, which were clad in denim cut-off shorts. 'The boys are off doing football training with Kev right now. And then they're visiting Granny after that, who's making their tea. All four of them, Kev included. Says she never sees enough of the boys these days, what with school and everything. She's looking forward to spoiling them. So, for one day only, I've got free rein.'

Andreas appeared with the nibbles on a tray brought from their flat – honestly, they'd just about brought the kitchen sink with them, it was no wonder he'd turned up shattered after carrying everything – plus a jug of fruity sangria, and a stack of small drinking glasses. The drink gleamed ruby red in the sunshine, and was filled with fragrant orange and lemon slices, diced apple and strawberries.

'Oh, and life just got even better.' Nikki grinned.

'At your service. Sangria by the sea.' Andreas took a bow.

'Wow, this is fantastic.' Cath was delighted. 'I see we're going Spanish, hey? A bit of a departure from your usual Greek-Cypriot style, Andreas.'

'Oh yes, Dan has taken the lead with the menu today.'

Andreas and Dan came up with such great ideas for their dining experiences. And *experiences* they always were!

So, it wasn't Tropicana cocktails, after all, thought Cath, though that might yet come to fruition later. And a Spanish theme, hey. It wouldn't surprise her if Andreas came out sporting a sombrero with some maracas and a castanet. Flamenco on the beach might even be on the agenda for later, she mused merrily. She'd better keep schtum, or she'd be giving the pair ideas. The lads were guaranteed to bring an element of joy to every occasion, and looking over at a now-smiling Will, in the midst of his troubling health issues, this was exactly what the both of them needed.

Nikki held her glass aloft. 'Cheers, or should I be saying "*Salud*" or "Olé"!'

'*Salud*.' 'Cheers.' Lily and Cath chorused.

'Thank you, lads.' Will had taken a small glass. With his health concerns, he was keeping alcohol to a minimum just now.

'Thanks, Dan,' Nikki called out towards the kitchen zone, where the 'head chef' was still full-on at the camping hob.

'You're welcome.' his voice drifted out over the sounds of sizzling. 'And I'll be joining you soon. Though mine'll be a 0 per cent lager.' Dan had agreed to drive them home later.

More mouthwatering scents, now of seafood and tangy tomatoes, were reaching the deck area. Ah-hah, Cath had an idea what might well be on the menu. When a slightly-sweaty looking Dan appeared with his oven mitts on, brought from Tilldale for the task, she was delighted to see a huge pan of – yes, she'd guessed right – paella. Prawns and peppers, mussels in their shells, chorizo, chicken, olives and wedges of lemon adorned the dish. 'Supper is ready.'

'Wow, that looks a-maz-ing,' said Lily. 'Wait, let me take a picture.' And she pulled out her mobile phone and snapped away. 'Okay.'

'Oh, I'm gonna have to stand it somewhere to serve,' explained Dan. 'Your kitchen space is a challenging area, Will.'

'I realise that, sorry,' Will agreed.

The paella dish was placed on a large bread board out on the wooden deck, where Dan crouched down to serve it out into cute Spanish pottery-style bowls.

'Ooh, aren't they pretty,' commented Nikki.

'We carried these all the way home from the Costa Brava, on our jollies two years ago,' Andreas explained. 'And the huge paella pan. Seemed a bargain at the time. But it cost us fifty quid in excess baggage.' He laughed. 'We hadn't thought of that, had we, love?'

'We do love a paella, though. It was well worth it,' Dan added with a warm smile.

'Dan's the paella pro,' enthused Andreas proudly.

'Well then, let's have a toast to the chefs,' said Will, who was looking more relaxed than Cath had seen him in days.

'Hear, hear,' said Cath, feeling such warmth for their wonderful friends.

'Yeah, thanks so much, lads. Can't wait to dig in,' said Nikki.

'Looks delish,' said Lily.

With a stunning sea view set before them, they tucked in. The flavours were divine. It was indeed as good as it looked. Perfect for a summer get-together on the coast. The lads had pulled off 'The Seaside Supper Club' perfectly. With no cooker, no real kitchen to speak of and only a portable gas camping hob, they'd done a sterling job.

'Cheers,' said Nikki.

'Cheers, and thank you,' said Will.

'This is exactly what the beach hut needs. Friends, fantastic food and . . .' Cath started.

'Fun.' Andreas finished, before Cath had a chance to find the right word, and then he pulled out a pair of castanets from his pocket and clacked away with dramatic arm gestures, almost knocking his food bowl off his lap! 'We brought back these little beauties, too.'

Cath shook her head as she giggled, fork in hand. The rest of the group chortled away at his daft antics.

Chapter 13

The fab four guests stayed until the sun began to dip low behind the dunes, setting beyond the golf course behind them to the west. Long shadows were cast over the deck area and the bungalow, the heat from the day now fading. A salty sea breeze rippled through the marram grass, and cooled their skin, as the tide rolled back in, making them reach for their jackets and light fleeces.

Giving the cheffing duo a break, Cath, Will, Nikki and Lily began clearing the glasses and dishes from the deck, washing and drying them at the little kitchen sink, ready for the gang's departure. Will and Cath intended to head off soon after the others, too. The hut wasn't really in any condition for a sleepover as yet.

With the crockery now stacked on the side, Andreas popped his head in to advise that the colourful Spanish-style dishes, which they'd served the paella in, were to stay as a 'hut-warming' present.

'But they're your special holiday ones. We can't take them,' said Will.

'Of course you can,' insisted Dan, appearing at his partner's shoulder. 'It seems very fitting that their new home is here by the sea.'

'That's so kind of you, lads,' said Will, evidently touched.

'That's wonderful, thank you. They are gorgeous,' added Cath.

'We think they've found their rightful home in the beach bungalow,' Andreas told them, with Dan smiling warmly on.

It also meant they wouldn't have to lug them back over the dunes, confessed Andreas more pragmatically to a chorus of laughter. After farewell hugs all round, Andreas was once again looking like a pack mule as they set off; loaded with the huge paella pan, sangria jug, Tupperware items and a rucksack filled with a heap of kitchen utensils. Dan had two half-empty cool bags; one packed carefully with the sangria wine glasses, tea towels and some spare ingredients. The girls were also loaded for the return walk, with the fold-up chairs, picnic rug and Nikki's wine bag filled with several empties, ready to recycle at the local bottle bank.

It couldn't have been a more joyful day. And Cath's heart, bruised from the news of Will's PSA test and impending scan, felt like it had been lifted with love.

Their supper club gang were waving merrily as they set off, calling out 'Bye', 'Thanks', 'It's been brilliant!', 'Love the beach bungalow!' and were soon on the trek across the dunes once more, back to the little car park behind the pub, and then on to Tilldale.

'Well, that was really lovely,' said Cath with a happy sigh.

She couldn't help but feel a touch of sadness, however, as she watched their friends go. It had been such a fun and magical day. The quiet that moved in as their gorgeously sociable supper gang moved out, left space in their minds for concerns about the impending MRI scan, and what it might reveal, to shift uneasily back to the forefront.

The beach below them was emptying, with just the odd dog walker about, and an early evening calm took over the bay. Eider ducks bobbed on the gentle waves, and terns glided across a sky that was now an inky-mauve-blue with hints of faded gold and peach as the sun began to dip lower. The ruins of Dunstanburgh Castle stood shadowy on the far headland.

The bungalow deck was now a space for two. It seemed right to stay a while longer. To ease into the evening, and make the most of this view, this place, before they inevitably headed home and back to reality.

'That paella was amazing, wasn't it,' said Will, as he topped Cath up with a glass of Rioja wine. He'd switched to sparkling water.

'Yeah, it was *really* good. Delicious.'

'I'd go as far as to say it's the best I've ever had. The lads always do a brilliant job of catering. And you know, it's really helped take my mind off things, today.' Will's eyes had a hint of their gorgeous sparkle back. Today really had been a light in the shadow of his recent news.

'I can tell. And that's so lovely. Yeah, having everyone here has helped me too,' agreed Cath. It had been a welcome relief. Even though their supper club friends hadn't known a thing about their current worries, their kindness and their friendship, and of course their sense of fun, was support in itself.

'I had a really good time,' acknowledged Will.

'And just think how many more wonderful times we can have, especially when we get the bungalow shipshape. Perhaps we can freshen it up with a lick of paint, and find some more furniture.' It was nice to make plans, to think of the future. And there *would* be a future for them with all sorts of things to look forward to, once they got past this hurdle. Cath felt her resolve strengthen.

'Yeah, it'll be good to get my girls over here, once I've got it a bit more sorted too. They'll love it.' Maddie and Sophie, though curious on now hearing about their dad's inheritance, hadn't made it over to see the hut in the dunes as yet. Will hadn't been in a big rush to show them either, to be fair, until he'd had chance to get some of the work done, making it look and feel a little more the part. He didn't want them to end up disappointed.

Talking of his daughters, Cath was jolted by the thought that the results of the scan which was booked for later this week, could change all of their lives . . . She tried to keep those fears down. Why spoil such a lovely day. But surely Will couldn't help but think about that, too. It was like life was on hold for them both until this next step. Cath sent a silent prayer to the golden-hued evening sky that all would be well for Will, and that perhaps, hopefully, it wouldn't come down to having to tell the girls at all.

She reached a hand out to his, and held on. Neither said anything as they looked out across the bay. There was almost too much they might say, and somehow right now they didn't feel the need to. Who knew what was next in life? What curveballs and pain, and what moments of joy and love, might lie over that next horizon.

They stayed in the now, holding hands, with the most stunning of North Sea views before them. One day, and one moment at a time.

Chapter 14

Cath found the wait excruciating. Being asked back in for results was, in her experience, never a good sign. She was pacing the hospital corridor whilst Will spoke to his doctor. Though Cath had offered to be there by his side, Will had wanted to face this one alone, heading into the consultant's room by himself.

The past couple of weeks had been tough. And since the wonderfully uplifting beach bungalow paella day, Cath and Will had had to plough on at work and at home, until the scan day finally arrived. Both of them hoping against hope that all would be well, and that this nightmare they'd suddenly been plunged into would end. But that wasn't to be.

After that, the biopsy had come next, and again, yet more days to get through. More nights at Cath's in each other's arms, words often failing them. Cath couldn't help but notice that Will didn't seem to want to be intimate in his own home, not more than a brief kiss and a cuddle. Perhaps the ghost of Jane, and his family ties felt so strong there, that it still seemed inappropriate for him, somehow.

And then, he'd had to deal with presenting cheery-faced video calls to his girls, trying hard to hide any trace of his fears or this dilemma he was facing. He was determined to protect them for as long as he could. Cath could understand that, respecting his decision, especially after all they had been through as a family, but she couldn't help but think that if she was in his daughters' position then she'd have wanted to know. And unable to offload her stress and fears in a private chat perhaps with her sister, steadfastly keeping her promise to keep Will's health scare as a secret until they knew the outcome either way, the tension for them both had been palpable throughout.

And here they were. The outcome imminent. What kind of conversation was going on between those consulting room walls? A relieved or extremely difficult one?

The sound of a door opening from along the corridor. Cath was on high alert. Oh, here he was. Will was coming out. His face looked pale. Her heart felt all jittery. The sucky swish of his trainers on the grey lino floor filled the corridor as he approached, sounding very much like the swishing of her own stomach.

Cath was trying to read his facial expression, his posture. If anything, he appeared rather dazed. He wasn't smiling. *Oh dear God, please let him be all right.*

She stood up instinctively as he neared, focusing on his beautiful hazel eyes, afraid of the words that might come next.

'Wi-ill.' His name caught in her throat. It came out sounding like a question.

He pursed his lips before starting to speak, 'It's cancer, Cath. I've got it. I've got prostate cancer. Stage T2.'

'Oh my God, Will.' The 'C' word snatched her breath away. No, not her gorgeous Will. And oh, dear God, not after everything he and his family had already been through. It seemed too cruel.

She took him into her arms.

As she held him, her mind was buzzing: *What did that even mean, T2? And what did this diagnosis mean for him? What next?* But she sensed this was not the moment to quiz. The questions, and some answers, would come soon enough. Time seemed to stand still for a few seconds. They hugged in this starkly-lit, white-walled hospital corridor, with other patients sat waiting their turn, a nurse walking purposefully by, clinging on to each other like they were clinging on to hope.

As they finally shifted apart, Will took a long, slow breath. It was evident he was struggling to take this in, trying to work out how to process, to deal with, this shocking news. His voice trembled as he finally spoke, 'I-I don't know how I'm going to tell them, Cath. I can't do this to them . . . not all over again.'

And she knew exactly who he meant. His girls. They were still reeling from the bomb of their mum's death, after all. And now this . . . Cath's heart felt sore for him, for them. At this moment, life seemed too bloody unfair. How could it be happening again to this grief-stricken family?

'I know, my love . . . we'll find a way,' she tried to soothe him with her words, but it was as though he'd hardly heard them.

A fucker of a cancer curveball had hurtled in. The impact of this frightening diagnosis was about to crash with wider consequences. Despite her personal fears – and she really didn't want to allow those thoughts headspace right now – she needed to step up and be strong for Will, for his family. As of today, there was a whole new future to face.

First, they needed to head back, to get Will home. 'Come on, let's go back to the car.'

Cath was glad she'd been the one driving, as Will seemed in shock. He was almost too quiet as they took the lift down; Will clutching a couple of leaflets, she noticed, one of them from Prostate Cancer UK, another Macmillan Cancer Support. It was all so hard to take in.

They'd talk later, process this more, when Will was ready. When the initial thoughts and fears had had time to settle. Dammit, she wished she'd gone in with him now, but he'd insisted on facing the consultant and his diagnosis alone. They were at such an early stage in their relationship, they weren't married, weren't even living together, and she hadn't forced the issue. But this was the kind of news you needed someone by your side for. Well, she was here now.

Cool fresh air hit them at the atrium glass door exit. Will paused.

'You feeling okay?' she asked.

'Bit sick, sort of giddy . . . I'll be all right to get to the car.'

She was feeling that, too. A bit spaced out. Like she was here, but also that she was watching it all unfurl like a movie . . . a nightmare.

'I can't stop thinking about the kids.'

'Oh, Will.' She held his hand as they weaved through a trail of slow traffic, that seemed to be kerb crawling but were actually hunting free spaces, into the row of parked cars where Cath remembered hers was. It was a relief to reach the Mini, and sit down. It felt familiar, safe.

Taking a slow breath, and deciding that she was okay to drive, she announced, 'Let's go.'

Will merely nodded, and off they set. Words failed them for a while. There was enough going on in their heads with trying to absorb this news, that chitchat seemed both irrelevant and irreverent. Cath focused on the drive, navigating the busy Newcastle City bypass, aware she was still reeling.

Fifty minutes later, driving over the brow of the hill, with the country landscape rolling like a patchwork of fields before them, and the Cheviot Hills in the distance, they could see Tilldale nestled in the valley. It felt a relief to be home.

Back in the village, they parked roadside and headed into Will's semi-detached house. Into this home, that had already witnessed so much pain and grief.

Cancer, it was real. Will had cancer. Cath felt haunted by the thought. He seemed so healthy, so vital. He'd only had the mildest of symptoms, and there she was, thinking he'd had a virus or was overdoing the cycling.

As they took off shoes in the hallway, unsure what to do next,

Cath offered, 'Umm, shall I make us some coffee?' You had this seismic news, and then you didn't know what the hell to do with it.

'Yeah, please.'

In the kitchen, the everyday task helped shift her focus for a short while. She'd make it strong; they certainly needed that. Froth up some milk. She'd been there enough to know how to work his fancy coffee machine. A rhythmic hum filled the kitchen, as it filtered through, along with the whizzing sound of the milk spinner.

She took the two filled cups, and found Will sitting on the sofa in the living room, head in hands. He looked up, rubbed the salt-and-pepper hair at his temples, and reached for his coffee, muttering, 'Thanks.'

'You're welcome. Better than the hospital stuff.' The hospital . . . and why they'd been there swamped their minds. They'd persevered in the waiting area, with a thin plastic cup of instant coffee from a corridor vending machine. It had been pretty tasteless. The only thing comforting about it had been the warmth.

'Will, I'm so sorry it was bad news.' She sat down beside him on the sofa, consciously leaving a few centimetres between them, giving him a little space.

'Yeah, bit of a shock. I'm the healthy guy. All the cycling, I don't smoke, don't drink that much, eat pretty well. I feel fine. It seems crazy.' He was shaking his head.

'Yeah, it does. But at least it seems like you've caught it early. What did the consultant say exactly? You mentioned Type T2?' Now seemed a better time for those questions.

She so wished she'd been in the room with him. She could have listened on his behalf, taken things in, made notes even, as his world had folded in like a pack of cards.

'Well, it's not the worst type, thank God. There's one to four. Two means the cancer's contained within the prostate, and not spread.'

'Okay, well, that's hopeful, I guess.'

'Yeah, guess I got lucky.' He sounded bitter, sarcastic even. 'Sorry,' he added swiftly, looking up at her, confusion and pain in his eyes. 'I didn't mean that. There'll be lots of others having this conversation, who aren't so lucky.' He paused, sighed heavily, then took a sip of coffee. 'Jeez.'

'So, what happens next?' she gently probed.

'Umm, I need to have a more detailed talk, soon, with the team . . . multidisciplinary or something. We then decide whether we go for surgery or radiotherapy as the first option. There was also something about active watching – keeping an eye on it. That's not going to happen here. I want it out. It's fucking cancer, it's going . . .'

'Yeah.' Cath nodded, understanding that he'd want to do everything he could to get rid of this tumour as soon as possible. Taking no chances that it might spread.

'There are loads of possible side-effects to consider, too. It was hard to take it all in . . . There's a letter they gave me. A website too. It'll all be in there, I suppose.'

'Okay, so we can look at all that. Get the information we need.' Cath's tone remained calm, even though she was tearing up inside for him.

He held her gaze with a haunted look. 'Cath, I can't tell the girls, not yet.'

'I do think they'll need to know, Will . . . they'd want to support you.' They were adults, and this was their much-loved dad.

'I know, I know, but not now. Not yet. Sophie's got her big law exam coming up. Her degree hangs on this. I-I can't do this to her, not again. She's already had her A levels wrecked.' He sighed heavily, exasperated by the position he found himself in.

'Yeah, I understand that, but I do feel that they'd want to know . . . to help. To be there for you.' Cath tried. It was such a big thing to keep from them.

'Leave it, Cath,' he snapped. 'We need to keep this to ourselves for now. And yeah, maybe later, when her exam is done, maybe then it'll be better news. Once it's gone, once it's removed. I'll have the surgery . . . We can tell the girls, then. In a couple more weeks.' He was determined to protect them.

'But surely, they'll want to know that you're about to undergo surgery, if that's the way it goes?'

His face was fixed, his decision too. 'No, there's no way I'm jeopardising Sophie's exam. And if Sophie can't know, then neither can Maddie.'

'All right, of course, it's your decision. Your family.' God, this was so difficult, but she had to concede. 'I can see your point with exams involved. Though I bet the girls will be bloody cross with you, once they find out that you've been holding back on this.'

'Probably, but that's nothing new, me doing something to annoy them . . . and hey, we can cross that bridge when we come to it.' He managed a wry smile.

'Oh, Will.' Cath leaned in beside him, closing the gap between them on the sofa. His arm came around her, and they sat side by side, battered by worry and shock, and yet harboured by the warmth of their love. 'We'll get through this. We will. Together.' Cath's voice held strong, in a world that had just turned upside down.

Chapter 15

An hour later, still at Will's place, having found some comfort in togetherness, he seemed restless, admitting to Cath that he felt both shattered and yet oddly alert. He had evidently been blown away by today's news, with the sudden blast of excess energy that had followed the shock having no real outlet.

'I think I might go out on the bike. Just a short ride. I need some air, some space. Something normal,' he said. 'I can't just sit in and put life on hold whilst I wait for this next appointment.'

'Yeah, I can understand that. That sounds a good idea,' agreed Cath.

They'd now looked up the website, read his NHS letter and browsed the leaflets. So much information, and yet it was still so hard to digest the fact that this was real. It was late afternoon by this time. A mild late May day, with bubbles of cloud, the chance of a shower. It'd do him good to get out. Clear his head a bit, if that were possible.

'I'll nip home then,' said Cath. 'Unless there's anything I can do here? Or that you want? Come back to mine later, if you'd like.'

She didn't offer a meal. Right now, Cath didn't even feel like cooking or eating. Her usual hearty appetite felt like it had been bludgeoned.

'Ahm, I'll let you know, when I get back. I just need a little space right now,' he responded.

'Yeah, I understand.' And Cath did understand, much as she felt like wrapping him up in cotton wool, he was still – oddly in the light of today's news – a fit guy, who needed the physicality of exercise. And, she knew him well enough to realise he was also an emotionally guarded man, who needed some time on his own. She so wished he was able to open up more with her, though. Perhaps if they'd been living together, and were further on in their relationship, they'd have more of a safety net in place, to work through these things as an established couple. It admittedly hurt to feel excluded in this way, when she had so much to give in support. But she told herself this wasn't about her. Right now, Will needed to get his head around this by himself. Despite feeling a bit wobbly after the shock of today, she tried not to take it personally.

After an extra-long hug, and a forced cheery-sounding 'Perhaps, see you later?' which was more of a question than a statement, Cath returned to her Mini and drove back to her cottage.

Sitting alone on her back garden patio, with her thoughts and a small glass of gin and tonic, which she'd caved in and let herself have, she deliberated. What did *she* do in the face of this news? This terrible news that the gorgeous man she'd fallen in love with, the boy she'd known all those years ago, was facing cancer. She brushed a tear, then another, from the corner of her eye; the silent ones she'd been keeping back all these hours. All that time wasted being unsure about each other this past year, the will-they-won't-theys now seemed so futile, and all those wasted years since meeting in their teens . . . Had she just found the love of her life, to lose him all over again?

When times were tough, she'd usually offload by chatting things over with someone she trusted. Yet, she knew she couldn't tell their friends, not yet, not Nikki, not even her sister. It was a secret she had to keep for Will's sake. It wouldn't be fair, or right, to share any of this before his girls were told.

Dammit, sitting about moping didn't feel right, either. And with the clouds massing, it felt a tad chilly sitting still, even with a cardigan wrapped around her shoulders. She really ought to start tackling the to-do list for the upcoming Tilldale Tea, now the date was fixed, but her brain was feeling like mush. That would have to wait for another day. She spotted a couple of pesky weeds in the garden border. That'd keep her busy, a spot of gardening. She went up to the shed, where she kept a few basic garden tools. The place where, just over a year before, the supper club had first started. Memories of her and Will and the others forging new friendships flooded her mind. She couldn't help but smile to herself, almost hearing their laughter, the chatter and clinking of glasses . . . and then, oh yes, that night under the stars, just the two of them, her and Will. The night when everything seemed to change between them. And the buds of their love emerged, and began to flourish. When, after those painful divorce years, life had started to seem magical once again. Will had given her back that joy in life.

Cancer wouldn't beat them. It wouldn't steal their magic, their second chance in love. It was very likely that surgery would work for Will, and if not – and she'd already looked it up – then radiotherapy could follow it. They were going to fight this. She'd do absolutely everything she could to support him through this, to get them both to the other side. There was no way she was going to let this cancer curveball stop them now.

She found her border fork and tackled those weeds, releasing some of her frustration as she turned the earth, picturing those tangled roots as Will's cancer cells, determined to dig them all out. As she stood tall, twenty minutes later with a creaking back, she couldn't help but notice that the borders had burst into a riot of summertime floral colour. There were jewel-shaded stocks, and big white daisies, tall purple delphiniums alongside delicate yet bold lacy-pink peonies and pretty peach roses in bloom. As she neared the rose patch, digging and pulling out dandelions by their long thin roots, and strands of what she knew of as 'sticky willy', she could smell the roses' perfumed aroma. She stood for a second and took in a deep heady breath, whilst gazing at all these gorgeous flowers that Reggie would have planted many years before. She must remember to tell the old gent all about his beautiful, scented roses when she next visited.

It was grounding being outside, tending the earth, with mud beneath her fingernails. Despite having been hit with the toughest of news, she found herself beginning to calm. They would cope with this. They had to. There wasn't a lot of choice in the matter, after all. It happened to so many people . . . cancer. Of course, you dreaded it touching you or yours. But if it did, then you just had to bloody well face it head-on.

'Cath, is it still okay to come around?' His voice sounded fragile.

'Of course. Whenever you like.'

'Right now?' Will checked. It had just gone seven-thirty in the evening. Cath had begun to wonder if he'd prefer to be alone tonight.

'Yes, right now is fine.' How might he think she'd have ever said no? On *any* day . . . and certainly not on the day of his diagnosis.

'Okay, see you soon.' Cath felt a sense of relief that he'd reached out. That he trusted her, and wanted to be with her, when he must be feeling at his lowest.

Wine and words followed, as he arrived bearing a bottle of chilled sauvignon blanc. He told her about his cycling, doing a twenty-mile lap of his favourite hill route and getting drenched in a heavy rain shower – she'd spotted the clouds massing earlier, as she'd finished her gardening, and had wondered about him. Will said that he'd come back feeling a bit tired, but that getting out had helped. He'd imagined he'd want a quiet night in. But then, he confessed, as he'd sat on his own in the living room, he'd felt all wrong, suddenly realising that Cath was the one he needed to be with.

Cath snuggled up beside him; needing him too.

She put on some chilled piano music, and they talked, Will admitting to feeling uneasy about his next FaceTime with the girls, wondering how he'd be able to sound relaxed and normal, knowing he'd not be able to mention a word of what was happening in his life. Cath reminded him that he could always tell them the truth straightaway, but he assured her that he was holding back for the right reasons, and for their sakes. She took his hand and reassured him that he'd find a way to get through that call.

They also touched on today's trip to the hospital, with the next step being a meeting with the multidisciplinary team, and the big decision yet to be made about surgery or radiotherapy. They talked more generally too, about Adam, about doing up the beach hut, the tea event, the weather, managing to shift the conversation and move it to lighter notes. It was as though they intuited that an easy-going night with some regular chat was now what they both needed.

And so to bed . . .

Not alone, as it transpired, after all.

Standing face to face in her white-walled bedroom, with its old wooden beams above and rays of hope and fragility in their hearts, his lips met hers. The pressure tender at first, then deeper, filled with need. The salty hint-of-wine taste of him, filling her from her tingling toes. They stood and kissed for a long, slow time, as if they needed to absorb every beautiful second.

How many more kisses might they have in this world? Such chilling thoughts rose unbidden to Cath, yet she knew he had every chance of getting through this fine. Still, those spidery thoughts kept creeping out of the corner of her mind. What if he didn't? What if he wasn't one of the lucky ones?

Calm, Cath. Don't wreck these precious moments. It took a while to still her troubled mind, to let her body relax and for touch and passion to take over.

They removed each other's clothes slowly, no need to rush. Their middle-aged bodies; the skin softer now, etched with lines, moles and blemishes, having lived a life already. Thank God for low-lighting, Cath mused wryly. Yet still, every touch from Will ignited something within. Love and longing soon filling her with warmth, and need, and pleasure. Hearing his soft groans at her ear, as her fingertips traced his stomach muscles just above his hips, lit something within her. He was definitely feeling all of this, too.

Holding on to each other, they made love slowly and sensually. The world dissolving, for this precious time at least, into this room for two.

Chapter 16

Waking together the next morning, after an understandably restless night, the realisation was that strangely and yet necessarily, normal life must resume. Will went off to work at the cycle shop. And Cath, after taking a 9 a.m. tuition, found herself looking forward to her drop-in at the Kirkton Care Home. It felt rather comforting to be going and chatting with her elderly friends, who'd know nothing of yesterday's troubling scenario, nor her and Will's private pain.

After being buzzed through at reception by manager Julie, who said she'd catch up with Cath before she left to run over a couple of details on the tea event, Cath entered the day room. She gave Reggie a big wave, and said her 'hellos' around the lounge. Spotting Joan lifting her face to smile at Cath broadly and expectantly, she couldn't resist choosing the wingback chair next to her this morning. Cath tried to share her time around the room, and its various occupants, as fairly as she could.

'Good morning, Joan.'

'Hello, pet. And how are you?'

'I'm fine, thanks.' The phrase that covered and smothered a thousand feelings, and let life carry on. She managed a smile. 'And you? How are you doing, my lovely.'

'Eeh, I'm getting by. Stiff in the joints, but that's all those turnips I pulled, back up in the day. No wonder I'm all bent up. Hard work that was.' Joan loved reminiscing about her Women's Land Army days, the reason she'd left Newcastle-upon-Tyne and came up to the Kirkton area in the first place. 'Aye, I remember getting off that bus, on the Kirkton High Street, and thinking, "*Crikey, there's only one street. Where are all the shops, and the people?*" I'd come from Newcastle, you see. "*Well, I'll not be here long,*" I declared to myself. And look at me. In my nineties, and I never bloomin' well left.' She gave a chuckle.

Cath grinned. She'd heard the story before and loved it. Joan had also told her all about meeting and marrying the handsome young farmer, and about their two children, a son and daughter. Cath'd even met her daughter, Joanna, here on a visit. Oh yes, life's rich tapestry of experience and history was jam-packed within these walls, if you just took the time to sit, listen and chat . . . between the inevitable naps, that was.

Linda came in with a trolley laden with teacups and biscuits, and a big stainless-steel pot. 'Tea time, everyone.'

'Morning, Linda. Hope you're fine?' asked Cath, as the carer reached them. 'Joan, would you like a tea?'

'Yes, lass.'

'And I'd love a cup too, please, if that's all right,' said Cath. She felt more than ready for a brew.

'Of course, petal,' answered Linda, adding, 'Biscuits, ladies? Help yourselves.'

Joan's shaky hand reached for a couple of Bourbons. 'Don't mind if I do.'

And Cath chose a comforting custard cream.

'Have we had lunch yet?' Joan then asked. Her day-to-day memory poor, yet the distant past still crystal clear to her.

'No, pet, that's coming later,' Linda responded kindly. 'Tea and biscuits for now.'

Joan gave a nod. Then said, 'The food at the hostel was good.

Filled you right up after a hard day's work.'

'I bet it did,' said Cath, realising that Joan had drifted back to the past.

'Oh, and we couldn't wait for a Friday night . . . the weekend. Hard times, hard work, but we also had so much fun.' Her weathered face broke into a smile. 'We had dances and everything. Friday night at the Archibold Hall and a late pass 'til eleven. The German Prisoner of War chaps played all sorts of instruments. And then at the RAF base . . . Milfield, they had a band and everything. Oh, and the music, it was wonderful. The dancing . . .' She paused, to look up at Cath. 'It was like we knew times were bloody hard, but we had to make the best of it . . . No use crying over spilt milk.'

'It sounds an incredible time. Difficult, but filled with so many special moments and memories too,' said Cath.

'It was, pet. It truly was.' The old lady took a sip of her tea.

And Cath thought of how they'd had to deal with all that worry back then, with husbands, sons and lovers going away, and you never knew if you were going to see them again, or what horrors they were facing. And yet still they danced, and looked forward, and believed in the better! Cath felt enchanted and touched by these memories of the war-time tea dances. This lovely, nostalgic conversation, over a nice cup of tea and a custard cream, was already buoying her up. Even though Joan had, of course, no idea about the worry she was holding within about Will.

'Aren't we having a dance soon, so I heard?' Joan then asked. 'Is it back at Milfield?'

'No, not Milfield, but we are planning a dance and an afternoon tea at the Tilldale Village Hall in a few weeks' time.'

'Oh yes, that's it. We've been asked to put our names down. Is mine on the list, Linda?' she called across the room.

'Yes, you're on, Joan. We wouldn't dare miss you out,' the carer called back.

'Splendid. Will that lovely couple from the shop be there? The two boys, proper gentlemen they were. And the little lads who were elves . . . when was that now? I'm getting rather confused.'

'That was our Christmas lunch, Joan. And yes, I think they'll all be there. Perhaps not dressed as elves though,' replied Cath, with a warm smile.

'Oh, well, I'm sure it'll be lovely, anyhow. Be like the good old days. Those Land Army tea dances.'

'Yes, the tea party, it's proving very popular, after your wonderful Christmas do!' exclaimed Reggie from a few chairs down, with an excited twinkle in his eye.

Cath was ready to head over there next, remembering to tell him all about his gorgeous garden in bloom.

'It is indeed,' added Linda, bringing the upcoming event back to mind. 'In fact, we might need to order an extra minibus.'

Oh crikey, Cath could feel another batch of scones, and a request for more of Lily's strawberry-cream sponges, and in fact anyone who could help out with bakes, coming on. But bless, it was lovely that the residents here were all so excited about the afternoon tea. Life was short – and oh, how much more was that sinking in now with Will's troubling diagnosis. It was a lesson to enjoy life while you can. So yes, Cath thought, the more the bloody merrier.

Chapter 17

A few days later, and the multidisciplinary team meeting had taken place, with a follow-up appointment with the consultant urologist, to talk everything through with Will.

He and Cath were now back at his house, after the hospital trip, Cath still feeling a whirl of emotions. Will had asked that Cath be with him at the hospital meeting this time, which had felt like a major step forward. She was so pleased that he'd wanted and trusted her to be there. That he'd realised the strength of her commitment and love, and that they could move forward as a team on this.

There was so much to take in, however. The decision to be made was a difficult one. It was tough hearing about the delicate operation to remove the prostate and its likely side-effects, and the alternatives – or follow up, if required – of radiotherapy options, along with hormone therapy. She could almost feel Will cringing beside her on learning how it might affect him. There was, of course, no easy fix. The consultant and specialist nurse gave their opinions, and their best advice formed by years of experience. And then, the decision was ultimately Will's to make.

Even before this meeting, he'd practically decided that surgery was the way forward for him – getting the cancer out there and then, in one go, was his way of thinking – but the team had advised him to go home and carefully consider his options. The implications would affect his future, his life. All of their lives.

'Shall we escape to the sea?' he asked her, as she was about to offer to make coffee, which seemed to be her default action these days.

'Are you planning to take me on a cruise?' Cath jested fondly.

'I wish. Well, that would be rather nice,' he responded. 'But I might miss my rather important date with the surgeon.'

'Who might yet be a machine . . .'

'Yeah, that was a bit weird when they said it might be a robot doing keyhole.'

'It's a whole new world these days.'

'As long as he . . . it, I suppose, does a good job, I don't really care. Bring it on. Anyway, I'm downgrading my offer to fish and chips and a walk on the seafront.'

'Ah, okay. That does sound a fine idea, actually.' Something normal in the new scary world of tackling cancer they'd found themselves in. Cath had to admit, the four walls of his kitchen, with the photos of Jane and the girls (who still didn't know a thing about all this), were making her already mushed-up brain feel a bit overcrowded. The sea air might help clear both their heads. She could still smell the clinical aroma of the hospital on them. It'd whip that away, for sure.

Will had grabbed a few essentials, changed his shoes to trainers, and snatched up his car keys. They'd then paused at Cath's cottage so she could do the same. Now, as they rounded the moorland hill that led down to the A1, the North Sea was in their sights. An indigo-blue strip drawing them enticingly to it, there on the horizon, past a zig-zag of green fields, and beyond the towering outline of Bamburgh Castle.

'Seahouses for fish and chips?' he suggested. 'They have the best ones there. Sat on the harbour, and straight out of the bag.'

'Oh, yes. Happy with that. You *so* know how to spoil a girl.' She gave a grin.

Sitting with piping hot, salt-and-vinegared, crispy fish and chips on their laps, whilst looking out over the fishing and tourist boats bobbing in the harbour, they chatted. Will was going to phone the consultant first thing in the morning. His decision on proceeding with surgery was final.

With a couple of hours yet to spare this afternoon, Will having asked Josh to fill in at the cycle shop today, they decided to take a drive further along the coast. It was only fifteen more minutes to get to Low Newton. The beach was so lovely there for a walk, and Will suggested they might go and check the beach bungalow, having popped the hut keys in his pocket, back at the house, just in case. They stopped to buy soft drinks at the village shop in Beadnell en route, thinking that it might be nice to sit outside on the deck for a while.

Strolling the sands holding hands – which meant so much more now, togetherness . . . support . . . *I'm here* – and with no rush at all, they took in the summer sights and sounds feeling the sea breeze on their skin. They then headed up the wonky wooden steps, away from the families and the dog walkers and the holidaymakers into what they now felt was their special part of the dunes. And there it was, Will's wooden hut, which today especially very much felt like a haven.

Unlocking the door to the bungalow, Cath was relieved to see it mice-free – woohoo! – and just as they had left it those few weeks ago, when they'd all been there for the glorious paella day. Those happy, easy-going days would come again, Cath buoyed herself with the thought. Even in the midst of uncertainty and Will's difficult medical choices, they would continue to find moments of joy. Cath was more determined than ever to seek them out.

The sun streamed onto the deck, in contrast to the rather cool and dark interior, so they took the two director's chairs back out with them, and Cath fetched a couple of glasses for their drinks.

As they settled down, sipping refreshing ginger beer, looking out to sea, Will began to open up. 'Did you hear the nurse suggesting I give it a name, my cancer?'

'Oh, yes, . . . r-ight.' It was coming back to her now. It had sounded rather odd at the time.

'Apparently, it makes it less scary. I wondered about Colin.'

'Well, it's certainly not a scary kind of name, but it does make me think about cake and caterpillars,' said Cath, with a wry expression.

'Ah, yes, hadn't thought about that. Better not desecrate Colin the Caterpillar, that was always the girls' favourite birthday cake.'

This was such a bizarre conversation to be having pre-surgery. But weirdly it was actually helping to lift the mood.

'I've got it!' he announced. 'Clive. I'm gonna kick Clive's ass the hell out of here,' he said with an American drawl.

'Yep, that works.' She couldn't help but smile.

And they sat there grinning and sipping ginger beer in the sun, amidst the worry, the pain and confusion, the what-ifs and the what-nexts.

Will then puffed out a slow sigh. 'Ah, but it's a real shame that all this, *here*, is going to have to be on hold for a bit. My dreams of doing up the bungalow this summer are pretty much stalled.' The reality of his surgery and the time he'd need for recovery, that he'd learned in much more detail today, was sinking in. 'It might be weeks until I'm able to get back to any physical work. Bastard Clive.'

'Hey, there's no need to pressure yourself with any of this, my love, the renovations can wait. And this bungalow has been standing a long time, in a far worse condition. It's been waiting years for its second chapter, a couple more months won't hurt.'

'Well, my heart's not really been in it these last few weeks, I suppose. And today, finding out how I'm likely to feel post-op, well, I'll hardly be able to get to work in the cycle shop for a while, let alone do any painting and decorating.'

'It'll be frustrating, for sure. But you really don't want to be taking on too much, too soon. After that op, you'll need to give yourself the chance to heal. That's the most important thing.' She reached a hand to brush his bare forearm, reassuringly. 'And all this' – she gestured at the wooden hut – 'it'll still be here, when you're feeling back to yourself again. Doing the place up, well, it'll be something to look forward to. At least the main structural repairs are done. That was such a good move, getting the roof sorted. And you said the joiner'll be back next week to fix those last rotten slats. It'll stay sound. So, there's no need to pressure yourself.' Cath was ever the voice of reason.

'Yeah, you're right . . .' he conceded, glancing back inside with a longing gaze, as though he wished he could wave a magic wand over it all and transform it, there and then.

'Give it time . . .' added Cath, gently. She meant the hut, and his healing.

Will looked right at her, his beautiful hazel-brown eyes seeming troubled. His real fears bubbling to the surface. 'I can't knock the NHS, but having been through that hell with Jane, I just want it out. It's a nightmare knowing I'm walking around with a cancer inside me. I mean what the hell are those cells doing right now? I want it over with. The op. Like, let's get on with it, get the bloody cancer out of my body, so it can't cause any more trouble.'

'Yeah, I can understand that.' Her tone was gentle, caring. After everything he'd been through with his wife, it must be extraordinarily tough to know you had cancer, too. To be reliving that nightmare. But this was different, she told herself. Will's cancer was very different.

'If it's still to be two weeks yet . . .' – which was what the consultant had mentioned – 'then they're going to seem bloody long ones,' he admitted.

'For sure. But you've got your work to focus on. And you can maybe do some of your shorter cycle rides.' She didn't want him to overdo it with his long-haul trails, right now. He may not have had many symptoms, but he needed to keep sound and look after himself before surgery. 'And hey, I'll be around too.'

He nodded, but didn't look convinced. Naturally, he was bound to be so very worried about everything yet to come.

In contrast to the storms they were facing within, it was a beautiful afternoon at the bay, with only a few wisps of cloud streaking the azure sky. If they'd have thought about it, and brought a few practical things with them, it might have been nice to stay over. Watch the sky melt into the flame colours of sunset, listen to the gulls and the hush of the waves as dusk fell, Cath thought longingly, and stay up to watch the stars come out. Oh, and then, make the most of the sofa bed. While everything was as it was . . .

Cath took a slow breath. Making love might change very much for them. They'd been informed by the specialist nurse, that after surgery it might be several weeks before Will might begin to feel like sex, and even then, physically it was likely to be a very different experience, with erection problems and urine leakage – the joys – to contend with. Will had seemed to shrink into himself in the consulting room at that point.

The physical and mental impacts were not going to be easy or pleasant for him. Cath had already looked up the likely side-effects online, too. Soaking in every grain of knowledge, spending ages on the Prostate Cancer UK site which was so helpful; reading the blogs of prostate cancer survivors, and learning about their experiences, the problems with peeing, the inevitable loss of libido, dealing with erectile dysfunction . . . It didn't make for easy reading.

What fate lay in store for her gorgeous Will? She couldn't help but worry for him. But hey, she told herself, any of that could be countered, be given time to heal, if they could only stop the cancer in its tracks. Keep Will safe, alive and well. Give him, *them*, their future back. That was the name of the game here.

They'd face what they had to, together, one day at a time, resolved Cath.

Trying to be more positive, she suggested, 'We could maybe come back over this weekend? Make a small start here. Maybe paint the loo, or something, on your next day off. Perhaps tie it in with when the joiner's here doing those repairs. If you promise not to take on too much.' It might well help take his mind off things.

He gave a small smile. 'Yes, shall we come back? Make a start . . . And, we could have that night over here, whilst the weather is warm, and before . . .'

Before it all changes . . . they were both thinking.

Chapter 18

Will had a dusting of white paint over his hair, and a fleck or two stuck on his eyebrows. He'd tackled the beach bungalow's ceilings, lightening them to a bright white to lift the space; thinking it made sense to do that first. Whilst Cath had started small and achievable, focusing on the toilet's walls – with the repairs to the wood having been completed the day before – choosing a white with a hint of pebble grey called 'Whisper'. If they liked it, they figured they might, in time and post-surgery, follow that shade through to the living space.

Cath grinned, looking at his speckled hair, thinking that he looked like an older version of himself. A glimpse of the grey-headed, still rather gorgeous chap, he might become in time. *If they had time . . .*

Of course, they did. Cath shook off that morose thought. All would be well. Being Sunday, the appointment for his surgery, with Will having confirmed the decision to go for the operation, was only four days away. She reached out to dab at the paint flecks on his brows, but they had set. She smiled. They were so very close, his eyes smiling amusedly back, and the air suddenly felt charged between them. Like the only natural thing to do right now was to steal a kiss. Their lips met tenderly at first, and then all those heightened emotions became channelled into that caress. Her heart felt so damn full of love and fear, right now.

They were soon lost to the moment. His hand clutching her back, drawing her even closer to him. Her hands ruffling through his paint-dusted hair.

'Oh, Will.'

'Cath . . .' His voice sounded husky with need, and love. Those myriad emotions of the past weeks rolling into a wave of longing.

They'd already set up the sofa bed for later, and the two of them tumbled back onto it. Will kissed her once more, whilst expertly undoing a button at her chest, slipping a hand inside her cotton blouse, finding her breast. Every nerve end in her body now on high alert and exquisitely tingling.

His lips moved away from hers, tracing her chin, her neck, to follow his hand . . . *Oh my*. Zips undone, clothes discarded. His hips and lower body moving to press, oh so firmly, against her, like a promise, as she lay beneath him.

The smell of fresh paint, and the salt sea air. A shaft of sunlight coming in and over them. Cath only then realising that the door was still open to the deck . . . and the dunes. They were merely part-covered by a light cotton sheet.

'Oh, what if someone walks by?' Cath whispered.

'Shhhh.' Will's index finger moved firmly yet gently, to press her lips closed, and that felt so damned sexy.

Sod it, a passerby would have to be bloody nosy, and very close to the deck, to be able to peer right in . . . she thought, and hah, serve them right if they did. They gazed at each other, Cath giving a giggle, and then carried on regardless, swept up in their need for each other. More than ready to seize the moment. Oh yes, and it was the most heady and sensual moment, as she blissfully felt him enter her. Their bodies knowing just where to take things from here . . .

Curled up together in the afterglow, they'd dozed in each other's arms.

A beautiful port in a storm.

* * *

Afternoon rolled into early evening. They reluctantly left the haven of the surprisingly comfortable sofa bed and managed to finish a second coat of paint on the loo's walls, as well as glossing the skirting board in there. One small job done, on a mammoth to-do list for the bungalow, but it felt good. Today had felt good. And keeping busy had kept them from overthinking.

They'd taken a stroll along the beach, and up to The Ship Inn, where they'd sat outside on the bench on the green for a casual and tasty supper of crab sandwiches and chips. And here they now were, back at the deck of the beach hut with some nibbles and a small glass of fruity-red Rioja to hand; the lads having left the last bottle for them after their gorgeous Spanish-style supper.

The sky had clouded, but that only served to add soft layers to the blush of colours that were diffusing the sky as the evening drifted towards dusk.

A few seconds of quiet passed, as they gazed out over the bay. Will seemed more thoughtful, as though he were drawing back in on himself.

'Hey, are you okay?' asked Cath, aware of the hefty weight that her partner was trying his best to manage.

'Ah, it's just the waiting for this op . . . It's killing me . . . hah.' He managed to laugh at his own ironic joke, that really wasn't funny.

'I know. That must be so difficult.' Cath reached to take his hand. 'Not long to go now, my love.' It was frightening for her too, but she was trying so hard to stay positive, to look on the bright side, and not listen to that 'What-If' voice of doom inside her head. She had to stay strong for Will.

Will had sent a couple of pictures of the hut and the beach view to his girls, with Sophie and Maddie responding that they couldn't wait to come and see the family inheritance for themselves. This was evidently on his mind, too. 'It's getting harder, keeping it from the girls . . . They've been talking about coming up. Jeez, what if they turn up out of the blue the same time as I'm booked in for the op? I've been putting Maddie off . . . pretending I've got stuff on with cycling competitions for the last couple of weeks. But I can't keep stalling them for much longer.'

The moment would soon be here to tell Maddie and Sophie about their dad's cancer and his operation. His daughters really did need to know, Cath was certain of that. She had tried to persuade him to at least warn them that he was having some kind of surgery beforehand, perhaps without having to spill all – she was sure the girls would never forgive themselves, or her and Will for that matter, for not being in the know if something were to happen or God forbid go wrong. And yet, she knew this was Will's call. She had to respect that. Knowing how much of a shadow this news was about to cast on them was so hard. It would certainly dim that new sense of hope they'd been trying so hard to build as a family, trying to reinforce their lives positively for the future.

'They'll soon get suspicious. It's almost time,' Cath agreed.

'I know. As soon as Sophie's exam is done,' he confirmed. He intended to tell his girls this news in person, together. He'd ask them to come home. None of it was going to be easy. He gave Cath a nod, glancing her way with a look that was filled with a mix of love, fear and trepidation. 'Maybe you can help me with that, telling the girls, when the time comes?' he continued.

She felt a little nervous about how the girls might react to her being there for that particular 'domestic' scene, and yet answered, 'For sure.' The girls might in all honesty prefer her *not* to be there, but if Will needed her support in this, then that was all the encouragement she needed.

Cath's hand squeezed his. Cath was looking forward to their first night staying over at the bungalow, even with the limited arrangements. But hey, who needed a posh hotel with that sea view. She was also excited about waking up together, and if they were perhaps early enough, watching the sun rise over the bay.

Sitting here this evening, side by side on the wooden deck, sipping wine and watching the flame-coloured tones of sunset begin to settle over the bay, despite all the fears, the surgery to come, it still felt magical. The beauty of nature was awe-inspiring; the dramatic transition of sea and sky, with colours and motion ever-shifting, ever-changing . . . very much like life.

Once they got through this next difficult chapter, once Will was well again, this place really would feel like the gift it was. A fresh and beautiful new start. And Cath couldn't wait to share it with him.

Looking out over the tranquil sea, that now reflected the molten peaches and golds of the summer dusk, this run-down little bungalow felt a place to pause, a place to just *be*. A place of hope . . .

Will seemed tired now. It had been such an unusual and stressful few weeks. As the light outside began to fade, Cath took the storm lantern in with them – a great find she'd discovered in the Kirkton charity shop. It was stylish as well as practical, as of course, they still had no electric. No TV here to settle down in front of, and their phone batteries might just last 'til the morning, though the signal wasn't great here, anyhow. But that was refreshing in itself. It left them time to talk, or just quietly to be.

With its fresh white cotton bedding on, the opened-out sofa bed looked rather like an island in the brown wood interior of the seaside hut.

It was too dark inside to read a paperback by mere candlelight. Her Kindle Paperwhite was the thing to bring next time, fully charged; Cath made a mental note. And, they hadn't thought to light the log burner – or even to bring logs for it – on such a gorgeous summer's day. Lesson learned, that was the thing to do, to light it in the evening, so the hut was warmed inside for bedtime. Even in early summer, there was a definite chill in the air once dusk had passed.

So, for now, it was a time to tuck themselves in under the duvet. With the sofa transformed to a bed, this was the only comfy space. But hey, it wasn't a bad one. Cath had actually brought pyjamas in her overnight bag, thinking she might need them whilst padding about in the morning, picturing herself sitting outside on the deck with a coffee. The pyjamas were in fact needed for the chill tonight.

Will was already naked as he leapt into bed. Once she got in beside him, he didn't waste any time in nestling up close to her.

'Pyjamas, hey? Sexy. Now there's a challenge.' In the dim light she could make out the cheeky smile that played on his lips.

She broke into laughter. It was great that he'd seemingly parked his worries, for a few hours at least. 'They're a pretty good choice considering how damned cold it is in here,' she responded.

'And I have the perfect way to warm you up,' he whispered in her ear. And here, in his vulnerability, with life so uncertain right now, the need for closeness was stronger than ever. He needed to lose himself in her.

And they got lost together, in a world of touch and taste and tenderness. Here in the dark, in a sensual world of two, in a chilly wooden hut by the sea.

Cath woke. It was still dark and hushed, other than the rhythmic shush of the waves rolling to the shore. The quiet coastal calm of the early morning hours. They must have been asleep for some time. She could hear Will's breathing, steady beside her, but it didn't sound deep. He was lying on his back, with a rigidity to his position. Might he be awake, too? Thinking? He had a lot to think about, bless him.

'Will?' she whispered, quietly enough not to wake him if he actually was asleep. Heaven knows, he'd need the rest. This surgery week to come was a big one. But there was something, something she so needed to say . . . It had been burning away like a fire in her heart for weeks now. He really ought to know.

'Ah-hah?' His tone was groggily gentle.

'Ah, you're awake too.' She nestled a little closer. 'Will . . .' She hadn't said these words often, at all. She'd hoped that he knew. The pain of her marital betrayal, the crushing hurt that followed, had taught her to keep all those promises and declarations down. She felt nervous, putting her emotions out there and on the line. But more than anything she felt that it was time. She took a breath. 'I love you, Will.'

In the dark, she heard a catch in his throat. 'A-ahh, darling Cath. I love you, too.'

The emotion in his voice nearly broke her, in such a beautiful way.

At the end, with Trevor, those words had sounded so empty from her husband, coming from a place of mere habit, or perhaps guilt. But with Will, this sounded so sincere, and also vulnerable. Love could lift you, leave you and make you feel so fragile. And yet she was so happy to hear those words. She'd never imagined she might fall in love again, or that anyone would love her back.

Will turned on his side to shift closer, as she moved onto her side, too. Cuddling around her in a 'spoon', his arm draped tenderly over the top of hers, above the soft, white duvet, holding her close. In a comforting love-warmed huddle, they drifted off to sleep once more.

'Morning.'

'Uhm, morning,' came Will's groggy reply, as he buried his head swiftly back down into the pillows.

Pale streams of light were coming in through the two small front windows. There were no blinds, and on their clearing-out day, Will and his mate had taken down and binned the original scraps of mildewed ditsy-floral curtains. It felt early. All was quiet except for a seagull's cry outside.

Dawn came early in Northumberland now they were into June. Cath glanced at her wristwatch, making the time out to be just after four. Despite the crazily early hour, she felt the urge to get up. To go and look out over the bay. It might be her first opportunity to see the sun rise over the sea here. Oh, but it may in fact have already happened, she realised.

As she sat on the edge of the bed, a chill began to envelop her as she realised that she, too, was now naked. Ah, there they were, her pyjamas discarded down on the floor. Hmm, their lovemaking last night had been slow and sensual, and she still felt fuzzily warm inside remembering it.

PJs now on, and with her feet bare, she crossed the cool wooden floorboards heading for the door, and quietly turned the key in the lock. She slipped out onto the deck. The colours before her were incredible. The sun was already part-way up, and the sky was softly aglow with burnt orange, peach and hazy purple hues, laced with delicate drifts of smoky grey. All the while, dazzling light came from behind the wisps of cloud, catching the crests of the waves turning them into ripples of white gold.

Cath took a slow breath, filled with awe at the panorama. Smelling the tang of salt in the air, and listening to the rhythmic beat of the waves.

Perhaps she'd make herself a coffee, and just sit for a while. Will was evidently in no rush to come out and join her, and fair enough, it literally was the crack of dawn. But for now, she didn't want to miss the moment. She stayed as she was, her feet bare on the cool dewy damp of the outdoor wooden deck, watching the sea and the coastal birds as they dipped and swooped and paddled at the water's edge. The sky slowly yet constantly changed, its colours shifting with each passing second.

Oh, and coffee. The realisation hit her; no coffee machine here, no electric kettle. It would be good to sort some basic electricity at the hut for the future, she mused. She was sure she'd spotted other bungalows with solar panels on the roof. Perhaps when they next came back over, she and Will might strike up a conversation with some of the chalet owners here and find out what was allowed. Perhaps Nikki's Kev would know about setting a panel up, just enough to make staying here more comfortable.

Ah-hah, and for now, it dawned on her, there was the camping stove and pan in the little kitchen area. She'd brought her cafetière and some ground coffee over. There were ways and means.

She spent a few more magical minutes outside, with not another human soul in sight, soaking in that glorious view. Crikey, it was still only 4.20 a.m., she realised as she glanced at her watch. No wonder Will wasn't rousing. And, yeah, as a yawn escaped her lips, she actually felt kind of tired. Coffee could wait. Cath snuck in, closing the door softly behind her, and slipped in beside Will's warm and waiting form, snuggling up. As she nestled against his back, he seemed to register her presence and gave a soft sigh. She soon drifted off into a surprisingly settled and steady sleep.

Will was up when she next came to on that Monday morning. She woke to see him standing in the kitchen area heating water in the pan, the high-pitched whistling of steam stirring her from her sleep.

'Hey, sleepy head.'

'Hi.' Cath smiled, before adding, 'Hey, I actually beat you. I got up to watch the sun rise over the bay just after 4 a.m.'

'Oh, crikey. That's impressive. Was it worth it?'

'It was indeed. Absolutely stunning looking out over the sea.' She opened her phone and scrolled to show him a couple of the photos she'd taken. Luckily, the battery had held out.

'Ah, amazing. That's so beautiful.'

It was. And she felt like she'd remember that view, and this last day and night, for all of her life.

It wasn't their usual Monday morning, by any means. Joining him for strong, rich coffee and croissants – straight from the pack, with there being no oven – on the deck overlooking the bay. Will in yesterday's T-shirt and his boxers, and her in her handy PJs. And it was still only 7.30 a.m.

The blues had won over, the sky now a bold ultramarine with just the odd puff of wispy high cloud. The dog walkers were out on the sands, plus some early hikers. Spaniels were bowling around in a whirl, Labradors lolloping in and out of the sea, border collies – so in tune with their owners – making a disciplined ball chase and return. Another gorgeous day on the coast beckoned.

But all too soon for Cath and Will, it was time to pack up, head back over the dunes, and set off on the country roads back to Tilldale, and to work – this evening for Cath, who had several online tutorials booked in, and this afternoon for Will. Back to reality for a short while at least. Will was already thinking about having to put a sign up in the cycle shop window, that 'due to unforeseen circumstances' he'd be closed later this week. He'd wondered whether to put that same message out on his shop's Facebook page, too. But his girls were bound to spot that, he realised, and then they'd be asking questions. He was not going to share his health news, not until the op was over. Thursday he'd be in hospital for surgery, and Friday back out, with any luck. And that also meant that Sophie's exam would be finished by then, too. He'd let the girls know on the weekend, ask them to come up, when it was all done and dusted. Hopefully with the reassuring news that the cancer was all safely removed.

Will and Cath couldn't escape reality for much longer. The hut had been a wonderful haven for these past twenty-four hours, but now it was time to face the future, whatever that might hold. Will tried to calm his fears, knowing he had to face this head-on, but his grip on the steering wheel as they headed back was a little tighter than usual.

In the passenger seat, Cath couldn't help the nauseous feeling rising in her gut, though she tried her utmost to hide her concerns from Will. She needed to be his rock in these coming days, and she would be. They both knew that this next journey in life for them wasn't going to be an easy ride.

Chapter 19

'Cath, I've just had a text . . . from Sophie.' Will sounded stressed. 'Her exam's done, and she's only gone and jumped on a train all excited, and is on her way home.'

'Oh, shit, that's going to be tricky, isn't it?'

'Don't I damn well know it.'

'At least her exam is finished. That was your big concern.'

'But I didn't want to have to tell her like this . . . And what about Maddie? It's not right to tell one without the other. I'd wanted to do it in person. Both at the same time. It'll be a big deal for them.'

'Yeah, I can see that. Ring Maddie now. Ask her to come up. I don't think she was working today, was she?'

'No . . .' His voice trailed with the sudden enormity of it all.

All the planning, all the secrecy was about to be blown apart. But he couldn't exactly lie anymore when his hospital bag was packed and he was going to be off first thing in the morning, Cath realised. The time had come for the truth.

'Okay, I'll ring Maddie,' he conceded. 'Tell her it's something important . . .'

'Umm, I was coming around to yours anyway after my lesson. Shall I make supper for us all? Would you still like me to be there?' Their earlier plan of a simple stress-free evening pre-op, had evidently been shattered. And she'd so wanted to make everything pleasant and comfortable for him, being the night before his surgery.

'Of course, and yes, it'll be good to have your moral support. And supper, yes . . . thank you.' He sounded distant, like his brain was a whirl. Poor Will. His emotions were about to get put through the sieve.

Cath let herself in with her spare key. Will had left for the train station twenty minutes ago, and Maddie who, thankfully was free this evening, was on her way up too; an hour's journey. The house seemed so very quiet. Will's trainers in the hall, but otherwise all was neat and tidy. The photos of Jane, of the family together, smiling at her from the walls. Cath stood for a second to look. The family unit they had all been . . . on the beach, on holiday, the snaps that held those precious happy moments in time. And then, they had all been put through so much, Cath's heart felt a sharp pang. Life and death, love and loss, what a curious, rollercoaster journey we were all on . . .

Cath gathered herself, with a gentle sigh, and headed for the kitchen. The place she felt most comfortable, especially in difficult times. She'd cook for them all, with love. Armed with her basket of ingredients for a chicken and mushroom risotto, plus some fresh sourdough bread bought from the lads' shop earlier today. Comfort food at its best. They'd surely need it.

She was ladling in another spoon of stock, and stirring the rice dish, when she heard footsteps outside, and chatter as the front door opened. So, this was it, Sophie's arrival. Cath took a breath. Her relationship with Will's youngest could be tricky at the best of times. It was an awkward one emotionally, a new woman coming into her father's life after such trauma for them all. But they were both working on it.

Cath took the pan off the heat and headed into the hall with the wooden spoon still to hand, saying a cheery, 'Hi, Sophie.'

'Hey, Cath. Hi. Ahm, something smells good.' Sophie gave a cautious smile. It must have been strange for her seeing someone else in her mum's place, cooking.

'Yep, I'm cooking a risotto for us all.' Cath tried to sound casual. But she couldn't help but feel uneasy about was going to happen very soon, once Will broke his troubling news.

'Nice. Oh yeah, Dad was telling me about Maddie heading up, too. That's pretty cool.' The poor girl was oblivious.

'So, how was the big exam? Go okay?' Cath asked, soldiering on with the conversation.

'Yeah, I think so. Couple of tough questions, but I'd studied hard on the corporate law stuff, which can trip you up, so I was happy with that part. Fingers crossed.'

'Well, I'm sure you'll have done well. You've done your best at least, and that's all you can do.'

'Here, let me take your bag up to your room,' said Will, squeezing himself past them, and, Cath noted, looking slightly anxious.

'Thanks, Dad. Yeah,' Sophie resumed, 'an end-of-term ball to head back for, and that's me done for the summer. Though we've still got the let ongoing in York, so I'll probably to and fro for a bit.'

And with Will recovering from surgery, what a different summer it was going to be for them all, mused Cath.

It was only fifteen minutes later when Maddie arrived. Dumping her bag and coat in a heap in the hallway, she fell into a welcome hug with her dad. She pulled away with a grin, just as Cath came through to say hello.

'Hey you, Mr I'm Too Busy. All of a sudden, I've got to drop everything and come up right away, tonight. So, what's all this about?' Maddie, ever forthright, was straight in there.

Will's face dropped a little. 'Umm, let's eat first. Cath's been busy making us all a lovely risotto, haven't you,' announced Will with forced joviality.

Cath had been grateful for something to focus on; chopping the onions, the chicken breast, and preparing dried and fresh mushrooms. Once the Arborio rice was in, it had needed stirring and checking constantly, and now the rice was creamy and *al dente* as it should be. The olive bread was now warmed through, too. Cath was relieved to find, that despite her nerves, she could still cook on autopilot.

Earlier today, she'd imagined it was going to be just the two of them. A casual cosy supper together, the night before surgery, the last food allowed before his op; not the easiest of evenings for them, but she'd hoped for a quiet and peaceful pre-op. They might have talked, or tried to watch something easy-going on the telly. She'd have been there in steady support. Would he have wanted her to stay? she'd wondered earlier on. She wasn't sure. It would have been the first time ever at his house, if so. But she certainly hadn't expected anything quite like this. And crikey, the hardest part of this re-jigged evening was yet to come.

Sitting together around Will's dining table, polite conversation filled the void. The food looked lovely, but Cath found she could hardly taste it. She wondered how Will was getting on opposite her. Both of them aware of the ginormous, and as yet unsaid, elephant in the room.

It was time. With supper now eaten – Cath wasn't quite sure how she'd managed to stomach it, though she had purposely given herself a much smaller portion – the moment had come to tell Maddie and Sophie about Will's illness and his imminent operation. The girls absolutely needed to know. Yet, both Cath and Will realised how much of a shadow they were about to cast on them, dimming that new sense of hope for the future they'd been trying so hard to build together as a family.

'Girls, there's something I need to tell you,' Will started.

Cath felt herself freeze for a second, holding her breath, then she gave him a gentle supportive smile.

'Oh . . .' Sophie looked up, glancing from Will to Cath.

'I thought there was something,' said Maddie. 'That phone call out of the blue, and you wanting me to come up tonight.'

Will took a breath, seeming to stall. Yet, Cath felt it wasn't her place to intervene. Not unless he specifically asked her to, anyhow.

'Come on then, spill the beans, Dad,' prompted Maddie. 'Oh, hang on, you're not getting engaged, you two . . .' Her eyes flicking straight to Cath's ring finger which was tellingly bare.

In that instant, Cath spotted Sophie's face drop like a stone. So that wouldn't have gone down well with his youngest, would it? But this wasn't the time to be worrying about that sort of thing. The next piece of news was going to upset the girls far more.

It felt so tough and unfair for Will to be forced into this situation. But here they all were.

'Okay, so there's no easy way to say this. And I hadn't told either of you yet because I wanted Sophie to get this exam done with no pressure, no extra worry . . .'

'Dad, you're scaring me . . .' Sophie said in a hushed tone, looking pale.

'So, I've got cancer. Prostate cancer.' There, it was out.

'Oh, shit,' whispered Sophie.

'Fuck,' said Maddie.

'It's okay. It's going to be okay.' Will tried his best to reassure. 'It's contained. It's Stage 2, which is good. It's treatable. I-I . . .' His eyes began to mist, as his voice cracked.

Cath felt this was now the time to step in. 'Your dad's going for an operation, girls. Surgery to remove the prostate and the cancer within it. Tomorrow.'

'*Tomorrow?* Dad, why the fuck didn't you say anything? How long have you known?' Maddie sounded cross.

'We could have helped you. Come up and seen you, supported you,' added Sophie. 'I'd have been okay with the exam. Dad, it's not right that you've had to deal with this all by yourself.'

'I've had Cath. She's been great.'

A flicker of tight emotion – concern, that might have been laced with jealousy – crossed Sophie's face. 'We're your family,' she stated coolly, which was pointedly meant to infer that Cath wasn't.

Cath remained calm, despite her own storm rolling inside. The risotto hit a wave of nausea. The girls were bound to feel gutted, and emotions were riding high. This was never going to be easy, after all. 'Your dad's just been trying to do the best for you both,' she said gently.

Will nodded, giving a weak smile.

'Look, we need to all work together on this. Be a team for your dad now,' Cath continued, sensitively taking the lead. 'He's got a big operation tomorrow, and it's likely to take weeks before he feels himself again. But listen, in the long run, the prognosis is very positive. The consultant has reassured us of that.' She wanted to set the girls' minds at rest that this was a very different journey than the dreadful one they'd been on with their mother.

'Oh, Dad.' Sophie got up and moved over to him to give him a big hug. Maddie was soon there with them, too. The three of them, in a huddle.

This was the key, Cath suddenly understood, watching them cling on to each other. Her role was to keep reminding them all of the things to look forward to, whilst soldiering on through this together. She would be there, supporting this precious family that she so wanted to become an integral part of in time, through Will's treatment. Keeping that sense of hope alive, and loud and clear throughout, *that* would be Cath's mission in helping them all. And providing a tasty supper or two, of course.

'I'll just go and put the kettle on for us all,' she said softly. Giving them a little more space to process this news.

They were standing together on Will's doorstep, in the fading light. Time to get home, Cath thought, feeling such a reluctance to leave. She looked up at him. This man whom she'd fallen in love with all over again, since that very first time, way back in their teens. Her heart felt so tender, it almost hurt. She'd so wanted to stay over with Will this evening, to be there in support . . . But everything had changed with that call from Sophie.

And now, the pair of them needed some rest, before the big day tomorrow, though she wasn't sure how likely rest was for any of them. She had a feeling that sleep might prove elusive. Cath was still on to collect Will at 6.15 a.m., ready to take him to the hospital for the appointed 7.30 a.m. arrival time. Though Maddie had offered to drive him there, he'd insisted it was Cath who'd take him. After that, they weren't quite sure what time his surgery might be; it depended where he fell on the surgeon's list, apparently.

'I'm sorry, I hoped you might stay tonight,' said Will, his voice hushed.

'Me, too,' admitted Cath. 'It's okay. I understand things have changed. It doesn't seem right now, does it.' *Understatement of the year*, that'd feel like stirring a hornet's nest with Sophie and Maddie home, to be honest. 'But the girls needed to know. That's done now. It's a big day tomorrow, and then we can all move on. Onwards and upwards, hey.' She forced an encouraging smile.

'Yeah, hopefully.'

'I'll be there for you, Will. Whatever you need . . .' Her throat felt tight with emotion.

'Come here.' And he folded her into his arms in a warm and loving embrace. They held on extra tight and extra long. Squeezing every second out of it.

Will's world had already changed with this diagnosis. But tomorrow felt pivotal, and so significant. How the surgery went could affect the rest of his life; all of his tomorrows . . .

'I love you, Mr Matthewson. And don't you forget that.' Saying those words felt easier now.

'Love you, too, Ms Taylor.' And in the midst of so much angst, somehow, he managed to make that sound a little bit naughty.

Cath went in for a second hug, pulling away reluctantly to say, 'Sweet dreams. Take care. And I'll see you in the morning, 6.15 sharp.'

'Yes, ma'am.'

Chapter 20

The early morning air was chilly, and a little misty, as she stepped out of her car to walk up Will's front path. Such a different start from her magical morning at the beach.

The day was here. And so was Cath, ready to take him to the hospital for his op. Though she felt anxious, there was also a sense of relief that this was it. That the surgery would be happening. And that somehow, they'd forge a path from here. Cath had shifted a few tutorials around this week, to be there with Will when needed.

He was at the door by the time she lifted her hand to knock. Aware of the early hour, and with the girls at home, she wasn't sure whether to use the doorbell. There'd have been no worries about waking them, however, as they were both here, still in their dressing gowns with bed-head hair, ready to see him off. And that was lovely. They were here for him, too.

His hospital bag was in hand, with a few essentials packed.

'Okay? Ready?' asked Cath, straightforwardly.

'As ready as I ever will be.' He gave a cautious smile.

'Oh, Dad. Take care.' Sophie rushed to his side.

'Go smash it, Dad. Hope the op goes great. Get the fucker out,' said Maddie.

'Will do. Clive is to be forever banished.' He must have shared its name with the girls last night. 'And hey, I'll be fine,' Will reassured.

'Ring us as soon as you can, yeah? Let us know how it goes,' added Sophie, concern creasing her brow.

'Or get Cath to, if you're not feeling up to it,' added Maddie.

'I will, of course,' stepped in Cath.

'And we'll come down and see you later, of course,' said Maddie.

'Love you, Daddy.' Sophie gave him the biggest hug, reverting to her childhood term.

'Love you, Dad,' followed Maddie, keeping it simple.

The journey had thankfully been a straightforward one. They'd given themselves plenty of time, as Cath was aware that parking could be an issue, even at this early hour. But five floors up in the hospital multi-storey she finally spotted a space.

Finding the ward was another small challenge. The Royal Victoria Infirmary was such a big hospital. But they tracked it down and were buzzed in, Will announcing himself at the nurse's reception desk. Ushered to a bed bay on a four-bed ward, with clinical aromas abundant, a nurse, who introduced herself as Annie, ran through the procedure again. She then gave Will the medical consent form to sign with the many side-effects listed. A stark reminder of what might lie ahead.

Will was then asked to prepare himself for surgery. After a trip to the loo, he put on his gown – one of the gorgeous NHS ones, white with a geometric pattern, and the gappy strings at the back. And to Cath he suddenly seemed so vulnerable there, even though he was smiling, if a little tautly.

He gave Cath his phone and watch for safekeeping, and left his overnight things in his bedside locker. The nurse had returned asking about next of kin, and Cath froze for a moment waiting to hear Will's answer. Where the hell did she slot into all this? His *girlfriend* – she hated that word – hardly covered it. Yet, if they thought she wasn't closely involved with Will, they might not allow her to be at this bedside at all; how crazy.

'Umm, there's my two daughters, Maddie and Sophie,' he started, 'and of course, Cath here . . .' He stalled for a second, before adding, 'She's my partner.'

And how did that fit in the scheme of things NHS-wise nowadays? They weren't married, hadn't even been together as a couple that long, Cath feared.

It seemed to work, however. Not everyone was married, after all. Annie took down all three telephone contacts, and confirmed, with Will's agreement, that the ward staff would ring Cath as soon as he came around in recovery after surgery.

Then the porter rolled a trolley bed in, the nurse announcing it was time to go to theatre. Will seemed pretty chipper, keen to get on with it, his chin up and ready to go. And after a kiss on the cheek, a hand clasp that meant so much, and a cheery 'best of luck' from Cath, onto the trolley he clambered and off he was wheeled. The porter talked away with him; no doubt trained in easy-going diversionary chat. His hand appeared from the side of the trolley, giving a small wave; the cannula evident there. Cath felt a huge lump in her throat. 'Bye for now, my love,' she whispered, more to herself than him. *Take care.*

She took a long, slow breath and felt her eyes misting. *He'll be okay*, she told herself. A few minutes later, she was still sitting quietly on the ward he'd been taken from, on a plastic chair beside his empty bed, feeling a little dazed. Nurse Annie popped her head around the part-drawn bay curtain. 'You okay, my love? Can I get you anything? A cup of tea perhaps?'

'Ahm, no thanks, but thank you for asking.'

After a few quiet moments, Cath switched to feeling restless. Time was going so slowly. It might yet be ages before Will even went into surgery. The operation was a delicate one, and could take around two hours, they'd been advised, and in more complex cases sometimes up to five.

Will had suggested, before he'd been taken to theatre, that she went off shopping in the nearby city centre to fill the time. How the hell could she wander around John Lewis and Next looking at bloody clothes and shoes? She then remembered there was a park nearby on the Town Moor and decided to head out of the hospital and go for a walk.

She found the entrance to Exhibition Park, and headed in beneath its Victorian-style metal-arch sign. Discovering the lake and the old white-domed brewery building, she walked on past a traditional bandstand, and then spotted several young children running about and playing in the park. This made her think back to when Adam was little, and to reflect on when Sophie and Maddie would have been youngsters, too. Those original family units now smashed to smithereens. Who'd have guessed the diverse paths they were all to go on. It was a good job you didn't know what was going to happen in life, she mused. But she wouldn't let herself get morose. There was always good in this world, too. It was so nice to hear the children's laughter here.

Now that the girls had been made aware, Will had wanted her to advise their supper club friends of his surgery, and the reasons behind it. They were going to find out soon enough, anyhow. Nothing stayed secret in Tilldale for long. It'd be pretty obvious something major had happened once he was back in the village and recuperating.

Cath had been walking for a while and it had been a good distraction. Feeling suddenly weary, the emotions of the day no doubt taking their toll, Cath found a park bench to rest a while. Now seemed like a good time to make that contact with their friends. Taking out her mobile phone, she decided a group message seemed the fairest way of letting them know, all at the same time. She decided short, sweet and to the point was the best way forward, and then pressed send.

Within seconds her phone began buzzing in her palm. 'Hello.'

'Oh, petal, how are you?' Andreas's warm and caring voice came down the line.

‘Oh, Andreas. I’m okay, I think. Just playing the waiting game, whilst he’s in surgery. I’m sat in the park.’

‘What a shock for you both. That was the last thing I expected to read . . . We’re still reeling, so goodness knows how you’re feeling. We’re on speakerphone, by the way, Dan’s here, too.’

‘Hi, lovely. Sending a great big hug,’ Dan came in.

‘Thank you.’

‘So, what’s happening today?’ queried Andreas. ‘Surgery obviously, and then . . .?’

‘He’ll stay in overnight, for sure, for monitoring. And depending on how he seems to be recovering, he should be allowed home later tomorrow. He’ll need a few weeks off work. He’ll have to take things steady for a while.’

‘Of course. It sounds a delicate operation.’

‘Yeah, it is.’

‘And the cancer? Sorry, tell me if this is too much . . .’ Dan asked cautiously.

‘It’s fine to ask. It’s a relief to be able to talk about it, to be honest. We’ve had to keep the whole thing secret up until now for the sake of Will’s girls. Sophie had an exam, and we only told them yesterday evening. So, thankfully, the cancer seems to be contained, and removing the prostate today, fingers crossed, removes it all. I think they do further tests thereafter, to check . . .’

‘At least, it sounds like they’ve caught it early,’ remarked Dan.

‘Yes, the team seem to think so.’

‘Thank God. And I hope it all goes really well for him today,’ said Andreas.

‘Send him our love and very best wishes,’ added Dan.

‘And if there’s anything at all we can do to help, just shout,’ confirmed Andreas.

‘Absolutely. Anything at all,’ Dan echoed.

Their kindness got to her, and she felt all choked up as she said, ‘Tha-nks.’

‘Lots of love, petal. We’ll be thinking of you both,’ Andreas continued. 'Oh, and send us a message . . . when you get chance, once he's okay and out of surgery.'

'Will do.'

'And we've all just sent messages to Will, on the group chat, too,' he added. 'For when he comes to. I'm sure it'll all work out fine.'

'Thanks so much, lads.' Right now, she'd *really* needed to hear that strand of hope.

Cath took a slow breath as she closed the call, wiping a tear from her eye. She'd been keeping herself strong for far too long. Aw, bless them, their support meant everything.

After only a few seconds, Nikki was on the line. 'Hey, hun. What's all this that's been happening? And today . . . surgery is *today*?' Nikki sounded somewhat incredulous. 'Are you okay? How's Will doing? What a bloody shock.'

'Yeah, we're still reeling from the diagnosis. He's in, he's most likely under by now, and God, do I feel weird,' she confessed.

'Aw, bless. Shall I come down? Keep you company? I can easily shift a few jobs around.'

'Oh, that's so sweet, but I'll be okay. It might not be too long, the operation, and then I'll be heading back to the ward. You might end up having a wasted journey.'

'Hey, I don't mind. Being there for you is never a waste, hun.' Nikki's words were heartfelt.

'Thanks, I'll keep in touch, and I so appreciate the offer, but honestly, don't come rushing down.'

'Okay, but let me know if anything changes.'

'I will.'

'And hey, why didn't you tell me before? I could have been there for you both.'

'I know, sorry, Will's prerogative. He didn't want the girls to know too soon, not after everything they've already been through . . .'

'Ah, of course . . .'

'And Sophie had an important uni exam coming up.'

'Ah, right.'

'We told them last night.'

'Ooh, only then. How did they take it?' Nikki well knew the background to the family's loss. She'd known and liked Jane, too. It was, of course, a small village. A close community.

'Not too bad. Gutted, of course. But, hey, we're all trying to be positive. And it does sound like they've caught it in time. Fingers crossed.'

'Thank Christ for that. Look, I'm mid cleaning job, but I couldn't not call you. I'm sending heaps of love, huge hugs, and fingers crossed for the op, and everything.'

'Thanks, lovely.'

'I'll call back later. See how the patient's getting on.'

'Thank you.'

'Love you loads. Take care. Hang on in there. He'll be out and driving you nuts again soon enough.'

'Yeah.'

'And please, let me know if I can help in any way.'

In the midst of her own already hectic life, it was so lovely that Nikki was there for them, and happy to help.

The message that had just come in from Lily was touching, too:

Hey, guys, so sorry to hear about your sad news. Sending loads of love and support for today! Let me know how I can help. Xx

Cath felt filled with such a sense of warmth. If she was now acting as Will and his girls' safety net, then she knew, as sure as anything, that these guys, these wonderful supper clubbers, were there to be *her* safety net, too. And that meant the world to her.

After a further twenty minutes sitting on a park bench, watching the world go by, a rain shower set in, and having only come away in a thin jacket, Cath headed back to the hospital. She shook off the raindrops, and finding a coffee shop in the main foyer, she sat nursing a latte, watching the ins and outs of patients, of porters and carers. Hearing the wail of an ambulance siren, the frustrated tantrum of a crying toddler. The waiting and wondering. Day appointments, check-ups, major surgery, all going on at the same time. Life and death, and the miracle that was perhaps a dozen surgeons' hands, right now, working on patients, fixing and healing, as well as the committed care of the nurses in the many wards around her. It was pretty mind-blowing. And you never really gave it a second thought until you were there, plucked out from your everyday life and thrown suddenly into the mix of it.

She took her Kindle from her handbag, and settled down to read for a while, choosing an easy-going romantic comedy to help take her mind off things.

A while later and her phone was ringing. She scrambled to pull it from her pocket. A Newcastle number . . . the ward? *Oh.*

'Hi, it's Cath.' *And breathe . . .*

'Hello, Cath. It's Annie. Good news, Will's out of surgery and doing fine in recovery. He was lucky to be one of the first in.'

Oh, praise the Lord.

'They'll be bringing him back up to the ward soon. I'd say give it fifteen minutes, and then come back up whenever you're ready.'

'Thank you. Thank you so much.' She felt a weight lift from her. This was the start – and yes, there'd be a hill of healing to climb – of life heading back up. Of more tests, and checks for cancer on the way, but he'd got through the op okay, and this felt like the first step to finding happier days.

She raised her latte mug in a mini 'cheers' to herself.

Chapter 21

He looked so pale and fragile as they wheeled Will back in from recovery. But the worst was over, the operation done. Cath gave him the gentlest of hugs, afraid of hurting him.

Will was to stay in overnight. The girls arrived early evening with relieved kisses, a cycling magazine and a couple of his favourite chocolate bars. They took up the two seats at his bedside, and started chatting. Cath took the opportunity to go and grab a sandwich, suddenly realising that it was teatime already and that she'd missed lunch altogether, offering to get the others something from the coffee place or handy hospital shop. Will said he fancied a packet of salt and vinegar crisps, something with a bit of flavour. The girls replied thanks but they'd just eaten, and then shared their plan that Sophie was to stay over with Maddie in her Newcastle flat that night, so they'd be on hand for visiting.

Cath intended heading back up the road to home, but not until she felt Will no longer needed her. She'd return to her cottage and bed, hoping for a few hours' sleep, ready to get up early and back to the hospital, to collect him the next day.

'We could bring him home,' offered Maddie. 'We'll be coming back up to Tilldale anyhow. I've moved my shifts this week to have a few days free.'

'Oh yes, that'd be nice for us to take Dad home,' Sophie added, almost territorially.

Or was that Cath being supersensitive, she mused, before responding, 'Oh, it's just I'd imagined I'd be taking him back with me. I'm going to be here visiting again in the morning.' She needed to know he was okay, to be there for him. That's how she'd imagined things would pan out. But she wasn't the only lady in his life who felt it was her responsibility to support him. Of course, his daughters would want to care for him, too.

It was oddly beginning to feel a bit competitive, in a who's-looking-after-him-the-best kind of way. With the patient, Will, piggy in the middle. The three of them were seemingly now wrangling for who did what, from his bedside. The tension was palpable, and that wasn't good, Cath realised. This wasn't the way forward in helping his recovery. 'Right, well, okay. The main thing is he gets home fine,' she said calmly and measuredly.

'Umm, girls, why don't you let Cath take me back,' Will interjected. 'She brought me down here, after all.'

The raised-eyebrow looks the girls gave each other, over the top of their dad's head, were unmistakable. If they could have got away with rolling their eyes, they would have.

In all kinds of ways, it would be a relief to get Will back home.

'We come bearing gifts of baklava, coffee cake and quiche,' announced Andreas. 'There are also the obligatory grapes, a couple of juicy satsumas and the latest copy of your *Cycling Weekly*.'

'Blimey, it's like the Three Kings bearing gifts.' Will managed a smile, from his position propped up in his armchair. He'd got back from the hospital last night, and despite feeling extremely sore and struggling to get up and down from his seat, was bearing up.

'Hah, pretty sure we're not the Wise Men, anyhow,' chuckled Dan.

'I'd agree with that!' Laughed Nikki, as she and Lily trooped in behind them. Lily brought homemade rocky road and millionaire's shortbread traybakes, and Nikki declared her promise to come round once a week whilst Will was convalescing, to give his house a lovely freshen up and clean, adding, 'Along with my new trusty helper here – Niece Lily.'

'Well, my exams are finally over,' Lily added, giving jazz hands. 'Woohoo! And other than my restaurant shifts, there's not that much going on.' She didn't mention her various social life commitments, hoping to make Will feel better about receiving their help.

'Ah, well done on your exams, Lily,' said Will. 'Bet that's a huge relief. And thank you so much, but my girls have said they'll help out, too.'

'Oh, it's no problem. That way, they can concentrate on you.' Nikki was adamant that she was going to help, and that this was the best way she could.

Sophie was still there since arriving Wednesday night, and Maddie, who had a nursing day shift today, was coming back up tomorrow. The girls wanted to do everything they could to support their dad, too. Whilst that was admirable, Cath quietly confessed to herself that it all felt a little crowded. It was almost like she and the girls were battling it out as to who could help Will the most. And that wasn't a thought she was proud of, or even liked to admit to herself. Bloody hell, she needed to pull up her big girl pants here – her role of being the family's safety net needed to be reinstalled immediately.

'Right, I'll go and put the kettle on for everyone,' said Cath, ready to make herself useful.

'Thanks, petal,' said Andreas.

'Hey, are you lot trying to fatten me up?' Will looked at the coffee table now laden with treats.

'Perhaps, but it's more to cheer you up than fatten you up. And hey, if there's too much, then you can always share. I'm sure your steady stream of visitors will be more than happy to tuck in,' said Andreas.

'Hah, so you bring all the goodies, and then sit and enjoy them yourselves. I'm on to your game.' Will sounded amused.

It was lovely to listen in to their banter as she bustled about the kitchen. Their visit was definitely helping to lift Will, who'd been a little quiet this morning up until now. No doubt the pain, and an element of post-surgery blues, hitting. The reality of his wound, and having a catheter in place, could not be pleasant at all.

As Cath headed back in, a few minutes later, with a tray of coffees, milk and sugar, Sophie was chatting away with Lily, which was great to see, whilst the others talked with Will, who was admitting that he was going to feel extremely cooped up for a while. No cycling for a bit, and complaining that he wasn't allowed to drive yet, either. Mr Active was on hold, and it really didn't suit him.

The chat over coffee and traybakes moved on to the subject of the beach house, and their fun paella day. Will was talking about the coastal bungalow with longing. 'Ah, it'd be the perfect place to relax and recuperate, with the fresh sea air and that glorious view.'

'It is wonderful there,' agreed Andreas.

'That day we had was mega,' added Lily. 'Sangria by the sea.'

'Oh, right,' Sophie cut in, a little sulkily. 'Seems like I'm the only one who hasn't been to see it, yet.'

'We can go, soon, Soph . . . once I'm on the mend,' Will appeased.

'Your dad will need a good rest before heading off anywhere,' Cath warned, sensibly, but regretted chipping in when she saw Sophie instantly giving her one of her cool looks. Oh dear, had she said the wrong thing again? Cath mused, but she couldn't help feeling superprotective of Will just now.

Will then mentioned the hut's condition and how it needed a bit of work, as if letting Sophie down gently, reminding them all there was no means of electricity, only basic furniture, a tiny kitchen and its interior was rather dark and dull. 'Other than that, it would be perfect,' he added wryly.

Cath gave a tentative smile whilst holding back a sigh; more than aware that her partner's hopes for the renovations were now going to be very much on hold.

That particular conversation, and Will's yearning to be back by the sea, hadn't passed by their friends unnoticed, however.

On the way out, pausing at the threshold beside Cath, as the group made their farewells, Andreas said, in a hushed voice, 'You know we'd love to help Will with those renovations. Get the beach bungalow shipshape for him again.'

'We would indeed,' agreed Dan.

'We understand how careful he's got to be, just now, of course,' continued Andreas. 'No reaching or bending, painting and decorating, for him. But it seems such a shame for you two not to be able to use the beach house . . .' he sought the right word ' . . . *comfortably*, yet.'

'I know, but it's just one of those things. No point in Will worrying about it,' said Cath.

'Exactly. Hmm, leave it with me. I'll get my thinking cap on.' He gave a wink.

Back home in her cottage, later that evening, Cath heard her phone buzz. She answered it to find it was a video call from Andreas.

She was tucked up in bed, propped against her pillows with a book, doing her best to try and decompress from these full-on, emotional and unusual few days. It hadn't seemed right to assume, or even ask, to stay over at Will's with Sophie now there. Will would likely prefer the comfort of having the double bed to himself, and some privacy to sort his catheter, anyhow. In these early post-op days, intimacy was naturally off the agenda, but Cath would have happily stayed in one of the spare rooms to be on hand to help.

'So how are you doing, lovely?' Andreas brought her back to

the here and now. 'All this with Will must have hit you so hard. Oh . . .' He peered at the screen. 'Are you in bed there?'

'I am.' She smiled. 'You've caught me having an early night. It seemed very tempting.'

'Well, I don't blame you, petal. You've been through the mill lately, I bet.'

'Ah, I'm all right. Tired, but fine. Just need to get the patient on the road to recovery again.'

'And that's exactly why I'm calling. So, we've been talking, me and Dan with the supper club girls . . .' And he began to tell her all about their incredible plans.

Cath listened with her heart swelling. 'And you'd really do all that? It sounds amazing, but that's a big job. And you're all working . . .' She didn't want them to feel under any pressure. There'd be a whole host of tasks involved with organising the Tilldale tea event as well, which was creeping up all too fast. She'd naturally put that on hold these past few weeks, but they'd all have to get back on track with that soon enough.

'Yep, we've discussed it as a group, and we have some time at the weekends, and in the evenings, too. After all, the summer days are long just now.'

Dan, hovering beside Andreas, added, 'And it'll surely be at least two weeks before Will's feeling up to making that walk to the hut from the car park.'

Andreas commented, 'Oh yes, watching him try and move today, oh my, I've been wincing for him.'

'I know, the poor soul,' Cath agreed. 'So yeah, he won't in reality be able to get over there very soon.' And, she mused, if much of the decorating plans that these guys were talking about were completed by the time he did get there, it might well stop Will trying to do too much too soon.

'Lily's on board; she agrees it'll be wonderful to help Will. The cancer news, and his surgery, that's been such a lot for you both to deal with. She and Nikki are right up for this,' Andreas confirmed.

'Oh, my goodness.' Cath was still trying to take in their generous offer.

'If you can get the keys, we'll aim to please,' added Dan with a quirky smile, delighted with his rhyme.

'It'll be a lot to take on, quite a challenge,' warned Cath, still wary of them overloading their already busy lives, yet feeling delighted that they'd come up with such a kind project.

'Oh, go on, let us do it. It's all for Will. I can feel another DIY SOS coming on,' urged Dan with enthusiasm.

'A beach hut-athon!' announced Andreas.

'Okay. And of course, I'll try and help out too, where I can.' Cath found herself grinning, despite the thought of yet more work ahead. 'And please don't go too wild with the decor. Remember Will's a lot more reserved than you lot.' She raised a smile, remembering the talk of cocktail bars and pink flamingos at their paella day.

Their offer of help was amazing. Will would so love this. And she could just picture taking him down there, once it was all completed and he was feeling brighter. Their friends all there, ready for the big reveal.

And so, the 'Beach Hut Challenge' was born.

'You okay to talk?' Nikki's hushed tones came down the phone line. 'Did you manage to get the keys?'

It was two days later, and on hearing her friend's voice, Cath moved to the downstairs loo at Will's house. 'Ah, hi . . . Yes,' she then whispered back. 'I found them in the kitchen drawer. They're safely in my handbag. Shall I drop them in to you shortly? On my way back to the cottage.'

'Hold fire on that. I've gotta leave for a job in a few minutes. I could call at yours on my way back, in an hour and a half or so, if that works.'

'Yes, perfect.' Cath kept her voice low, feeling like an undercover cop.

'Umm, are you all right there? It sounds kind of echoey?' Nikki asked. 'Are you hiding?'

'Hah, something like that, I'm in Will's downstairs loo.'

'Brilliant. Make sure you flush. Make it sound authentic.'

'Will do.' Cath stifled a chuckle. 'Bye.'

A while later, it was lovely to open her cottage door and see a smiling Nikki on her front step. Cath'd been so wrapped up in the build-up to the op and now looking after Will, that she'd had to step out of the norm and leave her own life behind.

'Hi, hun. Oh, and these are for you, freshly picked from the garden.' Nikki offered over a posy of fragrant and colourful sweet peas. 'Kev's made his own trellis and put in some seeds. They've gone crazy.'

'Oh, they're so pretty. Thank you. Hey, it's good to see you,' said Cath, suddenly feeling all emotional.

'You all right?' Nikki asked caringly, going in for a hug. Then adding, as she drew away, 'Bless, you've had so much on.'

This was the first chance they'd had to chat face-to-face since Will's surgery without anyone else around.

'Ahm, so-so,' Cath answered honestly, sounding shattered. 'It's all been a shock. And I'm trying my best to look after Will and the girls, but I have to confess, it feels a bit overwhelming at times . . .' She chewed at her lower lip.

'I bet. Hey, this sounds like the ideal time for a cuppa and catch-up, then. And after that you can hand over those beach house keys, ready for us to hit the hut.'

'Of course. And that's amazing . . . your offer of help.'

'You're more than welcome. We can't wait to get started.'

They were soon sat on the back patio with mugs of strong tea, chatting initially about the plans for the bungalow.

'Yep, we're all primed to go over to the hut tomorrow, late afternoon,' Nikki announced. 'Me and Lily are looking at paint colours en route. And then, on Wednesday' – that was the day after – 'the lads have managed to organise some help in the shop, so we've got a full day to crack on with it.'

'Oh, thank you so much for this. It sounds brilliant. But hey, please be subtle with the colour scheme, won't you?' Cath didn't want to sound ungrateful, but was still remembering all the chit-chat on their paella day about bright Hula-style florals and a grass-skirted bar. 'Will's far more conservative than Andreas and Dan. He'd want a relaxing atmosphere, I'm sure. Think coastal chilled, cool neutrals and easy-going tones.'

'Never fear. I'm with Will on this. I'll try my best to rein the lads in.'

'Hah, that's no easy task.' Cath had to smile, whilst feeling a sense of trepidation. For the revamp to be a success, Will would have to like the changes to the decor they were about to make. She had to trust the team on this, though. And they were doing it from a place of kindness.

The Beach Hut Challenge, she now learned, had been Andreas's idea initially. As soon as he and Dan had found out about Will's cancer and surgery, they were determined to help in some way. Doing up the Low Newton bungalow had become their mission, with Nikki and Lily jumping on board as soon as they'd heard the lads' plans. Nikki now promised to give the place a lighter, coastal yet still cosy feel. Ideal as somewhere to recuperate, she confirmed.

'Okay, so tomorrow, Sophie's seeing a close friend who's just back from uni, so I'm holding the fort with Will.' Cath was looking forward to having a little time to themselves to be frank. 'But Wednesday, as long as Will seems fine, I'll try and get over to help you. I can feign some last-minute extra tuition classes for my GCSE students, or something. I'm sure he'll enjoy having a little father–daughter time with Sophie, anyhow.' She had a feeling that Sophie would like that, too, with Maddie having had to go back home to work for a couple of shifts.

'And how are things on that front? With Sophie?' Nikki asked, with a note of conspiratorial caution, te pair of them having previously discussed some of the tricky moments Cath had had with Will's youngest daughter earlier on in their budding relationship.

'She'll probably be glad to get rid of me for a few hours,' Cath responded openly. 'To be fair, it's a tough time for all of us. I can't blame her feeling a bit prickly towards me. She must feel like I'm trying to worm my way in to her dad's affections . . . pushing her mother's memory out. But it's never that simple, is it. There's room for love after loss; there has to be, or life would be just too damned sad. But she's young, she's still hurting.'

'She needs to buck her ideas up, that's what I say,' Nikki retorted, feeling protective of her friend. 'You do so much for them all. If she's not careful and keeps on pushing, she might get some witch of a stepmother when you've had enough of it, and *then* she'll know about it . . .'

Cath could never envisage walking away, but she loved hearing her friend's support. 'We'll work through it, I'm sure. The important thing is that we concentrate on Will, right now.' She paused, gave a sigh, and then added confessionally, 'Though even that seems a bit of a bun fight between us all . . . trying to prove who can help him the best. It seems to have a very competitive edge, this care.' It felt good to be able to open up about the stresses she'd been facing within the family home.

'Oh, crikey. Families, hey . . .'

'Yeah. But at least they care. We'll get there in the end.'

Whatever the *end* might be. Cath couldn't let herself dwell on that too much. For now, it was one day at a time.

Chapter 22

Cath arrived at the beach hut two days later to the sounds of sawing – *really?* – and more predictably Wham's 'Club Tropicana' blaring out on a portable speaker. *Oh my, what was going on in there?* She bloody well hoped the lovely surprise for Will wasn't going to end up being a shock, for all the wrong reasons. She suddenly remembered the infamous episode of *Changing Rooms*, where the homeowners walked in for the big reveal, and ended up shouting, 'I hate it. Get this mic off . . .'

She had messaged Nikki yesterday, reminding her of her promise to keep Andreas's 'creative flair' under control. Nikki replied that she was still working on 'The Hamptons' theme, but with Andreas in the mix, who knew what else might happen. And *sawing*? Surely the professional builders had done all the woodwork repairs that were needed when they'd sorted out the roof and walls?

Spotting a heap of what looked to be old chipboard, intriguingly piled beside the deck, Cath took a steadying breath, and then cautiously poked her head in through the main door. 'Hel-lo!'

The sofa bed in the centre of the room had a dust sheet over it, thankfully. Behind that, Dan looked up, with screwdriver to hand, from a half-built kitchen cabinet unit . . . in, phew, a stylish off-white. The old kitchen section had been totally ripped out and was gone, wow. So, that was the pile outside.

Across the other side of the room, Andreas, was in fact the one sawing, umm, what looked to be thick bamboo canes. Goodness knows what they were for?

'Hi, petal.' Andreas beamed, as he reached to turn the music down a touch.

'Hey, lovely,' said Dan. 'How's Will getting on?'

'Okay, he seems in pretty good spirits. Well, as much as he can be, right now. Still sore and rather frustrated with life.' Will had actually been a bit grouchy these past few days, understandably. But the catheter was due to come out in a day or two, and she figured that should help him feel a little more comfortable, and more like himself.

'Oh God, having surgery down there . . . it just doesn't bear thinking about.' Andreas was being brutally honest.

Dan gave him one of his looks.

'Sorry, hun. That was probably a bit tactless in the circumstances,' he added.

'Don't worry,' Cath responded. 'And yes, it's a very tender area, the poor lad. Anyhow, what's been happening here? That new kitchen unit's going to look great, Dan.'

'Thank you.'

'But, umm, I thought we were just giving things a lick of paint?' she ventured. The lads evidently had grander plans. 'And what *are* you making, Andreas?'

'Now that's a surprise.'

Cath raised her eyebrows. It was damned hard reining that man in.

'Just wait until you see it all come together. No need to stress, we're sticking to the script on neutral wall shades. In fact, I think Nikki's found the perfect white plus a moonlight-grey for an accent wall. She and Lily are off to Homebase to collect the tins. But hey, admit it, it does need a little livening up. I'm working on a special feature, that's all.'

'O-kay, well, I'll reserve judgement on that until I see it.' Hopefully it might be something that could easily be taken down, or moved, should Will not like it. 'Right, well, how can I help? Give me a job.' Cath was keen to get busy.

'Well, before you get started, I'm desperately in need of a coffee hit. If you don't mind putting the kettle on, that'd be amazing,' asked Dan.

'Kettle?' Cath quizzed. When they'd left the last time, there was just an old pan. Dan had shifted the portable hob down to the floor, whilst he worked on the new unit, and there on the camping stove was a lovely, traditional-looking black and chrome, kettle. 'A gift.' Dan smiled.

'Oh, you shouldn't have. You're already doing so much. But, that's wonderful, thank you. That'll come in so handy. Coffee it is then. I've brought a new cafetière over with me too, to leave here, and some ground rich-roast Italian.'

'Oh, a rich, roast Italian sounds good to me,' called out Andreas giving a naughty laugh.

Dan, shaking his head, then added, 'There's a carton of milk in the cool bag, lovely.'

They carried on with their toil, whilst she found three mugs and began to make the hot drinks.

'We're back! With our gorgeous 'Pearl White' and 'Grey Whisper'. The Hamptons, here we come.' Nikki strolled into the hut grinning, with two large paint tubs to hand.

'More like a "Careless Whisper" the way Nikki paints,' chortled Andreas, ever the Wham fan.

'I'll have you know I decorated our lounge and dining room, single-handedly. I'm quite the pro,' came Nikki's retort.

'And I can do all the delicate skirting boards and edge bits. It'll be like piping a cake,' Lily chipped in.

'Or there's always good old masking tape,' added Dan practically. 'There's some in my rucksack there.'

‘Ah, okay, thanks. This bungalow glow-up is going to be so cool,’ said Lily.

‘A bunga-glow,’ came Andreas’s pun, quick as a shot.

‘Hah, that’s brilliant,’ said Nikki.

‘Even I have to confess to liking that one,’ agreed Dan.

Cath chuckled.

Lily glanced over to where she was pouring coffee. ‘Hey, hi, Cath. How’s Will?’

‘Hey, hun.’ Nikki came over, pulling her friend into a warm hug.

‘Yeah, he’s okay. One day at a time,’ she responded. ‘But it has knocked the stuffing out of him.’ A sigh escaped her lips.

‘Aw, bless.’

‘We’re all rooting for his speedy recovery,’ responded Dan calmly and supportively.

‘And he’s going to love what we’re doing here,’ added Andreas.

With Andreas likely working on some quirky feature, Cath wasn’t quite so sure about that. But hey, these were their friends and every hammer, nail and brushstroke were absolutely being done with love. If that wasn’t enough, then nothing would be.

After finishing their reviving drinks, more dust sheets were laid out on the floor, which was to stay as the original brown wooden planks, apparently. Some original features were to remain, at least, which was slightly reassuring, and Nikki had mentioned finding a gorgeous rug in shades of sea and sand for the living area, to go beside the log burner.

With all the talk of extras, as well as the paint, Cath couldn’t help but feel concerned about mounting costs. Nothing had been said about the money side of all this, and whilst giving up time and skills for free seemed fine and was so lovely of them, letting them cover the costs for all sorts of expensive additions such as a new kitchen unit and soft furnishings, well, that didn’t sit easily with her at all. She vowed to broach the matter before she left, but for now it was time to dip that brush and go!

Cath’s first brushstroke with the supper club gang felt

momentous, the pearly-white shade on the wall looking so fresh and new. This felt very much like a second chance for this place. A fresh start for the beach hut, with more adventures and stories for bungalow 12A to come. She crossed her fingers that these would be Will's adventures for many years yet, and if she was lucky enough, that she'd be a part of them, too.

With the music on – Lily requesting a change to some Taylor Swift – and Andreas switching tracks to a beaty rendition of 'Shake it Off', within the hour, the first coat on wall one was done!

Although Cath was occupied, time also seemed to move slowly. She was wondering how Will was getting on, and if he might try and contact her. What they were doing here was great, but she'd never made a good liar; secrets not being her forte. She'd had enough of lies and deceit from Trev. She was meant to be doing online tuition at her home in the village, and here she was, on a mad dash to the coast, undertaking what now felt like a DIY 'experiment' on his inheritance. Oh blimey, she hoped Will would like it. It had seemed such a good idea at the time. Perhaps her nerves about his recent surgery and ongoing recovery had left her reeling and feeling anxious about everything. Life was looking so good for the two of them, their relationship was going so well, and then suddenly with the cancer news, they'd found themselves on a knife-edge.

She dripped a blob of paint from her brush onto the floor. 'Damn it.'

But of course, Dan's dust sheets were down. The safety nets were there. Like her friends were, she realised. Her heart gave a big thank you as she looked around the room; Dan screwing a drawer together ready to place in the new unit, Andreas lining up sawn sections of bamboo, Lily and Nikki painting away, as Lily sang and Nikki hummed to the tunes. Their friendship life raft was in place. They just had to hang on in there.

It was time to head back to Tilldale.

'Well, I'll have to love you and leave you, guys. I've said I'd be back with Will by late afternoon,' said Cath. 'And I'm making supper for them all tonight as Maddie is coming up.'

'Oh, that'll be nice for them. You're so good. Send the patient our love,' said Nikki.

'Tell him we'll pop in and see him again soon,' said Lily.

'I'll bring baklava. It's a cure-all treat. And we'll get these keys back to you soon,' added Andreas.

'Not quite yet, though. If that's okay, Cath?' added Dan. 'I've a feeling we might need to hang on to them for a couple more days. There's a few more hours work, yet.'

'Thank you, and no worries, I'm sure Will won't be looking for them for a while, at least,' she responded.

'He'll still be busy licking his wounds,' said Nikki.

'Bloody hell, I hope not,' Andreas retorted, unable to hold himself back, then collapsing with laughter. He quickly apologised, but Cath was laughing too – as was everyone.

In the midst of the gloom was Andreas's humour, like a daft beacon of light. Cath was shaking her head, whilst they all grinned. What was he like?!

'And hey, thank you all so much. For this . . .' Cath scanned the room which was already so much brighter, the light now bouncing off the walls. 'And I'll send over some money to help out with the paint and everything. But well . . .' She started to fill up. 'You're just brilliant. I don't know what we'd do without you.'

These friends had only been with her for a year, since her traumatic life upheaval and her move to the countryside, and yet she knew already that they'd be friends for life.

'Group hug,' said Nikki, downing her paint roller and tray. The others downed tools too, and they made a huddle of love around Cath, buoying her up before she left.

Chapter 23

Two days later, and it was the first chance she'd had, since Will's surgery, to get back to making her regular visit to the care home. Still feeling a little raw emotionally from this turbulent week, and knowing she'd enjoy his company the most, Cath decided to go and sit with Reggie first.

'Hello, Reggie, how are you doing today?'

'I'm grand, lass, and you?'

'I'm okay.' It seemed to be the easiest answer.

'You sure? You look a touch peaky, if you don't mind me saying.' Reggie then sweetly added, 'And how's that young man of yours?'

And that simple question caught Cath off guard. Her voice was a little shaky as she said, 'Oh, Reggie. He's been in hospital, actually.'

'Well, what on earth are you doing here?'

'It's all right. He's back at home. I've been helping these past few days. His daughters are both there now, and his mum and dad are visiting this morning. So, I thought I'd leave them to it.' Will had only just told his elderly parents last evening, breaking the news gently when he felt well enough to see them without appearing worryingly fragile, knowing they'd want to come over straightaway.

'Ah, I see. He's got plenty of nurses and helpers, then. And what was wrong, pet? If you don't mind me asking? What was he in hospital for?'

Cath felt her eyes misting, and tension tightening her throat. She took a breath before making her response. 'Prostate cancer, Reggie. It was so out of the blue.' There, it was said. And oh my, she couldn't stop a tear or two welling, and spilling over. She swiftly brushed a hand to her cheeks. 'He's had to have surgery.'

'Oh, that's so very difficult for you all.' He reached to pat her arm gently. Having lived in the village, Reggie would have known about Will's family, their terrible struggles with Jane's cancer, and their sad loss.

Reggie and Cath sat quietly for a few moments. The stillness between them broken only by her sniffs, and her fumbling for a tissue, which she didn't seem to have. Reggie produced a clean pocket handkerchief and passed it to her. 'Here, pet.'

'Thanks.' She sniffed. *Oh my, she was meant to be cheering these elderly folk up, not bringing her troubles in with her*, she thought.

'I'll go fetch you a cup of tea. You sit there.' Reggie was slowly getting up to his feet.

'Oh, I can do it, Reg,' she countered.

'No, no, let me help.' He was insistent, as he got up and headed off to the residents' small kitchen area.

Betty who'd been watching from across the way, then shuffled over to take up Reggie's seat, asking Cath if she was okay. And Vera called out to offer her box of tissues, which were duly passed around the day room, chair to chair, like a pass the parcel to stop with Cath.

Linda, who'd caught up with Reggie in the kitchen, then came in carrying the cup of tea that Reggie had made. As well as being concerned about Reggie perhaps spilling some, and hurting himself, she was worried about Cath too. 'How are you, love? I'm so sorry to hear about Will's illness and surgery. Send him all of our best wishes. He was such a darling with everyone at the carols and the Christmas lunch.'

'Oh yes, Will. I remember now. He's the rather handsome one,' said Joan. 'Had a look of the film star Charlton Heston, I thought.'

Cath had to smile, as she snuffled the last of her tears into Reggie's hankie, apologising for her unexpected reaction. She hadn't bargained for that flood of emotion. It had taken her very much by surprise. One kind question from Reggie had toppled her like a house of cards. She must have been trying so hard to hold it all together for Will and his family these past few weeks, keeping her own feelings bolted down for all their sakes.

'There's no need to apologise, lass. You must be going through a lot,' said Reggie on his return with a plate of comforting custard creams and shortbread.

After chatting with Reggie over tea and biscuits, and having a few minutes each with Joan, Vera and Betty, Cath felt her emotions settle. And it was soon time to head off.

Manager Julie caught up with Cath at the entrance to the day room as she was about to leave. 'Oh, hi, Cath, just to let you know we've got the minibuses reserved for the third. Twenty-six of our residents have their names down for the afternoon tea event. That's nearly a full house, how marvellous. What time do you want them to arrive and be collected for, so I can let the company know?'

She then paused, giving Cath a concerned glance, no doubt spotting the blotchy-red eyes, and Reggie's hankie that she was still clutching, intending to give it a wash at home. 'Oh, are you all right, love?'

'Ahm, yes, thanks.' Cath released a gentle sigh. 'It's just been a tricky couple of weeks.'

'Oh?'

Linda and the others all knew, and it wasn't exactly a secret, so she explained, 'My partner, Will, has been diagnosed with cancer. He's had surgery just a week ago, to remove his prostate.'

'Oh, lovey. I'm so sorry to hear that. And I know just how you feel.' Julie placed a hand gently on Cath's shoulder, the gesture filled with kindness. 'My husband, Simon, went through the same. It was such a difficult time. He's right as rain now, though.' She gave a smile filled with hope and encouragement. 'But going through all that, it's not easy. I'm sorry for putting even more pressure on you, just then. Hey, are you sure you're still okay for this tea party? We can postpone, or cancel.'

Cath glanced back to the room where several of the residents were listening in, their wonderfully aged faces filled with anticipation. 'Not a chance! We can't let these guys down.'

And her elderly friends were smiling and nodding with relief at her response.

'That's the way, pet,' called out Reggie.

'Oh, it'll be so lovely,' from Vera.

'I love a bit of tea and cake, me,' added Betty.

A chorus of vigorous support for the afternoon tea rang out from the day room residents.

Reggie then added caringly, 'But only if you're sure it won't be too much for you, pet.'

'It won't.' Cath was adamant. 'It's several weeks away yet. And I think this might be just the tonic we'll need to get ourselves going again, something to plan and look forward to.' Though, she'd personally make sure that Will didn't take on too much of the physical work involved that day.

'Thank you so much, Cath.' Julie walked with her out through reception. 'It would have been a disappointment for them if it had to be put off. But if anything changes, or I can do anything to help you, in any way, not just about the function, please let me know.'

'Thank you. I appreciate that.'

As Cath left the home, her step felt a little lighter. Her heart had been lifted, surrounded by the love and support in that day room. Her visits were meant to be helping the elderly by chatting and cheering them up, she mused. But today, when she'd needed it most, they'd done exactly that for her.

Chapter 24

Back at the ranch – aka Will's house – later the same day, Cath still couldn't help but feel rather put out. It was lovely that Maddie and Sophie wanted to be there to support their dad, but it was evident that they wanted to take charge, or more exactly, take over; or that's how it felt to Cath.

Here, where Will was convalescing, wasn't Cath's home, and she knew that, but she'd become an integral part of Will's life these past months. And she'd hoped the girls had come to realise that, too.

It was now Friday, and eight days since Will's surgery. Cath was there for the afternoon, chatting with him, checking he was comfortable, and generally keeping him company. He seemed to prefer being in his armchair than resting up in bed, though trying to get up and down to the loo still seemed rather difficult for him. It was good to be on hand to help. Cath was more than happy to hang on for a while, and make some supper for them all.

Whilst Will was taking a nap, Cath caught up with his daughters in the kitchen. She'd brought round all the ingredients to make a cottage pie and had left them in the fridge. There was a cool atmosphere as she walked in, their chat pausing instantly.

'All okay? He's finding it a bit tough, isn't he?'

'Yes. It's to be expected though,' said Maddie, who as a nurse, was of course well informed. 'He's just gotta take things steady.'

Sophie was merely looking on, and nodding, at that point.

'Uhm, I was wondering about making us all something for supper,' Cath ventured.

'Thanks, but it's all right.' Sophie jumped in. 'I was thinking of ordering some pizza. Something nice and easy. Dad's favourite pepperoni might perk him up.'

It seemed rather pointed of Cath to now insist on cooking the healthier cottage pie with veggies that she'd planned. Also, one of Will's favourites.

'Ah, okay.' Cath was pretty certain she wasn't included in these pizza plans, either. There wasn't a mention of 'do you want to join us?' It seemed churlish of her to push to stay. But she felt odd, like she wasn't part of this support gang. Or perhaps she was tired herself, she reasoned. Her feelings too tender.

'Thanks, Cath. You've been great. But we've got this. Dad's done so much for us, and for Mum too, now it's our turn. We want to be here for him,' added Maddie, matter-of-factly.

The sentiment was great, that the girls were there and ready to support their dad, but Cath couldn't help but feel piqued.

'Well, I'm happy to help, and if there's anything at all, please, just say . . .' Her words drifted uneasily.

'Thanks, appreciate that, we'll let you know if we need anything but we've got it all in hand. I am a trained oncology nurse, after all,' Maddie reminded her.

'Of course. Well, I'll get off then. Just wanted to make sure you were all okay. But well, it looks like you're sorted.' She was trying so hard to sound upbeat, but she felt like a bloody spare part. 'Hope he has a good night. I'll see you all tomorrow.' She got that in, on purpose. There was no way that she wasn't going to do her bit and look in on him daily. She wanted to be there for him, too. Perhaps she'd do a kitchen takeover, and make that bloody cottage pie then.

Her handbag was in the lounge. Popping back in, she saw that

Will had now opened his eyes.

'Hey, I'm heading back home this evening, now. The girls will look after you. Take care, my love. I'll see you in the morning.' Did she dare kiss him? A peck on the cheek at least? The girls had followed her into the room by then, and Cath felt the heat of two pairs of eyes on her, as she leaned in for a farewell kiss.

'Thanks for dropping by, Cath,' Will said a little groggily. He was probably sleepy but his words ended up sounding polite and rather distant, as though she was a mere acquaintance.

Of course, he'd just woken up, but she couldn't help feel a bit put out . . . *pushed* out. How much was she a part of their lives? She certainly didn't yet feel like family. And she had to admit that that hurt.

Cath let off steam with her sister, Susie, calling her when she got back in. Her sister knew of Will, being privy to the ins and outs of their developing relationship, and was now fully aware of his recent cancer shock and surgery. And being her big sister, she knew Cath inside out, too. She was absolutely the right person to call. It was good for Cath to be able to vent without judgement. To be able to be totally frank.

'Argh, it's making me feel like the Wicked Witch of the West. When I'm there, it's like they can't wait to get rid of me. The girls, that is. And I'm only trying to bloody well help. I feel like they want to take over. To keep it to their little unit of three. They're not even subtle in treating me like a spare part. Will's too knackered even to notice, let alone to stand up to them. And then I feel terrible that I'm even thinking all these things, because it's a shitty time for everyone.' Cath ran out of steam then. It had well and truly been vented. Perhaps in a jumbled mass, but it was out there.

'You've had a good day, then,' Susie uttered wryly. 'And hello to you too, lovely Sis.'

'Hi. Sorry, I just needed to let that all out.'

'It's okay. That's what I'm here for.'

'Thank you. It's just so damn frustrating. And all I want to do is help Will get better.'

'Well, keep that as your focus. The rest of it is annoying, and hey, you should expect some respect at least from the girls, but it's not the time to go demanding an equal footing in their house. Maybe it *is* a bit too soon, and in the circumstances, everyone's emotions are bound to be heightened.'

'Yeah, I suppose you're right.' Cath felt herself coming back down. 'And it probably brings back difficult memories, too,' she conceded. 'Of when their mum was trying to get through her cancer treatments, and they'd hoped it would all turn out right . . . and it never did.'

'There's always a bigger picture, Cath. But hey, it's understandable how you're feeling too. You just want the best for Will. And I bet you'd imagined you'd be the one caring for him, nursing him through this. You were always like that . . . sparrows with broken wings, mice half-dead that the cat had brought in, trying to nurture them back to health in a cardboard box. Nurse Cathy. If you hadn't been a teacher, I bet that's what you would have done instead.'

'Hah, probably.'

'And how is Will doing?'

'Sore. But he's okay. Slowly, but surely, I suppose. It has knocked the stuffing out of him, mind. That's what's really hard, for him and me, seeing him so frail now. Yet when he went in, he was such a healthy, active man. Cancer is weird like that. Hidden. Lurking. You feel fine, and then getting the bloody thing out and treating it, makes you feel horrendous.'

'Yeah, I hadn't thought of it like that. But yes . . .' Susie sounded contemplative.

'Anyway, we'll work through it,' said Cath, sounding far more positive than at the start of her rant. 'So how are all of you? And what are your girls up to lately?'

‘Ah, we’re all fine. Hectic, as always. Hannah’s enjoying all elements of the uni life down at Bristol. On the netball team, too. She seems very happy. And Beth’s been off to Paris for a few days with her legal work. Sounded very glamorous, though she swore she hardly had time to see any of the city or sights. Had a very fancy dinner, all paid for, mind. All champagne and canapés, duck à l’orange, and something elaborate and chocolatey to finish.’

‘Sounds fabulous. We never got any of that treatment in my secondary school maths department.’

‘Hah, no.’

‘Oh, you’ll have to come up again soon.’ With their easy chat, Cath realised how much she missed her sister.

‘Yeah, once all this has settled with Will and his family, I’d love to. I’m sure you’ve enough on your plate just now. But it will be lovely to catch up again properly, and your little village is so beautiful.’

‘Yes, it is a bit hectic right now,’ Cath conceded. ‘And, on top of all this, I’ve got the Tilldale afternoon tea event, I told you about, to get organised.’

‘Oh God, yeah, you’ve got all that to prepare for. You must be bloody mad.’

‘Yes, well, I didn’t know any of this was going to happen when I suggested the idea, did I? I’ve got around thirty expectant attendees on the list. I can’t let them down.’

‘Oh heavens. Good luck.’

‘Cheers. I’ll need it.’ She *was* bloody crazy, she silently agreed. But Cath would park her concerns on that one for another day. Her brain might well implode otherwise.

‘Right, lovely, well, I’d better go,’ said Susie. ‘We’re off to The Bull for a drink with friends. It’s quiz night. And we’ve got a team together.’ The Bull was their local pub.

And didn’t that sound wonderful. A bit of carefree fun at a pub with friends. Cath suddenly yearned to go back to those easy days. They’d had a quiz night at The Star Inn here; Cath, Will and the supper clubbers in a team. A lot of fun, firing answers like bullets between them – not all of them right – along with a few cheeky beers and vinos. How the world had shifted. How much you took for granted. She'd give anything to be back there now, with a cancer-free Will and her buddies laughing. *It'll come again*, a small but steady voice rose inside her. Like the tides of the sea, good times, bad times, ebbs and flows. This too shall pass . . .

'Aw, have a great time. And thanks for listening, Sis.'

'It's been good to catch up. And you take care now. It can't be easy. Send Marti my get-well wishes, and my love.'

That made Cath grin. When Susie had come up to visit her in Tilldale, before Cath and Will were even an item, she'd insisted he looked like Marti Pellow from Wet Wet Wet. And hmm, that wasn't a bad look at all.

Closing the call, with her fears and frustrations aired, Cath felt so much stronger. The situation was the same, but she was ready to forge back in with a clearer mindset. A problem shared, and all that . . .

Talking with her sister had felt like pressing a reset button.

Despite feeling riled by the situation at Will's, and after letting off steam with her sibling, Cath knew that going forward she was stronger and more generous than her frustration had made her feel. Will's family were absolutely struggling with all this, too. And perhaps, if the girls were still making her life difficult later down the line, then, when Will was feeling much more himself, they could tackle it together. But for now, Cath understood that it was better to stay calm, keep visiting Will as and when she could, to be kind, and keep the peace.

It was now eight o'clock in the evening, and she sat outside on her back patio with a cosy fleece on, a glass of chilled pinot grigio to hand, watching swallows dip and turn, as she pondered. How best could she help Will and his family? That was what was important here. She needed to stitch up the holes that had recently formed in her safety net for them.

If she wanted to be a more permanent part of their lives, she had to be patient.

The next afternoon, Cath headed back to Will's with resolve, fortitude and her wicker basket to hand, bearing a home-cooked meal – the mince she'd left there last night could go in his freezer – and some additional goodies from the shop for them all.

'Hey, how's the patient?' Cath found Will in his armchair in the lounge, watching a football match on the TV. 'Andreas and Dan send their love, and I've picked up your copy of *Cycling Weekly*.'

'Ah, I'm okay, and thanks.'

'And there's some refreshing ginger beer, and a couple of 0 per cent lagers for you. I'll pop them in your fridge in a mo.'

'That's great.' He seemed a little distracted by the match.

Cath continued chatting for a while despite his eyes drifting to and from the players on the pitch, leading in to, 'Oh, and I wondered about getting some fresh air . . . a short walk or a drive out somewhere perhaps. How does tomorrow sound?' She planted the seed. She'd been getting updates from the supper gang, and the big beach bungalow reveal was imminent. 'It'll be good for you. To get back out,' she mooted. He needed to build in a little exercise at this point, anyhow, a little getting back to normal.

'Hmm, yeah, perhaps.'

'Okay, well, I'll have a think what might be nice.' She tried to sound casual, whilst smiling at her idea beginning to take shape. 'Right, I'll get this stuff into the fridge.'

She caught up with the girls, who were in the kitchen chatting, giving them her carefully chosen gifts of a mini candle each and some artisan chocolate from the village stores. 'Here you go, ladies, a little something to chill out with. I think we all deserve a treat, don't you?'

'Ah, that's sweet of you Cath,' said Maddie warmly. 'Ooh, and I love a candle.'

'That's so lovely, thanks, Cath.' Sophie seemed genuinely grateful.

'Oh, and I've got a meal to leave for you in the fridge. It's a lasagne, made fresh, so it'll keep for a couple of days, if you don't fancy it tonight. I've got a busy evening with tuition, so I'll be off shortly. Last blast of the exam season with my GCSE students.'

'Aw, thank you. That'll save us from getting a takeaway,' Maddie responded.

'Hope that goes well, your tuition,' added Sophie.

And Cath gave a smile. Small acts of kindness. Small steps forward.

She stayed a while to chat about Maddie's recent nursing shifts, and what plans Sophie had ongoing for the summer. Some easy conversation. Cath then asked how they felt Will was getting on, interested in their take on his progress. Though he was able to physically get up and down, and walk around the house more easily, these past few days he'd seemed a bit low if anything, a bit lethargic.

The girls had spotted it too, Sophie saying she'd have thought he'd be getting restless by now, eager to get back out on his bike or something.

'Yeah, it's knocked him a bit. But I see this often with my work,' commented Maddie. 'There's a real positivity and energy pre-surgery, like you're ready to face this thing head-on, and then afterwards, it's like the shock of it all, the realisation that you're really dealing with cancer hits your body, your mind too. It's hard.'

It was early in his recovery though, and goodness knows how sore he must still be feeling, Cath thought. 'Yes, you're right,' she agreed. 'He's had so much to cope with.'

He no doubt needed time, they all needed time. And perhaps, a little something to cheer him up . . . And Cath had just the tonic.

Chapter 25

'I wondered about a visit to the beach hut today,' announced Cath, when she called back the following morning, trying her best to sound casual about it.

The trip was planned. It was Sunday, they were now ten days in to Will's recuperation, and eek, this was the big reveal. After her secret mission to help start painting the interior with the gang, she hadn't been able to get back over to the hut and help. The supper clubbers were very much keeping schtum about any further details, too. She'd tried to wheedle some snippets from them on the design, or even better a photo or two, but they'd frustratingly said she'd just have to wait along with Will. By now, she was desperate to see the finished glow-up herself. 'Just a little drive out,' she added hopefully. 'I've bought one or two things to leave at the bungalow, mainly kitchen stuff.' And she did in fact have a set of puffin-print tea towels, and a couple of new pans to help make cooking there that bit easier in the future. She was especially excited to try out the newly refurbished kitchen zone. But of course, Will knew nothing of this as yet . . .

Will looked up at her, from his sofa seat, through rather jaded eyes. 'Oh.'

He didn't appear that keen on an outing at all. The op and the implications thereafter had naturally taken it out of him. And, even with the post-surgery catheter now removed, he'd admitted to Cath that things were still a bit of a nightmare on that front. He was having to use pads permanently. Oh dear, was this all too soon? Perhaps she should have left the outing for a bit longer. But it was all organised. She'd been keeping in touch with Nikki over the past couple of days. They were all primed . . .

'Sorry, I just thought some fresh air . . . perhaps a gentle stroll by the sea . . .' she mooted tentatively.

Damn, she should have realised he'd have concerns about going out so soon. Not to mention the practical implications that might be worrying him. But she did also believe that getting out, doing something more normal, might be good for him. The fit, young-for-his-age man had disappeared overnight on that operating table. But he had every chance of making a full recovery. 'There's a loo at the bungalow.' She caringly reminded him. 'And I'm not meaning a hike, Will, just a short stroll on the sands. The nurse did recommend some gentle walking. Or perhaps, we could just sit for a while, on the deck there, take in the view and some healing sea air. But hey, it's up to you.'

She backed off, letting him have a little think. He didn't need any extra pressure just now, she understood that. And hey, she supposed they could always reschedule if he wasn't happy. It would be disappointing but all it would take was one quick WhatsApp message.

Maddie had left early to head back down to Newcastle, and Sophie, who'd been making some toast in the kitchen, then came through to the lounge. She must have heard the end of their conversation. 'Everything okay?'

'Yes,' Cath replied, trying to smooth things over.

'Cath's trying to get me to go out . . . over to the beach hut,' said Will.

'Well, it'd probably do you good, Dad,' she prompted. 'You have been a bit cooped up here. Hey, I'd love to go and see it, but I've promised Lily I'd go over and help her with something this afternoon.'

The two young women had struck up a friendship since Sophie had been back at home, messaging mostly, which was nice. And Sophie had called there for a couple of hours the other day. They'd probably all been feeling a bit stir crazy, to be honest. But this did confuse Cath a little. Wasn't Lily going to be over at the hut with the rest of the gang this afternoon? But perhaps they both wanted some time with people their own age this afternoon instead.

Will looked up shortly afterwards, their words of encouragement seemingly working. 'Actually, yeah, you're probably right. A short drive out might be good. And we may as well take a look at the beach bungalow.'

'Great.' Cath struck whilst the iron was hot. 'Let's have a quick bite of lunch here, first. Then I'll call in at mine, and collect the kitchen bits on the way. About an hour's time sound okay to set off . . .?'

'Yep, fine.' He gave a small nod, the corners of his mouth lifting into a small smile.

The wheels were in motion.

They'd walked the track steadily through the dunes, and were now approaching the rear of the bungalow. Cath had sneakily sent a warning 'Thumbs Up' emoji from the car park.

'Okay, so there's something I need to do at this point,' Cath announced, feeling a buzz of excitement, as she reached from behind to cover Will's eyes with her palms. They were about to round the building's corner and approach the deck.

'Hey, what's going on here?' Will queried.

'You'll find out very soon.' She was smiling as she spoke, and suddenly felt a bit nervous, too. She wasn't quite sure what to expect. With so much on lately, with caring for Will, the girls, and keeping up with her tuition, plus the gang's reticence on letting her in on the finished results, she hadn't got a clue what the final renovations were like. She and Will took a few more slow paces onto the hut's deck.

The bungalow's door began to open from the inside, as Cath slowly pulled her hands away, all the while peering over Will's shoulder.

'Hello!' Dan stepped forward, with a gathering of excited faces crowded in behind him.

'What the heck are you doing here?' Will asked bemused.

'Don't worry, it's just a touch of Hula,' Andreas called out, as the others then shouted, 'Surprise!'

And there stood, Nikki, Dan, Lily, Sophie . . . how on earth was Sophie here? Oh, and Gemma too, their plumber friend.

Cath felt as stunned as Will looked.

'Come in, come in.' Nikki beckoned, looking delighted.

It was the lightness of the interior that hit Cath first. The pearly-white paint that Nikki had chosen was the perfect shade for three of the walls, and oh, the gorgeous soft grey feature wall behind the stove. The space in the living area looked so cool and airy. Coastal hues of calming blues and greys filled the room, above the umber browns of the original wooden floorboards which had been sanded and freshened up with a touch of natural varnish. A touch of teal caught her eye on wonderfully striking starfish-and-shell-patterned blue-and-white cushions, that were now plumped on the navy sofa bed. Oh, and there were new curtains, fluttering gently at the two front windows, that matched the cushions. The supper club gang had gone above and beyond, by far. And Sophie, who was grinning away besides Lily, was somehow in on it too. Cath was momentarily speechless as a wave of emotion rolled right through her.

'Am I at the right bungalow? How's this all happened?' Will seemed shocked, happy and confused all at once.

'It's incredible,' said Cath, feeling awestruck. 'It was nothing like this when I left you all that day.'

'Ah, so you were in on it, too.' Will looked to Cath bemusedly, yet couldn't help the smile that lit his face.

'The key bearer,' explained Dan.

'And Cath started the painting with us,' added Lily. 'Sophie's helped to choose the cushions and curtains, and then came down to put them up with us.'

'Oh yes, we've been up to all sorts of mischief whilst you've been recuperating, mate,' continued Dan, with a twinkle in his eye.

'Hey, how're you feeling, Will?' asked Gemma, who now stepped forward from the kitchen area – where there was a shiny brand-new sink. All set in Dan's fresh white kitchen unit, with its extra cupboards and work space. Something else that had totally changed.

Will was struggling to take it all in. 'Well, I'm getting there, thanks,' he replied after a short pause. 'Mind you, I think you lot have put me in to shock with all the carry-on here. It's fantastic, but oh my days . . .'

'Oh, and there's a new toilet installed, too.' Gemma gave a wide grin.

'I don't know how to thank you, all of you. It's just amazing. So how do I settle up for all this?' Will was still gobsmacked.

'No need for any of that. It's a gift. A get-well present,' said Andreas proudly.

And then, as the grand finale, their eyes moved to the 'Hula' corner, where he was now standing: Andreas's DIY semi-circular bar, with its wooden countertop and bamboo sides.

Ah, so *that* was what the bamboo had been for, thought Cath. The counter held a beautiful vintage blue cocktail glass filled with mini cocktail stick umbrellas, a stainless-steel pineapple-shaped ice bucket, and a flamboyant, oh yes, pink flamingo ornament. To the front, Andreas had pinned an opened-out raffia grass skirt for added humour. There were several glasses lined up and ready. Andreas then took his place behind his bar, with the biggest grin on his face, ready to pour his celebratory cocktails.

'Anyone for a pina colada? Or for those driving or still on meds, I have a pi-no colada mocktail.' There he was, in his element, sporting a Hawaiian-style shirt with colourful fake-flower garland teamed with chino shorts. Cath then spotted the tropical-plant paintings gracing the wall behind the bar.

The Hula bar was a triumph; a splash of bold colour and a bit of fun, in the midst of the coastal calm. It really shouldn't work with the rest of the interior design, but somehow it did. Perhaps that came from knowing it had been created with flair and love, mused Cath.

But what did Will think, was the million-dollar question?

'We did try to rein him in a bit,' Nikki added with a smile.

'But you can't keep a good man down.' Andreas gave a wink. 'So, what do you think, Will?'

There was a pause, as Will scanned the bungalow's interior once more. 'I actually love it. All of it,' said Will. 'I still can't believe it. When did you get time to do all this?'

'A team effort. We started a few days after your op, had a full day to kick things off, a few evenings after work, and a big bash yesterday with Kev lending a hand too, to bring it all together,' explained Nikki.

'I fitted the new sink and loo this morning,' Gemma added proudly.

'And we've only just finished putting up the curtains about ten minutes ago,' said Sophie, going over to give her dad a warm hug.

'But you were at home . . .' Will was still trying to work it all out.

'I left about thirty seconds after you!' She laughed. 'Lily's dad gave us two a lift over. We passed you as you stopped at Cath's.'

'Wow, just wow.' Will was still utterly gobsmacked.

Cath found herself getting teary. It was beautiful in here. A world away from the ramshackle, mice-ridden hut they'd walked into two months ago. A gorgeous place to chill as a couple or on your own, somewhere to sit and just be, watching the constant ebb and flow of the sea, and equally a space to have fun with guests, or to party perhaps – once Will was up to partying again, of course. And for now, a space to heal, to find a little calm and hold on to that hope for the future. That's what Will needed more than anything just now. And these very special friends had made this possible.

'Thank you,' Cath started. The words felt so little, but meant so much. 'Thank you all,' Cath repeated, her throat tight with emotion.

'Thanks so much, everyone,' added Will. 'I still can't quite believe it. No more dodgy dark-wood interior.'

'You're very welcome, my lovelies,' said Dan, his arm around his partner, and scanning their friends and Sophie, he spoke for all of them.

'Okay, it must be cocktail time, so who's for the real deal and who's on the mocktails?' Andreas called out as he began to pass around glasses filled with the creamy pineapple and coconut coladas, with vivid paper umbrellas and straws in. 'It's a *hut-warming* moment.' He smiled at his pun.

'And a big heartfelt get well soon from all of us,' added Dan earnestly.

'Yes, time to celebrate,' said Lily. 'And to wish you well, Will.'

'Absolutely,' added Nikki. 'To a speedy recovery.'

'Cheers, to you both,' said Gemma.

Oh, the lump in Cath's throat thickened even more.

'Music, maestro!' Dan then instructed.

Andreas took up his phone, ready to play something on the mini speaker, and Wham's 'Club Tropicana' blasted out. 'Oops, no, hang on, your first song was meant to be this . . .'

They all had to laugh.

After fiddling with his mobile, Andreas found the right track. The beat began, and the unmistakable chords of The Drifters' 'Under the Boardwalk' played out. The gang were soon swaying gently along, sipping their summer drinks.

'We've made a beach-inspired playlist for you,' added Dan.

'Aw, that's brilliant,' said Cath.

'Oh, and we mustn't forget the nibbles,' Nikki added. 'Lily's made Doddington cheese straws, there are also king prawns with a lemon-garlic mayo dip and sea-salt Kettle crisps.'

'And I have feta and spinach pastry parcels, and honey-spiced nuts,' said Andreas.

'Sounds delish,' said Cath.

'Don't forget the mini chocolate brownies too,' added Lily. 'In case anyone wants something sweet.'

'I'm in for those,' said Sophie with a smile. It was lovely to see her looking so happy.

'And I've brought the loo roll.' Gemma laughed. 'As well as the loo, of course.'

The group mingled, chatting about the new decor, and how this had all come about, with Andreas telling them that the germ of the idea had started with Will back at home, post-op, expressing his regret at being unable to make these changes for himself for a while. The group so wanted him and Cath to be able to start using the place as a bolthole for Will's recovery. The freshen-up with a lick of paint Andreas had initially suggested, grew into a bigger job as Dan remembered how drab and tiny the original kitchen unit was, and fancied putting his DIY skills to the test. After that, it had kind of morphed into a full interior design 'Beach Hut Challenge', Lily explained, with Sophie getting involved too. The crowning glory being a chance chat with Gemma at the village stores, who offered to help with her fabulous plumbing finale.

On that note, Will went off to inspect the new loo – a shiny white throne – needing his privacy for a short while. He hadn't quite imagined having a party going on while he changed his pad in the beach bungalow water closet, but at least the external noise made him feel a little less obvious. He'd been left feeling so damn debilitated by the operation. And yet, in the small yet light space, despite his ongoing physical discomfort and bloody annoying 'leaky tap' peeing syndrome, he couldn't help but smile, caught up in the sense of joy at the unexpected renovations.

Later, once the others had gone – with Sophie deciding to head back over to the village with Lily and Nikki – following a happy chorus of 'take care', 'get well soon' and 'goodbye', and big thanks all round, the hectic afternoon began to catch up with Will.

With a yawn, Will admitted to Cath that it had been a wonderful but exhausting day, so soon post-surgery. She set up two chairs for them outside on the deck, and left him to rest a while. They didn't need to rush back to Tilldale, though staying here on the sofa bed was a no-no whilst he was still feeling discomfort. In all honesty, it was so lovely here, Cath wasn't quite ready to leave, either. She was still soaking in all the wonderful new details: the shell-patterned cushions and curtains, the sand-and-sea swirled pattern of the abstract rug by the fire.

Cath popped the singing kettle onto the camping stove, and set out mugs and a cafetière. She then spotted the old brown-glazed, now sparkly clean, teapot, which had been artfully placed with an art deco cup on the kitchen side, and gave a smile. Hardly an heirloom, but a thoughtful memento saved from Will's family's past. Opportunely, she also noticed that a couple of chocolate brownies were left over, and once Will had had a little shut eye, they sat sipping soothing, mellow coffee out on the deck overlooking the sea.

'What a day. And you were in on it all along, I suppose?' Will gave a warm smile. 'I still can't bloody well believe it. What a transformation.'

'Yeah, well, I knew they were intending to paint the place, and I'd seen some woodwork being put together by Andreas and Dan, but I had no idea of the extent of the project. Not all this . . . the whole house through. I really don't know how they've managed it. And, they've done their best to keep up with their day jobs all the while, too.'

‘Yeah, there must have been some late nights going on.’

‘Yes, I bet. And then Lily teaming up to get Sophie on board, I had no idea of that development until I saw her here. But that’s lovely, too.’

‘Yeah, Sophie looked so happy. It’s great they’ve made friends. It’s all amazing.’ Making the most of the chance to rest, Will put down his almost-empty cup and closed his eyes again for a while. Cath sat contemplating, thinking how life had changed so very much these past months, all the while mesmerised by the sea in motion. Her gaze then followed a trio of terns in flight as they swooped and dipped across the bay. Her breathing slowed as she began to relax, too. It was such a beautiful place.

After the reveal, they’d stayed socialising with the others in the main living space. She had looked briefly in on the bedroom earlier, noticing that, too, had had a fresh lick of paint. With Will dozing once more, she couldn’t resist another peek in there. Heading back, and opening the door, the room was so lovely and airy. The walls were painted the same fresh white as the living area, and oh, one wall – the one you might rest a headboard against – was now a soft powder-blue that made her think of a coastal springtime sky. The shell and driftwood artworks – that Will’s distant relatives had likely made – which had been hanging in the living space, were now here. Aw, such a pretty memento and nod to the past. A further seashell-patterned curtain, to match those in the living area, had been put up at the little window. Of course, there was no furniture in here as yet.

But now, she could picture it as it might be. A double bed was in fact on order, in a reclaimed pale-wood finish that she and Will had chosen, but they were still waiting on a delivery date. Choosing it online together, before Will’s surgery, had felt like an act of hope, of something to look forward to. They could take nothing for granted, of course, with further PSA tests and follow-ups yet to come, but buying furniture for the beach hut felt like a firm commitment to the future. A happier future, together, with beach days, chilled days, family days, friends over days, and at the end of those days, a comfy bed to look forward to.

She smiled to herself remembering how completing the bed's delivery instructions online had kept the pair of them entertained. After having to give the car park as the delivery address, Cath filled in an explanatory message under 'Access Information' on the unusual residence, highlighting the necessary trip across the dunes to reach the property. Cath still wondered if a large tip might help persuade the delivery men to help shift the no doubt heavy item all the way to the bungalow. As a back-up plan, they'd figured on having a couple of strong mates on hand at the car park, just in case.

She headed back through to the living space, a gentle smile on her face as she gazed again at the hut's brand-new interior, which turned into a daft grin at Andreas's cocktail corner.

Sat back down beside a still-snoozing Will, she settled to watch the remaining beachgoers on the sands below; birds, animals and humans. She'd let Will rest some more; it had been a busy day, and he evidently needed it. It was lovely to think that from here on in, with all the works done thanks to their fabulous friends, they'd be able to come over and unwind more often.

Glancing at his sleeping form, Cath wondered if it wasn't just the surgery Will needed to heal from; after losing Jane he was still carrying a ton of grief. These past few years, he must surely have felt as if he'd been buried in an avalanche of loss. Though his own diagnosis and surgery had been a huge blow, it was very much something else to deal with on top of all that had come before. At least now, he . . . *they* could slip away and escape to this very special seaside place, which had been brought back to life with love, and a lot of hard work.

Sitting here with the warmth of the June sun caressing her skin, the salt in the air, and a magical view of the ruins of Dunstanburgh

Castle, Cath could already feel the place working its magic on her. She so hoped it would do the same for Will.

Onwards and upwards. With small, steady and gorgeously salty steps.

Chapter 26

Sunday, 3rd August was marked in red and loomed on the calendar. Now that they had hit July, it was only one turn of the page away. The Tilldale Afternoon Tea was coming around, and way too fast. Cath could feel her anxiety levels ramping up.

With the challenging health events for Will in May and June, and the weeks rolling by with Cath's continuing efforts to support him and his girls, time was moving on. In fact, it had blooming well steamrolled on. It was great that they had the date and venue fixed for the community afternoon tea, but numbers were constantly growing. As well as the large group coming from the care home, the lads had confirmed that since they'd put a poster up advertising the event in the shop window, the complimentary tickets were being snapped up from the village stores. Firm plans for the catering and entertainment needed to be made, and soon.

With Will still recuperating, only finding enough energy to venture out to check on his cycling shop which was opening on shorter hours, it would be down to the remaining supper club five to put the practical wheels in motion. Cath wanted to ensure the tea was another wonderful social event filled with fantastic food, music and dancing. Could they match the brilliant cuisine, fun and atmosphere of the Christmas lunch? It was a tall order. They'd set their own bar very high. This called for a supper club get-together and brainstorm. Cath felt a bit mean pushing her gang to help out yet again, so soon after all that hard work renovating the beach hut, but this was too big a task to face on her own.

She had already jotted down some thoughts and ideas. Her notebook in her phone listed:

50s music – confirm the band. One that's not too expensive! Live music would make the event extra special, and help give that traditional tea dance feel.

50s clothes. Looking the part would make it much more fun. She was sure Andreas and Dan would be very much up for it. And, if any of the guests wanted to dress for that era, that would of course be wonderful. She'd give Julie at the care home the heads-up. They'd need to add that to any posters and event information, too.

Food? Proper afternoon tea style – dainty sandwiches, scones with jam and cream, mini cakes and bakes. She'd added *LILY* in capital letters. The baking queen might fancy taking a lead on this one, and they'd yet to firm up who exactly was cooking and making what.

FUNDS?? More capital letters. Funding was going to be her biggest dilemma. Again, they'd agreed to host this as a free event, keeping it accessible to the elderly and those who might feel isolated or a bit lonely, including both young and old from the area. Tilldale wasn't a big village by any means, and they strongly felt it was important to try and cater for everyone who'd like to join in. At least, with ticketing via the shop, it meant that they had a track of numbers.

Cath felt slightly panicky, realising she'd left all this a bit late. But her mind and energy had been diverted to caring for Will these past few weeks. The other supper clubbers had been focused on their own lives plus doing the beach hut renovations. School teacher mode began to kick in as she sat pondering over a cup of coffee, ramping up ideas: the raffle – they'd need to get that hamper of tea-time goodies out on display with tickets for sale, the tombola to organise, additional donations – where might she ask locally for help? And she needed to check up on those sponsorship ideas mooted at the last meeting, including the Brownies' bounce-a-thon and Nikki's boys' car-washing idea. Had anything in fact moved forward with those? Time was running short.

Her usual organised self had been flagging; of course she'd had a hell of a lot to cope with, and right now, it being late in the evening, her energies were low. She stifled a yawn, realising her mind felt rather mushy instead of productive. Right then, time for bed. She'd sleep on it. She knew better than to try to make important decisions with a tired brain. But she hoped to have some more concrete, and also inspiring, ideas to take with her to the planning session tomorrow. She also hoped that Andreas would have some baklava handy for the morning. She needed thinking fuel.

A baklava brainstorming session was indeed doing the trick.

In Andreas and Dan's flat above the shop, coffee was poured, and the sweet honey and walnut delights were going down a treat. Nikki had pushed her first cleaning job to an hour later, and the lads were going to take turns to mind the stores. Lily was there, looking like she'd just got out of bed – which she probably had done after getting used to post-exam lie-ins. She'd turned up with her kohl looking slightly smudgy, not quite as slickly painted as usual this morning (or perhaps it was still last night's, Cath pondered amusedly). And, terrier Shirley, their extra team member, was there acting as a crumb cleaner and foot warmer for Cath under the table.

'Right, guys,' Cath started with an upbeat tone. 'We have four weeks to go until the Tilldale Afternoon Tea, and so far other than a poster in the shop and handing out several tickets . . .'

'Twelve,' added Andreas. 'Twelve tickets, so far.'

'Plus, the minibus – correction, minibuses – coming from the home, which at the last count was –' she took a breath – 'twenty-six residents plus three carers.' Of course, they'd loved the idea, and word had spread within the home about the Big Christmas Bash, so there was a 'fear of missing out' factor going on. 'Well then, we have a venue, a date and plenty of guests . . . and, I'm sorry, I realise I've let things slip lately, but . . .'

'Hey, that's only natural. You've had important stuff going on. You've been caring for Will and his family,' said Nikki kindly.

'Yeah, we could have got going a bit quicker on this, and helped you out,' added Andreas.

'But you were already doing all of that fantastic DIY at the beach hut,' Cath countered.

'Okay, so we've all been pretty busy,' said Lily.

'Right, we need a plan and fast. Food, music – and as we discussed before, a band would be lovely if we can afford it – and yes, we need to sort the finances.' Cath was getting down to business, with her phone out ready to add some detail to her list.

'So, the band.' Lily jumped in. 'I've been chatting with the Swing Band I'd mentioned from school. With it being the holidays, some are away, but a core of about five or six can come along. I've said I'd check it out with you guys, but that we'd perhaps give them a small payment for their time, plus a free afternoon tea. I mooted twenty pounds each, hope that's okay?'

That was at least a hundred pounds to find on top of all the catering expenses. But hey, where would you get a live band for a hundred pounds these days? Cath figured.

'They're really good.' Lily vouched for them. 'I heard them perform in a show at the Alnwick Playhouse at the end of term.'

'Oh, it would be brilliant, having a real band to dance to,' said Dan.

'And they can play the 50s stuff?' Nikki clarified.

'Yeah, that's what they do. It's like their thing, Big Band Swing,' confirmed Lily. 'After their concert earlier in the year, they've stuck with it. And I'm sure they'll do extra requests on the day, too, if it's something they know.'

'Ah, the oldies will so love it,' said Andreas with a smile.

'Okay, let's go for it. In for a penny, in for a pound,' agreed Cath. If they were going to do it, they'd damn well do this thing properly. 'Get them booked in, Lily.' It felt good to have a decision made. 'And now, let's get some detail on the food.'

Andreas launched into singing 'Food, Glorious Food', as he passed around more slightly warm baklava. He'd been up early baking this morning.

'Afternoon tea.' Lily jumped in. 'This sounds *soo* like my kind of thing. I'm looking forward to this, it's so cool. I can make loads of mini cakes and bite-sized pavlovas. They'll have to look really pretty and dainty, too. Maybe something lemony, a summer fruits one, and there has to be something chocolatey or caramel.'

'Oh yes, we absolutely need chocolate in there,' agreed Nikki, her eyes lighting up.

'Okay, leave this with me,' confirmed Lily, seemingly in her element. 'I've already had a word with Mum, and she's agreed to help bake. We'll do the top tier of cakes and fancies.'

'Are you sure? That's an awful lot of work. You do realise we'll be catering for forty plus people. How about if I make a big batch of scones, then,' Cath offered, feeling that she needed to do her bit with the baking.

'Why don't I do a batch of chocolate tiffin,' Nikki chipped in. 'We can cut it into cute bite-sized squares. My mam's got a brilliant recipe. The boys just love it.'

'Okay, great,' said Lily. 'So that's the chocolate option sorted.'

'Thanks, Niks,' added Cath.

'We could bake some additional scones, too,' added Andreas. 'I take it we'll be having a cream tea.'

'Of course, how can you have afternoon tea without supersoft scones with jam and cream?' confirmed Cath.

'And I can do loads of little sandwiches,' offered Nikki. 'I can get the boys to help. They'll be off on school holidays by then.

It'll be good to keep them occupied. And though they moaned a bit last time, they really did enjoy helping out. Hmm, I'd love to see them dressed up smartly as waiters. Mind you, I'll have to peel them out of their trackies and trainers.'

'On that note,' added Cath, feeling far more animated about the project already with the buzz of enthusiasm around the table, 'I'd love for us all to dress the part too, 50s tea dance style. Dresses for the ladies, and suits or smart jackets for the gents.'

'Oh, and stylish hair. That gorgeously glamorous Grace Kelly and Sophia Loren look,' added Nikki.

Lily gave a groan. 'Really? And how do I achieve that with a crop?'

'Think vintage,' added Andreas. 'Yes, I've got it, what about Audrey Hepburn, she was certainly cool with her pixie crop. I bet we can get a good haul of suits, and styles, over at the charity shop in Kirkton.'

'Hah, yeah, cos most of the townsfolk there are ancient,' added Lily, sarcastically. 'Probably been wearing it all since the 50s.'

'Well, I think it's a great idea,' said Cath. 'No one needs to spend a fortune that way.'

'I suppose I could try the Hepburn thing,' Lily conceded, having quickly checked out the icon on her phone, and evidently liking the look.

'That's my girl,' said Andreas, adding, 'Right, my time is up. We said we'd switch after twenty minutes. I'll go and relieve Dan. Ooh, now then, fancy.' He gave a cheeky grin. 'I didn't mean it to sound like that.'

What was he like? The girls shook their heads at him, unable to hold back the grins that creased their lips.

He headed out of the room, chuckling to himself. With the swap made, Dan was now in the brainstorming hot seat. And funding was at the top of the agenda.

'Okay, we did agree at the start of all this that it should be a free event for all those coming along. So, any ideas?' Dan prompted.

'Well, we originally thought of the raffle for a hamper of tea-time treats, perhaps with a bottle of bubbly,' started Cath. 'I'd be happy to approach a few local businesses for donations towards it. And we can do a tombola on the day. That'd be fairly easy to organise and everyone seems to enjoy that.'

'We can certainly gift some items for the raffle and tombola from the shop. We have some great local produce that would be wonderful for it,' replied Dan.

'That's great, thank you, Dan. But we can't let you provide it all. Any other thoughts, anyone?'

'Hmm, let me have a think. The boys did start on a few car washes. I've got twenty pounds in the pot, so far from that,' started Nikki. 'Their enthusiasm seemed to wane after the first weekend, but I'll get them back on to it.'

'Great, yes, and make sure they're still down to do mine and Will's, whenever they get a chance,' said Cath.

'Will do. Hmm, and maybe we could do something sponsored with their junior league football team, too. Perhaps with half of the funds raised for the team, and half for the event? A kick-a-thon, or sponsored fitness session, with extra laps of the football pitch or something. They'll be mightily impressed with that idea, not.' She gave a wry smile. 'But hey, all for a good cause. Leave it with me for now.'

'Thanks, Nikki.'

'And I'll see if we can wangle a reduced price for the hire of the hall. After all the work we put in for the renovations, I'm sure they'll be amenable,' Dan suggested. 'I'll chat with Veronica. She might also have some good ideas for fundraising or sponsorship.'

Veronica, the rather bossy chairperson of the village hall committee, had her heart in the right place. She could come across as rather scary at times, a force to be reckoned with, and a stalwart of the Tilldale community. She was always good to have on board.

'Yes, I think she'd mentioned about the Brownies doing

something. I'll follow that up and have a chat with Brown Owl,' added Cath.

'Okay, so food will, of course, be the biggest cost,' said Lily. 'And we'll need a firm idea of the final numbers for catering, very soon.'

'Yes, of course,' said Dan. 'I'll let people know they need to get their tickets early. We could put a 'two weeks to go' limit on, or something. I'll flash up a date on the poster, and put out a post on the village Facebook group.'

'Sounds a sensible idea,' agreed Nikki.

'I have my moments,' said Dan. 'Okay, so who's on for another cup of coffee?'

Thanks to her supper club posse, the event was beginning to come together. Cath felt so much better than she had last night, when anxiety over the tea-time bash had sent her thoughts spiralling. She'd need to start making some serious lists. A mammoth shopping list for ingredients for one, and a to-do list extraordinaire. She was committed to making this day a special one for everybody involved. To give the hall, the villagers and the care home guests, another wonderful event to remember, with more pictures and mementoes to add to the memory board she'd started there at Christmas time.

'Thank you so much, guys,' said Cath, filled with a warm sense of gratitude. 'You're all stars. I actually feel like we might be able to pull this off, after all.'

And, with one very special person missing from this planning session, Cath hoped Will would feel up to making it there to join them. A few weeks should make a huge difference in his recovery. Perhaps being a part of this event might mark the start of a new chapter for him, too. A sign that his recuperation and health were on the up. He might not be quite up to dancing a jive, but perhaps a slow dance together, swaying to the beats of Lily's school band, well, that really would make it the most marvellous of days. She could dare to hope, couldn't she?

Chapter 27

Cath had suggested a lunch out in a café on the coast, thinking it would be nice to have a change of scene. She missed their walks and those lovely 'dating'-style day trips spent together. She strongly felt that it was time they ventured out more, here and there locally, nothing too challenging, as a couple. Will seemed to be getting a little morose cooped up at his house, with only the occasional morning going to work at his cycle repair business, which he'd had to leave ticking over until now, in the hands of his friend, Josh. She was even finding it hard making conversation, day in day out, when Will hadn't really been doing much.

She was aware things were still tricky for him toilet-wise, but he seemed much more able around his home. Making cups of coffee, doing a few small chores, getting up and down from the chair well, and managing the stairs far more easily. It was the confidence to go out that was lacking, she was sure, rather than the ability. The operation had undoubtedly changed him, he was a shadow of the active, cycling-mad man she had met. But perhaps he just needed a gentle nudge in the right direction.

Cath had offered to drive, and they'd taken the winding moorland road across country, and then down to the coast past Bamburgh and Seahouses towards Embleton, where there was a sweet little tea room she'd been wanting to try for ages, called Drift. It wasn't actually that far away from the beach bungalow. So, if it turned out to be good, it'd be a lovely place to head for when they stayed there, she figured. Though, chance would be a fine thing. Since their outing for the big beach hut reveal, Will had seemed almost reluctant to venture back.

Will had his rucksack with him. She'd seen it left open in the house and she'd spotted several incontinence pads. He had admitted that things were still 'not great' down there, and Cath had urged him to have a word with his specialist nurse. She wasn't sure if he had taken her advice as yet. She didn't want to nag him, so had left it, for now.

They pulled up kerbside in the coastal village. The coffee shop was so pretty inside. All blues and whites, and mix-and-match reclaimed furniture, the colour indeed of driftwood. Wooden painted puffins and gulls adorned the walls and shelving, along with a host of local crafts for sale. Ooh, she'd have to get a little memento for the beach house. A huge glass counter was filled with inviting-looking cakes, quiches and treats. Will took a seat near the window, as Cath went for a closer look to see what was on offer.

Cath ordered a flat white coffee for them both, and from the varied menu Will decided on a rather basic ham salad sandwich. Cath went for a brie, avocado and chicken toasted panini, and had eyed up a slice of deliciously tempting raspberry and white chocolate cake for afterwards.

Will shifted in his seat, seeming uneasy, then suddenly blurted out, 'I'm not sure why we're bothering with all this . . . coming out, having lunch. It seems a bit of a farce, that life's all jolly, and we're having a good time.' His tone was exasperated.

Oh heck, it seemed the trip wasn't lifting his mood at all.

'Ah, I just thought it might help. Get us out for a bit. I've been wanting to give this place a try . . .'

He puffed out a sigh. 'It might well be nice for you, but it's a bloody nightmare for me.' He got up, rucksack in hand, and headed for the toilet, which was off to the back of the café. Cath could hear his huffing and puffing continuing as he tried the handle only to find it locked as someone was already in there.

Oh dear. Was this all too soon? Was she being a bit selfish? But she was trying to find a bit of normal. A bit of hope. A small treat, a drive to the coast, the chance to get them out of the house. Perhaps she was trying too hard.

She'd mooted earlier that they might also call at the beach hut, which was only a few miles away. But wondered now, how might that go down? Will didn't seem in the best of spirits. When he finally made it back from the loo, she cautiously mentioned her idea. 'Shall we call by the beach bungalow? Check on it. I brought the keys just in case.'

'Not today. I just need to get back home.'

'Are you okay, my love? Are you having bathroom issues?' Her voice was hushed, discreet. She just wanted to understand, to be able to try and help him as best she could.

'Not here, Cath. For Christ's sake.' His tone was terse. 'I feel like an old man as it is, and you're sounding like my bloody carer.'

'Sorry . . . I'm sorry,' she apologised, feeling flustered. God, she kept getting this wrong.

Will downed his coffee, and pushed the last corner of ham sandwich to the edge of his plate. 'Come on, let's get out of here.' He shoved a twenty-pound note onto the table top and was standing, ready to go.

'Oh, but I was going to pay. It was my treat,' she said. *Some bloody treat, this was.*

'It's okay. It's sorted now.' And with that, he was off.

She quickly shoved the remaining piece of panini in her mouth, grabbed her jacket, called out 'Thanks' to the waitress, catching her eye and gesturing to the payment on the table, and followed him out to the car. All the while wondering what the hell had just gone on. It couldn't be easy for him right now, but sometimes that man was so guarded – not telling her what he was feeling or struggling with – he didn't help himself. If he really hadn't wanted to go out for lunch, then he should have said so back at home. She wasn't a frickin' mind-reader.

Then, as she watched him walk rather uncomfortably to the car, she reminded herself, he was only a few weeks post a delicate surgery. He'd also had to cope with learning he had cancer, after everything he'd already been through with his family, and she felt a bit rotten at getting frustrated with him. But dammit, he was just so in on himself sometimes.

There was a frosty atmosphere in the car, both lost in their own thoughts. She didn't dare say anything more about dropping by the beach bungalow. It was hardly worth it anyhow, with this 'wobble' going on between them. Another time . . .

Chapter 28

The welcoming jingle of the store bell rang out.

'Good morning,' Cath called out cheerily. Almost two weeks had now passed by since the Tilldale Tea planning session and she was back at the stores in a different role, behind the counter.

'Oh, hello, Cath. I was expecting to see one of the boys.'

'Morning, Kenneth. They're taking a well-deserved break and having the day off, so you have the pleasure of my company, today. Would you like a cup of tea before you do your shopping?'

'Oh, yes, please. That'd be grand, lass. Two sugars.'

'And shall we push the boat out with a custard cream or two?' Cath gave a warm smile.

'Why not indeed.' The gentleman's eyes lit up.

Cath knew his routine well by now. Elderly Kenneth came in primarily for the chat and company, which he needed far more than the few supplies which he'd finally take home with him. He even had his own special chair to sit and 'bide a wee while' by the counter.

Cath had agreed to step in at the shop, as the lads were planning a day trip to Edinburgh with a lunch out. A rare treat, and one which Cath was happy to accommodate. They'd done so much to help her and Will lately, after all. And after their own difficult trip out last week, she thought Will might be glad of a little space. She'd been left feeling bruised by the whole thing, to be honest.

She liked to keep her hand in at the shop from time and time, anyhow. It was a great way of keeping up with village life, and she enjoyed chatting with the locals, the occasional tourist and workmen, who called in. Tilldale Village Stores was the unofficial community hub, and was generally open seven days a week, with Andreas and Dan only closing for a half day on Wednesdays and Sundays. It was a big commitment from them. But they loved their rural life and running the shop here, despite the long hours, after changing track and moving up from the hustle and bustle of London eleven years ago. Under their care and commitment, the shop had indeed become the beating heart of the village, but sometimes like everyone else, they needed to recharge their batteries, and today was the day.

Cath enjoyed helping there. As well as giving her a chance to interact with the locals, the money was handy, supplementing her online tuition. Her deputy head pension didn't kick in yet for a few years, and her early retirement dreams of leisure and travel had been kicked out of the park by her ex-husband's affair and their subsequent divorce. But hey, she'd travelled in a whole new direction since then. Moved to Northumberland, found her gorgeous Cheviot Cottage and made it home, changed her life, and made some lovely new friends here, so she wasn't complaining. Sometimes the curveballs were the things that gave you the courage to begin again, to reevaluate your life and learn to really live.

'I'll just go pop the kettle on then, Kenneth.' Cath pulled herself back to the here and now, and headed through the door to the back of the stores. 'Won't be a mo.'

An abundance of freshly baked goods sat lined up on the kitchen's side, looking deliciously tempting. Andreas and Dan had evidently been up and baking early, despite having a train to catch. There was a handwritten note from Andreas reminding her to warm some of the croissants, ready for the morning drop-ins, so she popped the oven on. Then, kettle on, mugs at the ready, and finding the biscuit tin which was always filled with traditional favourites, she popped some custard creams and a couple of chocolate Bourbons onto a tea plate.

Tea made, Kenneth was in situ with a large mug to hand and a gentle smile on his face. She'd warmed a half-dozen croissants through, which smelt deliciously buttery, ready to lure her morning customers in. And, sure enough, as soon she was back at the counter, in came a couple of builders who were on their way to work. She'd mastered the coffee machine, after a tricky start a few months' back, and two freshly ground cups of rich frothy roast were soon made ready to take away.

'Busy day ahead, lads?' she asked, as she popped two of the warm croissants, which of course they hadn't been able to resist, and a couple of steak pies into brown paper bags.

'More'n likely. We're up at Middleton Barns doing the conversions there.'

'Oh, we used to live up that way, back in the day.' Kenneth joined the conversation. 'Me and Dot, my wife. We had one of the little cottages by the farm there. Pretty place. Bloody cold and damp in the winter, mind. No central heating back in those days.'

'Aye, well, these'll be all insulated and cosy once we're all done.'

'Sounds just the job,' said Kenneth.

'Here you go, and have a good day,' said Cath, handing over their items.

'Cheers.' The lads paid, and were off.

The early morning newspapers, coffee, Danish pastries and croissant run had begun, with a flurry of customers dropping by. Cath enjoyed the buzz, warming another batch of pastries, as well as some pies and quiches, when supplies began to get low. Between times, she managed to chat with dear old Kenneth, too, of course. Sitting there on his chair by the till, he was like the shop's mascot.

There was a lull, and Cath's eye was drawn to the raffle prize that the lads had kindly now organised for the Tilldale Afternoon Tea. It looked wonderful; a huge wicker basket filled with a treasure trove of local produce, all cellophaned up and tied with curls of golden ribbon. Nikki had given a fancy bottle of Prosecco, and Lily was going to make up a couple of bags of millionaires shortbread and chocolate truffles, ready to add to the hamper at the last-minute, so they'd still be lovely and fresh. Andreas and Dan had generously raided their shelves to provide local shortbread, savoury biscuits, jams and chutneys, heather honey, plus Northumberland Tea and Rington's coffee, making the whole basket a tea-time extravaganza.

There were more items, too, stored beneath the counter, for the raffle: with donations of a meal for two from Bill, the landlord at the village pub, and Rachel, from The Pudding Pantry near to Kirkton, who had links with the care home, had gifted a voucher for Afternoon Tea for Two, plus Will who'd given a brand-new cycling top and a free bike service. With raffle tickets already selling well, apparently, funds for the event were picking up.

'So, are you looking forward to the afternoon tea, Kenneth?' she asked.

'I am indeed, lassie. Ah, it was such a lovely do, your Christmas luncheon that day. You really brought the village hall back to life. Marvellous it was.'

'Ah, that's so good to hear.'

And a full two hours after he arrived, and two large mugs of tea later, Kenneth finally left, taking a can of tomato soup, some wholemeal rolls and two strawberry yoghurts with him. 'Lovely to see you, lassie. Thanks for the tea.'

'You're very welcome, Kenneth. Enjoy the rest of your day.'

In a flurry of activity, Veronica, 'mistress' of the village hall, was the next to call in to the shop, with some very welcome news.

'We've rallied the troops!' she called out. She had been on a mission, she explained. 'So, I've asked every group that hires the hall to come up with a fundraising or sponsorship scheme over the next two weeks. They all agree that your community afternoon tea sounds a splendid idea. So, the Brownies are doing a sponsored bounce and assembling a small trampoline in the hall for their next session. The indoor bowls club are holding a bowl-a-thon. The Autistic Society are donating prizes for the tombola, which I'm more than happy to organise by the way, and the pilates class are doing a sponsored '500' – that's instead of the '100' apparently. No idea what that means.'

Oh my, Cath tried to look delighted with that fantastic support, but *that* was her pilates class – and she knew exactly what the 100 was, and that was painful enough. But 500 – really?! But hey, it was all for a good cause, she reminded herself. Cath was sure she'd find out more about it at her Tuesday pilates session, next week. Her core, and no doubt her purse, was going to be pounded, for certain. *Abs of steel*, Cath, *abs of steel.*

'That all sounds amazing. Thank you so much. And it's great that all the clubs are getting involved. That's such a lovely idea. And it'll boost our finances for the event. We'll be sure to make the most delicious spread for everyone, a real treat.'

'Oh, and the Brownies are more than happy to help out on the day too, Brown Owl asked me to pass that message on,' Veronica added. 'And there was something about them baking scones for it, too.' Naturally, scones with strawberry jam and thick cream were an essential part of any afternoon tea. And offers of help with making some extra ones – especially with the numbers attending rising daily, so she'd heard – would be more than gratefully received.

'That's brilliant, thanks. I'll give her a call. And thank you, Veronica, you're a one-woman wonder.' She really was a force to be reckoned with, and it was fabulous when her talents were put to good use.

'No need for any fuss. It's the least I can do. And well, I think it's a big thanks to you and your group that we've got the hall back up and running in the first place. Oh, and the hall hire that day will be free. That's all sorted. The committee is in full agreement.'

Cath had to smile. She had a good idea that no one on that committee would dare to challenge that particular proposal by Veronica, anyhow.

With the same speedy turnaround as her arrival, the door jangled as she left with a 'Just off to get the hall set up for indoor bowls.' The refurbished village hall seemed to have given Veronica a new lease of life, and sense of purpose, too.

It was almost 5 p.m., and just as Cath was about to close up, after a busy yet satisfying day, a couple in their sixties came dashing in.

'I hope we're not too late? They haven't all gone, have they?' The lady, who Cath recognised as living in a small hamlet nearby, sounded rather flustered. 'Only our Milly – that's the dog – has been poorly, and we clean forgot. I was just chatting to Joyce next door, and she mentioned it.'

'It's been a race to get here before closing time,' her husband added, looking rather red in the face.

'He was doing a good impression of Lewis Hamilton in those lanes. I was hanging on to my seat by the end.'

It suddenly clicked with Cath that it was officially the last day to get tickets for the Tilldale Afternoon Tea. The poster had been duly amended after their last meeting. She pulled out the list from behind the counter, spotting dear old Kenneth's name right there at the top. There were, oh wow, eighteen tickets already dished out – and that of course, was on top of the care home group numbers.

'No worries. You're fine.' Cath found the metal tin that Dan had been using for the tickets. 'Here you go.' She pulled out two of the tickets – that Lily had designed so prettily for them – from an elastic-banded bundle, and recorded the numbers and the couple's names on the sheet. She then gave a smile. 'Not long to go now.'

'Yes, and we heard how fabulous the last do was. Joyce told us all about it. We couldn't possibly miss out this time.'

'Well, be sure to bring your dancing shoes along. As well as the tea, we've got a band and dancing.'

'Oh, it sounds wonderful. We can't wait. Thank you. Oh, and how much do we owe you for the tickets?' added the lady, who Cath now remembered was called Sue.

'It's a free event, but . . .' Cath seized the opportunity to bring in some extra funds, 'we are holding a raffle, and there's a tombola on the day to help cover costs. Raffle tickets are a pound a strip, and the main prize is this wonderful hamper, right here. It's filled to the brim with tea-time treats.'

'And oh, what a hamper,' declared Sue.

'Put us down for ten then, pet,' said her husband, as he pulled out his wallet with a flourish. 'And the tea is all free you say, that's marvellous. It's not often you get something for nothing, nowadays. Thank you to whoever's organising it.'

'Well, that's actually me and my friends.' As well as a swirl of pride, Cath also was hit by a tug of anxiety. The pressure was on to live up to expectations.

'How fantastic, well done.'

Cath handed him ten strips of tickets for the raffle, after taking his name and a contact number.

'Fingers crossed, then.' He nodded at the tickets now in his hand.

Cath was crossing her fingers, too, hoping that they could manage to pull off another smooth and very sociable event.

'Joyce is coming along,' remembered Sue. 'I'll get her some raffle tickets, too. Let's take five more. She's recently lost her husband, you know. I think this event might help get her back out, cheer her up a bit.'

This was what it was all about, Cath thought, cheering people up, brightening their day, sending them away with a smile, a full tummy, perhaps a few new friends and some heartwarming memories. She just hoped that she and her supper club team could pull it off all over again, and make it as good, or even better this time. No pressure there, then! What could possibly go wrong?

With Dan and Andreas away all day, Cath had promised to look after Shirley as well as the shop. She'd taken the terrier out briefly over lunchtime. And, after closing up, she was now in the flat above the stores, clipping the little dog on to her lead, ready to head out to the fields beyond the village, and take a stroll down by the river. Cath stifled a yawn after her hectic day, but she had a feeling this walk would do her good, as well as the dog. She felt more than ready to decompress a little.

With a week now having passed since she and Will had had their difficult outing, though things had settled somewhat and she'd popped in to visit him each day, she was still feeling a little angsty, and couldn't put her finger on exactly why. Perhaps her mind would settle and begin to work it out as she rambled. She made her way down the stairs, with Shirley trotting eagerly beside her. After locking the side door, they turned the street corner, passing the village green with its stone cross memorial, and strolled by several traditional honey-grey stone cottages; their small front gardens in full bloom, with scented roses, tall hollyhocks, and pots and hanging baskets filled with purple and pink petunias, trailing begonias and delicate dark-blue lobelia.

Leaving the village behind, the pair made their way along the lane to drop down through a small wooden gate into the pastures that bordered the river. All around was farmland; fields of green where cattle and sheep calmly grazed, alongside crop fields now turning to barley gold. Away in the distance were the moorland hills. The sky above filled with bulbous clouds that were slowly scudding by, with a promise of summer blue beyond.

With nature all around, and Shirley happily sniffing and scooting about on a loose lead, Cath's thoughts began to settle. The Tilldale Tea was looming, of course, with all of the organisation that would entail. When she'd thought up this madcap afternoon tea scheme, she had no idea quite how popular it would be, or that Will would become ill with cancer and would have to undergo surgery, and be facing a slow recovery. She already felt tired to the bone, and despite all the wonderful offers of sponsorship and fundraising she'd received, there was of course a whole heap of planning to do and tasks to undertake. Juggling all this with caring for Will, plus the prickly atmosphere shifting momentarily from her to between him and his girls – just last night he'd accused Maddie and Sophie of 'ganging up on him' as they tried to persuade him to get back out and do some exercise on his bike again. With Cath privately agreeing with them, yet trying her best to keep his battered spirits up, it was taking its toll.

Her online tuition was still ongoing, though that had slowed down at this time of year – at least until the new term started – but still there was a lot of prep needed to keep up to date with any changes in the curriculum. She was making her weekly visits to the care home, too; she couldn't imagine letting the residents down. That was an awfully big life 'to-do' list in itself. Throw in a full day at the shop, which had been fine and she was glad to help out the lads, but she was more than ready to crash out on the sofa. Instead, here she was still going strong-ish, giving Shirley her exercise.

Cath's pace wasn't as brisk as it might have been. Snatching a yawn, she took a pause, gazing at the cool cola-brown ripples of the river flowing by. Her energy levels were definitely at a low ebb. The emotions of these past weeks surrounding Will's diagnosis and surgery had evidently caught up on her. Though she tried to keep bright and cheery for him and the girls, the disturbing thoughts that troubled her at night still managed to worm their way to the surface. She hardly wanted to acknowledge them. They were like doom-mongers. What if they hadn't got rid of it all, the cancer? What if it might already have spread? How did they know for certain that the surgery would work? Was cancer

'Clive' going to prove to be a bit of a bastard in the long run?

And what if she'd finally found the love of her life, and he wasn't going to be here for that long? These were the fears that she hadn't dared to voice to anyone.

She felt a prickle of tears.

'Hey, Shirley.' She bent down to stroke the soft-white fur of the West Highland terrier. 'Enjoying your walk, little lady?' Okay, she was aware she was talking to a dog, but there was no one else around to hear her, after all. And perhaps a chat with her canine pal might help shift these negative thoughts. Shirley snuffled her damp black nose against Cath's palm in response, and then stood still beside her, happy to receive more affectionate pats. The warmth of the mid-July sun was on Cath's back, the smell of grass and earth filled her nostrils. The sound of a tractor humming in the distance, and oh, the close hum of a bee as it passed by like a drone on its busy nectar-seeking way.

By the time she'd returned to the shop, Cath's head felt a little clearer; being surrounded by nature, her canine companion and the simple act of walking had calmed her. Everything would work out somehow, she told herself, as she hung up the lead and watched Shirley settle down into her snug bed. Keep the faith, find a way. No use fretting about what might go wrong. Appreciate the now; plan, plan, plan for the afternoon tea party; and a big two-fingered 'V' sign to Clive.

Chapter 29

At last, two weeks on, and they had the house to themselves for a whole evening, hopefully giving them the chance to relax a bit as a couple. And hopefully, after all the ups and downs of life after surgery, also the chance to be a little more honest with each other.

Maddie had settled back in at Newcastle, coming up only for the odd day off to see her dad, which was more about keeping him company than hands-on care at this point. And Sophie, who was living back at Tilldale for the uni summer holidays, had arranged to go out this evening with some old school friends, into Alnwick for a meal and drinks, eager to try out a new bar that had just opened. She was to stay over for the night with one of the girls who lived in the town.

Cath had bought some nibbles from M&S, prepared an easy chicken pasta dish ready to warm through at Will's, and planned a chilled evening. Without a third wheel, they might in fact be able to feel like a couple again and chat a little more openly. They still hadn't talked about his outburst at the café. Although, later that day he had apologised about being off-hand with her, though he hadn't seemed to want to go into it any more than that. And with Sophie around at the time, she hadn't felt inclined to push him.

Cath poured them both a glass of wine, and they sat chatting in his lounge about Adam's latest call – she'd guessed right, he and the dark-haired girl she'd spotted when she'd visited those few weeks ago had become a bit of an item, and Adam was taking her out for a drink this evening. Cath also filled Will in on her day yesterday working at the shop, and Veronica's amazing spons-a-thon challenges from the local groups for the afternoon tea event.

'Do you think you might make it? To the event. No need to have to do anything too strenuous, but more to be there. Perhaps help by chatting with the ones from the home. They'd love that.' Cath really felt he needed to start getting back out there. Stepping back into normal life.

'Ahm, yeah, I might do.' He was positively noncommittal, but at least he sounded like it was a possibility.

'That'd be great,' Cath encouraged further.

The atmosphere between them was pleasant enough, though Will was still rather quiet. They enjoyed their tasty supper, and there was only a hint of Will's ongoing discomfort with him having to make a couple of rather swift trips to the loo.

All in all, it had been a lovely evening. It was past nine-thirty, and Cath was sitting beside Will on the sofa with some beautifully relaxed piano music playing, by Ludovico Einaudi, so Will had informed her. It seemed only natural to move a little closer. Cath reached an arm up across his chest and shifted to snuggle up. God, she'd so missed that easy closeness they had not so long ago. She wasn't expecting anything more from him physically or sexually, not yet. She was well aware, after all, that making love naturally was very unlikely to happen for many months post-prostatectomy. But a kiss and a cuddle, that would be perfect.

After edging nearer, she looked up to catch his gaze. He seemed a little uncertain, bless him. Crikey, this was weird, like going back to the start. She tilted her face up towards his, her chest leaning against him now, her lips ready to brush his. Needing so much to feel that passion again, that intimacy. To show her love physically, if only in her kiss.

That was when he seemed to freeze.

'Please, don't, Cath.' Will sat up straight, raking a hand through his hair, 'This . . . *us*, it's not helping. It's too much.' It was evidently all too soon for Will.

'Umm, I was only looking to cuddle . . .' Cath pulled back, feeling hurt. She knew he'd been having a rough time of it since the surgery. But what the hell was he saying? What did he mean by that '*us*', exactly? Confusion swirled through her guts. 'Look, I know you're having a tough time, Will. You're only a few weeks post-surgery. We knew it was never going to be easy . . . *physically*. And I don't expect it all to be wine and roses just now, but please . . . *please*, don't shut me out again.'

It wasn't just the discarded kiss, the guards were going back up emotionally, too. Things should be getting easier for him, for them, but instead she felt it was all getting harder.

'I just want to help,' she added, when he didn't respond.

He'd cut her off before, earlier on in their relationship, when times had got difficult. It seemed to be his defence mechanism. However much she tried to be understanding – and of course, he'd been through so much with his wife's illness and passing, and now this massive upheaval with his own health problems – Cath couldn't pretend any longer that it didn't hurt. Not when he pushed her away like this. She thought they'd moved on from that closed state, that they were a team now. Before the cancer diagnosis and this operation, these past months together had been wonderful. Filling her with hopes and dreams for the future . . . *their* future. But jeez, this evening, and the day in the coffee shop, felt so very different from that. It was like a black cloud was settling over them.

'I'm not shutting you out.' In contrast to his words, his voice had a harsh, steely tone. 'I just need some time to deal with this. Time just for me . . . now and again.'

'Will, what's bugging you? Have I done something wrong?' She hated this wall that was mounting between them, that despite what he said was absolutely there. Since his surgery, he seemed to be building it back up, brick by brick.

'Ah, of course, you haven't.' He seemed to soften, pausing to look up at her with those dark-hazel eyes. 'But it feels too much, you being here all the time, fussing around me. I-I just need a bit of space, I suppose. Some time to get my head around what's going on.'

Oh, how that hurt . . . when had caring become *fussing* for him? Okay, so she'd been coming around daily, sometimes twice a day . . . checking if he was okay. Bringing him meals that he and the girls could easily warm up, offering hugs along with the lasagne and the homemade curry. Putting the washing on, changing bedding. Someone for him to talk to, if he needed, or that was the bloody idea . . . a shoulder to lean on. She'd spent time chatting and trying her best with the girls, too. She thought she'd been providing comfort and support for them all. She was the safety net, or so she'd hoped.

But the two of them hadn't kissed, other than a peck on the cheek, and she hadn't stayed over at all since the op, nor he with her. These past few weeks, she'd offered for him to come to her cottage, but other than a brief coffee when he'd ventured out once for a walk through the village, he hadn't seemed to want to spend time at hers. They hadn't even made it back to the beach house. Other than receiving the odd hug, if somewhat stiffly, he seemed to be rejecting physical contact.

It was like he needed to try and cope with all of this on his own. She knew that toilet problems were an ongoing issue. She'd seen the many urinary pads in the bin. His trousers tellingly a little bulky. Had he hoped things might be back to normal, quicker than they were? Was this a lot to do with what was troubling him? It must be bloody awkward to deal with. Perhaps he'd just needed some privacy to cope with that.

'Are you having problems, my love? Is it your bladder? The nurse warned all of that might take time,' she probed gently.

'Hah, that's just the bloody start of it . . . honestly, you haven't a damn clue!' He'd flushed red.

'Well, tell me. I can't help if I don't know what it is that's troubling you.'

'Maybe that's just it, Cath. You've got it at last. Maybe it's because I don't *want* to tell you. I don't want you to see me to the bathroom. Or have you looking after me like I'm an old man. Maybe, I just want a bit of peace and goddam privacy.'

Dammit, he was hard work when he was like this. He was in such a dark mood. And she wasn't at all sure how best to bring him out of it. But still his words stung.

She wished they'd had the chance to get to know each other for longer before all this had happened, to be more established as a couple – well, of course she wished it had never happened. But if they'd had that level of everyday intimacy, it would surely have helped at this stage of his treatment, with the difficult side-effects to deal with. Her mind flitted to Trevor, and pondered on the steadiness of a long marriage, that long-term knowledge of each other. When you knew each other inside out, little fazed you. But hey, that hadn't stopped Trev from jumping ship, had it? she reminded herself sourly. She felt her own mood darken. She was trying her best to help, but bloody hell, at this point it seemed to be driving Will further away from her. He was exasperating.

Okay, so Will was evidently feeling extra vulnerable right now. But dammit, she wished he could find it in himself to open up and talk. How could they be a team without communicating?

'So, that's it. I try my best to look after you, and you just throw it all back in my face. Well, thanks for that,' she responded bitterly. *Oh*, an awful thought hit her as her words spilled out, *did he no longer want to be in this team of two?*

'Cath, this isn't getting us anywhere. Please . . . can you just go.' He looked downbeat.

Was this just a moment of sheer frustration, on Will's part? He was once again putting up the emotional shutters and pretending – even to himself – that he could totally cope on his own.

'Okay then, send me away. Shut me out if you must.' Cath vented her frustration. 'But I'll not be far. You don't get rid of me that easily. I'll be here when you're ready, Will . . .' Somehow, she made it sound like a threat.

She sprung up off the sofa and stood, ready to go. She'd had enough of this, too, for tonight. They were going around in stressful circles, and it didn't feel at all good.

She gave a parting glance, before she turned on her heel, and she wasn't sure if it was relief or shock that she spotted on Will's face at that point.

Grabbing her jacket from the coat hook, she marched to his front door ready to let herself out. He trailed behind in the hallway, his face ashen. Not that Cath could see it at that point, as her back was firmly set against him. Pausing for a mere second on the threshold, her parting words were, 'You don't get to tell people if they can love you or not.' And she stomped out.

As she marched off down the path, filled with a heady mix of both love and fear, she began to wonder, *what if he really meant it?* What if they weren't to be a couple anymore? What if her love, once again, went unanswered . . .

Chapter 30

Cath had enough on her mind with the Tilldale Afternoon Tea event rolling in, and oh my, now only four days away. Focusing on that would at least give her time to let the dust settle on their harsh words. Her heart felt bashed and bruised. But perhaps she and Will did need a little space, just to breathe, and to get perspective back on everything once more.

She knew Sophie was there with Will should he need anything care-wise, and he was managing well getting about within his own home at least. A couple of brief text messages asking how he was – one a day, she rationed herself – were like a little rope between them. It seemed churlish to cut off totally. Yet his responses were short and to the point. Feeling torn up inside, she hoped to goodness he wasn't trying to sever that tie.

Cath told herself to treat it as a cooling-off period, praying all the while it wasn't to end up as a cutting-off period. Don't go there, she told herself, keep charging full steam ahead with the event planning. That, and only that, needed to be her focus right now. She wasn't sure how she'd get through it all otherwise.

With only one day left to go, Cath headed off with Andreas for a supermarket sweep in Alnwick; filling the large trolley with multiple bags of flour, butter, eggs, sliced loaves in both white and wholemeal, cucumber and smoked salmon for the sandwiches, raspberries, blueberries, cooking chocolate, tea bags, coffee, and literally litres of milk, and much more from her very long list. Coming back to the village hall to unload the many items onto the pantry shelves and into the fridges there, as well as using their own personal ones as overflow, all up to the gills. In the hall's kitchen, it was like a game of fridge Jenga; dare to shift one item and the whole lot might come down. She'd have to warn the rest of the team.

The afternoon brought a visit to the butchers in Kirkton for delicious thin-cut local ham, another finger-sandwich filler, this time, taking the trip along with Lily. Followed by a visit – including an essential and reviving cuppa-and-cheesecake stop for them – to the marvellous Rachel's Pudding Pantry in the hills beyond the town, to collect their order of twelve pots of homemade strawberry jam and lashings of local cream from the farm shop and tea rooms.

'Oh, is this for the Tilldale Afternoon Tea, tomorrow? Best of luck with the event, ladies.' Rachel, the owner, whose family also ran the farm, caught up with them at the counter. 'Watch out, you've got my Granny Ruth coming along this time. She put her name down for a ticket, when she was at the home for a spell of respite care. She's back in her cottage now, but is coming along on the minibus with the others. Look out for her – she's short, with a slight Scottish twang and a bit of a character. She keeps saying how much she's looking forward to it.'

'Ah, that's wonderful,' said Cath. And Ruth, yes, she had been chatting with a new lady at the home by that name a little while back. A rather feisty and interesting lady, she remembered her talking about the family farm, and all sorts of puddings that they made there. 'Actually, I think we may have already met,' added Cath. 'I visit there most weeks, and yes, I remember her. A lovely lady. I'll look forward to seeing her again.'

'Sweet,' added Lily. 'We'll be sure to seek her out. My Grandma Liz is going along, too. I'll introduce them. And we may well get everyone up dancing, if they're up for it.'

'Oh, I'm sure Granny will be.' Rachel smiled, amusement shining through her warm green eyes. 'It's sounding wonderful already.'

Cath hoped so much that it would be, feeling the weight of expectation on her already loaded shoulders. She had her purse to hand, with some of the event funds at the ready.

'Oh, no need for that, the jam and cream will be on the house, of course. Oh, and why not take a couple of jars of Granny Ruth's chutney. It's her latest recipe made with spiced plums and apples.'

'Are you sure?' Cath felt a bit cheeky accepting all that.

'I'm certain. I really don't know how you're managing to put it on all for free, like Granny said, but thank you. It's such a lovely event to organise for everyone. Ruth will so enjoy her afternoon with you. It's the least we can do.'

'Well, in that case, thank you. That's very much appreciated. But I will settle up for our delicious cheesecake and tea.' That was so generous of Rachel, thought Cath. And she was more than happy to pay for their personal treats.

The pair left with a spring in their step, despite hefting the huge cardboard box filled with preserves and cream.

Simple acts of kindness, spreading sunshine along the way.

With no time to lose, that evening, Cath, Andreas and Dan were back at the village hall getting a head start with the prep for the big bash tomorrow.

The tea plates, cutlery, and cups and saucers they'd discovered in the kitchen's storeroom prior to the Christmas lunch – originally from Women's Institute in the village – had come in mightily handy. They'd left them all neatly stacked back then. Hopefully, they'd helped at other functions and group activities since. Cath decided to freshen them all up by running them through the dishwasher. It would be great to have everything sparkling clean for their tea. They also rinsed the tea and coffee pots thoroughly, and placed them in position by the hot water urns, ready to fill and brew.

Cath had even found a reel of old Jubilee-style bunting in red, white and blue flags, tucked away in a cardboard box at the back of the storage area. 'What do you think, lads? Shall we put this up?'

'Oh yes, it'll give it a celebratory feel,' said Andreas.

'Go for it!' added Dan.

And opportunely enough, Nikki and husband Kev called by a few minutes later, to see how they were getting on, offering to help with anything.

'As it happens . . .' Cath grinned hopefully as she gestured towards the colourful flag-filled box.

'A-ha,' responded Kev. 'Go on, then. Where do you want it putting, and where are the ladders?'

Nikki found the tall stepladders for him, tucked away in the boiler room, and then she began orchestrating the fixing of the bunting across the top-front of the stage and along a further two sides of the hall's walls. Being an electrician for many years, Kev'd got used to heights and was unfazed. After he'd finished the job, Nikki let the others know, and Cath peeked in to the hall. Fixed in gentle loops, the bunting gave a gorgeously colourful summer fete feel to the hall.

'Aw, that's so pretty. Love it!' She gave a thumbs up to Kev. 'Oh, and while you guys are here, shall we get the trestle tables out and set them up? Leaving room, of course, for the all-important dance floor area below the stage.'

The more they did now, Cath figured, the less stress for tomorrow. There'd be more than enough to do with all the food preparation in the morning; a zillion scones to freshly bake for starters.

After having dried and re-stacked all the crockery, plus setting out the tiered afternoon-tea stands that Nikki had collected earlier,

'Why do we do this to ourselves?' Dan asked, stifling a yawn.

'Ah, we love it really. And we want to make it special for everyone. That's why we put in so much effort. Think of all those happy faces tomorrow,' came his partner's response.

'Yeah, I can't wait to see them all when these stands come out, filled with delicious treats. I want it to feel like the Tilldale Ritz,' added Cath.

'No pressure here, then,' replied Andreas with a chuckle.

A sense of anxious expectation thrummed through Cath. And ten minutes later, after thanking the lads, Nikki and Kev, they made their farewells. Being the last to go, she switched off the hall's lights one by one, closed the heavy oak main door behind her, then turned the lock with the old metal key. It was all going to be fine, she told herself, keeping her thoughts positive.

She was in fact heading home to weigh out all the ingredients ready for the morning's scone-making session. There was no resting on her laurels this evening. At least that was the final job on her to-do list for today. Tick.

She just wished she had a tick list for her relationship with Will. A swirl of anxiety hit her. Whilst the tea was a lot of work, she knew the steps she had to take to make it a success. She wished so much that she had a plan like that for her relationship with Will. Whilst not being able to put in a full day of graft for the event, Will had messaged the group on WhatsApp, saying that he intended coming along a little later, to help out where he could. He hadn't even told her personally, which again felt like another crack in their relationship. And this would be the first time they'd come face to face since he'd so abruptly asked her to go. She couldn't help but wonder how that would feel, and how he'd be with her.

She really didn't want to dwell on it, but a strange sense of gloom fell like a shadow over her.

Chapter 31

With thankfully little time to dwell on her relationship issues, Cath had been up bright and early, prepping and baking since 6 a.m. The scones for the cream tea needed to be soft and fluffily fresh, and for the quantity required, she decided it'd be easier using the big school ovens in the hall. Oh, my word, had the final catering numbers risen, like the scones she'd just baked! She'd caved in when she'd heard that the Brownies group were to help, and she'd asked them to stay for the tea, too.

Tea was to be served at 2 p.m., with guests due to arrive at the hall for one-thirty. And she still had the fresh cream to whip for the *fifty-four* scones! It was now one-ten, and the five supper clubbers, with the addition of Hamish, Nikki's eldest son, and minus Will who was to pace himself by coming along later, were going full pelt within the village hall.

Cath was in the kitchen, electric whisk to hand, and a big stainless-steel mixing bowl before her. She emptied four large pots of cream into the bowl and started to whisk, trying to hold her concentration, despite the time running away with itself. The cream would take a while to thicken but once it did, it went quickly and was easy to overwhip. She wanted it to be the perfect consistency to spoon on top of the scones without any messy drips, but lusciously smooth rather than a solid mass.

Lily was working at the other side of the kitchen, plating up the marvellous mini cakes and bakes on to the top layer of the three-tier stands. Using her artistic touch, with dainty strawberries and some pretty viola flowers picked from her parents' garden, she laid out squares of Nikki's chocolate tiffin, mini honey-nut baklava – an extra touch care of Andreas – individual cream-and-fresh-berries pavlovas, salted caramel choux bites and slices of sticky lemon drizzle. The platters soon began to look like works of art; the perfectly pretty plates that Cath had dreamed of serving for her special guests. 'Tea at the Tilldale Ritz' was taking shape. When Cath took a pause mid-whipping, and glanced over, spotting the stunning arrangements, she felt a tear mist her eye.

'Oh, Lily. They are just beautiful. Perfect, in fact. Thank you, lovely.'

'Fa-bu-lous, darling,' boomed Andreas's voice across the room, from his finger-sandwich stand, lined-up alongside Nikki and her eldest son Hamish, who'd been tasked with buttering the bread.

'I think the Saveur restaurant vibes must be rubbing off on me.' Lily gave a smile. 'They always make things look so artistic.' She'd been enjoying working at the delightful restaurant part-time between her studies for the past year now.

The tiered stands, borrowed from Ellie at Claverham Castle, were looking fantastic. All they'd had to do was collect them yesterday – Nikki had gone on a trip for those – and then return them all washed for Monday. It was those touches of generosity that helped bring the event, and the community, together.

Cath went back to her cream whipping, Dan took over the sandwich station from Nikki who was desperate to put some finishing touches to the hall's decorations. Lily began to fill white porcelain pots with candy-cotton-scented glossy strawberry jam and then set out more dishes ready for the cream. A batch of six scones had already been positioned on layer two of each stand. A production line of finger sandwiches was now being finished by Dan, Andreas and Hamish at the far end of the kitchen – a selection of local ham, egg mayonnaise and cress, smoked salmon and cucumber, and grated cheese from the nearby dairy teamed with Granny Ruth's chutney. All kept under a cling film wrap to keep them fresh, ready to put out at the last-minute, on tier one. And all the while, the clock on the wall kept ticking away.

'Oh, Andreas, we need to dash. We're still in our working scruffs. The wardrobe awaits,' exclaimed Dan, as he placed the final finger sandwich under wraps.

'Of course! We need to look the part.' Andreas grabbed a holdall, and they made a swift exit, most likely heading for the gents' loos, with Cath and Lily left chuckling.

Lily had come wearing her 50s-style outfit, and was looking striking in a vintage white-spotted maroon A-line dress she'd found on Vinted, at a bargain price of five pounds. It was rather unusual and lovely to see her in a dress. With her pixie-cropped dark hair, a maroon floral hairclip positioned to one side and her trademark bold make-up and red lips, the style really suited her. There was more than a hint of Audrey Hepburn going on. The Dr. Martens boots were her own individual touch; though somehow it still worked.

With the fresh cream finally at the right point, Lily whizzed it away to dish out. Cath then realised that her own 50s-style attire was still in a bag on the floor of the kitchen's storeroom. With now less than ten minutes to go, and early guests and the band arriving at any point, she decided it'd be better to finish clearing the kitchen, pour cold milk into the jugs to go out with the tea and coffee, and warm the teapots ready to fill. She could make a quick outfit change once everyone was settled in the hall, she decided. Her navy-spotted apron would have to do for now!

The kitchen was soon cleared, the dishwasher buzzing away, and with disinfectant spray to hand, Cath was giving the surfaces a wipe down. Talk about cutting it fine. But she knew after checking on the hall earlier – where two long rows of trestle tables were now covered with crisp white tablecloths (double sheets that Nikki had ironed and brought in), and set with fifty-four places of tea plates, cutlery, and cups and saucers, it was all looking grand.

She couldn't resist a further quick peek, however, before the guests came. And oh . . . bud vases were now placed down the centre of the tables too, filled with the fragrant pink and yellow roses that Cath had brought from her garden – a nod to Reggie who'd have planted those rose bushes years ago – along with pretty pastel shades of carnations and delicate white sprigs of gypsophila, that Nikki had bought yesterday from Wendy, the Kirkton florist.

The tombola was set out, with volunteers Veronica and Dorothy, from the hall committee, having spent the last hour sticking the raffle-ticket labels to each of the donated items, with zeros and fives being the winners. The duplicates had been folded and placed in a wicker basket for the lucky dip. Young and old seemed to love this game.

Oh, and there on display at the end of the stage was the pièce de résistance, the raffle prize, a tea-time bonanza hamper. Many tickets had been sold in the shop already, but Lily was later to do a sweep of the room to check everyone who'd wanted to join in had had the chance.

Cath was just about there with covering the costs, phew, and anything left over from the various sponsorships that were still coming in, was to go rather fittingly to the village hall funds.

'Well done, team,' said Cath proudly, realising the lads and Lily were now at her shoulder scanning the room too, and catching Nikki's eye as she stood tweaking a teacup or two to make perfect symmetry.

Tilldale Hall was ready, ta-dah. All it now needed were the guests to fill it.

'Hey, Mam, we're here.' In trooped Scott and Angus, dressed smartly (if somewhat reluctantly) in their school uniform black trousers and white shirts, ready to help serve the food and drinks, waiter-style. The young trio of Nikki's sons had enjoyed helping out at the Christmas event, despite having been unenthusiastic recruits to start, and were back working with the supper club team for the 50s-style tea. Will had insisted on helping at the event too. Cath and the others agreeing, over the group chat, that he shouldn't come in too early only to wear himself out. His recovery being the most important thing.

Cath couldn't help but wonder how awkward today was going to be for the pair of them, coming face to face for the first time since what she'd been calling 'Will's wobble'. But hey, she'd deal with that when it happened, for now, guests were imminent.

Anxiety was nipping at her. She couldn't shift this feeling that she'd forgotten something. She'd had the biggest to-do list ever, and had been working her way through it all week, even down to making sure there was plenty of loo rolls in the toilets. But was there something obvious, something she might have missed? Perhaps she was just so determined to get this right for everyone who'd helped and everyone who was coming along, that it was only natural. She'd done her best, she reassured herself.

'It's going to be fantastic,' said Lily with a smile, as if reading her thoughts.

'The minibuses are here!' came a shout from the corridor, that sounded very much like Nikki's husband, Kev. This was followed by a call of, 'Oh no, and so is the rain!'

Drat it.

But in true organised Cath fashion, after having checked the weather app this morning and spotting the chance of heavy showers, she had thought to leave several large umbrellas at the hall entrance, just in case.

'Okay, everyone, go and grab a brolly, and we'll help see the care home guests in,' came the command from Cath. 'It's all systems go!'

'Here we go again!' echoed Andreas; Cath now registering that he was dressed smartly in a Gene Kelly, 'Singin' in the Rain'-style dark suit. Stood with, oh my, a Danny Zuko-styled Dan with a Brylcreemed quiff, his *Grease* black leather jacket, white T-shirt and black jeans. Amazing!

'Love the look, lads!' She grinned, giving a big thumbs up.

So, this was it! She popped back to the kitchen to scan everything on a final check: the tiered stands all dressed and looking deliciously tempting, the extra sandwich platters all done, teapots and milk jugs at the ready. Cath took a deep breath, then she headed on out to join the welcoming committee. If she'd forgotten anything, it was too late. She steadied her nerves by reminding herself that they had plenty of good food, tea and coffee galore; the raffle and tombola organised; the band were here and setting up; and very soon to be joined by the magical addition of the cutest of choirs, being the Brownies group. Cath had heard from Brown Owl that they had made some gorgeous felt flowers to hand out as buttonholes for everyone, too. An activity they'd completed at last week's session, to help with their community and creativity badges.

Stood with a welcoming smile at the big oak door, Cath was ready to open an umbrella, and go and greet her guests. Dan and Andreas were already out there ushering two elderly residents gently down from the first minibus. She recognised them as Joan and Vera from the home, looking smart in their best floral dresses.

Cath went to join them, ready to take over at the minibus steps. The driver was also there, kindly assisting the new arrivals, along with Linda who worked at the home. Next in line was Betty, looking lovely in a smart navy twin set and wearing her pearls, followed by a very dashing-looking Reggie in a grey pin-striped suit and red-and-navy-spotted tie.

'Hello,' she greeted them with a smile. 'Shame about this rain, but we'll soon be inside and dry.' Cath popped her umbrella over their heads, and letting Betty take a hold of her arm, and giving Reggie a moment to sort his walking stick, she assisted them along the pavement.

'Ah, don't worry pet,' said Reggie cheerfully. 'A little rain's no bother at all.'

'We're so looking forward to our afternoon out,' said Betty. 'Thank you very much.'

'We are indeed,' agreed Reggie. 'And we're in for a real treat. This lady and her friends are the bee's knees of the catering world, Betty. It'll be like having tea at The Ritz, I'm sure.' Reggie gave a wink.

And Cath smiled, as that's exactly what she'd been hoping for too, though she did warn, 'Now, don't go raising expectations too high,' as she helped the pair of them up the steps and into the village hall's entrance.

Cath left her brolly at the entrance door, and led her duo through to the main hall, and their places at the table.

'Oh, this looks wonderful.' Betty's face was a picture as they entered the room. 'The flower posies are delightful, and look, we've got tablecloths and the best china out, too. I bet this is even prettier than The Ritz.'

'It's grand, lass.' Reggie's simple words warmed Cath.

She felt proud of how they'd pulled together as a team to make this hall into somewhere rather magical, the perfect setting for an afternoon tea.

'And how's your young man? Very much on the mend, I hope,' Reggie asked kindly.

'Yes, he's on the road to recovery, thankfully. It's kind of you to ask.' Cath thought it best to keep the conversation light, and Will was indeed making progress, even if life was more than frustrating lately for them both. Will hadn't as yet arrived. She hoped he'd keep to his promise to come along, even if it might be awkward between them.

And then Reggie followed up with, 'I've been thinking about you two lovebirds.'

'Oh.' Cath paused, unsure of what to say, and then quietly confessed, so only Betty and Reggie might hear, 'Well, I'm not sure if we're quite lovebirds, right now.' With everything going on with Will of late, she felt like they'd tumbled out of that particular nest.

'I'm sorry to hear that, dearest Cath,' responded Reggie kindly.

'I'm sure we'll get through it all, somehow.' She tried her best to sound positive. But deep inside she felt so torn and confused by Will's recent outbursts.

As if he'd been summoned, Will then appeared at the hall's entrance. He must have slipped in while she was busy at the bus, as he was holding a teapot and approaching the table where Reggie and Betty had just taken their seats. Cath felt herself freeze, whilst her heart thumped rapidly. She and Will gave each other what felt to Cath like a curt smile. Maybe, it was that freezing sensation affecting her mouth momentarily, she mused.

Kenneth and Cath's neighbours, John and Mary, were settled at the table too, having been ushered in by Kev.

Will politely offered, 'Anyone for tea?' He looked very dapper in his dark-navy suit, white shirt and pale-blue tie, thought Cath, realising that she'd never seen him in a suit before. Smart casuals, or his cycling Lycra were his norm. The 50s fashions were so stylish, and oh yes, she had yet to make her own quick change, she realised.

'Thank you, young man,' said Betty, with Mary and John next in line, and Kenneth holding up his cup at the ready.

'And how are you doing, Will?' asked Reggie when Will had reached him. 'Very much on the mend, I hope.'

'I'm doing okay, thanks, Reggie.' Will evidently didn't want to expand on his recent health issues here, but he seemed to appreciate the caring question.

Cath had shifted slightly back, ready to head away and make her escape to the kitchen. With several of the guests now having arrived and in situ, they'd need to crack on with the catering. But she couldn't help herself stealing a glance over her shoulder at Will before leaving the hall. Despite his recent surgery and with all the issues he was facing, he'd made it here, and was looking to help others and be a part of his supper club team, taking care of this Tilldale community. And despite their personal difficulties and recent falling out, she appreciated that he hadn't wanted to lct anyone down.

As Will moved on to the next table, Reggie called Cath back over, patting his top pocket as he said, 'I've brought her with me, you know. I've chosen this one specially; it's the letter about when we went dancing. We used to love to dance back in the day.' Her elderly friend's eyes had misted a little, filled with sweet nostalgia, and love, and loss.

'Oh, Reggie . . .' Cath found she couldn't say any more. She remembered the lost love letters, and how she and Will had finally found them in the loft of her cottage. Elsie and Reggie's loving history recorded over time. With all that had happened with Will, since they'd met the second time around just over a year ago, flooding her mind, emotions were filling her to the brim. Her eyes were dangerously close to filling, and perhaps spilling. 'That's so lov . . . lovely,' she managed to croak.

With an introductory hoot of a trumpet, the youthful band from Lily's high school struck up, taking the pressure off Cath and the sensitive nature of the conversation, with some relaxing tunes. Starting with a couple of Frank Sinatra tracks – Cath recognising 'I've Got You Under My Skin', which seemed pretty apt.

More guests began to arrive, Cath spotting several faces from the village and surrounding areas, including the final ticket holders, Sue and her husband, along with their neighbour Joyce. Lily was escorting her glamorous-looking Grandma Liz to a seat just along from Reggie. And two young mums with their toddlers from the newly started playgroup came through, which was fantastic to see. Young and old, all were welcome.

And there was a short grey-haired lady in a purple floral dress, who looked to be in her eighties, chatting loudly with Vera from the home, the pair of them laughing away about something. The slight Scottish lilt and the feeling of déjà vu suggested to Cath that she was Granny Ruth. Cath went over to say hello, deciding that the food could wait another few minutes, to give everyone the chance to settle and get sociable around the tables. She and Ruth had a lovely chat about The Pudding Pantry tea rooms, Cath telling her how wonderful the raspberry cheesecake had been when they'd called in for the jam, and Ruth chuckling as she revealed her great-granddaughter Maisy's latest antics on her new pony.

With teas and coffees served, and most of the seats now taken, Cath politely said she needed to get back to her tasks, and dashed to the kitchen. Along with Dan, Andreas and Lily, final touches were made to the platters and cake stands, and ta-dah, they were soon ready to be served. Nikki rounded up her three boys, and they began to carefully carry them into the hall. Angus, Nikki's youngest, had the most serious look on his face, his concentration fixed as he was determined not to drop a thing. Middle-child Scott merely beamed at everyone, and said a cheery 'hello' as he took it all in his stride. Stands and platters were placed mid-table ready to share between the guests. With 'oohs' and 'aahs' and 'wonderfuls' filling the room.

Will, Andreas, Dan, Cath, Nikki and Lily then brought in a final tiered stand each, and the room burst into an unexpectedly rousing round of applause.

There was a ding of a teaspoon against a cup, bringing a hush to the proceedings, and young Hamish announced rather formally, as though he'd been practising, 'Afternoon tea is served. Please help yourselves.'

'Thank you, young man,' responded Kenneth, as he reached eagerly for a finger of ham sandwich.

'Oh, important question, jam or cream first?' quizzed Cath's neighbour Mary, diving in for a scone.

'Now then, I'd go jam first, that's the Cornish way, apparently,' said Betty.

'Oh no, it has to be cream,' interjected Kenneth. 'Sort of acts like butter then.'

'Who cares, it'll be delicious whichever way,' pronounced John with a smile.

'Oh, and look how pretty all the cakes are!' exclaimed a delighted Ruth.

'Beautiful,' said Betty.

'These are a work of art,' added Reggie, unable to resist a slice of lemon drizzle, straight from the top tier.

'You're supposed to go savoury first,' hissed Vera, giving him a nudge.

'Ah, don't you go worrying about that, pet. No need to stand on ceremony here. I'll be working my way through the lot anyhow . . . in whatever order takes my fancy.' He gave a cheeky wink.

Vera merely shook her head in exasperation.

Cath stayed a few precious seconds to watch everyone delightedly tucking in, then saw this as her chance to nip out, ready to make a swift wardrobe change in the storeroom. All was quiet in the kitchen area now with everyone out in the main hall serving and chatting. Though she was a little late with her 50s outfit, she was determined to join in and look the part. She'd found a gorgeous dress, a couple of days ago, in the Kirkton charity shop. A ditsy print, pink-and-green-floral affair, that nipped in at the waist, showing just enough décolletage, and swirled out in a fabulous A-line skirt. She slipped out of her trainers and got her navy ballet pumps ready – pretty yet still comfy and practical, with all the running around she yet needed to do.

Closing the door on the little store, she took off her apron, and her long-sleeved T-shirt and jeans, pulled the dress out of the bag, and thrust it over her head. Hmm, perhaps she should have changed in the bathrooms where there was a mirror, she suddenly thought. Oh well, today wasn't about her, was it. A swipe of soft-pink lipstick went on. She decided to let her dark wavy hair down out of its ponytail now that the cooking was over, and ran her fingers through it to loosen it up a bit. Sorted. She'd do. She'd better get back out to the hall and give her gang a hand.

Will glanced over just as Cath was making her way back in through the hall's double doors. She saw him look and then look again, as a hint of a smile creased his lips, and his eyes seemed to widen. But then, as though he'd remembered their falling out, his face fell rather stonily once more, and he turned away to serve some more tea.

At that point, a troop of young girls dressed in their brown and yellow uniforms walked briskly in through the doors. Brown Owl lead the way, instructing them to gather just below the stage. Veronica, who was in on the Brownie troupe's singing, and had spoken with the swing band members earlier, gave a nod to the band to take a well-earned break. They then wrapped up the 'Fly Me to the Moon' tune they were on. Brown Owl turned choir-master, and with her back to the audience, began some vigorous arm signals. Dan made a loud ding with a teaspoon on a cup, to draw the guests' attention to the new arrivals, and a respectful hush filled the room.

The pianist had stayed back as agreed, to start the opening notes to lead them in, and a nine-year-old girl took a step forward from her pack to start with a solo introduction. Her voice was so clear and beautiful as she began the first chorus of 'Somewhere Over the Rainbow', the rest of the Brownie choir joining in thereafter. The look of joy on the guests' faces was mesmerising. And though Cath had known this was to happen, the gorgeous singing and its effect on the gathering was wonderful. 'If You're Happy and You Know It' came next with the audience joining in with the actions, and then a great version of Bruno Mars's 'Count on Me', to huge smiles and much applause, and a 'woohoo!' from Andreas.

And then, something totally unexpected happened – not part of the supper club's plans for today's event at all. Reggie stood up first, and then Betty, and one by one several of the care home residents filed into line behind the Brownies. And Reggie, who stood a little to the side of the choir, started to sing. His voice a little shaky to begin with, but then it rang out loud and clear with the first line of 'Stand by Me' by Ben E. King. And then the elderly guests who'd filed behind him, plus the Brownies, joined in to sing the most wonderful rendition of one of Cath's favourite songs. She looked across to Will instinctively, but then had to look away, as the tears that were fogging her eyes were threatening to spill over. This moment was so magical and touching, and unforeseen. The lyrics summed up everything about the event today, about her love for Will, and for their families and friends. It was so wonderful and so bloody moving, that it made her want to cry – in the best of ways, and also want to go over and somehow shake Will out of his dark and gloomy, cut-off place.

The hall burst into thunderous applause as the rendition by both young and old came to a heartfelt close.

'Bravo!' cheered Kenneth.

'Marvellous,' shouted Dan.

'More,' called out Vera, who being rather frail and finding standing for long a challenge, had remained in her seat, but had sung along heartily with them.

Reggie took a small bow, enjoying his moment in the limelight, then said, 'Thank you, and I'm sorry all, but that's the only one we've practised.'

'Well then, that calls for another cup of tea, and we'll get the band to strike up again shortly,' said Andreas. 'There's plenty more scones and cake to go around, too. And don't forget the baklava.'

Cath, still brimming with emotion, stepped forward to address the singers. 'Thank you all so much. And thank you, Brown Owl, and your fantastic Brownie choir. That was just wonderful.' She added, 'We've left some spare seats at the end of each table for you. And there's still cake and scones galore, and a drink of lemonade for the young ones, too.' Cath was so glad that she'd thought to include them in the tea. And she knew the elderly would enjoy having a little chat with them, too.

'Ooh, and we've got our crafted buttonholes to hand out. We'll do that first,' exclaimed Brown Owl gathering up a big hessian bag. 'Come on, girls.' The children took several of the bright pink, purple, red and yellow felted flowers each, and gave everyone a gorgeous floral gift to clip onto their outfit, and to take home and keep. The smiles in the room got even broader.

'Oh, and there's one more thing.' Brown Owl dug into her cloth bag again.

The youngest of the group, walked up to Will bearing a small gift bag, announcing herself as Olive and saying that she and her dad had worked on this together. Cath watched with intrigue as Will opened the bag, pulling out a hand-sized metal craftwork. As he turned it in his hand to study it, Cath could see it was a man on a bicycle, made of twists of metal strips, nuts and bolts welded together. 'Daddy loves your cycling shop,' the girl added. 'We heard you've been poorly, and we made this for you . . . to cheer you up.'

Small kindnesses that meant so very much. Well, that was it, Cath's tears spilled over. The dam had bloody well burst.

Will was evidently feeling it, too, as he took a sniff before replying, 'Thank you so much, I love it. You and your daddy are very clever to make this. It's going to have pride of place in my cycle shop.'

'You're welcome,' her sweet voice came back. The little girl looked so happy with a huge smile on her face, as she turned to join the rest of her pack, ready to find a seat, sip some fizzy lemonade and dive into the cakes and bakes.

Reggie called Will over, then, and they had a little chat. The room settled with the warm buzz of conversation, laughter and tinkling spoons stirring as teacups were refilled by Dan and Andreas. Lily made her move around the venue with the last of the raffle tickets for sale. The tombola of treats (and veritable tat!) was drawing some eager punters too.

A short while later, with the tea-time treats savoured, the band came back on, bursting into a lively 'In the Mood'. With John and Mary up on their feet in no time, swiftly followed by Reggie and Betty, the old-time dancing had kicked off. Everyone who was mobile was soon up on the dance floor, and those a little less able were nodding, clapping or hand-jiving along in their seats.

It had a real 50s feel as 'Rock Around the Clock' was played next, followed by 'Wake Up Little Suzy'. Reggie began twirling Betty rather vigorously to that one, considering they were a pair of octogenarians. Carer Linda was looking on carefully, ready to step in and steady either of them, if need be. But also, not wanting to spoil their fun. Next up was Elvis's 'All Shook Up' and a lively version of 'Hound Dog'. Grandma Liz had partnered up with Kenneth, and Land Army Girl Joan and Edna from the home were having a jig. Andreas and Dan joined in with that one, too. It was a shame terrier Shirley wasn't there to join in, but food hygiene and health and safety issues had kept her at home today. Cath held back a frustrated sigh, as she caught sight of Will. They'd managed to pull off a fantastic event here, and yet she couldn't fully enjoy it as he was still acting like Mr Bloody Frosty. She had to admit in the midst of all the fun and frivolity she was feeling a bit lost.

The band then moved to slow things down with 'You Send Me', which is when Will looked over at Cath, who was now busying herself collecting up the used plates and cutlery. He looked rather unsure of himself. Cath felt her stomach dip. She remembered wanting to slow dance with him so much at the end of the Christmas Bash, and it hadn't happened, and here they were – eight months later, with all the ups and downs that life had decided to throw their way – still hesitant.

It was then that Reggie called out cheekily, 'Come on, Will, Cath . . . join in.' Then giving a big wink, he added pointedly, 'The clearing up can wait.'

She paused to gaze over at Will. Wishing he would walk across the hall to her, to take those tentative steps back to togetherness. And for Cath, the room seemed to hold its breath.

A second or two wait that seemed so long, and then Will began to move slowly towards her. Of course, it would have seemed rude not to act on Reggie's prompt. She placed the stack of plates she'd gathered gently down on the table beside her, feeling a lump form in her throat.

'Cath?' was all he said, his voice husky with emotion.

'Of course.' They'd missed much of the song already, but he took her hand and led her towards the space at the front of the hall where the others were dancing, gently drawing her close to him, and oh, they were about to experience their first ever dance together. She reached her arms up around his neck as his circled her waist. Did she feel a hint of resistance, a stiffness of his limbs? Was he doing this just to be polite? Yet here she was in his arms. Will's body warm and close, his breath gently tickling her ear, and she dared to nestle her head softly against his shoulder.

And as they leaned in, Will seemed to soften into the movement, and the slow swaying motion. Cath was trying hard not to think too much, making the most of the dance, and the music and the moment. But oh, how she'd missed his closeness, the scent of him . . . so very familiar, and despite all the ups and downs and curveballs, how they still just seemed to fit. The far end of the hall now filled with couples swaying, Dan and Andreas, Kev catching up with Nikki, Lily and her younger cousin Hamish doing a twirl, elderly ladies holding hands, the mums dancing with their toddlers, Reggie gently swirling with Betty . . . but Cath was sure he'd be imagining that it was his Elsie there with him as he felt the crinkled warmth of the treasured letter in his pocket resting against his heart.

Love didn't go away when someone close to you died, it stayed like a light in your soul. No wonder at all that Will was still finding all of this difficult, Cath understood, but couldn't help but want so much more. He had so much of life left to live, he needed more light, more joy. If only he would let it in . . .

Chapter 32

The afternoon was drawing to a close. Dan gave the band the nod and they announced the last dance, striking up with the chords of 'True Love Ways'.

Cath and Will drew apart fractionally. Would their love find a way? The thought swirled in Cath's mind. Did they carry on and dance again? Or might that be *their* first and last dance? It was a gorgeous song, and the lad from the band stepped forward to sing the lyrics. Cath didn't want this moment to end, their closeness to end.

'Shall we?' asked Cath, almost afraid of what the answer might be.

It was almost four-thirty, and the minibuses for the care home were due to arrive at any minute. Cath should really be making a start on the clearing up, and of course be helping the elderly with their coats and preparing them for their trips back home, but glancing around, most of them were still on the dance floor, too. She wasn't ready to break apart.

Their faces were still close, and his eyes were hazel pools of mystery. Cath gave a small hopeful smile.

'All right, then.' They weren't the most romantic of words, but they were better than a no – or worse, a grouchy response. The two of them leaned back in for the last dance of the event.

Would this be the first of many, or the only dancing they'd ever have? So close, yet still so confused. She could feel the beating of his heart against her chest, as they swayed. What was his heart wanting to tell hers, was it very different from his mind? Cath took a long slow breath as the song moved to its finale. The music soon came to a close, along with the Tilldale Afternoon Tea event, and those on the dance floor stopped their swirling and looked to the stage, giving a hearty round of applause for the high-school musicians, who stood up to take a bow with broad grins on their faces. Kenneth was still dancing with Ruth, an interesting new development, giving her a final twirl, and then calling out, 'Bravo'.

Cath and Will stepped apart, Will giving a careful smile, as Cath said a rather formal 'thank you', perhaps sensing how hard that had been for him. Despite those beautiful moments being held in his arms, he was still frustratingly unfathomable.

The raffle, which had been drawn a while before, had been won by a delighted and deserving Linda who was excited to take home her hamper prize. The tombola table had been stripped, the Brownies' floral buttonholes were being jauntily worn as the guests prepared for home, and there were plenty of smiles.

Nikki's lads were busy helping to gather jackets and coats ready to reunite with their owners. And Dan and Andreas were now escorting guests out of the hall and towards the main entrance doors, offering little cardboard boxes of spare scones and cakes to take with them. Kev was ready to do a return 'taxi' service along the street and out to the local hamlets, and was standing with his car keys at the ready. Now they'd had a moment's pause, several of the elderly had realised the wonderful dancing had in fact taken it out of them, and were more than grateful for a lift up the street. Time for a late afternoon nap, in fact. And time to reflect on a gloriously sociable afternoon . . . for the supper club team as well as the guests.

In the midst of the farewells and thanks, Cath caught up with

Reggie in the entrance hallway. 'Thanks for coming, Reggie.'

'Oh, Cath, you did it again! What a marvellous event, thank you so much.' He was beaming away. 'It really has been wonderful. And pass on my thanks to your friends. You've all worked so hard. I've so enjoyed being back here in the village again, and this hall . . . the dancing, it felt rather like the good old days.' He gave a watery-eyed smile, the emotions of the occasion evidently catching up on him.

'You are so welcome,' said Cath, as she took him into her arms for a hug. When she'd moved into Cheviot Cottage, she'd never imagined that a magical friendship might develop with its previous owner. And, it felt all the more special having sadly lost her own parents a few years back. 'And I'll be there at the home to see you all next week, Reggie.'

'Oh, and we'll have lots to talk about after today, won't we?'

'Absolutely. You and Betty jiving for a start.'

Her regular visits to Kirkton Care Home had become part of her new life here in Northumberland. So much had happened in these past eighteen months, so much had changed in her life, that sometimes it was hard to comprehend. Even with the ups and downs with Will, overall, she felt so much happier of late. She felt like she was putting down roots, finding her way. Like somehow, whatever twists and turns that might yet come, life would work out okay.

Cath watched from the steps to the hall, her hand lifted ready to wave, as the first minibus was about to set off with its merry load of passengers. Andreas and Dan were standing out on the pavement, waving, where they'd been helping the elderly on board.

'Bon voyage!' called out Andreas as the vehicle started to moved off.

'They're only going five miles,' chuckled Nikki, who'd appeared next to Cath.

'Yes, but it's been a momentous occasion for them,' he countered jovially, having overheard.

And he was, in fact, right. Today would have been very special, and so unlike their normal day-to-day routine at the home. Cath filled with pride thinking how they'd managed to do that for everyone, given them a day to remember.

'You all right, hun?' asked Nikki.

'Yes, of course. It's all worked out lovely, hasn't it?'

'Yeah, the do's been brilliant.' That evidently wasn't what she was getting at, however. 'Ahm, I saw you and Will dancing . . . but that was after he'd been avoiding you all afternoon.'

Oh, it hadn't gone unnoticed then, this ongoing rift between them. But of course, their friends were invested, they'd given her and Will the final matchmaking push to get together, after all. And they cared . . . 'Oh, Nikki, things are a bit tricky just now. But hey, we'll work it out, I'm sure.' Cath kept her response short. She appreciated her friend's concern, but this really wasn't the place to go into details about her love life.

Nikki added warmly, 'Well, you know where I am if you need to chat, hun.'

'I do, and thanks.' Cath put an arm around her pal's shoulder.

After waving the second minibus off, Cath turned to go back in, heading for the kitchen and the no doubt mountainous clearing up. She discovered Will there, drying and stacking up plates. His movements had slowed, and she couldn't help but notice that he was looking pretty shattered. She walked on over to him, feeling a little hesitant in case he felt she was treating him like an invalid again, but concerned enough to ask, 'Hey, are you feeling okay?' She was about to place a hand gently on his arm, but held back. Still unsure as to where they now stood.

'Bit tired, but I'm all right.' He carried on with his drying up.

'Honestly, get yourself away,' she urged, feeling worried that he'd overdone it. 'Time to head on home.'

'But there's all the clearing up to do. I can't just up and leave.'

'Yes, you can. We can take it from here. The others are around to help. You look whacked.'

'I'll be okay,' he persevered, stubbornly.

'You might well be okay, but there's no point pushing it.' Cath was adamant. It was great that he had turned out to help, but not at the expense of his ongoing health.

'Okay.' He caved in. 'Well, I suppose I'd better go and say bye to the others.'

Shortly afterwards, Cath followed him through, intent on seeing how much clearing up there was left to do. The hall had emptied out, other than Kenneth – the first and last – who was saying his farewells. Kev was about to set off with him.

Will made his farewells, too.

'Well done, Will,' said Nikki.

'Thanks, mate,' said Andreas.

'Go and have a rest, pal, you look a tad peaky,' from Kev.

'Yeah, time to zone out and relax,' said Lily, giving him a hug.

'Bye,' said Cath gently.

'Bye,' Will answered.

Did she kiss him on the cheek? Go in for a hug, too? But in her indecision, she missed the moment, and he'd turned to leave.

They were then down to the supper club five, plus Nikki's three lads left clearing up. They shifted the remaining tea sets and cake stands to the kitchen, ready for the mammoth washing-up session; the dishwasher alone couldn't cope with this lot. Nikki stripped off the tablecloths, and the trestle tables were folded and stacked away by Dan and Andreas. The young boys were handed the broom and a hoover with orders from Nikki to tackle the hall's floor. A begrudging groan came en masse from the trio. The novelty of helping out was starting to wear thin. But they'd done an amazing job whilst the guests were here; chatting with the elderly as they served their teas and bringing top-ups of food and drinks throughout the afternoon. Hamish even stepped in to dance with Janet from the home, when she didn't seem to have a partner, evidently making her day, judging by her broad smiles.

In the meantime, the supper club five hit the kitchen, Lily

putting some upbeat music on, starting with a Sabrina Carpenter track. Washing-up liquid was poured into hot running water in the original school kitchen sink, soon frothing up into pine-scented bubbles. The rubber gloves went on for Dan, and tea towels were brandished by the others bar Nikki, who was ready to put everything back on the shelves once dried. She was hoping she'd remember where it had all been to start with.

'Hey, how's Will doing?' Andreas asked as he stood beside Cath, drying the first dish. 'He left saying he was sorry but he needed to get going.'

'Yeah, he looked pretty knackered, to be honest,' added Dan.

'Man, he was wiped,' agreed Lily.

'Yeah, I noticed that, too,' answered Cath. 'He was determined to help today. Ahm, he has been doing pretty well in the scheme of things.' She paused, she hadn't told them anything about their falling out, hoping against hope that it'd just blow over. Concern was nipping at her, however, not only about their personal issues, but another check was due soon with the consultant for any ongoing indication of cancer. 'But God, I so hope the next PSA results come back clear.' Her words felt like a little prayer. Whatever was happening between them, the main thing was that Will got better.

'We all do,' Nikki said, giving her arm a reassuring squeeze.

'Well, if we can do anything to help, please shout. Either of you, that is,' said Andreas.

'Yes, that goes for us, too,' said Nikki, meaning her and her family.

Lily was nodding beside her. 'And me.'

'Thank you.' Cath so appreciated their ongoing support. All she really wanted was for Will to get the 'undetectable' news on the cancer, at the end of this stage of his treatment. Fingers and everything crossed for that. That was the best you could hope for at this point, with further tests ongoing. And whatever happened next personally for them, a clear check would at least mark a fresh start for Will, after weeks of worry with his health.

The dishwasher had done its cycle with an earlier load, and the enormous stack of tea plates and cups that Dan had handwashed was finally coming to an end. Cath grabbed a cloth and her spray and did a full disinfect of the now-cleared kitchen surfaces.

'Hall's all done,' Hamish announced, as he and his brothers trailed in to the kitchen.

'We're starving. Any of the scran left?' asked Scott, with a cheeky grin.

'There wasn't much left over after the takeaways were handed out, and it's all packed up now. There's no way I'm getting this kitchen all messy again,' warned Nikki.

'Uh-hhh.' The young lad's shoulders sagged dramatically.

'Hang on,' interjected Cath. 'There's a box here with some cake in.' They'd shared out the last of the goodies between them. This had been her portion to take home; three slices of cake exactly. Perfect for the three lads who'd worked so hard.

'Aw, thanks, Cath.' Angus grinned, as Scott gave Hamish a high five.

'Take them outside!' warned Nikki. 'Not a crumb to be spilt in here. We're nearly done.'

'Okay, thanks, guys.' Hamish looked delighted as he took the box, along with three napkins that Nikki handed them, and the youngsters scampered out.

With Veronica organised to come back and buff the parquet flooring tomorrow, all they had to do was give everything a final check over. Cath looked into the hall. The trestle tables were all packed away, and the lads had done well with their sweeping. The band had left the stage as it was. You'd never have known they'd been there, nor that there had been a tea and dancing, other than the memories still circling in Cath's mind. She felt happy-tired and gave a gentle sigh. Wondering about Will, hoping he was all right after his hectic day. And wondering too if they might ever be right as a couple. She felt totally shattered, after her early start and extremely full-on day, but thinking about the smiles on the faces of their guests, it had all been so very worthwhile.

Heading back into the kitchen area, with the last of the crockery and cutlery put away, and her friends still there, Cath spotted two bottles of fizz left out on the side. 'Oh, whose are these?' she asked.

'Ah, I won one on the tombola,' said Lily.

'And the other was a gift from your neighbours, Mary and John, as a thank you for all our hard work,' explained Dan.

'Aw, how sweet. Well, don't forget to take them home,' said Cath.

'You keep it, Cath.' Lily offered hers kindly.

'Yeah, and hold on to this one, too,' said Dan.

'But that one was to share,' she countered.

'Hmm, then perhaps we can use them when we next get together?' suggested Andreas. 'Maybe another trip to the beach hut? I'd love to go back there, while we've still got some summer.'

'Yeah, it's such a cool place,' added Lily.

'And, fingers crossed for that clear result for Will. Hopefully we'll be celebrating some good news by then,' said Nikki.

'Yes, absolutely.' Cath knew that the test was due in a couple of weeks, another hurdle. Not wanting to dwell on that, she moved the conversation on. 'And hey, have you lot just invited yourselves over?' Cath smiled, but felt mighty awkward. It would be down to Will, if he wanted the group to visit the bungalow again. But oh my, how would things be for the two of them? 'Ahm well, yes, that sounds a lovely idea,' she added feeling flustered, and hoping it didn't show.

Why did everything have to be so damn complicated? If this was it . . . and Will had made his mind up, that they were no longer to be a couple, it didn't bear thinking about. Dancing with him, being back in his arms, had made her miss him even more. And if it was a bit of a mess between the two of them, how the hell did that leave them all as the supper club? Cath felt a wave of nausea.

The friends collected their bags, and any cooking utensils,

food storage boxes and spare ingredients they'd brought with them. The last of the takeaway cartons were gathered up, too. It was time to head home.

'Well done, team supper club. Thank you so much!' Cath said, putting her personal worries aside for a moment.

'We did it!' said Nikki.

'We did indeed. Tilldale à la Ritz.' Andreas beamed.

'Your school band were brilliant,' added Dan.

'And the Brownies, they were so cute,' said Lily.

'Oh, and Reggie and Co. dancing the jive.' Cath grinned, remembering the moment fondly. 'I thought his hips might go at one point.'

Five minutes later, as Cath stood on the hall's steps, about to place the big old key into the lock of the oak door, she gave a sigh. It had been a wonderful, if tiring – and for her and Will, an emotionally confusing – day.

The rest of the gang were gathered outside, ready to drift off up the street on their respective walks home.

'Well done, guys, great job. See you, Cath,' called out Lily.

'Thanks again for all your help, everyone. You've been brilliant as always,' she responded warmly.

'Thanks, chief. See you soon.' Dan gave a mock salute.

'Bye, my loves. Been a pleasure,' added Andreas.

'Awesome cake.' Nikki's Scott, who'd been waiting outside on the wall with his brothers, sponge crumbs tellingly smeared across his lips, grinned.

'Don't talk with your mouth full,' Nikki scolded, shaking her head.

The young lad merely raised his eyebrows, while his brothers sniggered.

Kev reappeared then, adding, 'Cake? What cake? Where's mine?'

'All gone, Dad.' Hamish grinned, exaggeratedly licking his lips.

'You didn't save me any. Darn it!'

'Just thinking of your waistline,' chipped in Nikki with a grin. 'Anyway, thanks all.' She turned to her fellow team members adding, 'We did it! Another successful event.'

'Team supper club,' said Lily. 'Aw, I'm gonna miss you lot when I'm away at cooking school. Fingers crossed on my Food Diploma and A-level results coming soon.' Her hopes were still pinned on Leiths.

'Ah, you'll do well, I'm sure. And then, you'll be away having the best of times,' responded Cath reassuringly.

'And think of all the new recipes you can try out on us, when you're back for the hols,' Dan responded.

Lily's smile lifted.

'Love you all,' said Cath, brimming with affection. Their farewells felt like a hug.

'You too, gorgeous one.' Dan gave a wave. And the four supper clubbers began their saunter home, with Nikki's lads having jumped in the car with Kev.

Cath paused on the steps. After today's frequent showers, the sun was coming back out, along with an arch of colourful rainbow brightening the sky, that made her stop in her tracks and smile.

Rainbows were a symbol of hope and of promise, of fresh starts. Cath mentally crossed her fingers. They also spread a little happiness. And that's exactly what team supper club had done today.

Chapter 33

Cath jumped. A loud knocking pounded from the cottage door. Jeez. There was an urgency about the thudding; not your usual parcel delivery driver. Cath was shattered after her hectic day; she'd been home a mere half an hour, and had just crashed out on the sofa with a big mug of tea.

She clambered to her feet, and dashed through the hallway. 'Okay, okay, I'm coming.' Was there some kind of crisis? Someone hurt out on the street? An incident on the way home with the elderly in their minibus, heaven forbid?

She pulled open the door. 'Oh.'

It was Will on her front step. He looked careworn, pale and tired.

Blimey, he must have really overdone it today, but why was he here, not resting up in bed or something? Was something else wrong? 'Are you all right?'

'Not really, no.'

Oh, God. Had he had some bad news? Had the results come in, and he hadn't dared tell her? Was that why his mood seemed blacker than ever? Cath's mind was in full spin.

'Cath, I-I've done this all wrong . . .'

Whatever did he mean? Oh, was he breaking things off? Her

heart plummeted. Whatever it was, she didn't need to be having this sensitive conversation on her front step. 'I think you'd better come on in.'

'Uhm, can we rewind a bit?' Will said. He'd reached the hallway now, and Cath was closing the cottage door.

Her pulse was racing, her emotions scattered like a gun had gone off, and she didn't know whether to flee or face them.

He was standing still, looking so earnestly at her. 'Cath, can we try again?' he asked.

'Oh, Will, what exactly are you saying?' After all the hurt and confusion, she needed to clarify this. To be a couple with Will was everything she'd wanted, and yet, she was tired of all this toing and froing, of all this emotional pain. 'What's changed?' Cath needed to know where this was coming from. If this was genuine, or if it was all just going to happen on repeat; Will letting her get close, then retreating again – until her heart felt sorer and sorer.

Will took a breath. 'That dance today . . . holding you close in my arms, just confirmed all those things my heart keeps on telling me, when my mind has been warning me to step away.' He sighed. 'Ah, it's so much more than that . . .'

Cath realised they had Reggie to thank for their dance. Their elderly friend had been instrumental in getting them together on the dance floor today. And he'd evidently been doing far more than that too, as Will began to explain. 'I was talking to Reggie at the event, he was telling me all about his Elsie. About the wonderful times they'd had, and some of the hard times too, and how much he missed her now that she'd passed. And even though it still hurt to lose someone so close, he told me he hadn't regretted a single second of it.' He paused, taking a slow breath, before admitting, 'I *have* lost someone already, and I'm scared, I really am, of letting love in again. I was worried I couldn't survive another ending. Or put you through the same. But then this evening, I'm sat there thinking, what the hell am I doing? What am I waiting for? Do I want to spend the rest of my life as a lonely old man, when I have this gorgeous woman right here, or do I risk telling her . . . *you* . . . how I really feel?'

'Oh, Will,' Cath began.

'Wait . . .' Will stopped her from saying more. 'I want you to know the truth first, *all of it*. Then you can decide.'

So, there was more to this. 'Come on, let's go through to the lounge,' Cath calmy suggested, though inside she was anything but calm.

And taking a seat, Will went on to admit his embarrassment about the urinary difficulties he was facing, and his fear that he'd never function well sexually again. 'All this, after the surgery, physically, it's been awful. Peeing . . . I thought it might be a bit of a dribble before and after going, but oh no, it's literally like a leaky fucking tap. That's made life so difficult since the op. I'm getting through pads like a baby in nappies. I even tried going out on the bike a couple of days ago, and it was a bloody nightmare. Ended up having to jump over a hedge to try and find somewhere to change the bloody thing.'

He looked up at her, the distress so apparent in his expressive eyes, before adding, 'And it's so hard knowing that I can't make love to you, not properly, for months yet . . . if at all. Not in the same natural way. How could you even want me like that? And I don't want you staying out of obligation, or just because you feel sorry for me.'

'Oh, Will.' She knew to let him carry on, to get it all out, now that he'd finally opened up.

'I told myself by cutting off, I was protecting you, Cath. All the questions whirring in my mind, sending me nuts: What if I don't make it through this cancer in the long run? What if it comes back, and you have to go through everything I had to with Jane? Could I put you through that? I'm so sorry, Cath, but I'd convinced myself you'd be better off without me. You still might be . . .'

'Isn't that my decision to make, though, not yours?' She held his gaze steadily. 'And, Will, I don't feel sorry for you, not in a pitying way, I just feel bloody frustrated that you've not told me all this before.'

He sighed, before adding, 'I did take your advice, finally. I rang the nurse . . . from that advice leaflet I had. She was brilliant. We had a good chat, and she reassured me that all this was quite normal post-surgery. That things really will improve over time, but it might be months, not weeks, before I begin to feel more like my old self. I'd been expecting too much. She reminded me of some of the exercises to try, too, which I've started.'

'Well, that sounds good. So, there's a way forward with that.'

'Yeah, there is. And, Cath, I'm so sorry I pushed you away the other night. I acted like a right twat.'

'Yep, you did.' Cath wasn't going to let him get away with it that easily.

'Oh shit, I've really messed up.' His dark eyes held hers, seemingly searching deep in to her soul. 'Cath, can we try again? Be a couple. If you still want me? Ah, but I'd understand if I've pushed you too far this time.' He stopped speaking, gathering his thoughts from their messy, post-surgery tangled web. 'The real truth is, Cath, at the bottom of all of this, I was trying to protect myself. I was, still am, terrified of losing someone I love, again.' He seemed so afraid of the deep emotion he was feeling, and all the hurt that might come should it ever go wrong.

'Today,' he continued, 'seeing all those fantastic people in the hall. Hearing the laughter, the chatter, it showed me that life can be good. Even if you're old, even if you're frail . . . even if you have lost the love of your life. They are still going strong out there, and grabbing life by the balls. Jiving, for goodness' sake. I came to realise that shutting myself off isn't the answer. It's just made me more miserable than ever.'

'Blimey, that must have been depressing for you,' Cath teased, lightening the mood, happy that they were finally talking honestly and openly again.

'Yeah, it bloody well was.' He gave a small chuckle. 'Cath, what I'm trying to say is that I miss you, *us*,' he finally confessed.

'Oh, come here, you bloody idiot.' She took him into her arms. 'I miss you, too.'

That hug, oh my. His arms came around her too, and they clung on. Feeling the warmth, the reconnection, the togetherness. No words were needed.

As they reluctantly pulled away, his lips creased into a smile. Those gorgeously sensual lips that she'd missed so much. She tilted forward, still holding his gaze, as she reached to brush her lips against his. The pressure returned from his was warm and welcoming, melding into a kiss. Woohoo! A proper heartfelt, passionate, tingly toes and oh, all sorts of other parts, kind of kiss.

Lying in bed, Will with his boxers on, essential pad in, Cath in her bra and knickers in support. The rest of their flesh bare, with a mere drape of cotton sheet over them. They'd not ventured to make love, not yet. This closeness was enough, for now. She could still trace her fingers over his abs, rest her head against his chest, hear the steady rhythm of his heartbeat.

And in time, she was certain they could get a little more creative . . .

Will's breathing had slowed, as he rested in slumber. Finding calm in the storm. Finding each other, once more.

For all the fear, surely it was better to *feel*, than to cut yourself off. To let in those moments of pure bliss, as well as the roller-coaster ones of doubt and insecurity. It was about being human; to love and be loved, in a world, a life, that was always going to have change and at times hurt in it, whether you wanted it or not. Putting yourself out there, opening up to the beautiful vulnerability of love, wasn't easy. But taking that risk, riding that wave, letting yourself really feel the joy, the bliss, as well as those inevitable moments of pain, had to be worth it.

Go on, open your heart to love, she thought, as she lay beside

Will, feeling a thrum of warmth and tenderness fill her from the crown of her head to the tips of her toes. It would surely be a bumpier ride, but oh my, what an amazing journey.

Chapter 34

Will picked up his mobile. A group video call was coming in from his two girls.

'Hey, Dad, how are you?' There was Maddie in her Newcastle flat.

'Hi, Dad.' Sophie joined in a second later, from her accommodation in York, having popped back down to stay with her friends – including Jess who'd apologised for being a pain during exam time – and check the flat out, being mid-August and the holidays still.

'Hey, girls. This is nice . . . seeing you both together.' Will's face lit with a smile.

'Well, we thought you might like to see us again soon in person, too,' said Sophie.

'Yeah, we're planning on coming back up for the weekend. Does that sound okay?' asked Maddie.

'Yes, of course. I'd love that. Ahm, Cath's here,' he added, as he beckoned her over to join in with the chat.

Cath moved to Will's shoulder, able to see the girls on the screen, as she also appeared in Will's mini frame. She couldn't help but spot the flicker of uncertainty cross Sophie's face. It was still there like an undercurrent; a sign of Sophie's ongoing unease with the situation, that her dad had found someone new romantically. And yes, Cath and Sophie were still working their way through that. It wasn't easy, but Cath got it. A new woman coming into Sophie's dad's life, in the place where her mum should have been, must feel so hard for her.

'So, shall we go over to the beach place? We're desperate to spend some time there, especially now it's all done up. Sophie's been telling me all about it. Are you up for that, Dad?' asked Maddie, sounding protectively caring. She was handling her dad's new relationship far more easily, even if it must feel strange for her too. 'We had the idea to make a special day over there.'

'Yeah, okay then, that sounds a really nice idea,' replied Will.

'And Cath can come too,' Sophie launched in, even though she then took a chew of her lip.

Maddie added, 'Don't worry, you two can chill, and we'll do the cooking over there for you. We have a plan, don't we, Soph?'

'Sounds like you two have been scheming,' Will responded, the corners of his eyes crinkling into a gentle smile.

'Perhaps, but it's all for the good.' Maddie grinned.

'That sounds lovely. Thank you, girls.' Cath came in to the conversation. 'But just a warning, if you're planning on cooking, the kitchen area is pretty small. There's only a gas camping hob – it's a pretty decent one, but there's no electricity in the hut.'

'Noted,' said Maddie. 'Yeah, I'd remembered about the hob from what Dad had mentioned a while back.'

'Well, I'm coming back on Friday night. I'll be on the train,' said Sophie, no doubt angling for a lift, then adding, 'But I can get a taxi from the station if you don't feel like driving.'

'Oh, I'm sure I'll be all right for that, love.' Of course, Will wouldn't want to let his daughter down. Taxis were expensive for Tilldale, too, being a half-hour away from the station.

'And if not, I can fetch you, Sophie,' offered Cath, jumping in.

'Okay, well . . . thanks.' She sounded as if she'd been caught out by Cath's kindness, seeming – perhaps naturally – nervous about some forced alone time together.

But Cath hoped that all these small steps might begin to add up to something, over time. A relationship, and with a little perseverance, a friendship with his girls. All she wanted was for Will and his family to be happy, and yes, she needed to feel that her place with them was a comfortable one. One that in time could grow, and maybe one day flourish, with some much-needed love and support. She'd keep sowing the seeds.

'And I'll be driving up Saturday morning, as I've got a long day shift on Friday,' added Maddie.

'Ah, it'll be great to see you, girls,' said Will. 'Something to look forward to.'

'Brill. Sounds like we're sorted then, Sis,' Maddie addressed Sophie, and they gave a thumbs up to the camera.

'And hey, thanks for everything you've done these past few weeks. Looking after me, and everything,' Will added, looking a little misty-eyed. 'Your mum would have been so proud of you both.'

Cath felt all choked up, too.

'Aw, thank you. Love you, Dad. Take care. See you soon.' Sophie started waving. 'Bye, Cath,' she added, simply yet rather touchingly.

'Thanks. Have a good week, Dad,' said Maddie.

'Will do. Love you, girls.'

'Love you, too,' said Maddie.

'Bye, and thank you. The weekend sounds lovely.' Cath gave a warm wave back, as Will closed the chat, saying, 'Ah, that was lovely of them.'

Perhaps those seeds were already making roots.

Plans had been tweaked, mid-week, when Cath had had a call from Adam saying he wanted to come up that next weekend, too. She'd felt in a bit of a quandary. She so wanted to spend the weekend at the beach bungalow with Will and the girls. Which felt like the biggest social family olive branch ever, but she didn't want to put off her own son coming up either. With helping to care for Will, and the Tilldale Afternoon Tea event to organise, it had been several weeks since she'd last seen him. Will saved the day, by being upfront, and asking the girls if they'd mind another guest at the beach house for the meal they were planning.

They'd been open to that, and learning that Cath's son was much the same age, he had an invite from the girls to join them. They'd since linked up on their socials, apparently.

The 'big kids' beach bungalow day was here.

'Right, you two, you can go for a stroll or sit out on the deck, but you're not allowed in here for the next thirty minutes while we do the cooking.' Maddie poked her head out of the beach hut door, and was being bossy, eldest child style.

'You know what it's like when we get in the kitchen,' warned Sophie with a cheeky smile. 'It might be wise to steer clear, or the mess'll do your heads in. I promise it'll all be worth it, though.'

From their chairs on the deck, Cath and Will gave each other a glance. Will was still looking rather pale, Cath thought, but slowly and surely, he was making a good and steady recovery. Yesterday, he'd even ventured out on his beloved bicycle again. Perhaps it had taken it out of him a little. He probably pushed the distance. They might take that walk a little later, but for now, sitting here in a comfy seat – making the most of the gorgeous bay view as the tide rolled in, hearing the splash of the surf and the families playing in the August sunshine – seemed the perfect place to rest.

'We'll stay here a while,' Cath answered, as Will nodded in agreement. 'But we'll be sure to keep out of your way.'

Adam was due to arrive at the bungalow shortly. On hearing of their beach hut plans, he was delighted to be asked to join them, and had offered to help out. He had been recruited by the girls to the culinary team. He was, apparently, organising the dessert, which he had stayed back at Cath's cottage to make, and was bringing along with him. Cath had hitched a lift earlier with Will and the girls, to make the most of the day. It was a wise move from Adam, no doubt, with no fridge facility here, and Will's girls on a compact kitchen takeover.

So, it was going to be a real 'family' day out. Cath was curious, and if she were totally honest, a tad anxious, about how the dynamics might work out. Adam had at least met Will before in the village, though she and Will hadn't been established as a couple at that point, and she knew her son was easy-going company. But yes, it was early days for them all. New family ties were about to be made. And as well as some inevitable nerves, that was exciting, too.

'Anyone for a beer or glass of wine?' asked Sophie. 'Or would you prefer a soft drink for now, Dad?' she added thoughtfully.

Will had been careful with his alcohol consumption since the diagnosis and treatment, wanting to give his body the best chance possible to get through this thing.

A muffled voice came from inside the hut, followed by Sophie saying, 'Oh, right, and Maddie says there's some 0 per cent lagers, too.'

'Yep, one of those will be great,' Will responded.

'I'll go for that, too,' added Cath. 'Thank you, girls.'

A chilled beer from the cool bag, on this sunny day, would be perfect.

Cath sat back in her chair. It was unusual for her to be the one resting and sitting down. Well, this was nice; the girls cooking for them, making the effort to do something special for their dad, and yes, air punch moment, for her too. It was gorgeous here at the beach bungalow today. The sun was peeking past slow-scudding clouds. A late-summer warmth to the air. And looking across at Will, she could see that he felt comfortable here. Maddie had been amazed by the refurbished bungalow. The new loo, thanks to Gemma, made life far more pleasant, too. And here on the re-oiled deck were the best seats in the house.

A pew with a view.

* * *

Adam soon arrived with hugs, and Cath's cool box which he'd carefully and levelly carried over the dunes.

'Hi, guys.'

'Hey, Adam.' Cath stood to give him a peck on the cheek.

'Hi, mate, how are you doing?' her son asked Will kindly.

'I'm good, getting there,' came Will's response. And they shook hands warmly. 'The girls are inside . . . Sophie, Maddie, Adam's here,' he called out.

'Great, I'll go say hi, and get this pudding into the cool.'

They could hear chatting, as they made their introductions.

And within a few minutes, supper by the sea was about to be served.

'Okay, here goes. Maddie's chilli con carne on the coast, and I've done the nachos,' announced Sophie. 'And before you mock me, yes, I know they came out of a packet, but I have made the guacamole dip all by myself.'

'Ah, that's brilliant, girls. And hey, no mocking here. Remember your good old dad's not exactly the chef of the family, either.'

'It smells delicious,' Cath commented, realising her tummy was rumbling.

Bowls of steaming hot chilli, garnished with a blob of crème fraîche, a sprinkling of black pepper and a sprig of fresh coriander, were passed out by Sophie. The colours looked vibrant, all rich-red, as aromas of spiced tomato filled the air. Adam followed with a bowl of crunchy tortillas and Sophie's luscious-looking green avocado-based dip.

He then nipped back in to bring out three additional fold-out chairs, as they gathered *en famille* to eat al fresco on the bungalow deck, sat overlooking the bay, with bowls on their knees. 'Head chef' Maddie appeared last, with a bottle of red wine to hand and a trio of glasses. 'Anyone care to join me in some vino?'

The girls were all in, Cath accepting a glass which would go perfectly with that spicy savoury supper. Will stuck to the 0 per cent beer, with Adam doing the same. Adam had offered to take the girls back to the village later, the plan being to leave Cath and Will to their own devices. Cath had packed enough clothes for them to stay over if they felt like it. Fingers crossed.

The food was simple and delicious, and halfway through the meal, Cath scanned the deck where the five of them sat; their grown-up children chatting away. It was great to see the three of them cooking, serving and having fun together. And as well as the warmth of the spices in her tummy, she had the heartwarming feeling that at last things might really work out. Adam and the girls, her and Will, this was the start of something new, something special, and hopefully something lasting. Is this how life could be? The grown-up kids getting on well, meeting up, having fun, sharing food, chatting . . . The youngsters would have their own lives, jobs and uni going on, of course, but might the three of them want to share some family time with Cath and Will?

In a beach bungalow by the sea, a blended family was growing its roots.

Later, with the empty chilli dishes cleared away by the girls, Adam popped in to the hut, coming out bearing a cheesecake-style stainless-steel dish. The zesty scent of lime filled the air. 'I hope you've saved some room. This took me longer to make than anticipated. Here's my Key lime pie. I figured the lime flavours might work well after the chilli.' He'd evidently picked up some culinary skills from his cooking-mad mother. 'Ah, wonderful. Great idea. Well done, Son.'

'Looks luscious, Adam,' said Sophie.

'Thanks, that looks fantastic,' added Will.

Adam went back in for serving bowls, a large knife and several spoons, and they were soon tucking into wedges of buttery-ginger-biscuit-based lime-and-cream pie with a sprinkling of dark chocolate shavings.

'Delicious' was Will's verdict. 'Thanks, mate.'

Maddie put a thumbs up, her mouth too full to speak.

Sophie smiled broadly. And Cath felt a burst of pride.

Cath suggested a post-supper stroll on the beach, but with Maddie and Adam intent on finishing the washing up, and saying they were ready to chill with a cold beer, and Will taking a brief nap, it was only her and Sophie wanting to go.

'Okay, well, let's leave these to it and have a wander,' said Cath, feeling happy yet still a touch anxious at the thought of it being just the two of them. She so didn't want to put her foot in it inadvertently, and spoil a really lovely day.

They scrambled down the dune bank to the front of the hut. And as they ambled along the sands, Sophie lifted her gaze, looking across at Cath as she spoke, 'Ahm, I wanted to say thank you, for everything you've been doing for my dad.'

Wow. 'Thanks. I wanted to be there for him. It's been a tough time for you all,' Cath acknowledged.

'I know . . . and . . . I'm sorry . . . if I haven't made life easy for you lately.' There was a second or two pause. Cath looked on quietly, gently smiling, to give the young woman the chance to find her words. 'Well, we've both seen how much you've done for Dad these past few months, and this meal today, it was our way of saying thank you.'

'It's been wonderful, Sophie. I really appreciate it. And I know your dad will have done, too. Thank you, both.'

'Hey, and your Adam's not a bad chef, too. That pudding was amazing.'

'Must have learned a thing or two from me, somewhere along the line.'

'Yeah, our mum was a really good cook, too. I used to love her banoffee pie.' And Sophie, for the first time, shared a happy memory of her mother with Cath. And those few words felt like a magical gift.

They both gave a broad smile. Having this chance to chat, felt like a cloud had been lifted. It was like the sea breeze had blown through the fog of their relationship, lightening it, and bringing with it a chance for change.

This felt like such a big step forward for Cath and Sophie.

Two sets of footprints were now running parallel, as they walked side by side in the sands.

The beach day had been a success; with two broken families coming together. And the fear currently hounding them about Will's health might soon, fingers crossed, lose its grip on their lives. The relief of an 'undetectable' diagnosis for him at the next round of tests, that was the goal. The hope that finally life could move forward, and work out for them all. Could she dare to dream?

Back on the deck, with the sky softening to a more subdued, rosy-hued evening light, Cath caught Will's eye, a glint of its old sparkle back, and registered his mellow smile as he watched the two of them return. Might he be wondering the same things? He was certainly enjoying the moment. Their grown-up kids had done so well, thinking this up and taking charge today.

Though he looked slightly tired, Will was still so very handsome. His dark hair, and the most sensual of hazel-brown eyes, that melted her insides when he looked her way. How could he think she wouldn't fancy him anymore, merely because of the present implications of his health and surgery? Ah, it had made her love him all the more. Seeing his courage and his determination through this most difficult of times. Witnessing how much he wanted to protect his girls, and how – even if rather foolish and grumpily – he'd tried to protect her from more hurt, too.

But this lady wasn't for backing down. And she knew when not to give up on a good thing, the best of things. If her tummy was full after that gorgeous supper, then right now, her heart was even fuller. Life could throw its bloody curveballs, but she knew who to stand by, and who she needed to darn well hold on to, when they started coming.

Chapter 35

Ten days later, and the news they'd been waiting for had come in at last. In an appointment with the consultant, Will had this morning received the confirmation that the operation and all subsequent tests had gone well, more checks would continue regularly, but for now he was officially 'in remission'.

The relief was incredible, so much so that he'd broken down in tears. Cath had welled up too; her heart, which had been broken over his illness, now felt welded back with hope. They shared a tender and relieved smile, and she placed a hand gently over his, as she sat beside him in the consultant's room. She appeared calm, but on the inside, she was giving a woohoo and a massive air punch. Will had been in such a dark place for so very long, trying to keep his remaining family together and supported, in the midst of devastating grief. It was no wonder that this cancer diagnosis of his, with the necessary surgery and side-effects, had hit so damned hard.

'Woah, that's so good to hear,' Will had said, once he'd had a chance to gather himself. Then he'd stood up to reach over the desk and shake the consultant's hand. 'Thank you so much. To the whole team here, too.' These surgeons and the team of nurses and health workers who commit their care, their skills, and gave people hope and their lives back, time and time again, deserve so much credit.

The two of them were now sitting on a rug on the sands. With that fantastic news still ringing joyously in their ears, they'd escaped to the sea. The new strand of fairy lights on the deck of the beach bungalow were twinkling gently from the hut in the dunes behind them. Supper was prepared and waiting to be warmed, and a cosy bed was ready for them later. The flat-packed double bed had made it across the dune track last week! It was all assembled and set up with fresh laundry.

The late-August sky was now deepening, with trails of mauves and peach, gold and orange, settling in molten layers against a backdrop of dusky-ultramarine blue. Smells of salt and a hint of seaweed drifted on the fresh coastal air. Cath and Will had strolled down to the beach to take in the view just as the sun was about to set, armed with creamy hot chocolates – laced with a tipple of Baileys for good measure; they were celebrating after all.

Back on the sands, nestled together on their blanket, they chinked mugs.

'Cheers!' said Will.

'Cheers. To good health,' replied Cath.

'And happiness,' he added.

'Absolutely.' And she could feel that happiness running through her veins like warm Northumberland honey.

'And, Cath . . .' He turned, his dark-hazel eyes now set on hers. 'Thanks for everything . . . for being there with me every step of the way. It's been a rough road these past months.'

'Oh, Will, I was so very glad to help, I wouldn't have had it any other way.'

'Perhaps we could have cut out the grumpy bastard bit,' he added wryly.

'Yeah, definitely.' Cath raised a smile. Being able to joke about it together, made them feel like the team they were.

He took her free hand. 'Will you stay . . . be with me . . . a bit longer? I don't want to go back down that lonely road again. Oh dammit, I'm not saying this very well. What I mean is that I love you, Cath . . . and I want us to have a future together.'

'I think you said that perfectly, actually.' She grinned. 'And, I love you too. I'd love to start a new road, and a new journey with you. Side by side.'

Epilogue

The sound of a cork popping echoed along the beach. The Prosecco they'd kept from the Tilldale Afternoon Tea had been nicely chilled in the new fridge – whoop! – that Nikki's Kev had installed at the beach hut last week, after having fitted a solar panel on the roof to provide electricity.

It was early evening, the week after Cath and Will's – rather sensual and a touch spicy as it turned out – sleepover by the sea, and the beach had virtually emptied.

Nikki and Lily held several glasses aloft, and Cath shared the bottle between them. The group were soon sipping the refreshingly decadent pale-gold liquid, the bubbles fizzing in their mouths.

'Delicious,' said Nikki.

'Cheers,' said Lily.

'Cheers,' echoed Cath.

'Good health, everyone,' added Kev.

'Abso-bloody-lutely,' Will responded giving a thumbs up.

'Well then, before we have too much of this, I reckon we should take a dip,' suggested Dan.

'Whey-hay, time for some wild swimming.' Andreas was tearing off his T-shirt as he spoke.

'Yay, let's take a swim in the sea!' Lily was up for it.

'Come on, folks,' Dan encouraged. 'All for one and one for all.'

Andreas's shorts were now off. He was showing a rather toned chest and was down to his fitted Y-fronts. It wasn't a bad sight at all, his abs weren't that far off those of his village stores' apron, but, oh my . . . his hands were reaching for the waistband.

'Hang on, what are you proposing here?' asked Cath, at the risk of sounding prudish.

'Let's let it all hang out, why not. We're all friends. There's no one else around,' he suggested flamboyantly, after scanning the beach.

'Woah.' Nikki was putting on the brakes, too. 'I'm up for a swim but honestly, we don't need to see you naked, hun.'

'True, I have enough of that at home,' added Dan wryly.

'All the jiggly bits,' added Nikki, screwing up her nose.

'Hey, I'm proud of my jiggly bits,' countered Andreas.

'Doesn't mean we all have to see them,' responded Nikki, laughing.

'Okay, undies it is!' agreed Andreas. 'Come on then.'

Cath felt rather relieved. It had taken enough courage to let Will see her naked, in her mid-fifties, though that had actually worked out pretty damn well. Speaking of which, Will was stood up and ready, rocking the boxer short look nicely. Things were beginning to settle down for him post-surgery at last. He'd lost a little weight from his frame, but was now cycling again, and was still looking good. Dammit, he'd always look good to her, Cath realised with a smile, as she peeled off her T-shirt, getting in to the spirit.

Tops and shorts and skirts and trousers were being tossed aside en masse to the sands.

'One, two, three and run!' Will announced.

'Hurrah!' shrieked Cath.

'Whoop!' Nikki.

'Yay!' Lily.

'Woohoo!' Dan.

'Feck, it's freezing!' howled Andreas.

They made a dash into the cool North Sea in a take-your-breath-away moment.

Six supper clubbers, side-by-side, all holding hands.

The Recipes

Cath's Comforting All-in-One Roast Chicken Dinner (Serves 4–6)

2 tbsp olive oil

6 large bone-in, skin-on chicken thighs

Salt and pepper
5 medium white potatoes, peeled and cut into 4 pieces
4 medium carrots, peeled and chopped
2 large parsnips, peeled and cubed
A large knob of butter
2 tbsp plain flour
150ml white wine – optional
500ml chicken stock – Knorr's stock pots are great (or 600ml if not using wine)
1 tbsp chopped fresh thyme
1 tbsp chopped fresh rosemary

Pre-heat oven to 190°C/170°C Fan

Heat a very large oven-proof pan over medium-high heat on the stove top and add 1 tbsp of oil.

Season, and then brown the chicken well on all sides, until nicely golden. Remove from pan and set aside on a plate.

Add the potatoes, carrots and parsnips to the same pan with any remaining meat juices, and allow the vegetables to brown on all sides. Once they've caramelised slightly, remove to a plate.

Turn the heat down to medium. Add a knob of butter and 1 tbsp of oil, then add the flour and stir with a wooden spoon until absorbed. Slowly add the wine and whisk (using a balloon whisk) to prevent lumps forming. Then add the chicken stock slowly, still whisking.

Add the thyme, rosemary and more seasoning, and stir. Let the sauce bubble gently, as it cooks for around 5 minutes.

Add the vegetables back to the pan, and then the chicken pieces, nestling them into the sauce and veg, keeping them skin side up with the tops out of the sauce.

Cover the pan with a lid, and roast for around 40 minutes until the chicken is cooked through.

Serve with green veg, such as tenderstem broccoli or dark cavolo nero kale.

Lily's Showstopper Strawberries and Custard-Cream Victoria Sponge

Cake ingredients:
225g baking spread (such as Stork), straight from the fridge
225g caster sugar
225g self-raising flour
1 tsp baking powder
4 large eggs

Filling and Topping:
½ 370g jar of strawberry jam
200ml double cream
150ml good quality ready-made cold thick custard
1 tbsp icing sugar, plus a little more to dust
250g fresh strawberries

Pre-heat oven to 180°C/160°C Fan. Grease and line the bases of two round and deep 20cm sandwich tins.

Measure the sponge ingredients into a large bowl and beat for about 2 minutes with an electric whisk until smooth. Evenly divide between the two cake tins.

Bake for around 25 minutes, until golden and well risen. To test, insert a skewer into the middle of the cake; if ready it will come out clean.

Leave to cool in the tins for at least 5 minutes, and then turn out onto a wire rack to cool completely.

Filling: Pour the cream into a large bowl and whip until you have softly stiff peaks. Sift in icing sugar and gently fold through, then fold in the cold custard.

Hull and slice the strawberries, keeping back a few to decorate the top.

Place one half of the cake on a plate or stand, spread the custard-cream over, add the sliced strawberries in a layer. Spread your jam on the underside of the other half of the cake, then sit this half on top, with the jam side down.

Decorate with a few artfully placed strawberries and a light sprinkling of icing sugar.

Enjoy with a cup of English Breakfast tea, or a glass of Prosecco, and friends. Truly scrumptious!

Dan's Perfect Paella
(Serves 4)

300g boneless chicken thighs, diced
3 tbsp plain flour
2 tbsp olive oil
200g chorizo ring, peel the thin outer layer of skin off and chop
1 medium onion, chopped
2 large garlic cloves, crushed
1 red and 1 yellow pepper, diced
200g paella or Arborio rice
600ml chicken stock
1 x 300ml can chopped tomatoes
1 tsp dried oregano
1 tsp dried, plus 2 tsp freshly torn basil
A generous pinch of saffron
250g cooked king prawns
12 mussels

Dust the chicken with flour and season. Brown on all sides at medium-high heat in a large deep frying, or paella-style, pan with 1 tbsp of the oil. Set aside.

Add the chorizo sausage to the same pan and brown for 5 minutes. Set aside.

Add a further 1 tbsp of oil and fry the onion for 3 minutes, add the garlic for a further 1 minute. Then add the peppers, and continue to fry for a couple more minutes. Add the rice and stir through for a further 2 minutes so it absorbs the juices.

Return the sausage to the pan, add the chicken stock and tinned tomatoes, dried basil and oregano, saffron, salt and pepper. Bring to the boil, add back the chicken pieces, and lower heat to simmer for around 25 minutes. (If it seems too dry, add a little more stock as necessary.)

Add the prawns and mussels, and stir through. Cook for a further 5 minutes, until the mussels open. (Discard any mussels that do not open.) Garnish with the fresh basil.

Buen provecho! Bon appetit!

Sassy Sangria

1 bottle dry red wine, something like a tempranillo or Rioja
60ml brandy
2 large oranges
1 lemon
3 tbsp caster sugar
350ml cold water
1 apple, 150g strawberries, 1 peach or pear, chopped
Fresh mint to garnish

Add the wine and brandy to a tall jug. Juice one orange and half the lemon, and add the juice to the pitcher.

Add the sugar, and stir until dissolved. Thinly slice the remaining orange and lemon, and add to the mix. Add the remaining fruit.

Stir, cover and chill for at least 30 minutes, to allow the fruit to infuse the wine.

Serve chilled, with or without ice as preferred, and a sprig of mint to garnish.

Andreas's Pina Colada

Makes 1
120ml pineapple juice
60ml white rum
60ml coconut cream
Ice cubes
Wedge of pineapple to garnish (plus a Maraschino cocktail cherry and paper umbrella!)

Pulse all the ingredients along with a handful of ice in a blender until smooth. Pour into a tall glass and garnish with flourish.

'Pi-No' Virgin Colada

Makes 1
120ml pineapple juice
80ml coconut cream
¼ teaspoon vanilla extract
Ice cubes
Wedge of pineapple to garnish (plus a cocktail cherry and paper umbrella!)

Method as above. Cheers!

Nikki's Mam's Chocolate Tiffin

175g digestive biscuits plus 175g rich tea biscuits, roughly crushed (leaving a few chunky bits)
200g unsalted butter
40g soft brown sugar
110g golden syrup
40g cocoa powder
180g raisins or sultanas
300g milk chocolate – melted on its own

Put the butter, sugar, syrup and cocoa powder in a large pan over a low heat and melt, stirring.

Stir in the raisins/sultanas, and then add the crushed biscuits until well coated.

Flatten the mixture into a greased and lined swiss roll style, or square 8"x 8", baking tin. Spread the melted chocolate evenly over the top.

Leave in a cool place until set, then cut into squares with a sharp knife.

The Big Kids' Cheat Chilli with Nachos (Serves 4)

2 tbsp sunflower oil
1 large onion
1 large clove of garlic, crushed
450g lean minced beef
1 heaped tsp chilli powder
295g condensed cream of tomato soup
200ml water
400g can red kidney beans, drained
To serve: half-fat crème fraîche, guacamole and tortilla chips

Heat the oil on medium-high and fry the onion for 2 minutes, then add the garlic and mince for a further 5 minutes until nicely browned, breaking up any lumps that might form.

Stir in the chilli powder, and cook for a further minute. Add the tomato soup, water and kidney beans.

Turn down the heat, and simmer gently, uncovered, for around 30 minutes until tender. Stir frequently. Season to taste.

Serve with the crème fraîche, guacamole and tortilla chips. Rice or potato wedges make a great accompaniment, too.

Adam's Key Lime Pie
(Serves 6–8)

75g unsalted butter
225g crushed gingernut biscuits
250g condensed milk (from a can)
250ml double cream
4 limes, zest and juice (plus 1 further lime to slice for decoration)

Melt the butter, and stir in the crushed biscuits. Press into the base and sides of a 20cm loose-bottomed flan tin. Chill.

In a large bowl, whisk the condensed milk, cream, lime zest and juice together with an electric whisk until thick.

Spoon over the biscuit base. Chill in the fridge for at least a half hour before decorating with lime slices. A grating of dark chocolate works well as an additional garnish too.

Zingy and delicious!

Will's Cosy Hot Chocolate by the Sea
Serves 2

500ml whole milk
2 tbsp cocoa (if you prefer it not so sweet) or hot chocolate powder
100ml Baileys or Irish Cream liqueur
Whipped cream
1 chocolate flake, crumbled

Gently heat the milk until almost boiling, and stir in the cocoa powder.

Add the Baileys Irish Cream, and stir again.

Pour into your favourite mugs, or glass latte cups.

Top with whipped cream, and a sprinkling of flaked chocolate.

Delish!

A Letter from Caroline Roberts

Thank you so much for choosing to read *The Seaside Supper Club*. I hope you've enjoyed spending time with Cath, Will and the supper club gang! If you did, and you'd like to be the first to know about my new releases, recipe tips, and see the stunning views on my walks with my spaniels, please follow me on Instagram @CarolineRobertsAuthor and on Facebook / CarolineRobertsAuthor, and sign up for my newsletter at https://carolinerobertsauthor.substack.com

The Seaside Supper Club is inspired by my beautiful Northumberland village, and the magical beach bungalows at Embleton Bay and Low Newton. Also, by my love of food and the way it brings people together, as well as the twists and emotional turns that life can take us through. I think we all deserve a second chance, and some good friends to buoy us up when times get tough.

I hope you loved this book, and if you did, I'd be so grateful if you would leave a review. I always love to hear what readers think, and it helps new readers to discover my books too. You'd make this author very happy.

Thanks, and all best wishes,

Caroline x

Keep Reading . . .

The Second Chance Supper Club

Could a new start heal her appetite for life?

When Cath moves to a rural Northumberland village to escape her husband's betrayal and a life that no longer feels her own, she's determined to embrace a fresh start. But the quiet charm of her new surroundings seems only to magnify the loneliness of being on her own for the first time.

On a whim, Cath suggests starting a supper club, transforming her garden shed into a cosy, twinkling haven where neighbours can gather. What begins as an effort to ease her solitude becomes something far greater – a circle of friends, each bringing their own stories, struggles, and laughter.

As bonds deepen over shared meals and mishaps, Cath discovers the healing power of community and dares to believe in love and joy again.

Christmas at The Second Chance Supper Club

The snow-dusted village of Tilldale comes alive at Christmas. Twinkling lights and carol singers make it the perfect setting for laughter, friendship, and the unexpected joys of the festive season.

But heartbroken Cath doesn't feel like she is sparkling. Finding herself falling for Will, a widowed former firefighter with whom she shares a history, Cath had been hoping for their budding romance to bloom. But with Will still caught in the depths of his grief, could this relationship be star-crossed before it even begins . . .

Determined to bring some happiness to herself and to the community, Cath decides to hold a village Christmas lunch, and with a little help from her supper club friends, brings everyone together.

But whilst they warm the hearts of their neighbours, can Cath and Will find their way back to each other during the most magical time of the year . . .?

Acknowledgements

A book is nothing without a reader, so heartfelt thanks to all my readers, the bookstores – staff and owners – the hard-working librarians, and the book community including those on social media, for promoting my books and supporting so many other writers, too. I do love hearing from you all on my Facebook and Instagram, so please continue to keep in touch.

The Seaside Supper Club is very much inspired by the magical beach bungalows set in the dunes at Embleton Bay. Thanks to Rachel Sinton for answering my many questions and showing me around her family's amazing beach house there. This book also recognises Northumberland village life and especially that of my local community who welcomed me into their fold over twenty years ago. I have to thank Ally and Shi-Shi of Chatton Village Stores, and a big hello to Pat and Sarah, who allowed me to interview and observe them as they served, chatted and baked.

Having sought information on Will's medical condition and subsequent treatment, the specialist nurse Sophie with Prostate Cancer UK was brilliant, not only in providing the medical facts but also advising on the emotional elements of dealing with this condition. I so appreciate your time and your invaluable insights.

Thanks to maths teacher and friend, Rebecca Moss, who helped me to understand Cath's working role and background, and whose dreams of becoming a teacher came at the same point as I was trying hard to get my books published – and yippee, we both very much achieved our goals! Also, warm thanks to Yianna and her Greek-Cypriot dad for their help with Andreas's character.

My writing community are so appreciated. Thanks to my Romantic Novelists' Association friends for their ongoing support, kindness and inspiration over afternoon teas, kitchen parties at conferences, and pooled lunches!

My publishing director, Georgina Green, thank you for being excited by this Supper Club series and taking me on, and Priyal for all your support in taking me forward, along with all those in the editing, marketing and creative team at HQ. Thank you for giving me an exciting new chapter with your publishing house.

Big thanks to my lovely agent, Hannah Ferguson, for believing in and guiding me with this new Supper Club series, plus all the team at Hardman & Swainson.

Any mistakes you may find are wholly my own. I endeavour to try my best but sometimes a typo or a piece of information slips the net! Writers are only human, too.

Last but never least, my family and friends, for their patience and support. I spend many hours on a laptop upstairs in the spare room in a world of my own with make-believe people. Thanks for giving me the time and space to create these characters and stories, which I hope you will love.

All best wishes,

Caroline x

Dear Reader,

We hope you enjoyed reading this book. If you did, we'd be so appreciative if you left a review. It really helps us and the author to bring more books like this to you.

Here at HQ Digital we are dedicated to publishing fiction that will keep you turning the pages into the early hours. Don't want to miss a thing? To find out more about our books, promotions, discover exclusive content and enter competitions you can keep in touch in the following ways:

JOIN OUR COMMUNITY:

Sign up to our new email newsletter: http://smarturl.it/SignUpHQ

Read our new blog www.hqstories.co.uk

X: https://twitter.com/HQStories

f: www.facebook.com/HQStories

BUDDING WRITER?

We're also looking for authors to join the HQ Digital family! Find out more here:

https://www.hqstories.co.uk/want-to-write-for-us/

Thanks for reading, from the HQ Digital team

HQ